Slaughter
DECK

Slaughter
DECK

A NOVEL

Konrad Karl Gatien & Sreescanda

IRP NOVELS u.s.a.

LOS ANGELES . CALIFORNIA

For information, contact: irpnovels@gmail.com

2011 PAPERBACK EDITION PUBLISHED BY IRP (USA)

FIRST PUBLISHED IN 2009 IN HARDCOVER AS
"SAVE THE WHALES PLEASE"
Kunati Inc. (USA) and Kunati Inc. (Canada).

Designed by Kam Wai Yu
Persona Corp. I www.personaco.com

ISBN 978-0-9845730-0-4
FICTION
1st Printing

http://www.irpnovels.com

Library of Congress Cataloging-in-Publication Data

Gatien, Konrad Karl.
Save The Whales Please: a novel / Konrad Karl Gatien & Sreescanda.
Summary: "A firebrand first lady and a notorious whaling pirate team up for an epic, high-
tech, high-seas adventure--a whale drive from the Arctic to the Antarctic of 1972 blue whales."
--Provided by the publisher.
ISBN 978-0-9845730-0-4
1. Whales--Conservation--Fiction. 2. Blue whale--Fiction. 3.
Whaling--Political aspects--Fiction. 4. Whaling--Japan--Fiction. 5.
Presidents' spouses--United States--Fiction. 6. Political fiction. I.
Sreescanda. II. Title.

D E D I C A T I O N

Wenda, who believed when nobody else did; for that, I will owe her forever.

Janice, who has been there through good times and bad.

And above all, Mom, of course. She can never be repaid. Ever.

—Sreescanda

To Mom, who raised me with great love and taught me the virtues of patience, silence, effort and courtesy ... especially patience.

To Dad, who has always supported my dreams, no matter how wild.

To my wife and children, who, through their unfailing love, bring untold joy to my life.

—Konrad

BOOK ONE

The whale is at the heart of a guerilla war of resistance that has spread over all the world: it is the symbol of the ecology movement and emblematic of the fate of all species on the planet. The battle line has been drawn here. If this amazing animal, the largest ever to exist on the planet, cannot be saved from the ruthless exploitation of a handful of men, what chance of survival have other species?

David Day
The Whale War

Norwegian Sea

The stench of death struck her like a backhanded slap.

Dr. Jan Everett recoiled violently. The pungent odor wrenched tears from her eyes. Bile rose in her throat. Her legs weakened.

Hundreds of carcasses of minke whales floated in the choppy waves. A red triangular flag was staked into each kill. The flags stretched like an undulating sea of headstones. Red LEDs flickered across this vast cemetery on water, one on each whale, radio beacons that beeped and flashed to help the killers keep track if any drifted off.

Jan was no stranger to the slaughter and abuse of wildlife, having eye-witnessed the clubbing of seals, massacre of wolves, skinning of foxes, shooting of grizzlies and other vile acts of cruelty and carnage, yet once again she felt unprepared.

"Jesus," breathed Dr. Raquel Ruppert, the black woman in braids and nose ring, who stepped up to the helm beside Jan. "Are you okay?"

Jan nodded wordlessly. As best friends who could practically read each other's thoughts, Jan knew Raquel anticipated a profanity-laced soliloquy. She also knew Raquel understood why Jan just locked her knees and held in her rage. They stood at the tip of the arrow-shaped prow of their Zodiac, a 14 x 14, outboard powered inflatable, flying the insignia of the world's leading environmental watchdog: GreenPlanet.

With a sputter of dying engines, two more Zodiacs drifted up on either side, carrying a pair of men each, David Boycott and Patrick Knight, GreenPlanet's videographer and reporter respectively in one, a couple of ecologists from the Scientific Committee of the International Whaling Commission in the other. Blood-streaked crests smashed up and over into the inflatables. With sunlight trapped behind the mile-thick stack of nimbus rain-bearers, the utter gloom and early morning chill deepened the pall.

"Start counting," Jan said, breaking her silence.

The two women and four men lifted scarves over their nostrils and breathed through their mouths as they steered their Zodiacs ponderously between the mammoth corpses bloated with air. The heat from the dead whales released tiny red geysers of blood. More oozed from the open harpoon wounds. Still more flooded from their bellies laid open by grenades. The rich, wet, fatty stench wafted up in a visible, nauseating pink mist. Jan stopped alongside the loosely flapping jaw of a cow. Her small teats dragged in a dense red sea. The explosion from a grenade-tipped harpoon had ripped a tunnel through her blubber, flesh and organs, all the way to an unborn calf. The fetus was horribly burned and the cow's long vagina oozed a river of blood.

Norway owned the dubious distinction of pioneering almost all the most brutal methods of killing whales. Earliest records documented them employing "drive fishing" to herd whales and dolphins into fjords, then draw nets across and either spear the leviathans to death or hammer wooden pegs into their nostrils to suffocate them. With the advent of guns, they pumped bullets into the trapped giants. In the nineteenth century, following the discovery of vast Antarctic herds, a British engineer was commissioned to invent a means of electrocuting whales to hasten the slaughter.

"Two sixty," said Jan totaling the counts from each Zodiac. Norway had been granted a permit by the International Whaling Commission to kill 212 minkes.

"But we don't know how many were towed before we got here," cautioned Raquel. Norway processed the harvest in whaling stations located along the shore. They may have arrived between tugboat trips.

"Looks like they are by no means done," said Boycott, peering at the horizon through his video camera.

"What do you mean?" reacted Jan sharply. "They're already over the limit."

"Yeah, and they are conscientiously counting," said Boycott with his usual sarcasm. The IWC trusted its member nations to embrace the honor system and monitor hunts. "Ten o'clock."

Everyone lifted the binoculars slung around their necks.

"A catcher." Jan noted the trademark catwalk from bridge to bow that allowed the gunner to rush directly to his harpoon when the crow's nest spotted the quarry.

"Appropriately called *Svend Foyn*," informed Boycott, zooming his long lens in on the writing along the front of the hull.

Svend Foyn became the godfather of modern day whaling when he invented the grenade-tipped harpoon in 1867, the devastating weapon that had destroyed over three million whales and counting. The catcher bearing his name fit his bloody legacy. Giant red droplets from the slaughter smeared most of the white, seventy-five-foot hull.

Jan's patience snapped. "That's it. Let's go."

"We have evidence of violation," said one of the IWC ecologists. "We'll take it up at the next session."

"And allow this slaughter to continue?" retorted Jan. "Like hell we will."

Ever since the creation of Cetacean Bay the previous year, the Antarctic whale sanctuary that now extended from the fortieth parallel below the equator all the way to the South Pole, discontent had been brewing within the IWC. Iceland quit. Japan was sly, staying in and launching a clandestine hunt in the protected waters for severely endangered fins and humpbacks. Word leaked out. The international backlash was swift and severe. Australia threatened to dispatch her navy and New Zealand considered suing. Fleets of eco-warriors confronted the secret fleet. Embarrassed and humiliated, Tokyo backed off but did not back down. They resumed hunting using a loophole called "whaling for scientific research," taking almost a thousand whales. At the last IWC meeting, Jan had successfully closed the loophole.

Fearing collapse, the IWC allowed whaling nations each to kill 212 minkes under the clause of "coastal and aboriginal whaling," which the US supported to appease Native Americans, a powerful lobby and voting bloc in the Northeast and Alaska. The move left Cetacean Bay untouched, placating the anti-whaling lobby, whose nations had strength in numbers, but apart from America, lacked the global, economic and political clout that drove all policy making in the IWC.

A week ago, GreenPlanet had received an anonymous tip that Norway planned to ignore the quota even though she did not depend on whaling to sustain her economy anymore. In 1959, a huge gas field was discovered in the North Sea. Today, Norway controlled 35 percent of known oil reserves in Western Europe and 50 percent of all natural gas. But fish remained the staple diet and Norwegians fervently believed that whales were big fish. Conservation came second to misplaced tradition.

Jan took the anonymous tip to the US Department of Commerce, demanding the threat of an embargo on Norwegian imports if the quota was violated. But the president balked because of Norway's strategic importance to NATO. Jan broke her promise to stay away from controversy, gathered her eco-warriors, practically kidnapped the two ecologists and crossed the Atlantic. Patrick Knight, the gangly reporter, gained access to the records of Norway's Bureau of International Whaling Statistics in Sandefjord, where the nation's whaling records had been maintained since 1938, including the approximate location of the current hunt. They had sailed up the coast all night, pinpointing the hunting coordinates this morning by monitoring the whalers' radio.

Raquel stepped across and started the motor with a toothy, exuberant smile. "So, we are going to do it?"

"I want the next news cycle to lead with us," said Jan vengefully.

Everyone around her looked at each other, then Boycott expressed their sentiment, "Welcome back! Woo-hoo!" He looked at Knight, "You owe me twenty." Back to Jan, "He bet me that you'd be lying low till November. I told him, no way. You can't cage the tiger."

Jan unleashed a steely smile. "Let's make headlines."

Raquel hurried aft, squatted down and plunged the control stick, kicking the Zodiac forward. Knight anxiously unwound an arm toward the throttle. The ecologists followed a distant third. The three inflatables leapt over the wave crests, their bounce evoking a sense of energy, spunk and rebellion.

Jan straightened in the blinding orange wetsuit that fit like a second skin over her lean five foot six frame. She planted her feet in a defiant wide-legged stance and grasped the flagpole. Rage blushed on her cheeks and glinted in her eyes. In that moment, she duplicated the signature image of her that was etched in the minds of millions— that of a firebrand animal rights militant who also happened to be the most famous woman on the planet.

BoomBoomBoomBoom!

Grenade-intensity explosions shot across the sky. Jan snapped her head up, startled by the close proximity of the thunder pursuing blue-white flashes of lightning. The Norwegian Sea stretched between unforgiving latitudes that rarely enjoyed fair weather, even in summer. This morning was no exception. The outward fringe of a storm system swept down from the Arctic and streamed off Norway's precipitous fjords. For the first time, Jan noticed the dark clouds were running really low. Wisps skimmed the water.

She gritted her teeth to fight off the chill that stung her pinched skin with the sharpness of a thousand needles. The women closed the gap with the *Svend Foyn* quickly. *Too quickly.* The catcher had deliberately slowed down. When the Zodiac entered the tail-stream, Jan knew why.

"Hold on!" she yelled.

The *Svend Foyn*'s screws engaged suddenly, churned up a fierce current and hurled it at the Zodiac. Behind the aft bridgescreen was an unshaven, ragged veteran of the sea, presumably the skipper.

"Don't let up!" Jan hollered to Raquel.

Both women pressed their feet into the wooden deck plate and hung on as the Zodiac skittered like a runaway car on ice. It took all of Raquel's strength to keep on top of the throttle and rudder. The Zodiac slipped out of the powerful wake and inched up alongside the *Svend Foyn*, which ran steady, its bow plowing in and out of the water with effortless rhythm.

Jan looked up when the skipper emerged from the bridge and leaned over the side. He drew his lips back in a menacing grin. She was close enough to see that his teeth were edged all around with black tartar.

He yelled down, "Fokoff!"

In her twenty-three years of fighting for animal rights, Jan had heard worse. More sailors appeared and sneered with an encore of "Fokoffs!" The skipper circled his arms, signaling the bridge to helm closer. Instead of being daunted by the giant vessel bearing down, Jan grinned up at the skipper and pointed a finger forward with a flourish.

"Show time!" shouted Jan.

Raquel plunged the throttle home.

The Zodiac leapt, streaked past the catcher and sprinted to

a quick lead. Jan looked over her shoulder. The catcher's aging engine could not gain on the souped-up little craft. In fact, the *Svend Foyn* fell further and further behind. The skipper raced out onto the catwalk in front of the bridge, shouting. Jan and Raquel laughed. They could imagine why he was so angry. He came from one of the oldest testosterone-driven societies, where men were men and women peeled fish.

Chunks of ice, frozen overnight, disintegrated under the racing Zodiac with the sharp staccato of machinegun fire. Overhead, the bottom threatened to fall out of the sky. The *Svend Foyn* trailed by more than three hundred yards now.

"Whales!" shouted Jan, looking ahead.

A pod of at least thirty minkes sunned themselves, blowing, leaping out of the water and re-entering head first in what was easily the most graceful arc to behold. Named after a German whaler called Meinecke, who mistook them for diminutive blues, hunters had ignored them. They weighed only five tons and were called lesser rorquals. The Schedule, an IWC document that laid down the "rules" of whaling, did not even include them until 1975, when larger whales had been all but destroyed. The hunt for the minke had been on ever since.

Jan circled a finger over her head. Raquel wheeled the Zodiac around about fifty yards from the minkes and cut the outboard to place themselves between the *Svend Foyn* and the hunt.

A teen loped along the catwalk to the gun mounted on the bow. His stride faltered when he saw Jan and Raquel dead ahead. He looked back quickly. The skipper hadn't moved from the catwalk in front of the bridge. Jan was counting on his ego to get the better of him. And it did. Instead of steering away from the women and continuing the hunt, the skipper drew his finger across his throat.

Boycott's camera recorded the hunters' every move.

The teen jumped on the gun platform at the forwardmost tip of the catcher. He strapped himself quickly and ripped off the tarp to expose an ugly, rusted, 90mm launcher. Lifting the heavy missile from a rack of others, he loaded it into the cannon's maw. When he swung it toward the two women with a grin, the catcher pulled to within two hundred yards.

PhatPhatPhat!

Jan's heart pounded synchronously with the GreenPlanet flag whipping above her head. A thrill coiled around her body. She looked over to Raquel, who appeared just as tense with nervous excitement. They leaned down together and lifted their sign: SAVE THE WHALES! PLEASE!

The stormy sky chose that moment to blaze alive. Lightning raged down, trapping Jan, Raquel and the *Svend Foyn* in a cage of electricity. Thunder blasted. Nature's sound and light show escalated. The bedlam in the skies transferred to the water. Giant swells climbed out of the sea like hooded snakes. The standoff would look like an epic mismatch in Boycott's camera: two women in a tiny rubber raft holding up a placard for mercy against a large, armed vessel climbing higher and higher on a gargantuan wave.

Thirty feet above the women, its scaly keel fully exposed, the *Svend Foyn* poised for what seemed like an eternity atop the foaming crest not yet ready to collapse.

"Fokoff!" shouted the teen at the top of his voice.

He angled the barrel of his gun down and fired. With a report that surpassed the roar of sky and sea, a four-foot-long grenade-tipped harpoon sizzled toward Jan and Raquel.

Simultaneously, the underbelly of cloud opened with a swirl. *WhopWhopWhop!* An unnatural growl grew so loud so fast no one had time to react. A black monster descended through the gaping vortex. *BangBangBang!* Starbursts bombarded down from it.

A US Navy Blackhawk dropped, firing.

The laser-guided shots met and detonated the grenade-tipped harpoon in midair. Tentacles of flame streaked away with an ear-rending blast. The minkes submerged as one.

The danger, far from over, was only beginning.

The giant wave disintegrated, hurling the *Svend Foyn* at the Zodiac. Jan and Raquel emptied their lungs in a scream. But they could have been miming, such was the noise of the weather, water, catcher screws and rotors. In that second of terror, when death seemed inevitable, Jan glimpsed a thread of hope.

A rope ladder unfurled from the helicopter.

"Grab it!" she shrieked to Raquel.

The *Svend Foyn* crashed toward them. The teen gunner clung to the barrel, twisting in front of the muzzle, still attached to the platform by the harnesses hooked into his belt.

The women blindly reached up for the ladder that curled toward them wildly like an attacking serpent. Jan closed her fingers the instant she felt the high tensile weave of a rung. But could they escape the *Svend Foyn*'s bow tip?

It came down like the hatchet of God.

The Blackhawk rose, lifting the two women a heartbeat before the catcher plunged below their feet and obliterated the Zodiac. Tendrils of burning diesel from the smokestack passing underneath enveloped, singed and blinded them.

A cross current buffeted the *Svend Foyn* before it could flatten to even keel, and the catcher flipped over. The skipper ejected into the water. Like all the sailors on board, he wore a life vest and floated to the surface. More heads appeared.

Aboard the Blackhawk, men in dark combat gear reeled up the rope ladder and pulled Jan and Raquel inside. The instant Jan straightened, the officer amongst them saluted Jan smartly.

"Lieutenant Hendrix, ma'am. United States Navy. Sorry about the close call. We were right over you all the time, but we did not expect them to actually make an attempt on your life."

"Don't sweat it," Jan said with a smile. "Neither did I. Rescue the others."

"Yes, Ma'am."

"Sure is nice to have your own personal eye in the sky," said Raquel.

Jan winked. "One of the better perks of being the first lady."

Washington DC

Darkness and Marine One descended at the same time. Inside the luxurious Sikorsky VH-3D Sea King making its final approach to the White House, President Carsten Everett sat by the window alone, pensive and withdrawn. The youngest chief executive since JFK, his stomach tightened nervously at the sight of about two dozen reporters on the South Lawn. Their necks craned up and around all together like a pack of hungry wolves, he thought, waiting to feed on his failure. Everett shrank away from the glass.

How had it all gone so wrong? His presidency had begun with such promise and optimism. He'd galvanized a nation, capitalizing on public discontent with the two major parties, convincing Americans to turn traditional politics on its head. They propelled him to a shocking, history-making win as an Independent.

Once in office, the narrowness of his victory was exposed. He became locked in a daily battle with a Democratic House and a Republican Senate. He'd won the election promising to run the federal government like a corporation but did not figure on Keith Leeds and Will Todd, Democratic and Republican leader of the House and Senate respectively, to be already positioning themselves for a White House bid four years down the road. Jockeying for the best poll numbers over every issue, the three men blackmailed each other into gridlock. But it was in the course of a few months last year that his presidency really began to unravel.

Already weakened by the Democrats and Republicans, who used their infinitely more versatile nationwide PR machine to brand this presidency as weak and irrelevant, he felt irreparably hurt by his most trusted partner, the only woman he'd loved, his wife, the first lady.

Jan.

She had turned the world against the Japanese by exposing their secret whale hunt in Cetacean Bay, and relations between Washington and Tokyo had been frigid ever since. So this three-day state visit to Japan to break the deadlock in trade talks drew intense media scrutiny, turning into a soap opera that crossed from news to entertainment when it became known the first lady refused to accompany him. It was too late to change the itinerary. More than a year in planning, the trip had been set up to coincide with the critical June-to-November stretch of the presidential race and hand Everett a badly needed foreign policy victory.

In recent years, the United States and Japan had played this game of chicken. When Washington cried foul, Tokyo tightened the screws on the dollar, which was still the most important currency but had lost its luster as a stable benchmark. Japan had always wielded some control and influence, but it was significant now, having purchased almost a trillion and a half dollars, or 10 percent of the US national debt. It did not help that the new prime minister had an agenda of his own: overtaking China and restoring Japan as the most powerful economy in Asia.

Everett could not forge a breakthrough, one that would have resonated in the Midwest where Japan was heavily invested and taken his current slim lead decisively beyond the margin of error.

He felt the soft bump of wheels. Marine One was on the ground. People materialized out of their seats to open the door, uncoil the stairs and kick off the security checklist before he disembarked.

"Don't answer any questions," a reassuring voice whispered in his ear.

Everett turned to look at his most trusted aide and confidant, George Pleasance, the White House chief of staff and CRP chairman—Campaign to Re-elect the President. Everett nodded and stood up.

The rotors were slowing when he appeared at the door. The sound was loud enough to give him a few more seconds of respite from the reporters. He saluted the marine at the bottom of the steps and started across the South Lawn.

Alone.

During the first six months of his term, the first couple had rarely been seen apart in public. Over the last two years, as his administration came under siege at home and abroad, rumors of marital discord grew louder when the more familiar picture became that of a solitary president shadowed only by his towering bodyguard, Anthony Trent. Trailing Trent by a yard, as always, was George Pleasance, lean, concave, hunched over, shy and awkward. He was utterly unremarkable—as memorable as a faceless working stiff among the ordinary millions who spent their entire lives in anonymity. He went largely ignored by the press, as did the president's senior counsel, Thomas Lhea, the African American who brought up the rear. He came off as a picture of efficiency, with his straight posture, crew cut, dapper suit and briefcase.

The rotors swept to a standstill. The reporters erupted.

"Mr. President, do you think Japan will follow through with their threat of a trade war?"

"How will this affect your campaign?"

"Are you concerned your approval is 28 percent five months before the elections?"

Everett wore a tight smile, said nothing and disappeared inside the White House. Out of sight of reporters, who dispersed under a half moon that flitted in and out of view, his stride lagged. Pleasance and Lhea came abreast of the president as they entered the West Wing.

"Leeds and Todd have to be licking their chops," said Everett, anticipating his opponents' attack ads highlighting his debacle in Tokyo.

"We're prepared for it," said Pleasance confidently, a stark contrast to his quiet and retiring public persona. Everett knew him as brilliant, mercurial and a master of damage control.

"Our ads will spin this as Congress's fault," said Lhea. A lawyer and media specialist, he coordinated the air wars. If there was a silver lining, it was the fact that the other end of Pennsylvania Avenue suffered even lower approval numbers. "We are listing all your campaign promises and how Leeds and Todd took partisan politics to a new low by blocking every one of them on the floor."

"We came up with a catch phrase that you should work into every speech," said Pleasance. "The do-nothing Congress."

Everett smiled for the first time. "I like that."

Zoe Zurich, the perky White House communications director and spokeswoman of this administration in the daily briefings to the press, appeared and said breathlessly, "We have a situation concerning the first lady."

Everett blinked anxiously. "Is she okay?"

Zoe gulped. "Actually, sir, she's expected to be on TV any moment now."

They hurried down to the Situation Room, a futuristic looking space dominated by giant screens on which officials from the State Department, Pentagon, Joint Chiefs of Staff and CIA were patched together for a video-conference in the event of an emergency. Pleasance turned on the TV news.

"First Lady Jan Everett and a whaling vessel were involved in a confrontation on the Norwegian Sea. Details are sketchy—"

Coverage abruptly cut away to the airport in Svolvær. A media circus greeted the US Navy Blackhawk as it landed to return the rescued whalers. A reporter put a microphone in front of Jan. Everett's heart sank. His wife lived for this. True to form, she went off, blasting Norway as a "nation of callous killers."

Late afternoon the following day, Marine Two brought Jan home. Everett emerged onto the South Lawn wearing an appropriate expression of relief. A mob of cameras, heavy on the paparazzi, jostled and strained against the ropes. Additional Secret Service agents had been brought to ensure no one broke through. Since becoming first lady, Jan's dare-devilry drew Princess Diana-type coverage. Her every mood was on file and there was probably nobody on the planet who did not recognize those stunningly light eyes, petulant nose and full lips.

Everett embraced his wife. Wearing a pleasant smile, he whispered fiercely, "Don't say a word."

"I can see you missed me," Jan hissed back.

Cameras flashed like it was a rock concert. The screaming questions overlapped each other. They waved and disappeared inside. Jan and Everett said nothing further until they were alone in the West Wing Sitting Hall upstairs.

"Jan," said Everett, releasing the gold draperies in front of the double arched windows, "you are going to tender an apology first thing in the morning."

"Like hell I am," retorted Jan. "What did I say that the facts did not bear out?"

"If you won't apologize, I will," said Everett flatly. "My statement will go much further." Jan glared at her husband for a long moment. Everett met her eyes evenly. "You're not a scrappy college campus activist anymore."

"You're not the man I married."

"I grew up."

"No. You became a politician, selling out the people who got you here." Environmentalists had poured money into his campaign because he was Jan's husband.

"Whales don't affect the lives of average Americans. The looming trade war with Japan does."

"All I want you to do is show some spine."

"You want me to be a bully."

"If that's what it takes."

"We are not playing regional politics anymore, Jan. A romanticized view of whales makes for a good platform in California. But Iceland and Norway are the sites of our advance warning radars. They're up for renewal in August and we cannot jeopardize the agreement. Especially with things deteriorating the way they are in Russia."

The Nationalist Party had won a narrow majority in the Kremlin. They had run on the platform of turning the clock back to Stalinist ways. Discontent brewed, which harkened back to those dangerous final days of the Soviet Union, raising fears once again in the West about the command and control of Russia's vast nuclear arsenal.

"The Norwegian people," Everett went on, "are well aware that public opinion, more than anything, drives the whaling issue. Pleasance showed me a recent poll—"

"That power-hungry weasel has a goddamn poll for everything."

"That's uncalled for."

"He's as much a part of your life as I am. Probably more. Hell, I think he loves you."

"That's enough."

"He controls every facet of your life with numbers. He's the son of a bitch who had the audacity to suggest your approval rating would go through the roof if I had a baby in office."

"Let's not go there."

"Why not? We always come back to it."

"Drop it."

Jan didn't. "I made it clear during the four years we were dating that I did not want kids. I had my life mapped out just as you had yours. So I tied my tubes."

"A week before we got married," Everett said.

"After the baby was born, would you have given up your career?"

"Someone had to make a living and it was not going to be you."

"You knew who I was, what I stood for and where I was going with my life. I did not force you to marry me. In fact, after you proposed, I asked you to sleep on it."

"I had no plans in politics at that time."

"Oh! Just because you make a career change, I'm supposed to drop my life's work?"

"This isn't about our marriage or Pleasance."

"Like hell it isn't! He's laying down the rules we have to play by until November. He suggested I apologize to Norway, didn't he?"

"I don't have a spectacular record in foreign policy."

"Jesus, you've changed."

"Before you point a finger at me, remember you'd be dead if that Blackhawk hadn't shown up when it did. How do you think that happened? Because you're the first lady. If you want to enjoy the perks, you've got to accept the restraint that goes with them."

"I'm not going to change because Pleasance doesn't approve."

"You are still going to apologize." Jan looked at her husband. He went on grimly, "I want to see a draft. We cannot afford new fires."

Jan left. She'll do it, Everett thought, entering the kitchen. Her practical side always wins out in the end.

He heard her start a bath, then took the elevator down to the Oval Office.

Done in deep reds, golds, greens and blues, it was supposed to reflect the president's youth and vigor. He poured himself a stiff drink, gulped it down, poured another and another. He was half way through his fourth drink when a soft knock sounded on the door.

Everett looked up. Two Secret Service men walked the outer office along with Anthony Trent, who periodically checked through the peephole of the white door from the secretaries' pool. There were a dozen other Secret Service agents and Executive Protection Branch officers on patrol inside and outside whichever part of the White House he occupied, day or night.

"Come in," he said tiredly.

Pleasance and Lhea entered.

Everett smiled, "Don't you guys ever go home?"

"To do what?" said Pleasance. He was single. Everett could not imagine his chief of staff married to anything but his job.

"Grab a drink and put your feet up."

Pleasance sat down with a gin and tonic. Lhea poured himself bourbon. He was divorced. Everett knew it had been a bitter court battle.

The president held up his drink. "Cheers."

He would blame the alcohol when he woke up tomorrow and reasoned why he broke his strict, self-imposed policy of separating his personal life from the affairs of the country. He had always kept his problems with Jan to himself, but tonight he stated flatly, "I think my marriage is over."

He caught Pleasance and Lhea by surprise. He suspected they were aware Jan and he were having problems, but the first couple presented a picture-perfect facade of happiness to the world, even the White House staff. Polls demanded it: 58 percent of Americans admired the "first marriage" and 67 percent considered Jan and Everett as role models for spouses with conflicting careers. He went on to bare all to his two closest advisors.

An hour later, Everett swung his feet off the table, gulped down the rest of his scotch and stood up. "I'm sure she's asleep by now."

"Goodnight," said Pleasance and Lhea together.

The instant Everett closed the door, Pleasance said, "This could become quicksand."

Insiders likened the power he wielded to that of Bob Haldeman in the Nixon White House. In fact, Pleasance had studied Haldeman's spectral movements inside the White House to gain complete control of all access to the president.

"What can we do?" said Lhea, the John Ehrlichman of this administration.

Pleasance was at a loss. "Call Lance."

Lhea dialed Vice President Lance Adrian, a fifty-year-old former three-term Senator from North Carolina. The lifelong Washington insider completed the triumvirate of the shadow power within this White House. Adrian's voice sounded gruff with sleep.

"What's the matter?" he asked in a Southern accent. "Is everything all right?"

"No," said Pleasance.

❄

Upstairs, Everett found Jan sound asleep. *She's still so damn beautiful.* He climbed into bed beside her. Instinctively, she turned and nestled her head into his chest. He lay awake. He'd grown up in an unusual single-parent home—a single father. His mother died when he was six. Everett Sr. was a boring, colorless mortgage broker. He never remarried, raising young Carsten alone with an iron, military hand. They woke up at precisely the same time every morning, arriving at school five minutes before the bell, ate dinner at seven and retired to bed by nine. Carsten grew tall, with the physique of an athlete. A hunk by any standard, girls fawned over him. His father—short and chubby and unsuccessful in finding another woman—equated good looks with stupidity. He relentlessly drill-sergeanted the boy into bringing home flawless report cards. But Carsten excelled in school because he hated the middle-class contentment and confinement of his youth. Ambition fueled him to a full scholarship in college, where he discovered politics as the ideal confluence of what he'd been deprived of: money and power.

As a mere sophomore majoring in finance, he ran for student president. Jan showed up to volunteer for his campaign. He was instantly smitten by this blonde bombshell, as smart as she was beautiful. Jan was a freshman, a year younger than he, studying to be a veterinarian. He discovered on their very first date that there was nothing understated or complicated about her. She was loud, stubborn and opinionated, with a temper on a hair trigger. He envied her upbringing, the diametric opposite of his. She came from an affluent, progressive family. An only child, her parents, both successful, well-traveled veterinary doctors with a world view, instilled the notion that her gender was not an excuse. They encouraged her to be uninhibited with her emotions and gave her unlimited freedom. So she grew up fearless.

Everett tried to tell himself that Jan's fame did not bother him, but in the back of his mind, he envied her. He was her equal in intelligence and looks, yet somehow she seemed to have more of both. Maybe because Jan was comfortable being beautiful, even shrewdly using it to her advantage. She was a well-known environmental activist on campus when they met. She helped him become student president to further her own green agenda. Jan was famous when they married. It got him elected to the US Senate, but it also helped her green cause and in the White House, it emerged front and center.

Once Everett became president, all facets of their marriage changed. It required ego and arrogance to run for and win the highest office in the land. The pressure of a wife who rivaled and even exceeded his public appeal got to him. Theirs was a complicated relationship—a marriage built as much on love as the love of causes, politics and policy. Insatiable readers, they would deliberately choose opposite sides and go at it for hours. Nothing turned them on like an invigorating debate. They had always been much too smart not to find a way around their differences. Not lately. Oil rights, fishing and other environmental issues that Jan stood for were unpopular in Alaska, Pennsylvania, Texas, the Northwest and industrial Midwest. The rest of the world was even more unforgiving. They stopped having intelligent dialogue.

The spark went out of their marriage.

They'd always tried to eat at least one meal a day together. Now they strived for the opposite. They continued to have intermittent sex, but had stopped making love. Their practice of actively participating in each other's work dwindled, and they settled into separate circles. When they did talk about what they were up to, it was well after the fact, invariably resulting in loud fights.

As he drifted off, curling his arm around her shoulder, he wondered what he wanted more: domestic bliss or a second term? The choice was simple, though it would be complicated in a way he never could have imagined by a man awakening to leave for his last day of work in the bitter cold of Alaska three months later.

Deadhorse, Alaska

Dan Sitka threw back the sheets and swung out of bed. He squeezed the last of the toothpaste—another omen it was his final day. He shaved, showered and climbed into the Gumby suit, a heavy neoprene survival uniform bearing a circular patch: Office of Aircraft Services, National Oceanic and Atmospheric Administration.

Downstairs, he went to the checkout desk and said goodbye to the staff. They did not hide their jealousy. He was headed for sunny San Diego, California. Temperatures at Deadhorse oftentimes fell to negative 55°F. With the wind chill factor that number dropped to negative 115°F. For fifty-six days, the sun never rose at this latitude. Located five hundred miles north of Fairbanks, Deadhorse was a town with a native population of 3,500. That figure rose to 8,600 when oil-field workers arrived at the Prudhoe Bay industrial complex. Traffic had been thinning all month because waters of the Beaufort Sea were icing up, reducing drilling.

Sitka made the detour toward the state-maintained airport two miles north of town. Signing over the jeep, he grabbed his bags from the back and boarded the only aircraft parked on the tarmac, a de Havilland Twin Otter Series 300.

"Good mornin' all," bellowed Sitka with an unrelenting smile. He stripped off the several layers of wool before he plunged into the pilot's seat on the left side of the flight deck.

"Morning," replied Kelly Cuomo, accepting his peck on her cheek. An attractive, happily married woman in her mid-forties, Kelly occupied the copilot's seat.

"Hey, Dan," greeted Jason Tractor. He sat directly behind Kelly, facing starboard.

"Yo," grunted Chris Hanson, looking out the port window aft of Sitka's seat. "No kiss for me?" Without missing a beat, Sitka twisted around, leaned over and gave him a wet one. Hanson grimaced. "I asked for a kiss, not a bath."

"I was overcome." Sitka logged in with the Control Tower and reached behind the throttles for the fuel and ignition switches. The Otter's engines roared.

Flight No. 45 to Survey Block 12 in the Beaufort Sea was born.

Following the discovery of oil and gas in the 1970s in the Arctic waters off the coast of Alaska, environmentalists lobbied hard to protect the last 2,000 of the most severely endangered of all whale species, the great bowhead. The powerful oil companies were forced to establish aerial surveys of whales to observe their numbers, conserve their habitat and implement drilling restrictions. The Chukchi Beaufort Sea was divided into twelve survey locks and for the past month, Sitka, Kelly, Tractor and Hanson had combed the waters between longitudes 140°W through 157°W south of 72°N latitude. This final flight was scheduled to survey a block of the Beaufort Sea between longitudes 154°W and 157°W.

"Flight OCS-oh-4-5," called Control Tower, "you are cleared for take-off."

The plane accelerated. The twin engines sucked in the icy morning air, transformed it into energy and spat out a searing blast that drew fluttering lines of heat in the atmosphere immediately behind. The nose lifted two degrees per second. Deadhorse, zip code 99734, receded into an indefinable cluster of lights.

"Dan," said Hanson, the port observer, after he'd set up his station, "I hear you have a new squeeze down in California."

"She's more than a squeeze," replied Kelly before Sitka could. She was team leader, navigator and forward observer.

"Tell all," urged Tractor, the starboard data recorder-observer.

"Allow me," Kelly jumped in again. "She's a professor and he met her when he was on assignment with the NMFS down in San Diego." The National Marine Fisheries Service.

"That was six months ago," said Tractor.

"He's been dating her since," grinned Kelly. "Where do you think he disappears every other weekend?"

"This month is the longest we've been apart," confessed Sitka finally.

"So, is this love?" teased Kelly.

"I'm going to ask her to marry me."

Daily flight paths were derived by subdividing each of the twelve survey blocks into strips thirty longitude minutes wide. A random mark was selected along the northern and southern edges of each block. The straight line joining these two points was called a transect. They flew as many transects as time and weather permitted.

"Coming up on Survey Block 12," said Sitka.

A large scale Beaufort Gyre moved the waters westward in a clockwise flow from the Canadian Basin. Kelly switched on the common communications system so that their commentary from here on could be recorded. "Descend to target altitude."

Sitka eased the Otter down through the light snowfall and freezing temperature to fifteen hundred feet, the height for maximum visibility and minimum disturbance to the whales.

"Thar she blows! Port ahoy!" hollered Tractor, as he always did, when he spotted the first whale of the survey through the Otter's bubble windows.

A lone bowhead leisurely swam on the surface. Black all over, the whale sported a distinctive white patch under the chin dotted with a series of black spots. Bowheads had no dorsal fin. Instead, they possessed twenty-five-foot wide flukes behind a yellow-tinged gray band. They fed on minute copepods inhabiting the surface of the water. Hanson quickly worked his handheld clinometer, an instrument used to pinpoint every sighting.

A cow surfaced beside the bull. Sitka diverted the Otter toward the two whales. Named for their most prominent feature, an arch-shaped mouth which extended almost a third of their length, a bowhead bull could accommodate a pair of elephants standing side by side when he lowered his jaw.

The crew observed and recorded their behavior, confirmed their number. Kelly observed, "No calves."

Tractor entered all the data into his laptop. The disks were shipped off to Anchorage, where specialized software analyzed the effects of ice cover, human activity and other oceanographic conditions on the whales' migration route. The US Department of the Interior then released detailed maps and tables.

In the course of the next two hours and several transects, Kelly, Hanson and Tractor made only three further sightings. Bowheads had been killed primarily for their baleen plates, the longest of any whale. Between 1850 and 1913, the bowhead population fell precipitously from 62,000 to a mere 4,000, after which they were considered commercially extinct. Alaskan Inuit, led by their village elders, were still permitted to hunt them. They took twenty bowheads annually as part of their traditional hunt. Conservationists pleaded for a total ban under the Endangered Species Act, but American law exempted native Indians and Inuit from any ban, labeling them "subsistence and aboriginal hunters."

The crew commenced their final leg back to Nome.

"I saw a copy of a memo from my beloved Congressmen from Alaska, seeking permission to harvest seventeen additional bowheads," said Sitka. Born and raised around the oil rigs here, where both his parents had worked before they retired to Seattle, he was one-eighth Native American. Still, he could not support the continued killing.

"It's election time," said Tractor with a cynical smile.

Aboriginal whaling was a major voters' issue in the Northwest. Even though Inuit and Native Americans could not be blamed for decimating bowheads, that dubious honor being owned by nineteenth century commercial whalers, every bowhead taken exponentially diminished the chances of sustaining the species.

"But Jan Everett is close to getting aboriginal and coastal whaling banned at the IWC meeting next Friday," said Sitka. It was the last remaining loophole that allowed whaling nations to hunt.

"I love that woman," said Kelly. "She's got balls."

"The MHA is predicting the IWC will fold if Jan wins," said Hanson. The Marine Hunters Alliance was an international pro-whaling lobby based in Reine, Norway.

A violent bout of clear air turbulence rattled the aircraft and the crew's nerves briefly. Kelly checked the control panel. The A5000 — a state-of-the-art, Department of Defense navigation system, with an internal GPS that could pinpoint the Otter's position to within fifty feet — was dead. It had been acting up the past two days. Fearing Maintenance might ground them so close to the end of the survey, Sitka and Kelly had decided not to include the problem in their daily reports.

Sitka caught her eye and tapped the control panel. That had been correcting the problem. The A5000 came back on. He set a course southwest and switched to autopilot.

They chatted idly.

Later, when he should have heard from the Air Traffic Control in Nome and did not, Sitka radioed in. "Nome CT, this is OCS-oh-4-5, do you copy?"

"Roger, OCS-oh-4-5," crackled the naturally reassuring voice of Matthew McGrath, the ATC specialist in Nome.

Sitka recognized McGrath's voice. "Matt?"

"Hey, Dan."

"You don't see us yet?"

"Negative, OCS-oh-4-5, you're not within my range yet," McGrath replied.

"That's strange," said Sitka. He double checked his coordinates.

"I'm showing we are forty-three miles northeast of you."

The Otter ran into an impenetrable bank of fog and heavy snowfall. Sitka stayed on the radio while McGrath called up the National Weather Service's downlink station at Gilmore Creek, where imagery of global weather was acquired from US meteorological polar and geostationary satellites. They pinpointed the leading edge of the fog and heavy snow.

"You're in the Bering Strait south of the Chuckchi Sea," said McGrath. The Otter was a hundred and eighty miles off the coast of Alaska and traveling toward Russia.

"How did we get so off course?" asked Hanson.

Sitka and Kelly exchanged a guilty glance. Sitka said dismissively, "That turbulence must have disoriented the A5000."

"Do we have enough fuel?" asked Tractor.

"Not enough to get back to Nome," replied Kelly.

"Let me make some phone calls," said McGrath. He returned a few minutes later. "We are going to fly you to Russia. Level off at oh-2-5. Take a breather. We'll be handing you over to them in fifteen minutes."

Sitka set the altitude select panel at 2,500 feet. Thick fog and heavy snowfall reduced visibility outside to zero. Everyone remained a little tense. Fifteen minutes later, Tractor's clinometer slid sharply off the counter, as did the computer on Hanson's station.

Kelly straightened, "We're losing height."

"The altitude hold light is on," observed Sitka. Barely did he confirm this, when six quick beeps shattered the tranquility of the cockpit.

"It can't be!" gasped Kelly, the color draining from her face in an instant.

"What?" asked Hanson and Tractor together, swinging around.

"Those beeps came from the radio altimeter," said a flustered Sitka. He grabbed his throttle. A fifteen-pound pressure on the column automatically shut off the autopilot. The switches and lights indicated he was in control.

"It's set at fifty-one feet," explained Kelly, "and sounds when the plane passes fifty feet above that height."

"So we're a hundred and one feet above sea level?" asked Tractor with a tremor.

"That's impossible." Uncertainty raised Sitka's voice.

He realized, for some reason, the altitude hold had never engaged even though the light came on. The altitude deviation warning had not sounded either, another malfunction that would have tipped him of the plane's loss of height, which was a parabola—a shallow, imperceptible curve to start. Neither he nor the others noticed the descent until the curve got progressively steeper and Tractor's clinometer slid.

The fog broke. Everyone gasped. They were arrowing toward the choppy waves of the unforgiving Bering Sea.

"OCS-oh-4-5, how are things coming along?" McGrath's voice crackled lazily over the radio.

It was the last thing Sitka heard.

The Otter flew into the water at 157 miles per hour.

The impact turned Sitka's head. He saw the right wingtip hit the Bering Sea first, then the right engine, then felt the bottom of the fuselage smash into the water. The plane plowed three foamy furrows.

His skull struck the side switch panel. His neck snapped his gaze forward. The Otter raced toward an iceberg. Sitka shut his eyes, anticipating a head-on collision and instant death. Instead, he felt a tremendous jolt. He opened his eyes and realized the plane had glanced the floater at over ninety miles an hour. The cockpit spun so fast, he glimpsed the midsection meet another block of ice. The crash preceded a blast of cold air. The berg had split the Otter in two. The cockpit, together with the wings, skewed off as one piece.

Inside, Sitka's eyes flew about. Everyone was alive, yelling reassurances. Their harnesses held, while the fuselage around them tore away like paper. The auxiliary fuel tanks ignited. A flashfire enveloped the right engine. The propeller blades sheared away in diverging directions.

Kelly's seat broke loose. Her hand smacked Sitka's face.

"Kelly!" yelled Sitka, grabbing it.

But she was being sucked out through a gash. He realized she'd lost her hand and he was holding the gory stump. He recoiled and threw it away just as he glimpsed the right wing take her out.

The engine detonated. The Otter listed powerfully. *Crrrack!* Sitka looked behind fearfully. The bubble window imploded, gone in an instant. So was Hanson's face. He died instantly.

A loud tearing sound followed. Lines spider-webbed across the floor and widened to cracks in the blink of an eye. Tractor yelled out! His seat was sucked into the water just as the fuselage passed over, decapitating him. Tractor's head rolled around Sitka's feet.

Horror took away his voice. Still trapped in the hurtling wreckage, Sitka rode to the top of a wild crest. Gas fumes in the near-empty left side tanks ignited. His seat ejected straight up, then plummeted directly into the inferno of sparks and shrapnel. He resigned himself to death, closed his eyes and opened them when he felt an icy wetness instead of searing heat. He was in the water, alive. He had time enough to register he'd fallen ahead of the burning engine, which barreled toward him.

He somersaulted forward still buckled in his seat and pressed himself face down as far below the water as he could. Fire rushed by inches above him with a numbing roar. He felt his hair singe and cool within seconds. He emerged from the water gasping for air.

The noise of the crash subsided. Sitka became aware of the bone-chilling cold of the Bering Sea. The powerful currents rapidly dispersed the wreckage. Sitka did not fight the sea. He freed the seat cushion which doubled as a flotation device and allowed himself to be carried by the waves.

After an hour, Sitka could see no evidence of the crash. All the pieces of the plane and its dead crew had either sunk or scattered. He lost feeling in his hands and face, the only parts of his body that were exposed. His Gumby suit, a requirement pushed by the Wives Association to reduce deaths among the 350 search-and-rescue cases off Alaska every year, could keep him alive for up to twelve days in subzero water, but the crash had ripped the integrity of the neoprene. He intermittently lost consciousness, slipping and emerging from extended periods of delirium.

When he came out of one such blackout, his eyes saucered in astonishment.

Los Angeles, California

Flashbulbs went off like fireworks when the first lady climbed out of a limousine flying the Stars and Stripes. The scene looked straight out of a movie premiere. But this was the dull Mark Taper Hall and the event a mundane GreenPlanet strategy session in preparation for the International Whaling Commission's Fall Session meeting next Friday to vote on her motion banning aboriginal and coastal whaling.

The GreenPlanet event would have gone unnoticed had it not been for the news leaks in Washington this past week. Reports surfaced that Jan sat in on an Oval Office conference attended by Japan, Norway, Russia and other pro-harvest heavy hitters. Everett sought a compromise. Determined to slam the door shut on further hunting, she refused to budge and dismissed threats of the IWC's demise. There had been similar dire prophecies prior to the successful 1982 moratorium vote and again when Cetacean Bay was created. The Japanese declared in a press conference afterwards that a ban would be tantamount to the US dictating their food, culture and sovereign right to harvest coastal resources. The Norwegian diplomat let slip that the meeting ended with the first couple exchanging angry words.

Catchy sound bites like "First Marriage in a Whale of Trouble," veiled economic threats from Japan which rocked Wall Street, a president who could ill afford any lapses in a tight race that was coming down to the wire, Norway flexing her NATO muscle and mounting dissent inside the IWC—all entwined and elevated her arrival in Los Angeles into the headlines.

Stepping away from her Secret Service, Jan looked straight off a glamour magazine in an emerald green skirt, gold blouse, simple pearls and high heels. Her hair cascaded in curls. Her lips, shaded lightly, opened in an easy, radiant smile. Serious correspondents and yellow journalists crowded the barricades, hurling questions about policy, politics and tabloid fodder. Growing up in the age of the 24/7 news cycle, Jan had always been media savvy. As first lady, she took it to a whole new level, ensuring maximum exposure by making the most powerful and most influential Top 10 list as many times as the best dressed and sexiest. She waved for the cameras and entered through the plain double doors.

Once inside, she became all business, shedding the Secret Service and walking into the conference room alone. It was a full house.

"Hi, Jan," GreenPlanet President John Chambers jostled to her side and greeted her with an oily smile.

"John," Jan replied flatly.

"We should talk," he said in a bearish tone unsuited to the enthusiasm all around.

"Afterwards." Jan saw Raquel approaching with Boycott and Knight.

"Now, if you don't mind," he insisted.

"I'm sure it can wait." She brushed past him. "Hey, guys."

"If looks could kill," chuckled Boycott, "Chambers just pulled the trigger."

"What did you say to him?" asked Raquel.

"Our usual pleasantries," Jan smiled.

Jan and Chambers had a history of confrontation that dated back to the day he took over GreenPlanet, which had, the year prior to his appointment, pulled off a seismic merger. Several hundred eco-groups, from major players to splintered grassroots efforts on every continent, joined forces to work under one umbrella. With offices in almost every major city of every country, it provided the kind of game-changing influence the green cause had always sought. But the coalition grew GreenPlanet suddenly from a tightly knit North American group into a global environmental megacorp.

With a track record of streamlining giant multinational companies, Chambers was narrowly installed by a deeply divided board. Jan led the opposition, pointing to environmental violations in his previous tenures. She openly called him a corporate whore who did not care about GreenPlanet's mission, just the challenge of reorganization and his $1.6 million paycheck.

Chambers directed money and manpower to create a bureaucratic hierarchy and central superoffice in Vancouver. He then set out to transition GreenPlanet from a scrappy outfit into a white-collar lobby group, clashing with the radical wing led by Jan. Prior to his arrival, she had garnered worldwide notoriety for shadowing a freighter carrying nuclear waste to be dumped without safeguards in a poor African nation, scaling a New York skyscraper which housed the world's most recognizable brand name in shoes to protest child labor in their factories overseas and seizing a North Sea oil rig that would have wiped out marine life over five hundred square miles if it had been scuttled as planned in the Atlantic. Her vigilante-style and classic beauty made for splashy covers and headlines.

Jan realized Chambers was not used to playing second fiddle. He was a rock star in the business world. When he took over GreenPlanet, governments shuddered and financial markets reacted because his accomplishments were the stuff of corporate folklore. He'd been named *Time* Man of the Year for recognizing, embracing and exploiting globalization.

She underestimated his cunning early on. He expanded his power base by tripling fundraising and swelling GreenPlanet's coffers. Her ego could not tolerate being sidelined either. When Everett won the White House, she went from personality to phenomenon and decisively wrested the spotlight from Chambers. GreenPlanet took on her militant style. Chambers could not buy attention. He fell into her shadow.

"Forget him," Boycott dismissed. "A pirate whaler was picked up on radio south of the Chinook Trough." A patch of Pacific Ocean about a thousand miles north of Hawaii and feeding ground for sperm whales. "There was one communication in Japanese."

"We can fly to Honolulu tonight," explained Raquel eagerly. "The time difference will get us there around ten PM local time."

"Guess what's waiting?" grinned Boycott. "*Earthforce.*"

Eight months ago, Jan had pulled strings and realized legendary eco-maverick Paul Worthy's long endeavor to procure a submarine, which would enable him to use both stealth and speed to pursue the faster tuna boats, driftnetters and elusive pirate killer-factory ships. Earthforce, Paul's sea-faring ecogroup, after which the sub was named, was the only major green name that had held out of the GreenPlanet merger. Worthy lived by his own rules. His methods constantly tested the fine line between protest and terrorism.

"They've been in Pearl for the past month, training to sail that sub," said Raquel. "They're ready for their first dive."

"It would be a coup," Patrick added, catching some of the enthusiasm, "if we can snatch the manifest. It'll embarrass the heck out of Japan this Friday."

"I promised Carsten I wouldn't stir anything up," said Jan, disappointed.

After the Norwegian incident, she had agreed to maintain a low profile. Publicly, these past three months, Everett and Jan had been the affectionate first couple, an image that endeared them to Americans. Privately, they couldn't have been further apart. They were cordial, even intimate every now and then, but she chose to be excluded from the politics of re-election.

As certainly as their marriage was in the dead zone, the president was in a battle for survival. With Everett and his two opponents, House Majority leader from Massachusetts, Democrat Keith Leeds, and Senate Majority Leader from Florida, Republican Will Todd, carrying the West, East and South, respectively, the Midwest's undecided industrial belt where Japanese investment was concentrated became the most hotly contested prize. A face-off over whaling could turn Tokyo hostile and take him out of contention altogether, ten weeks from the November day of reckoning. Already, Leeds and Todd were pointing to the increasing shift in power from the Executive to the Legislature and constantly characterizing Everett as nothing more than a titular head of state. This forced Everett to reinvent the relevance of his presidency.

"That doesn't mean Paul can't go get them," said Jan.

Raquel shook her head. "He's out of money after all those trial dives and refitting the sub. With you on board, he was hoping GreenPlanet would pick up the tab."

Jan bit her lip. "I'm sorry, guys."

Chambers tapped the microphone and called for order. He made a brief opening statement.

Traditionally, the fall session of the IWC was used by the Scientific Committee to present *The Report*, a bulky document of whale stocks determined over the course of the year through sightings, expeditions, catch figures provided by whaling nations and other studies. Debates and deals between pro and anti-whaling forces followed, determining the catch quota to be voted on in the annual meetings held the following May.

"But the Scientific Committee's computerized formula for setting catch limits," wrote Jan in her petition, "is a complex one that compares total whale stocks in small areas, historical information and most vitally, catch figures, a number that whaling nations submit and the Scientific Committee accepts as an honest and accurate number. However, as the enclosed deposition signed by two Scientific Committee eyewitnesses indicates, Norway not only exceeded its catch figures, but then lied about it, calling into question the integrity of *The Report.*" Jan went on to successfully argue that this fall session be declared "extraordinary." A three-fourths majority was required to abolish "aboriginal and coastal whaling," a fundamental provision in the IWC Schedule.

Media reports this morning placed Jan an impossible six votes shy.

Jan took the podium and shocked everyone. "We are one vote short."

The room erupted.

They discussed coordinating with GreenPlanet's offices worldwide to initiate a massive phone-and-fax campaign that would tie up the lines of the IWC Commissioners of governments still opposed. Starting tomorrow, protestors would picket the guilty embassies and consulates in every major media market. They broke for lunch and finished a couple of hours later.

"We have to talk," said Chambers, cornering her. Jan was about to dismiss him. He added, "You don't want to be the last to know, do you?"

Jan stiffened. "What do you mean?"

He strode away without another word. She followed him into an adjoining room.

Jan spoke first. "Is this about Norway? Does GreenPlanet Europe feel we stole their thunder? They were only planning to stand on sidewalks with posters. What we did is what we should be doing. Wage war. Make real change. If you don't like it, quit."

"I was hoping you would."

"And let GreenPlanet fall into your hands? No thanks."

"I can force you out."

Jan remained unruffled. "You need the board's support and it's full of CEOs and other special interests who spend a lot of time in

Washington, where, if you've forgotten, I have some influence."

"Then why did your husband's chief of staff call me to make it happen?"

That made Jan blink.

Chambers seized on her surprise. "You will not be representing GreenPlanet at the IWC meeting on Friday. I will. Here," he removed a piece of paper from his pocket. "Your resignation."

Jan took the letter. She looked at Chambers, then tore the sheet into shreds and rained them on his shoes.

"I have the votes on the board to make it happen."

Jan's eyes blazed. "Don't overestimate yourself." Her quick temper flashed. "Fuck with me and I'll nail your ass to the unemployment wall."

Jan climbed into the limousine. Raquel, Boycott and Knight lounged in the back seat. Jan told them what had just happened. It was a silent ride back to Malibu, where Everett and she owned a spectacular hilltop home. She barely noticed the refreshing sea breeze gusting up the lush canyon. Jan went straight to the phone. Her friends knew her well enough to escape onto the balcony.

"Hi, honey," said Everett, answering the direct line to his bedroom.

"Darling," Jan began tautly, disregarding the weariness in his voice from campaigning across four cities in the Midwest all day. "Did you know that my letter of resignation from GreenPlanet was waiting for me in Los Angeles."

"What?"

"Apparently it was drafted by the White House."

"I don't know what you're talking about."

"You're priceless, dear."

"Jan, I swear—"

"Our deal's off." She slammed down the telephone, rattling everything else on the table. She called out to the others, "We're going to Hawaii!"

Nome, Alaska

Dan Sitka came to in the hospital. The curtains were drawn on either side of his bed. A smile twitched at the corners of his mouth. *I'm alive.* He became aware of a dull throbbing around his thighs. Being a southpaw, he naturally reached out with his left hand. An excruciating pain came with the effort and a gasp wrenched out. He looked down.

And screamed.

From the elbow down, his left arm was amputated. So were both his legs below the knees.

A doctor and a nurse ran to his side.

"What the hell did you do?" he shouted at them.

"Calm down. I'm Dr. Myron."

"But why? What happened?"

"You'd been in freezing water for more than four hours," said Dr. Myron explained. "The frost bite was so bad we had no choice."

"This can't be happening," Sitka sobbed.

"Once you've had something to eat, the nurse will sedate you, get you some pain-free rest."

After the doctor and nurse left his bedside, Sitka lay staring at the ceiling. *Why me? Why this? On my last day!*

The nurse returned a few minutes later with a bowl of thin soup. Sitka insisted he could feed himself. She propped him up against the pillows, wrapped a hospital-blue paper bib around his neck and placed the bowl on a tray table across his stomach.

"Can I get a paper and pen after I finish?" requested Sitka.

"Sure," smiled the nurse.

Sitka wrote a letter using his right hand. The handwriting was unsteady but decipherable. He painfully folded the letter. A searing pain robbed him of his breath after he inserted it into the hospital envelope. Sweat and tears poured down his cheeks. His mouth was so dry he was barely able to form the words, "Can you seal the flap and mail it?"

"Yes, of course." The nurse smiled warmly. She daubed his right arm with wet gauze and injected him with morphine.

His world went black.

Chinook Trough, North Pacific Ocean

In the bloody golden dusk and orange-blue waters, graceful silhouettes rose in front of the evening sun. Plumes of water vapor, mucus and oil droplets spouted high. Giant plateaus of dark hide grew majestically out of the ocean, cascading water. With watery roars, tail fins cut the surface in far-reaching rains of fine spray. Droplets glittered brilliantly against the yellow and red palette. Airing twin flukes clear of the water like the wings of some majestic bird, sixty-foot bodies languidly arced and fell back into the water. In the span of seconds, with a fluid forward rolling motion, hundreds of tons of the most enigmatic mammals on earth surfaced, breathed and dived again.

Physeter macrocephalus, Greek for "blower with a big head," described that square-headed, grinning mammal most people immediately conjured in their mind's eye when whales were mentioned because of *Moby Dick*. The sperm whale was an atypical whale. Gallivanting alone under the polar waters north of Japan, the bull led a separate life for reasons still beyond human understanding and visited the tropics only to mate. He was joined by other bulls and they swam the giant arc past the Aleutian chain. In years past, several hundred made this trip. This year, the pod numbered only thirty.

Channels of water deep under the ocean carried their mating calls. Different species of whales used these channels to communicate with one another halfway around the globe. The language of sperms was a series of clicks, bangs and wheezes called codas. There were at least twenty-three different arrangements, invariably beginning with a coda of five evenly spaced clicks, which scientists believed to be the sperm's equivalent of "Hi, gimme five!"

Upon arriving at the Chinook Trough, there were the usual standoffs and fights. More than one bull wanted a particular young cow, who played hard to get. She flipped over belly up and placed her vulva out of reach of the circling males, a promiscuous lot, who gang raped her the moment she rolled over to breathe. Other females came to her aid, escalating matters into a free-for-all involving dozens of leviathans roaring, pounding and hurting each other with terrifying intensity.

There were few back-downs. They blew challenging streams of bubbles and flung their sixty-ton bodies against one another. The sounds of colliding blubber sent deafening dull slaps across the ocean. Water erupted with the intensity of storm waves when bulls buried their titanic snouts under rival suitors and ejected them clean out of the water. Weaker sperms used their teeth and barnacles to fight back. The losers slunk away, their flukes shredded, their magnificent bodies horribly bruised. The ocean was awash with blood, attracting sharks, who preyed upon the wounded.

By destroying the "gentle giant" image, recent behavioral research had eroded much of the awesome myth of sperm whales. And even though Herman Melville enthused "his great genius is declared in his doing nothing to prove it," marine biologists revealed that their IQ was nothing to write home about. True, the full grown bull possessed a brain three times heavier than a human's, but rather than intelligence, much of that brain was utilized to find food by echolocation—dispatching sound waves and processing the returning echoes. Sperms then stunned their prey with concentrated blasts of sound. On the other hand, like intelligent species, they were a close-knit, cooperative group of nursing females, yearlings and adult males. DNA sloughed off cows suggested that they cared for calves communally. Mothers staggered their forty-minute dives so there was always one adult guarding the young.

"Whale!"

Rending the peaceful evening air over the Pacific, this discordant human cry reverberated over the speakers of the *Stavenger*, one of the many killer-factory ships that disregarded international laws and regulations protecting whales.

Originally built and christened the *Kugolev* in 1968 as a high-speed catcher for the former Soviet Union's notorious Vostok whaling fleet, she had been purchased through a bank in the Netherlands and had since traversed the globe from the Arctic to the Antarctic under eleven different names. *Stavenger* was her current incarnation. Her "ownership" shifted with surreptitious regularity to post box companies in Norway, South Africa, Liechtenstein, the Bahamas and several South American countries. Her base of operations moved constantly around corrupt African and South American ports. She escaped legal action by altering her flag of convenience at will and docked only long enough to empty her ill-gotten cargo. Since she stalked alone, she moved quickly, stealthily and profitably.

Ecological detectives had exposed these brazen pirate whalers as far back as 1975. Even in this new millennium, they roamed the oceans with impunity, respecting neither national borders nor endangered species. It was open season on every whale all year round. The *Stavenger*'s pirates killed an average of seven hundred whales annually. If they were spotted, they cut loose their kill without a thought and outran their pursuers in the swashbuckling tradition of bandits on the high seas.

A bell rang on all decks. Most of the motley crew of the worst Africans, Asians, British, Norwegians, Latin Americans and Russians lounged in the Pig—a dingy room on the starboard side, where they gathered, smoked, drank and gambled between harvests. The unruly international cast was united by greed, cruelty and the English language, which they spoke with a multitude of accents and varying degrees of fluency. Crisscrossing shouts, laced more with obscene homespun expletives than recognizable words out of the dictionary, they took off with a thunder of boots to their stations.

Captain Arlov Vesprhein strode along the catwalk leading to the gun platform. Nobody embodied the breed of the pirate better than the *Stavenger*'s skipper. Freebooting, ruthless, arrogant, he brought to mind the handsome, dangerous heroes of Harlequin novels. His short blond hair drew attention to his cold blue eyes. A crooked, broken nose softened the square jaw. Perfectly even teeth flashed behind full, wide lips. He was forty-five years old and looked thirty. He insisted on being called captain and had even murdered a man who'd refused to address him as such.

He wore a pair of shorts, nothing else, proudly showing off a washboard abdomen. His bare body was a geography of rippling, carefully nurtured and beautifully demarcated muscles. Every inch of his back and arms was intricately tattooed with demons and gods in a gaudy rainbow of colors. He leaped down on to the gun platform.

His balls were killing him. They had brought three whores with them on this trip. The crew shared two women and he kept the prettiest one for himself. Even so, he wore two condoms. He was paranoid about sexually transmitted diseases, having seen his father suffer painfully from unprotected indiscretions.

Tightening the headset and microphone over his square, angular skull, he plugged the dribbling wires into the radio on his belt. He waved behind his head, a signal to the squat Korean cramped in the crow's nest. Immediately, the lookout's nasal voice squawked over the ship's speakers and Vesprhein's headsets. "Whale! Twenty thirty o'them!"

Vesprhein recognized them instantly as sperms by the forty-five-degree forward angle of their spouts. Instead of a dorsal fin, they had a series of humps corrugating their back.

He tapped the mouthpiece. "Bridge. Can you hear me?"

"Loud and clear, Captain," answered First Mate Alfonso.

"Decided to join us after all, Number One?" Vesprhein's law, which applied without prejudice to officer and deck hand alike, stated that every man be at his station within two minutes of the bell. The captain had spies who reported any tardiness, which he then punished with half rations, menial work and physical pain.

"I-I w-was—" stammered Alfonso.

"Getting fucked?" Vesprhein cackled.

The Korean laughed. They were hooked up to the speakers on the ship and their laughter resonated across the ship laced with static.

Vesprhein had named this son of a butcher as first mate only because his uncle was harbormaster at the port of Iquique, Chile, the *Stavenger*'s current base of operations. He didn't much care for the hairy, morose, twenty-six-year-old giant, whom he dismissed as a dumb prick and took every opportunity to degrade. The post of first mate on Vesprhein's boat suggested importance without granting any. It was a largely ceremonial and revolving one reserved to curry favors.

"Lady, do we have a count?" Vesprhein switched from humor to business.

"Yes, Captain," reported Derek Thatcher at once over the radio, "thirty whales straight ahead," The big-boned British scumbag was better known as Iron Lady.

He operated the *Stavenger*'s FishEye, a cutting edge device that used acoustics to paint a real-time 3D picture of the ocean beneath the waves. Resolution and sensitivity were such that the FishEye displayed the exact spatial location and size of their prey's speed, the water temperature, distance log, split-screen zoom, adjustable gain and contrast, alarms and a lot more.

"Full ahead," ordered Vesprhein, gripping the handles.

The telegraph rang and the bell in the engine room clanged all the way up to the deck. With a roar, the *Stavenger* surged forward, her bow plunging in and exploding out of the undulating waters. The sun, now an ocher ball, touched the ocean surface and gilded everything, including the *Stavenger*'s roaring spray. Vesprhein tightened his grip on the harpoon gun, bouncing with the wild bow. He'd been hunting whales longer than most of his crew combined. The bulls would sense the *Stavenger*'s noisy screws and flee. But the cows would not.

"Eighteen cows," reported Iron Lady, counting off the remaining adults who stayed with the calves scattering in panic.

"Calf gonna blow now," shouted the Korean. "Ten o'clock."

Vesprhein swung the gun over and tensed with the instincts and knowledge passed down across three generations of whalers. Fear drove the youngsters to dive without taking a deep breath. Consequently, they returned for air frequently. With a big splash, a gasping male surfaced square in the middle of Vesprhein's sights.

He pulled the trigger. The gun smoked with a loud report, releasing a cold harpoon, universally regarded as the most brutal weapon of death and outlawed by the Humane Killing Subcommittee of the IWC. It was a steel pipe, with neither a grenade head nor a line trailing back to the gun. Glinting wickedly through the low beams of the fading sun, the front of the shaft, which had an ordinary, machine-pointed cap screwed on, sliced into the calf's flesh by the sheer force of its impact.

He squealed.

Vesprhein knew exactly how the calf would behave. Reeling, bucking, thrashing with an agony his tender age left him unprepared to tolerate, he twisted into a dive. This only served to shred his innards. Gallons upon gallons of blood swilled into the water. Reeling and bucking and thrashing, he broke out of the ocean and rent the air with cries. An explosive would have killed the baby instantly, but Vesprhein wanted the calf alive to trap his mother.

Shrieking protectively, she emerged. Vesprhein did not kill her immediately. Her son would take an hour to die and she would not leave his side. She howled and rolled over and over in the crimson ocean. Vesprhein mortally wounded more calves, bringing all their mothers bleating with grief to the surface. Fiercely loyal, they gently caressed the dying young, some not even their own.

The *Stavenger* started a slow circle. Iron Lady called out the location of the cows as they surfaced and Vesprhein fired grenade-tipped harpoons. Sixteen inches inside the skull, the trigger mechanism—a barb connected by a wire—detonated a penthrite charge. The ensuing explosion rippled out powerful shockwaves, lodging shrapnel in the brain, killing them instantly.

It was dark when the last cow died. Immense floodlights lit up the ocean and the carnage. There were too many whales to tow, so Vesprhein dropped anchor. The *Stavenger* was modified to function as a processor. The reconstructed rear contained a slipway, an arched hole with a ramp, allowing whales to be dragged on to the long slaughter deck atop a quick-freezing plate. Refrigerated compartments packed every available cubic inch of the remaining space.

Vesprhein marched back and forth on the catwalk above like a CEO proudly regarding his million-dollar empire. Winches lowered cables with piercing scrawls. Wearing thigh boots, wielding hooks and chainsaws, the pirates leaped on the first sperm hauled aboard. The men would work through the night and much of tomorrow, hauling the dead whales up the slipway, one after another, skinning, hacking and refrigerating the meat.

Washington DC

White House Chief of Staff George Pleasance came in before anybody and left no earlier than midnight. Tonight was no exception. He was grappling with the president's stagnant poll numbers. As always, his manner reeked of concentration and intensity.

The son of a polygamist Mormon who had five wives and eighteen children, Pleasance grew up lacking affection or attention. His father neglected all his children equally. Pleasance inherited his mother's outward submissiveness and inner rage. As the first wife, she and her children receded further with each subsequent marriage. Born and raised in a fundamentalist compound, she was too afraid to speak or break out. Her misery hung like a dank odor over her children. So Pleasance wasn't a happy child, especially frustrated because he realized early on he was more intelligent than everyone else, including adults. He regarded home schooling as brainwashing the next generation of religious extremists for a life in the margins. He envisioned a greater destiny for himself.

Isolating himself, Pleasance spent hours in front of a computer— his lens to the world outside, one that came with an invitation to vote in an opinion poll on practically every web page. The concept of gauging approval from cold impersonal stats fit his quest to be important without the need for social interaction. He secretly applied to and was accepted by the University of Utah. A week after his eighteenth birthday, Pleasance forged his father's signature for financial aid, stole fifty dollars from his wallet on the one night he spent at the house and slipped out of the compound without as much as a note to his mother.

In college, politics married his love for stats and blogging. He launched a website that connected polls to campaign strategy. A local politician noticed and hired him. Pleasance did not complete school, graduating instead from local to state to races for the US Congress before he turned twenty-five, the youngest political operative inside the Beltway. This early success only swelled his ego, which he kept entirely internal due to his unshakable repression, but manifested in his cutthroat tactics to win at all costs. Coming off an impressive upset win of a rookie over an established Rep in the House, he moved to Washington, where he met Everett who was two years into his term as a young senator.

They connected at once, united by the common bond of a deprived childhood they both hated and escaped with their driving ambition. Each quickly recognized that the other filled missing personal and political blanks for the ultimate power trip they both sought: the US presidency.

In Everett, Pleasance saw the new breed of politician: an Independent, just like 41 percent of the electorate. The major parties had long since lost their majority in the voter rolls. But Everett lacked name recognition nationally. That belonged to Jan, Pleasance's research showed. She was born and raised in California, exactly the right place for her looks, activism and dare devilry. The right stuff for Hollywood. Daytime television had built her into every woman's hero. High profile celebrities fawned over her causes. She loved the idea of Everett as president and agreed without a thought to be the springboard to widen his exposure. They began to appear together on lightweight top rated shows.

Pleasance quickly learned that Jan was no fool. While they presented the picture of the "now" couple—spouses professionally on par with each other—she never overshadowed Everett, pulling back just enough to make every appearance a little more about him, even on glossy magazine covers. Pleasance made them play coy, so that, when Everett finally announced his intention to run for president as an Independent, the media ate it up. They hailed his candidacy as a testament to the growing wave of voter rejection of deeply partisan, career party candidates.

From start to finish, Pleasance ran a brilliant campaign of numbers. Taking the best from the left and the right, he engineered Everett's victory with enough of the middle. At 38 percent, it was the lowest fraction of the popular vote to elect a president. A micromanager, he helped pick Everett's Cabinet, an unprecedented mixture of Democrats and Republicans, then made it an event, having the president announce it from the same podium where he was sworn in to office. The salient features of the men and women they chose were their wealth, power and proven mettle in political combat. After the first hundred days, analysts chalked Everett's outline, reporting him a casualty of these partisan big guns, who had carved up Washington among themselves and left the idealistic entrepreneur-turned-politician with nothing but the White House.

Pleasance did not disagree. An unforgivable mistake, especially for an ardent student of the history of missteps by prior rookies. He'd grown close to Lhea and Vice President Adrian during the campaign. Together, they conspired to tighten the reins on the Cabinet. Creating their own special provinces, the three men became Everett's enforcers and purged all opposition close to the president—the biggest and earliest shakeup ever.

Pleasance appointed Adrian the conduit to the Oval Office for the secretary of state, defense secretary, National Security Advisor, the CIA and the Pentagon. Then he subtly reorganized the chain of command to place Thomas Lhea, Adrian's counterpart in domestic affairs, between the president and all the executive agencies from Agriculture to Veterans Affairs. Neither Adrian nor Lhea ever acted without Pleasance's authority. As Everett's friend and confidant, he took over the administrative reins of the White House. He supervised the staff, organized the president's schedule and granted time in the Oval Office to members of Congress, committees, the media and public. He decided who could and could not see Everett, even taking a seat to the president's immediate right during Cabinet meetings.

Pleasance turned his chair around to face the window. Rain beat down hard. Thunderstorms raged over most of the eastern seaboard. They could have done without the distraction of the upcoming whaling vote on Friday, particularly since the president and the first lady were widely publicized to be on opposite sides. Once in the White House, Pleasance had hoped Jan would moderate her views. Instead, she'd used the Oval Office to intensify her cause for animal rights. Never did a month pass without her getting embroiled in controversy. Recent polls showed cracks in her popularity. An alarming 40 percent considered her an environmental terrorist. The disapproval came mostly from men. Sixty percent of women still held Jan above reproach, but that was significantly down from 78 percent when the Everetts were inaugurated.

Pleasance disliked Jan from the moment they met. He'd had to fight for everything she'd grown up with. Unlike Everett's, Pleasance's jealousy was indignant and hateful, even though they had needed all that he despised about her to reach this pinnacle. But now, her strength was Everett's greatest weakness.

"George!" Everett stormed in.

Pleasance started and swiveled the chair.

"What the hell are you trying to pull? Jan called. She—"

"Was asked to resign from GreenPlanet," said Pleasance, recovering his composure as quickly as he'd lost it.

"Did you have anything to do with it?"

"Yes." When they were alone, they spoke like friends and equals. "I never thought she'd get so close."

The US position on whaling was decided every year by a show of hands in an interagency committee, which consisted of representatives of the Departments of Sate, National Marine Fisheries Service, the Marine Mammal Commission, other federal agencies and conservation organizations like GreenPlanet. Jan had been surprised that the department heads unanimously agreed on a complete ban of aboriginal and coastal whaling. Little did she know that Pleasance was confident the US position would be in the minority. So it came as a shock to him when Jan announced she was only one vote short.

"She's still one vote short," said Everett. "What's your point?"

"If she finds it, there'll be repercussions. In a close race, Alaska may be the difference between winning and losing if she gets aboriginal whaling banned."

"I've been working the phones too," said Everett.

"So she will lose?" insisted Pleasance. "Are you sure?"

"Yes," snapped Everett, then his shoulders sagged.

Here comes the guilt, Pleasance thought and nipped it right away. "She's gotten just as much mileage for her cause out of you being president."

Everett nodded. "True."

"A second term means she can do even more."

"I guess."

"You have to be cutthroat about this," Pleasance said firmly.

"It seems so ungrateful, George."

"She must lose for you to win. It's as simple as that."

"I still hate it. I hate hurting her. As tough as things are between us, I still love her."

"I know," Pleasance feigned.

"How could you even think you'd be able to squeeze Jan out of GreenPlanet? She's the face of that thing."

"Exactly. Chambers said Vancouver feels overwhelmed by the first lady's name and persona. Jan is GreenPlanet and GreenPlanet is Jan. His faction in the board wants her out, or at least minimized, but they were afraid they'd offend the White House. I told him the president did not interfere with the internal politics of a private organization."

"Jan knows you're behind it."

"I don't care, Carsten," said Pleasance gently. "My loyalty is to you."

The president's irritation subsided. "I know. I appreciate it. I am sorry to put you in the crossfire. But we need her if we're going to win again, George."

I wish we didn't, Pleasance wanted to say.

"Couldn't Chambers have waited until November?" asked Everett.

"I'm guilty of the timing. I thought Jan wouldn't do anything to hurt your chances."

"She won't. But red flags go up in her head the instant you force her into anything."

Pleasance nodded. "I'm sorry."

"I'm the one who should be. It's not fair to you my failing

marriage is complicating everything."

"It is what it is. What did she say when she called?"

"She said our deal's off and hung up."

Pleasance's eyes flickered with concern.

"Don't worry. I'll call her in the morning." Everett left, closing the door behind him.

Pleasance waited until the president's footsteps receded out of earshot. Then he telephoned the home of the assistant director, Protective Operations, US Secret Service. The call woke him. "Hello."

"This is Pleasance," he snapped. "Where is the first lady?"

Honolulu, Hawaii

Jan peered out of the descending plane. Day or night, the approach into Honolulu International Airport presented a magnificent spectacle. The most famous extinct volcano, Diamond Head, loomed as a dark silhouette west of Koko head amidst glittering lights from the eighty-six-square mile stretch of urban Honolulu.

In 1887 King Kalakaua gave the United States permission to develop a coal station at the confluence of the two mouths of the Pearl Stream, named for the once abundant oysters. The station grew and spread across 22,000 acres to become the Pearl Harbor Naval Base, the world's largest, best sheltered anchorage and the second largest source of income for the local economy. Deep cuts in the defense budget had forced Pearl Harbor to expand its once purely military operations to include civilian contracts, one of which was the refitting and trials of the *Earthforce*.

She had been originally built at the Electric Boat Company in Groton and commissioned on September 14, 1942, to serve in World War II. She remained one of the few submarines never to take a direct hit. Jan rescued her from the being scrapped altogether by negotiating her donation to eco-maverick, Paul Worthy.

About an hour after they landed, Jan stood atop the sail with Raquel, Boycott and Knight. Her Secret Service stood on the pier, watching the sub pull out. She had forbidden them from coming along.

Repainted with the same dull black that once afforded her maximum concealment from German U-boats, the *Earthforce*'s 283-foot length and sixteen-foot diameter was almost invisible in the beautiful, warm, humid Hawaiian night. They steered past active submarine piers, dry docks, tanks, faceless buildings and Hospital Point into the open ocean. The sounds and lights of Waikiki Beach receded. The currents sweeping across roughly heaved the submarine the instant she left the sheltered headlands.

Worthy leaned over the hatch. "All ahead full."

The bridge trembled with the vibration of the twin propeller shafts. Four clouds of vapor lifted out of the aft exhausts. The breeze strengthened, carrying everyone's hair aloft and billowing out their clothes by infiltrating the gaps.

"I'm beat," yawned Raquel.

"Me too," said Boycott.

"When do we submerge?" asked Knight.

"Not until we're close to our target," said Worthy. "Unlike nuclear submarines, which can stay submerged for months, the charge on our batteries lasts only about forty hours underwater."

"Then I'm going to get some sleep. Good night." Raquel dropped out of view. Boycott and Knight followed.

Alone together, Worthy and Jan stood in silence for several moments, then he asked tentatively, "How's Carsten?"

"Fine. I guess."

"Everyone's saying it's a close race."

"It sure is shaping up that way."

"Things okay between you two?"

Jan shrugged wordlessly. Worthy changed the subject. "You being at the top has really made a difference, Jan."

"But there's so much more we could have accomplished," she lamented.

"Come on, the president's job is hard. He's got to pick his fights and sometimes he's gonna drop the ball."

"Always me and my causes?"

"The comfort zone of marriage."

Washington DC

"No!" snapped Pleasance, rounding his desk and sitting down. It was nearly four AM and he rode the ragged edge. He hadn't gone home or slept. At the other end of the line were the two agents from Jan's protective detail, calling from the Honolulu office of the Secret Service. "Do not alert the coast guard. How much do the media know?"

"Nothing, sir. Nobody knows she's here." Jan had slipped by the press barricades outside her Malibu home by using her housekeeper as a decoy. She joined the others, who'd left early, aboard Air Force Two and deplaned at Hickam Air Force Base, headquarters of the Pacific Air Command and home to the 15th Air Wing in Honolulu.

Pleasance slammed down the phone. *Goddamn her.* He closed his eyes to settle his anger. He decided not to wake Everett and tell him his wife was in Hawaii aboard a submarine. He didn't want the president ordering another Norwegian Sea-style interference. His rivals were already charging Everett with turning the US Navy into the first lady's personal fleet.

Pleasance called Lhea. "I want to keep an eye on her without any overt deployment."

"Sure," said Lhea at once.

❄

A telephone rang in a house on Oxon Hill, Maryland, a neighborhood housing employees of the nearby Pentagon. The tall, forty-year-old resident of the tastefully decorated home blinked his eyes open. Nobody would call at this hour unless it was an emergency.

"Robert Random," he answered. He headed the National Reconnaissance Office.

The world of reconnaissance and surveillance in Washington was a Byzantine one, controlled by a security system known as Sensitive Compartmented Information. As the name suggested, the operations were elaborate, secret and separate. No individual was allowed access to all SCI activities. All that changed when Everett took office. Thanks to Random's friendship with Lhea, in the short span of a year they accomplished what no other administration had dared: they integrated the different SCI entities into the NRO. Irate committee chiefs argued that redundancy kept the powerful tool of surveillance out of a single entity's hands. Recognizing that knowledge was power in Washington, Everett backed Lhea and Random.

"Nobody," said Lhea firmly over the phone, "but nobody, has clearance except you, me and a need-to-know hierarchy."

In the concentric rings of power around this president, Random operated in the circle immediately beyond Pleasance, Lhea and Adrian. Random did not ask any further questions and swung out of the bed. He knew that if he played his cards right and won Pleasance's validation, he could be the next National Security Advisor if Everett won re-election. His wife rolled over sleepily. He brushed his teeth, showered and dressed quickly.

When he reached the office, his deputy waited with an initial report. "We don't have any overhead platforms where the first lady's headed." Platforms referred to spacecraft, satellites and reconnaissance planes. "The closest one is *Lacrosse 3*."

An incredibly versatile spy satellite, *Lacrosse 3* produced images by shooting radio waves to the target area below, processing the return signals and transmitting them to White Sands, New Mexico, via the relay satellite *Milstar*. But the National Security Agency owned a piece of *Milstar*. They would immediately notice if *Lacrosse 3* was moved, particularly to a remote region of the Pacific Ocean.

"It has to be a 5600," said Random. The number 5000 represented space-based imaging assets in general. The 5600 was a KH-14, the most advanced spy satellite. Random's NRO controlled all three KH-14s currently in orbit.

"The closest one is 5603 over China," said the deputy. The last digit represented the latest in the series.

"Don't we need to locate the submarine first?"

"There's a SOSUS station at Johnston who can help us." SOSUS was the Sound Surveillance System, a worldwide network of US listening posts that fed submarine activity of every nation on the globe to a large chart in the Current Operations Department within the Navy Operational Intelligence Center.

"Do we have somebody down in Johnston who can bypass NOIC?" asked Random. He didn't want the Navy Secretary, who was aligned on the side of the National Security Advisor, to find out.

"Yup."

North Pacific Ocean

"Captain to conn." The speakers on all levels aboard the *Earthforce* crackled with a loud voice, "Surface contact."

Worthy trotted down the passageway into the Control Room. The crew had taken turns to grab short spells of sleep throughout the night and this morning so that at least one person manned each station. Rorque Jr. was on duty now. Once an executive officer in Her Majesty's Service, he had since retired and taken up environmental protection as a cause.

"Morning, Rorque," greeted Worthy.

"Hey, Paul. Are we gonna blow his arse out of the water?"

"I think we should make sure he's the pirate first."

"Details, details," snorted Rorque and turned to peruse the array of diving and steering controls around him.

His dry, poker-faced humor tickled Worthy, who guffawed and started up the ladder to the conning tower, which housed the navigation, radar and sonar equipment. There were two periscopes. The forward attack periscope had a small, inch-and-a-half window. The other periscope had been modified for videography so that violations could be recorded.

Worthy stepped toward the blue-lit area equipped with sound equipment currently found on US nuclear submarines. Massive declassification of Strategic Defense Initiative programs had enabled Worthy to purchase the transducers that were mounted on the submarine's bow.

"I'm pretty certain it's our quarry," said the sonarman, pointing to a tiny blip as the tracer arm rolled up-screen. "The ship is not moving. Engines are stopped." Specialized software filtered out extraneous ocean and marine life noises to isolate the turbine, a complex, throbbing *whoosh*. "But I'm reading shrill metallic sounds."

"Flensers," Worthy recognized the power knives used to cut up whales. "Will they hear us coming?"

"I doubt it."

"Are you working on her ID?"

"Yup," nodded the sonarman. "We should have something shortly." Their computer contained an encyclopedia of sonar signatures of known pirate whalers and other marauders on the high seas. The data included "integrity" information, like condition of the superstructure and keel, recent damage reports and other details such as current base of operations, flags of convenience, ownership information and captain and crew profiles.

"I'll be outside," said Worthy.

Jan, Raquel and the lookout were already there. They'd woken up at the crack of dawn to chip in, making coffee and serving breakfast.

It was a clear day, quiet and calm. The sun was directly overhead, signaling noon. The *Earthforce* rocketed at maximum revolutions toward the continually receding horizon.

Stepping up and across, Worthy asked, "See anything?"

"Nope," said the lookout. He wore a bulky helmet with a thick, dark tinged visor.

He took it off and Worthy slipped it on. Called the Crusader II, the helmet was once classified and manufactured purely for US military use. Worthy had customized it with binoculars over the visor. It also went from regular field glasses to infrared high vision with the push of a button.

"Twenty miles to target," crackled the sonarman's voice on the external speaker.

"Time to go below," announced Worthy.

"Are we gonna submerge?" asked Raquel excitedly.

"You mean dive," chided Worthy.

"Excuse me."

Worthy leaned over the hatch and yelled, "Rig out the bow planes."

With a faint whirring sound, two slanted-down fins rotated and extended on either side of the bow until they were perpendicular to the hull.

"All set to dive."

An alarm sounded. Worthy followed the two women down the ladder into the tiny conning tower space. He slammed the hatch shut and rotated the wheel in the center, dogging it firmly into place.

"Green board," Rorque's voice crackled over the intercom from the Control Room below, referring to a hydraulic manifold monitoring the hatches and other hull openings called the Christmas Tree. Lights glowed red if open or green when closed. "We are rigged and ready to dive."

"Dive, dive, dive!" Worthy grinned at the women. "I love saying that."

The ballast tanks opened their vents with sharp blasts. Slender fountains of water erupted through the slotted deck. The bow tilted into the ocean, which rose along the sides of the conning tower and submerged the tiny eyeports.

Washington DC

Twelve hours after his request, Pleasance's phone rang. The caller ID blinked with Robert Random's name.

"Robert," greeted Pleasance tersely. "Wait." He conferenced in Lhea, who was in his office across the hall. "Go."

"I have recon photos," reported Random. "She's headed toward a pirate whaler called the *Stavenger*."

Jan's being on the *Earthforce* should have been brought up during this morning's national security briefing, but Pleasance had nixed any mention, hoping whatever she was up to would be resolved by the evening, when he and the president got together to wrap things up for the day. Everett was in and out of the Oval Office all day. With the campaign in full swing, his visits back to the White House were few and far between. This made everything so hectic he barely had time to catch his breath between meetings.

"Intelligence reports Worthy is carrying torpedoes," added Random.

"Sinking a pirate will boost the president's numbers," smiled Pleasance. "Make sure we do not lose her."

"No problem there," assured Random. The KH-14 was a natural sub-sniffer. "I'm not taking any chances. I ordered an electronic leash." A blue-green laser that penetrated the water and locked on to the submarine. "She can no longer shake our tail. Not even underwater."

Chinook Trough

The *Stavenger*'s pirates hauled the last cow aboard. Blood gushed continuously down the giant drains and slipway. As far as the eye could see, shark fins cut deadly trails, devouring not only the gigantic chunks of discarded meat, but also bewildered calves, who circled and rammed the side of the *Stavenger* ceaselessly.

The slaughter deck was slippery with gore and the men clung to lines lashed along the sides. A burly Colombian with a knife scar on his cheek stepped across the deep wrinkles behind the flippers of the last carcass. As he proceeded past the cow's postanal hump, he dug his flensing knife into her blubber to keep his footing. The wrinkles and hump were somehow responsible for her ability to dive as far as two miles and stay submerged for as long as forty minutes. The Colombian stomped across the signature white patch over her belly, now colored with her blood, and leaped across the crater carved out by the grenade that had killed her. He paused atop her nose, the biggest known to man, and ground his shoe into her lifeless left eye staring up at the sky.

A giant rivulet of moisture wept down, past her mottled white upper lip, toward her slack, all white lower jaw, where a Norwegian ex-felon worked with a chainsaw on her single row of teeth. Unlike baleen whales, sperms were hunters. The absence of teeth on their upper jaw suggested they used them to grasp, not chew, their prey and interact with other whales. These ivory pegs were the stuff of scrimshaw. During off hours, the more artistic thugs carved them. In days bygone, it was considered an original American art form.

A massive crane stopped overhead with a shrill metallic scrawl and lowered a giant hook at the end of a knot of chains. The Colombian plunged the tip into the cow's s-shaped nostril that caused her slanting spout. Barely did he leap off her rectangular forehead when the hook screeched onward with a powerful jerk, peeling the skin off her body. The vast reservoir of oil in her nose, mistaken for spermaceti by early Europeans, who gave the whale its name, gurgled out in a torrent. Rich in triglycerides and esters, it aided her in some unknown manner to dive deep, stay buoyant, control her body temperature and produce the sound blasts she needed to hunt and defend herself. The ex-felon stopped sawing and nonchalantly let almost a thousand gallons of clear amber liquid wash around his legs. He swayed to keep his balance in the powerful flood.

The hook continued moving with the ear-rending sound of unoiled bearings and a distinctive, sullen, brute force staccato of thick wet pops caused by millions of connective tissue strands breaking. Flinging giant gobs of blood every which way, a stubborn inch from the foot-thick subdermal blubber and underlying muscle came off too. Steam rose in a thick curtain. Her thin skin had dried quickly and cracked in the brief time she'd been on the cutting deck. Simply not adapted to be out of the ocean, she cooked in her own blubber. Thus sperms, who mysteriously beached in alarming numbers, could not be moved without harming them further.

The crane dumped the skin overboard. Heedless of the heat and stench, more pirates descended with whirring flensers. The myoglobin-rich meat, which helped the whale retain oxygen during her long dives, was excavated in large cubes and thrown on a conveyer. Packers at the far end of the belt hoisted them over their shoulders and into refrigeration compartments. The entire crew was on deck, either cutting or carrying meat.

Consequently, the slender arm of the *Earthforce*'s forward periscope broke the surface unseen.

"Estimated range?" asked Worthy.

"Eight miles," replied the sonarman.

"Bearing?"

"3-2-8," answered Rorque Jr. from below.

A new voice interrupted over the speaker. "We have an ID. *Stavenger.*"

"Arlov Vesprhein," said Jan at once. The pirate's notoriety was unparalleled. The repeater screen came up with a crew list, available photos and the latest info.

"I thought you said the pirate made a Japanese radio transmission," said Worthy.

"Probably the buyer."

"Says here he's operating out of Iquique, Chile," Raquel read off the scrolling text.

Worthy swung the periscope around. "I don't see anyone."

"Nope," confirmed sonar.

Jan pursed her lips thoughtfully.

"His is a pretty hi-tech ship. His FishEye can detect up to five hundred yards. Let's be careful," said Worthy. He lowered the attack periscope and raised the other, rigged for videography, above the water. The images from its powerful lens came up on the TV screen. He pointed to the *Stavenger*'s low riding hull. "They have a full load. The waterline is not even visible."

"Says they also carry depth charges," said the sonarman, perusing the bio. "None of his men are allowed to have weapons of any kind, but there is a gun room with enough firepower to arm all his men and more."

Jan looked over to Raquel. "Raq. That will be your team."

Raquel memorized the location. "We'll secure it."

Jan straightened sharply. "Vesprhein."

They watched him saunter down the catwalk from the bridge to the gun platform after a topless woman in a thong. The pair reached the gun turret. He pointed into the sea. She nodded enthusiastically. He loaded a grenade-tip harpoon and placed her behind the gun. Calves still roamed around the *Stavenger* in search of their mothers.

"Jesus Christ," murmured Jan, as every eye in the conn froze on the monitor.

A silent cloud of smoke puffed out of the gun. The harpoon pierced the calf's midsection. He leapt. The grenade, packed with explosives for a forty-five-foot adult, atomized the eighteen-foot calf. The woman clapped with glee.

"Bastards!" hissed Jan.

The sonarman looked up. "Their flensers just stopped working. They're ready to move out."

"Let's go!" ordered Jan.

"Wait," said Raquel. "Look at that." They were close enough to get a glimpse of the army of mobile, intersecting fins in the bloody water lapping against the *Stavenger*'s hull.

"Shark city," said Worthy.

"Shit," muttered Jan.

"We'll shadow him until we're clear of them."

"Then what?" asked Jan. "How do we stop him?"

"Kaboom," Rorque's voice crackled over the intercom.

"We intend to sink him, Mr. Rorque, but not until we've boarded him and grabbed his manifests." Worthy lowered the videoscope and turned on the com. "Make our depth one hundred feet. Secure for silent running." To his sonarman, "Monitor his FishEye."

The crew quickly fastened everything metallic and shut down the ventilation system, the air conditioning machinery and all nonessential mechanical equipment. The submarine gently dipped deeper and the depth gauge at Worthy's elbow slowly inched to seventy feet. "Increase speed to six knots."

"Another harpoon shot," said the sonarman, seeing the report of the gun squiggle across his screen. Jan clenched her fist helplessly. They came within a mile of the *Stavenger* and stopped. Silent Running raised the temperature inside the *Earthforce*, forcing the men to strip off their shirts. The women went to their tanktops.

"You should be heading down," indicated Worthy.

Jan and Raquel nodded grimly and took the ladder. Rorque, Jr. gave them a thumbs-up as they descended past him to the Diving Room. "Good luck."

❃

Aboard the *Stavenger*, Vesprhein walked onto the bridge with the naked whore. Alfonso and Iron Lady stood on either side of

Quvango, the charcoal black Angolan helmsman named after the town of his birth.

Vesprhein addressed the first mate with uncharacteristic geniality. "I'll take over now." He nodded to the whore. "She's yours. Take four hours off." He winked derisively toward Iron Lady, who earned his nickname not because he was the former prime minister's namesake, but for his willingness to lie face down on the giant steel drums in the engine room for the ship's sexually desperate. "You've my permission to make it a cozy threesome."

"I'll pass, Captain," hissed the Englishman sullenly.

Alfonso grinned, grabbed the whore and disappeared down the companionway.

"That be very generous, Captain," said Quvango, twisting his mouth in surprise. The nephew of a tribal chief, he had extraordinarily thick lips, the consequent accent even thicker.

"We are not going back to Iquique," whispered Vesprhein. Iron Lady did not belong to the handful who were privy to the fact that the position of first mate was a temporary one on the *Stavenger*.

Quvango did. "Trouble?"

"Better price," confided Vesprhein, not that he trusted Quvango. He did not. But the popular helmsman would spread the word that it was Alfonso's time to go.

Quvango's lips stretched from ear to ear in a toothy grin.

Vesprhein grinned back. The ship would be pleased the first mate's usefulness ended at sea. On shore, Vesprhein would have paid Alfonso and sailed away. This far out in the north Pacific, it was impractical to return to Iquique to drop off one man and now was as good a time as any to "terminate" his services.

As pitiless as Vesprhein's reputation was when it came to killing whales, he made sure he was not labeled a coldblooded murderer of men. Rather, he'd cultivated a reputation as a mercenary and loved the nickname he'd earned in the universe of seafaring thugs: Captain Roulette. Because he played Russian with his ship and command.

Like now. He was going to challenge Alfonso to a bare knuckles fight, give the Chilean a chance to win control of the ship *and* half the chief engineer's pot in the Pig, which could swell to $5000.

Just one catch: gladiator rules applied. Last man *living* won.

Vesprhein never worried about losing. He was still captain, five death matches later. The first mate never stopped bragging about his exploits as a Víbora—rattlesnake—Chile's deadliest street gang. If Alfonso was all he made himself out to be, and he'd sold much of the ship on his exploits, a win would seal Vesprhein's invincibility in the eyes of his men and reinforce the abject fear he used to run this ship.

❈

"She's moving," said the sonarman on the *Earthforce*.

"Match her course and speed," said Worthy, feeling the grip of excitement. All were veteran saboteurs, but there was something about stalking in a submarine. It felt predatory and he loved it.

"Paul," said the sonarman after they'd been shadowing the *Stavenger* for about fifteen minutes. "He's heading northwest, away from Iquique."

Worthy punched the two-digit extension to the Diving Room, where Jan, Raquel, Boycott, Knight, yeoman O'Hara and another crew member, Kyle, pulled on wetsuits and scuba gear.

"Jan," said Worthy. "Vesprhein may be headed for a midsea rendezvous to transfer his catch."

"I'll bet it's a Japanese ship," said Raquel.

"That's why *you* have the Ph. D.," quipped Boycott.

Raquel slapped him. "Shut up."

"He's doing only six knots. The buyer must be close by."

❈

Vesprhein stayed on the *Stavenger*'s bridge, pacing impatiently between the FishEye and Quvango.

"Captain," said Iron Lady, "I'm picking up a faint submerged contact. Very fuzzy."

"Must be a calf," dismissed Vesprhein.

"Surface contact!" Iron Lady jumped.

Vesprhein remained calm. "Radio, send out this message. Catch complete. Ready for transfer."

Iron Lady looked around and blinked.

Vesprhein's face turned to granite. The Englishman and Alfonso were friends he'd picked up at Iquique. "Warn the first mate and I'll kill you."

"N-no, Captain," the Englishman's lips trembled and he squirreled his eyes back to the FishEye.

"There he be, Cap'n," said Quvango.

A discontinuity marred the horizon, materializing into a large merchantman with four goalpost-like derricks and cargo hatches forward and aft. She had a giant crane and her squat stack polluted black smoke skyward. Her name, *Kagoshima*, was barely decipherable in Japanese or English under the peeling paint, rust and decay.

"Go downstairs and lock the first mate in his cabin," Vesprhein instructed Quvango.

The Angolan hurried off down the companionway. Vesprhein took the wheel. He picked up the phone and called down to the Pig, alerting the men to prepare for a meat transfer. Fifteen minutes later, the two ships pulled alongside each other, holds aligned. Rusting chains unspooled the anchors into the sea.

❄

In the *Earthforce*'s conn, Worthy hoisted the periscope out of the water. They had made their depth sixty feet. He watched the cranes on both vessels swing into action. A man Worthy concluded was the Japanese skipper lifted himself across to the *Stavenger*'s deck on the *Kagoshima*'s crane. Twin sacks—money, presumably—straddled his left shoulder front and back. He strode up the catwalk on to the killer-factory ship's bridge.

"How long do you think the transfer is going to last?" asked Jan over the intercom.

Worthy lowered the periscope and activated the intercom. "An hour, probably less. They have two cranes working."

"This is perfect," said Jan. The pirates would all be engaged in transferring the meat. Those who weren't would be dead asleep in their quarters after a night of nonstop work, harvesting meat.

"I have the bio on the *Kagoshima* and you're gonna love it," the sonarman whispered with hoarse excitement. "She belongs to Kaiyou."

The world's largest fishing company. Controlled by the Obata family, Kaiyou, whose characters in Japanese meant ocean, operated a fleet of over five hundred ships. Annual sales exceeded sixty billion dollars. Ranked sixty-seventh among corporate giants in the world, with subsidiaries and partnerships in twenty countries, the Obata family exerted formidable political clout in Tokyo. But Kaiyou also employed 26,000 Americans aboard their processing ships up in Alaska and four times that in three Midwestern states, where they manufactured parts for ships, including the US Navy.

"Yes!" said Jan, catching the sonarman's glee.

"It gets better. This is not their region."

Jan pumped her fist. "This is an unbelievable opportunity to weaken the WLJ."

Kaiyou was part of a conglomerate called the Whalers League of Japan. Formed in 1976 when whale stocks were depleted and pelagic fleets became uneconomical, WLJ's members divided the oceans among themselves. Kaiyou claimed the Antarctic. As the most powerful member of the WLJ, they had masterminded the secret hunt of fins and humpbacks in Cetacean Bay last year that eventually backfired on Tokyo.

"Exposing Kaiyou can trigger infighting," said Knight.

"This changes everything, doesn't it?" asked Raquel.

"No," said Jan. "Just the final objective."

She explained. It was a daring departure from their original plan of just seizing just the manifesto.

"Shit," grinned Boycott. "We'll blow up the IWC session this Friday."

"Oh, yeah," agreed Jan.

Synchronizing their watches, Jan, Raquel, Boycott, Knight, O'Hara and Kyle emerged out of the submarine. Everyone carried a gun except Boycott, who came armed with his camera as usual.

❋

On the *Stavenger*, Iron Lady watched the FishEye. The worrisome fuzziness was gone.

About half an hour had elapsed since the two vessels had drawn alongside. The Japanese skipper had returned to the *Kagoshima,* having stayed only long enough to exchange money and papers with Vesprhein. The two cranes continued to work, about a third of way done with the transfer

"I'm going to my cabin," Vesprhein said. Iron Lady looked up to find himself staring straight at the captain. "Chart a course for Luzon, Philippines. That will be our new base of operations." Vesprhein slung the moneybags over his shoulder. "Now, I'm going down to terminate our first mate's services. I will kill you next if he's warned."

Iron Lady said nothing. He had been languishing in Iquique after his ride, a freighter smuggling women and children for prostitution and slavery, sank. He eluded capture by jumping off the ship and swimming two miles to shore. He hung out at the dockside bar, where he met and got to know Alfonso, whose Víbora gang routinely stole from transit containers on tips from his equally corrupt harbormaster uncle. Six months ago, the *Stavenger* pulled in. Iron Lady introduced Vesprhein to the FishEye, which he'd stolen when he picked up a job power-washing a warehouse the US Navy used to stockpile parts. The captain loved the gadget and hired him. Inevitably, Iron Lady's acquaintanceship with Alfonso at Iquique grew to a friendship aboard the *Stavenger,* with an unspoken understanding to watch out for each other.

Vesprhein headed down the companionway. His heavy footsteps receded. Iron Lady stood uncertainly staring down the companionway. Then he looked away toward the cranes swinging back and forth. He wanted desperately to warn Alfonso, but he loved his own life more.

He bit his thumbnail.

Maybe I can tell the Colombian flenser, who owes his job to Alfonso also. Iron Lady rested his hands on either side of the FishEye. He decided to keep quiet. Alfonso was no angel. Having witnessed Víbora gang operate, Iron knew Alfonso's claim that he'd killed men was not an idle boast. The lumbering first mate was a vicious son of a bitch.

Iron Lady casually looked down.

A blip moved across the FishEye screen.

Iron Lady's eyes narrowed. The profile resembled … *a diver?* Reaching for the alarm, he lifted his eyes out the bridge window. The ocean was empty. He looked down again. A dense school of fish blanketed the blip. The school passed, so did the blip. Some kind of big fish, he figured, relaxed and quickly retracted his hand. Last thing he wanted was Vesprhein to think he'd raised a false alarm to create a diversion to save Alfonso.

❄

Below, Vesprhein locked the money in his cabin. Having lived amongst criminals most of his adult life, he knew they were all the same. Selfish. The Englishman would do nothing more than consider warning Alfonso. Vesprhein arrived outside the first mate's door.

Quvango, standing guard, grinned. "He don't even know he be locked in, Cap'n."

"Inform the crew we are having a burial at sea. Everyone's invited to the services."

"Yes, Cap'n." Quvango bounded out of there.

Vesprhein opened the door.

The whore crouched on her hands and knees with Alfonso behind her. So much sweat rained down their bodies, they looked fresh out of the shower. How could Alfonso not know they'd stopped? Not hear the deafening, metallic screech of cranes? Not feel the ship's herky-jerky listing as the cargo was transferred? The first mate had to be stupid, or sure he was in no danger, or both. Vesprhein cleared his throat.

"Fuck off," dismissed Alfonso without turning, bucking his hips. Vesprhein coughed again. Alfonso whirled furiously, saw the captain and froze. Alfonso roughly jerked himself out of the whore, who wailed. He swiped the back of her head and she whimpered to silence.

Vesprhein glanced down and smirked, "That's one shitty dick, Number One."

Alfonso laughed nervously. He grabbed his shorts off the floor and wiped himself. Then he climbed into them. "I don't know it was you, Cap'n."

"Now you do." Vesprhein landed a gigantic fist straight into Alfonso's nose.

The Chilean's bone gave with a sickening crack. Blood flew. Tears ripped out of his eyes. He crashed into the bunk. The whore screamed. Vesprhein grabbed the floundering first mate by his hair. As he did, Vesprhein felt a jolt of pain roar from his crotch to his head and realized Alfonso had thrown a knee into his balls.

Vesprhein rocked back on his heels.

❉

Outside, by the *Stavenger*'s stern slipway, the six divers surfaced quietly. The ramp was open as they knew it would be. Water cascaded down. Automated jets on either side of the cutting deck powerfully hosed off the blood and gore, a process that took about four hours. The thermal reader in Jan's goggles indicated no warm spots.

O'Hara and Kyle crawled up the ramp first, fighting the gush, which carried evidence of blood even after two hours of washing.

They helped up Jan, Raquel, Knight and Boycott. The collision of water on the deck lifted an opaque spray. It offered excellent cover but made the going slippery and treacherous. Jan struggled over to the ladder that would take them up one level. Energized with purpose, she went first, climbing the naked rungs quickly.

Fighting and winning eco-battles in enemy territory was sweet. It sent a clear and powerful message that, as first lady, she had not left the audacious street fighter behind. Rather, the additional visibility, notoriety and security her stature gave her emboldened her even more.

Jan rolled onto the catwalk. Staying low, she stripped off the scuba tanks. The others hurried up and did the same. They stashed their gear behind a heap of lashing and split into pairs. Having pursued and boarded other killer-factory ships through the years, they knew the general layout. They'd familiarized themselves with the *Stavenger*'s minor variations from Worthy's data banks.

Raquel and O'Hara slipped toward the Pig. It was their task to lock the occupants in, secure the gun room and seal midship access to the bridge. Knight and Kyle went aft, toward the engine room with the objective of securing the door from the outside and trapping the crew down there. Then they would work their way up, blocking the aft access to the bridge. Jan and Boycott proceeded forward to do the same.

Since Jan was the only one armed, she peered in. The upwinding stairwell was deserted. She nodded and led the way. They took the steps two at a time. At the landing, she curved her head around the hatchway. The passage was empty. They sprinted under fluorescents that cast a morgue-like blue-green wash. The bulkhead on either side reeked of age. Paint peeled to expose ugly rivulets of rust caused by decades of abuse from the ocean. They came upon another gloomy corridor. She stuck her head forward. Nobody. Jan frowned. Her earpiece crackled with Knight's whispered "Engine room's empty."

There should have been four engineers.

A moment later, Raquel reported, "Nobody in the Pig."

"What's going on?" wondered Jan.

Followed by Boycott, she headed up metal rungs. They stepped off at deck level. Another empty hallway. They hurried to the end, where it teed off. She turned right without looking left.

"Hoy!" a voice snapped behind them.

Jan whirled.

A squat Asian—the Korean lookout, she recalled from his profile on Worthy's computer—charged in on the run. Jan saw his eyes widen with surprise, then recognition. He pulled up hard. His sneakers slipped. He skidded awkwardly. Clearly, he wasn't expecting *her*.

He slid to within a yard of Jan. Prepared for a confrontation, she swung her gun. The gun handle nailed his temple. His neck snapped. Shielding his camera, Boycott bulled his body into the man, smashed him against the bulkhead. The Korean's arms splayed. He reached for the Fire Alarm.

Jan swung hard and swung fast, striking him just as his fingers grasped the handle. The blow knocked out him cold, but as he crumpled, he drew the handle down.

The alarm shrieked. Jan didn't flinch. She snatched open the nearest door, a closet. "Shove him in there."

Boycott put down his camera, grabbed the Korean's underarms and dragged him in.

"Trouble?" crackled Raquel's voice.

"Not any more," replied Jan. "Come on."

Boycott shut the closet door, picked up his camera and raced after Jan. The alarm still ringing, they came around the final corner to the foredeck. The daylight at the far end blacked out in a sudden rush of men.

"Fuck!" Jan exclaimed and pulled back out of sight.

A thunder of hard slapping feet approached from the other side.

Boycott and she were trapped in-between with nowhere to run.

✴

"The fire alarm just went off," said the sonarman urgently.

In the *Earthforce*'s conn, Worthy whipped the videoscope out of the water. The *Stavenger*'s crane heaved another load of frozen meat toward the merchantman.

"Oh, no."

The pirates suddenly broke into a run. *What would cause everyone to abandon their stations?* Worthy could think of only one reason.

The first lady.

Washington DC

Wiry and bespectacled, Bruce Wilhelmson was the prototypical nerd who'd been picked on all through school and dismissed by the pretty girls. He constantly wondered how they would react if they saw him now. He had an important job that entailed keeping national secrets. Anal and thorough, he was the TA—threat analyst—assigned to all images from 5603, the KH-14 satellite watching over the first lady in the North Pacific.

Wilhelmson peered closely at the color photographs being constantly updated on his computer screen. He absently switched to infrared as he sipped from a mug and grimaced. The coffee was cold. He stretched, then threaded between the cubicles, all equipped with terminals like his and manned by analysts like him, with SI-TK, or Signal Intelligence-Talent Keyhole security clearance. This permitted them to study imagery only. They were not privy to how it was obtained. Wilhelmson, who was beginning his tenth year at National Photographic Interpretation Center in Washington DC, had a pretty good idea, because each platform had its own idiosyncrasies.

He poured himself fresh coffee, opened the refrigerator and grabbed an apple. On his way back to his terminal, he swung into the Assistant Administrator's office.

"Hey good looking, what's cooking?" he said, closing the door.

He rounded the desk toward Bianca Stevens, thirty-three-year-old mother of twins, whose homely looks, like his own, drove her to overachieve. They'd been dating for the past six months. They kissed and made plans for the weekend.

Wilhelmson reluctantly headed back to his station. The first lady was known to be unpredictable and it wasn't a good idea to take his eyes off her. He dropped into his chair, took one look at his latest screen and turned ashen.

He grabbed the phone and dialed furiously.

❄

Fifteen minutes later, a midnight black Escalade and a silver Lexus with federal government plates, pulled into Federal Building 213 at the corner of First and M Streets, eight blocks from Capitol Hill. A cyclone fence, topped with rolls of barbed wire, ran around the site. Federal Protection Service officers manned the entrances. The neighborhood attracted few tourists—precisely why the site had been chosen. The beige bricked-in warehouse fit right in with the other aging structures of the adjacent Washington Navy Yard on the banks of the Anacostia River.

Pleasance and Lhea climbed out of the Escalade. Random emerged from the Lexus and led the way inside.

US space-based reconnaissance had come a long way. Thirty years ago, satellites ejected capsules of film after photographing a target. The capsules were snatched out of midair by C-130 aircraft, processed and analyzed. Today, seconds separated photography and computer analysis. To cope with the millions of images that poured in daily, sophisticated recognition capabilities ignored what had not changed, informing the analyst of aspects that had. It was this feature that alerted Wilhelmson to the fact that Jan and five eco-warriors had boarded the pirate whaler.

"Are you sure?" asked Lhea. Nobody sat down in the chairs Wilhelmson had for them.

"Positive," said Wilhelmson.

"Where's Worthy's submarine?" asked Pleasance.

"Underwater." Wilhelmson pulled up an insert screen. Microwave reflections from the sea surface detected internal waves in the ocean between layers of different density and showed the *Earthforce* as a cigar shaped shadow.

"What's her strategy here?" asked Lhea. "Going on board outnumbered like that?"

"Take them by surprise, I guess," said Random, "using the sub as intimidation."

"That's not all," Wilhelmson interrupted. He explained that minutes after she disappeared into the ship, the men suddenly rushed inside. Crew on the *Kagoshima* had also moved to the edge of her deck. It would seem the first lady had been captured.

Pleasance smiled coldly.

Chinook Trough

"We're trapped!" hissed Jan

"What's going on?" erupted Knight in her earpiece.

"Jan! Are you all right?" Raquel asked immediately afterwards.

Jan barely heard them. Even if she did, there was no time to respond. The fire alarm kept pealing. The noise of the crew thronging the narrow corridor reverberated into a deafening howl of voices. The footsteps from the other side advanced, just around the corner.

Jan pointed to the first door she saw. "In there!"

Boycott ducked through. His camera struck the jamb and dislodged the battery. There was no time to pick it up. Jan backed hard into him and they sprawled into a small storage cabin. It was dank and reeked of trapped moisture. Ropes, crates and supplies, held behind netting, were stacked up in a U, leaving a three-by-three-foot square to cramp in. As she fell, she saw Alfonso—she recognized him from Worthy's data banks—step on the fallen battery, slip and fly off the floor in front of her. She kicked the door shut just as he landed. His thud masked the slam of the door. In the subsequent moment, the pandemonium reached a crescendo outside.

The door handle jerked, pushed down from the outside.

"Lock it, lock it!" said Boycott in a hoarse whisper.

Jan punched her shoulder to the door as it began to open. *Click.* She heard the latch engage and turned the lock in the nick of time. *Slam!* The door shuddered again with a crash of bodies.

"They're trying to break it down!" he gasped. "They saw us!"

The fire alarm died abruptly.

"Shh." Jan held up her forefinger. "Listen."

Wham! Thud! Blows exchanged amidst rousing cheers and grunts of pain.

Jan pressed her eye to the keyhole. Alfonso was on the floor, swinging a weak roundhouse. His boot caught Vesprhein's knee, unbalancing him. Alfonso crawled away from the door and stood up. Vesprhein, steady on his feet, rammed his head into the first mate's stomach.

Jan pulled back sharply as the two rocked the door to its hinges again. "It's a fight."

So the men had rushed in to follow it. The slapping feet on the other side had belonged to Vesprhein and Alfonso, the captain chasing the first mate, who'd wrenched the handle down, probably to find his balance after tripping over Boycott's battery. Someone assumed the fire alarm had gone off as part of the brawl and turned it off.

Boycott breathed easy. "So we're safe."

Not for long.

Jan's eyes streaked to the floor. "Oh, crap."

A wire dribbled across the jamb. Her hand jerked to her ear. The earpiece had fallen out. It was on the other side of the door. The commotion would carry to the other two teams, who'd assume the worst.

"They'll come for us," Boycott said.

✳

A wild swing from Alfonso caught Vesprhein alongside the head. Lucky sonofabitch! thought Vesprhein, reeling. A fluke connect. Alfonso's head reared up and his eyes caught fire. Vesprhein smirked arrogantly to stoke the Chilean's pent-up hatred. But Vesprhein wasn't prepared for the fierce looping right that split his lips. He stumbled. Each blow the first mate landed seemed to double his confidence. When he connected on two debilitating punches—one blacked Vesprhein's eye and the other walloped into his kidney—all vestiges of fear and intimidation evaporated.

His jaw almost dislodged under another well-executed right. Vesprhein spun, his back to the first mate, who dropped a double-fisted sledgehammer into Vesprhein's spine. He kissed the deckplates violently. His teeth rattled. Alfonso squatted hard, flattening Vesprhein's guts, and yanked a fistful of hair. Pain snapped to extremities of every nerve on Vesprhein's face.

Alfonso sprayed spit into his ear, "You think you can take me, *gringo* mothafucka?"

Vesprhein shot a forearm under Alfonso's chin. The Chilean flew back. Vesprhein rose and bulled Alfonso into the bulkhead, landing punches that usually knocked out opponents before they could even get into the fight. More crew had money on him, so the cheers were twice as loud and intense. But Alfonso wasn't going down. He was younger, bigger, stronger.

Vesprhein discharged a powerful, fight-ending left. It encountered air when Alfonso ducked at the last second. The momentum twisted Vesprhein out of position. Alfonso jumped him. He couldn't hold Alfonso to the wall but wouldn't let the first mate pin him either. Vesprhein stumbled past the red-bearded chief engineer—the *Stavenger*'s official bookie. He was offering even money for the first mate to kill the captain.

✳

Jan watched the two men go toe to toe up the sloping corridor toward the daylight of the foredeck. The loud cheers amidst the sound of blows receded. She opened the door an inch at a time.

"Freeze!"

Jan whirled, swinging her gun. A head ducked, barely escaping her powerful swipe.

"Raq!" gasped Jan

"You're all right!" said Raquel.

"We thought you'd been taken hostage," said O'Hara.

Clang! Footfalls over grating. They turned their guns together. A pair of shadows curled around. Knight and Kyle.

"Thank heavens," said Knight. "You're okay."

"Brawl between Vesprhein and his first mate," Jan quickly explained. "The whole crew is following the fight. This is going to work out better than we planned. Close all entries into the ship. Lock the doors from inside and let the bastards have the best seats in the house for the big bang."

❋

On *Earthforce*, Worthy agonized. *Where are Jan and her team?* He leaned over the hatch. "Are we ready to shoot?"

The plan was to fire the torpedoes in exactly seven minutes. But he couldn't. Not without knowing the boarding party's situation on the *Stavenger*.

"Yup." Rorque replied at once. "Just have to open the outer doors."

The red light labeled CORRECT SOLUTION blinked boldly on the face of the angle solver. Tension mounted. Worthy felt wet around the collar. He realized now what the retired commander who'd trained them meant by "long seconds of taut expectancy" before every sinking.

Worthy looked at his watch again and raised the periscope. The meat transfer was complete, yet the *Kagoshima*'s showed no sign of departing, which only confirmed his fear that Jan had been captured. Also, she should have shown herself from the bridge three minutes ago.

"What the hell?" Worthy startled.

❄

For the first time, Vesprhein felt his age. His body ached. It had been a long time—*Jesus, not since I was ten*—that he'd been on the receiving end of a beating. He saw the doubt in the eyes of his supporters. Alfonso had accomplished the unthinkable: taken the captain the distance.

Vesprhein backed onto the foredeck so Alfonso had to emerge face first. The sunlight blinded the first mate. Vesprhein clubbed the Chilean's face with a right and dug a brutal left into his belly. Just like that he was in control again. Maybe it was a good thing he was being tested. He would emerge stronger in his own mind, loom larger over his crew and squelch any notion that he'd lost a step or weakened with age.

Alfonso found a crease and smashed two hands into Vesprhein's chin. The captain staggered. The first mate jabbed a hard left to the mouth, then a harder right to the body. The Chilean began to dismantle him.

❄

A pit opened in Worthy's stomach when the moving human circle emerged on the *Stavenger*'s foredeck. He instantly figured it was a hostage situation, with the first lady in the middle. Then he caught fleeting glimpses of two men in a savage free-for-all. He recognized Vesprhein at once from his tattoos. The other man was big, brown and hairy. The first mate. So, the rush indoors was to see the fight and the *Kagoshima*'s crew were being looky-loos.

The eco-warriors were safe.

A moment later, shit flew.

"Their FishEye found us!" exclaimed his sonarman.

❄

Alarm bells rang all over the *Stavenger*. Jan was aft, locking the last entry door from the slaughter deck into the ship. She froze. The

FishEye, she deduced at once, the only other alarm on this ship. It must have detected the sub. The boarding party was behind schedule. Worried, Worthy probably drifted too close.

"What now?" asked Raquel over the earpiece.

They had to abandon the mission. It was the sensible thing to do, Jan knew. Instead, she asked, "Status on the doors?"

"Secured," came the reply from the other five eco-warriors in quick succession.

The decision was hers. They all understood they'd never have an opportunity like this again. Considering the vastness of the oceans, pirates and buyers were phantoms, their encounters fleeting wisps, there one minute, gone the next. To catch them mid-transaction was an epic coup—a potential game-changer for Friday's IWC session.

"Let's go for it," Jan declared.

"I was hoping you'd say that," responded Raquel.

"Yeah," agreed Boycott.

With all the pirates locked out, an advantage Jan had not anticipated, they could complete her bold and audacious new mission objective if they controlled the only position they had not yet secured. Won, it would deliver them the ship. Lost, it nullified locking every entry door. By virtue of its location, it opened up the ship much like a lowered drawbridge did a fort. It was the proverbial hilltop.

The symbol of command.

The bridge.

❄

Vesprhein was staring at defeat and death when the FishEye went off. Alfonso distracted sharply. Not Vesprhein. He swore sperms sought revenge, claiming his father had been on a boat that was sunk by one. So he insisted on maintaining an alert for at least twenty-four hours after every sperm whale hunt. He figured this was one.

Vesprhein bored in, hitting the Chilean with a series of blows. He felt a rush. He smashed Alfonso in the ribs then launched an uppercut that sent the Chilean tottering. The specter of defeat lifted. The energy shifted in the ring of sailors. He fed off it.

❄

WhoaWhoaWhoa! The deafening peal continued. On the bridge, Iron Lady swiveled. He'd been standing at the bridgescreen with Quvango. They had not moved their eyes since the fight emerged outside.

"Your cap'n ain't winning this one," Iron Lady had just gloated, cackling like a hyena, a second before the FishEye sounded. He hurried to it.

"Yeah!" Quvango shouted.

Iron Lady glanced outside briefly then back at the display screen. He froze. The Englishman had set the FishEye to autoscan in a slow circle for an undersea approach by anything longer than forty feet.

"A submarine!" he gasped, recognizing the unmistakable profile. "Call the captain!"

"Fuck no," Quvango refused. "Cap'n be kickin' ass."

"Now!" shouted Iron Lady, killing the alarm. *Distracting the captain will give Alfonso the break he needs.*

"Fuck you," Quvango retorted.

Iron Lady reached for the microphone switch beside the wheel. Quvango smashed down on Iron Lady's wrist. The Englishman withstood the blow and rammed his other elbow into the helmsman's chest. Quvango fell backward. Iron Lady swiped again, cutting the Angolan's cheek to the bone. He swept Quvango's legs. The helmsman fell. Iron Lady landed a boot to the skull. The Angolan curled up defensively. Iron Lady didn't stop kicking until Quvango went still.

Then he stepped across him to the microphone.

"Don't," cautioned a new voice.

A well-built youngster, twenty-five, if that, rose out of the companionway. Handsome, clean-shaven, thought Iron Lady, linking the boy and the submarine instantly. But it didn't answer the question: *Who the fuck is he and what the fuck is he doing here?*

Quvango groaned. Iron Lady, a veteran of savage fights since he was a foster child growing up in the harsh back alleys of Glasgow, shifted his eyes suddenly. The kid's eyes followed. Iron Lady lunged, kicked the automatic from his grasp. Iron Lady felt fingers pinch tightly around his ankle. He pivoted and brought the other foot down into the youngster's face. The boy let go with a shout of pain.

Jan heard his cry as she sprinted across. She had glimpsed O'Hara turn out of sight at the end of the passageway bisecting the officers' deck. Her fears that the FishEye's alarm would prompt a response had been unfounded. Everyone reported empty passageways. Knight, working under the foredeck, said that the fight sounded even more intense after the bell.

She heard sounds of struggle as she stormed up the steep companionway of metal treads. Rounding the final switchback to the bridge, she loped up, two steps at a time. Jan's eyes cleared the top and her hopes died. O'Hara bled and squirmed on the floor. His assailant, a silhouette against the bridgescreens, flipped the microphone switch beside the wheel. It let out a high-pitched whine. He leaned down to raise a warning.

Jan fired before he could speak. The bullet struck the woodwork an inch from his thigh, ejecting chips clear across the bridge. He whirled. Jan recognized him at once. It took a moment for recognition to flood Iron Lady's eyes. He prepared to lunge.

Jan lowered her gun to his crotch. "I wouldn't."

The rest of the boarding party poured up and in around her.

On deck, Vesprhein crowded Alfonso against the railing under a hurricane of blows. He was going to punish Alfonso. The first mate had come so damn close to taking him out. Now he needed to destroy the perception this was a near-successful challenge. Even the vilest crew member must cringe. Vesprhein crash landed his knuckles into Alfonso's eye, swelling it shut, clobbered his ears till they bled, hammered a skinned fist into Alfonso's mouth until teeth ripped out of the gums and fell to the deck.

The power of the next blow turned the first mate around completely. He collapsed forward, almost tipping into the sea. Vesprhein wasn't going to let him drown. Alfonso had to die at the captain's hands. He came up behind Alfonso and checked the first mate's fall by grabbing his hair. Alfonso wheezed. Vesprhein coiled a massive arm around Alfonso's neck. Silence rippled around the half circle.

The men chanted, "Captain! Captain! Captain!"

Staring straight out, Vesprhein twisted Alfonso's head to break his neck.

Something glinted above the water.

His eyes, trained for the sea, spotted the barely discernible stem of the periscope. He released Alfonso and looked to the bridge.

Jan waved down. Quvango and Iron Lady appeared on either side of her. Then Vesprhein saw the guns to their temples and the rest of the boarding party.

Jan's voice boomed over the *Stavenger*'s outside speaker. "We are from GreenPlanet and we control this ship." She slipped into fluent Japanese, "Captain and crew of the *Kagoshima*. You are about to be sunk. Abandon your ship now!"

Vesprhein quickly realized what the first lady was trying to do. She wanted to capture both sides of the illegal trade. It had never been done in half a century of ecowars to save the whales.

❄

In the *Earthforce,* Worthy rejoiced, "Bearing, mark."

"2-2-4."

"Range, mark!"

"5-1-5."

"Open outer doors forward."

Worthy waited for Rorque's report. It came in about five seconds.

"Outer doors open."

Worthy's hands snapped around the handles of the periscope and his eyes grabbed the guard. Jan gave him a thumbs-up. The Japanese crew had been pulled out of the water onto the *Stavenger*.

"Fire!"

Rorque turned the firing keys one after the other.

The *Earthforce* shuddered twice in rapid succession.

❉

On the *Stavenger*'s deck, populated with the crews of both ships, Vesprhein saw a pair of sleek silhouettes rise to the surface. Alfonso, staggering against the railing, saw them too and emptied his lungs.

"Torpedoes! Two!" He held up two fingers and started running to the other side. "Jump! Jump!"

Heads turned in unison.

"No!" Jan's voice blasted over the speakers in English and Japanese. "You are safe on this ship! Stay here!"

But Alfonso was already leaping over the rails. He hit the water just as the twin fish struck the *Kagoshima*.

Two explosions tore across. The *Kagoshima* listed sharply. A mushroom of flame shot through a funnel. Multiple detonations tore through her. One of them took her bottom out. The merchantman sank within minutes. Vesprhein suffered none of the hypnotism that glued every other eye to the spectacular destruction. He was just sorry he had not killed the first mate. *Alfonso probably died without feeling a fucking thing.*

"Mr. Vesprhein!" Jan's voice came over the speakers again. "You and the captain of the *Kagoshima* will come with us to the IWC meeting and testify."

Vesprhein spat on the deck.

"I thought I'd ask nicely first," she replied.

Vesprhein gave her the finger.

Jan stretched out her arm and jerked her thumb skyward.

The Pacific rumbled, growled and then erupted. The *Earthforce*'s nose shot up at a seventy-degree angle, simultaneously twisting around along her long axis. Two-thirds of her 283-foot length rocketed clear out of the water, then she fell back, launching two tidal waves off each beam. Every mouth on the *Stavenger*'s dock dropped open, except Vesprhein's. His jaw locked tight.

"Cooperate or lose your ship," Jan commanded.

Washington DC

Dale Gabon loved designer clothes. Today, his ensemble included a white cotton shirt by Zeon, blue chalk-stripe wool suit from Bella, a red silk tie by Pierre and black leather shoes from Sole. He sported a pencil thin moustache and wore a very expensive, hard-to-discern, toupee. Standing in front of the mirror, he flicked invisible dust off his suit and left the men's room. Always fastidious about his appearance, he paid more attention than usual this morning because he'd received an unexpected call from the interior secretary, who said he was coming to see him.

Gabon strode down the corridor between the cubicles where he had begun his career as a bureaucrat under President Jimmy Carter.

"I don't want to be disturbed," said Gabon firmly to his secretary and reached for the doorknob. The frosted glass above it bore his job description: Under Secretary for Oceans and Atmosphere, National Oceanic and Atmospheric Administration, Department of Commerce. Unwritten was the exact job he performed. He was the IWC commissioner for the United States.

"Good afternoon," said Gabon, closing the door behind him and greeting the interior secretary. Even though he worked for the commerce secretary, Gabon was more familiar with the interior secretary. They played golf every now and then.

This could be your break, the interior secretary had said over the phone, filling Gabon with nervous anticipation. A bureaucrat all his life, Gabon had never been able to get over that last hump into the exclusive club.

"Hey, Dale," smiled the interior secretary.

Gabon offered him Darjeeling tea from an exotic collection in his drawer. The men talked about their handicap while stirring their cups. Washington's old boys' club showed in their easy camaraderie.

Gabon had been handpicked by Vice President Adrian, who had known him as a young assistant under Richard Frank, a lawyer chosen by President Jimmy Carter in 1977 to be the IWC commissioner. Nicknamed Big Dick by conservationists, Richard Frank had favored whaling and Japan. His closed-door meetings with the Japanese had removed the US from the forefront of the international drive to save the whales. When Ronald Reagan took office, Big Dick registered as a foreign agent with Whalers League of Japan.

Gabon was Big Dick's protégé. A picture of them with Adrian and Jimmy Carter during a 1979 White House soiree stood on the table beside that of his wife and daughter. He had furnished his office with Big Dick's desk and his swivel chair too, custom-built to accommodate his mentor's large frame but much too big for Gabon.

The two men took their seats. The interior secretary withdrew a folder from his briefcase and handed over a sheet of paper. "Read this."

An expression of delight transformed Gabon's face. He looked up. "How many people know about this besides you and me?"

"The pilot, Dan Sitka, and his boss, the director of the mineral management service, who went to the hospital to visit and wrote that report."

"Does anyone in the White House know?" asked Gabon.

"Uh-uh," the interior secretary shook his head. "This can take us out of the first lady's dog house." Since he wore corporate America close to his heart, he too had been at odds with Jan. His appointment was a reward for the record money he'd raised for Everett's election and re-election

"Or ensure a second term for the president," said Gabon.

The interior secretary tilted his head. "How?"

Gabon told him how.

The interior secretary's face glowed in admiration. "Let's call Pleasance."

✻

In the White House, Everett posed for the routine pictures with the prime minister of India, who was seeking arms and aid. The president passed the diminutive leader to the care of the secretary of state and went back to the Oval Office. His administrative assistant fell into step beside him and whispered that Pleasance, Lhea and Adrian were waiting for him.

Jan. He'd promised Pleasance last night to call her first thing this morning, but it had slipped his mind. Everett sighed and opened the door. The late afternoon sunlight, streaming in through the bullet proof windows, picked up some of the gold from the draperies and saturated the primary colors in the decor with warmth, a sharp contrast to the cold outside. The three men sitting on the two sofas across from the president's desk stood up with simultaneous greetings. Set into the wall between the sofas was a fireplace and above it a portrait of George Washington by Rembrandt Peale.

"Gentlemen," waved Everett, walking across the deep Prussian blue carpet that helped set off the lighter walls and curtains. The presidential seal on the carpet was repeated in bas relief on the ceiling. "Sit down."

They dropped back into the two deep cushions upholstered in cream and red striped fabric from Scalamandré. Everett leaned down to pour himself coffee from a tray the mess steward had left on the table. "George, I haven't had time to call Jan."

"Too late for that," said Pleasance.

"What's she done now?" asked Everett wearily, dropping a sugar cube into the cup.

"She flew to Honolulu last night." Everett stopped stirring. "Got on Worthy's new submarine and took off to confront a pirate whaler, the *Stavenger*."

"I'm assuming that's the good news." Everett headed for his desk, made from the wood of the British ship, HMS *Resolute*. He flopped into his chair and leaned into the Kevlar reinforced backrest.

Pleasance nodded. "Yes. When she arrived, the *Stavenger* was unloading illegal whale meat on to a Japanese merchantman, the *Kagoshima*. Jan sank the merchantman and boarded the pirate whaler with five of her friends."

"Is she okay?" asked Everett anxiously. "Have you alerted the Coast Guard?"

"No," replied Pleasance quietly and firmly.

"Why not?"

"We don't want a repeat—"

"These are pirates, George! Her life may be in danger. Get me the Joint Chiefs."

"No!" The whip in Pleasance's voice froze Everett's hand on the phone. "You cannot use taxpayer money to protect her with means and measures available only to a president."

"Damnit, George! She means more to me than this office!"

"Does she?"

Everett's expression retreated.

Pleasance softened and added. "You use the power of this office to help one person, even Jan, where does it end? How will it look? What happens when it turns out those resources were needed somewhere else? You're setting your personal agenda before your country's wellbeing. You'll be crucified."

"You're saying I do nothing?" Everett looked at Lhea and Adrian.

Their silence stated their opinion better than words.

Everett slammed his fist on the table. He turned. Atop the credenza against the wall were personal trinkets, all gifts from Jan. There were three Valentine's Day cards, one for each year in office, an Everett-Adrian button signed by her with best wishes that'd he worn throughout his first run, a bust of John F. Kennedy and a pet rock. His eyes rested on their wedding photo. A happy, beautiful couple. They looked like strangers to him now.

Still. Jan was capable. Frighteningly so. *She got herself into this mess. She can get herself out.* Everett turned around. "Keep an eye on her."

"The satellite we pulled to watch her was the one stationed over China," said Pleasance. "With the Korean situation as it is, we will be compromising national security if it stays over Jan any longer."

Everett nodded. Seoul, South Korea, had been under siege from violent demonstrations following the rape and murder of a teenage girl by a US marine. With North Korea disarmed, continued US presence seemed unnecessary and withdrawal had surfaced as a campaign issue. The Joint Chiefs of Staff, though, advised Everett that the troops were the only deterrent to China's lengthening arm of influence in the region.

Adrian stepped in with a soothing voice. "Jan is safe with Worthy playing bodyguard. His crew is well armed. His submarine is carrying fourteen torpedoes."

"Bringing us to the real problem," said Lhea. "*Kagoshima*'s owned by Kaiyou."

"Great." Everett shook his head. The owners of Kaiyou, the Obata family, had practically installed the New Frontier Party in office in Japan. They would want retaliation. The prime minister could assert Japan's economic might and appease the Obatas with two words that Everett feared more than anything else in these final months leading up to the polls.

Trade war.

"That should be our focus," said Pleasance.

Everett nodded. He hit his intercom. "Cancel all my appointments."

Within the hour, the President's Council of Economic Advisors arrived. Everett insisted on secrecy, so they used the underground passageway from the Treasury Department to the White House. News hadn't broken yet of what Jan had done and he wanted to get a full grasp of the consequences of her extreme action. The financial markets were nervous as it was, what with no deal between the two biggest economies. Any further tension could send traders running for cover.

Adrian, Lhea and Pleasance sat in.

"A trade war can spell financial meltdown here and abroad," said the treasury secretary, a former CEO of one of New York's prestigious securities firms.

"That's a bit extreme, isn't it?" Everett was an investment banker himself. Finance was his forte.

No one knew what a real Japan-US trade war would look like. The last time the two countries came close to one was in 1994, when the US sought a bigger share of the Japanese market. With 7 percent of the world's population, the two countries controlled half the stock and bond market and issued 60 percent of the currency in circulation. As always, the Japanese conceded just enough to turn the Washington paper tiger back.

"Not if we can no longer control interest rates, the dollar and our deficit," said the Federal Reserve Bank chairman. Americans were so concerned about China, they did not realize that the Japanese had quietly become the largest buyers of long-term US treasury bonds. During the housing and mortgage crisis, Japanese companies bailed out three of the top ten brokerages on Wall Street by purchasing a controlling interest in all of them. When the recession passed, they controlled 20 percent of all retail banking in the US. Exploiting the rock bottom real estate prices, Japan re-entered the market with a vengeance. Today, twenty-one million Americans worked for Japanese companies in the United States. Tokyo was on par with New York as a center of the financial world. The securities firm Takara, which was twenty times bigger than America's largest firm, had risen to number one in the world.

Everett continued, "The Japanese recently embarked on their biggest domestic economic expansion yet. A trade war can stall that."

"But it will hurt us more and they know it," said the treasury secretary. After sluggish growth over the past two quarters, a trade war could spell another recession, which nobody wanted to hear in an election year.

The commerce secretary nodded. "Our debt is approaching fifteen trillion."

So Washington depended on continued Japanese and Chinese investment in American bonds. Last year, interest alone to those two countries exceeded the combined budgets of the Departments of Agriculture, Education, Energy, Housing and Urban Development, Interior, Justice, Labor, State, Transportation and Veterans Affairs.

"They won't have the guts to play hardball, will they?" asked Adrian.

"Why not?" asked the Federal Reserve chairman. "Japan can insist on being paid back in yen." The weak dollar translated into more yen and runaway US debt. Financial experts likened the annual Japan-US confrontation to a loaded gun. This Japanese prime minister was the first to take the safety off and close his finger around the trigger.

Everett shook his head. "Even the best minds on Wall Street in their wildest dreams could not have imagined a bunch of whales might start the shootout."

The intercom buzzed. "The interior secretary and IWC commissioner are here to see Mr. Pleasance."

Everett shot a look at Pleasance. "What's this about?"

"I summoned them," shrugged Pleasance. "I wanted to speak with Gabon before he left for the IWC vote in Los Angeles. The interior secretary is from Alaska and may have to be our point man if the vote to ban coastal and aboriginal whaling goes the first lady's way."

Everett's eyes narrowed. Pleasance never granted a meeting without purpose. There had to be more. They'd discussed Jan's remaining one vote short just last night. He noticed the commerce secretary react. Rules of Washington politicking demanded the IWC commissioner go through him to set up a meeting in the White House. *So what was Gabon doing with the interior secretary?*

Pleasance left.

Everett looked around the room. He saw only one way to preempt Wall Street from knee-jerking into a tailspin. "We have to insulate the market. What she did cannot make a single headline."

"Easier said than done," said Adrian, "knowing the first lady wants just that."

Everett replied confidently, "I can kill this story."

Pleasance walked into his office. Gabon and the interior secretary rose from their chairs. Pleasance never engaged in pleasantries. He did not care to know about the personal lives of anyone if it had no bearing on his narrow world, which at this point revolved around getting the president re-elected.

"What's this?" asked Pleasance, looking at the folder on his desk.

"Sitka's report," said Gabon.

Pleasance looked blankly from Gabon to the interior secretary. "Should I recognize the name?"

"No."

Pleasance read it. Gabon outlined the scenario that could be generated with the report. The ruthlessness of Gabon's plan curved Pleasance's lips. Vintage Richard Frank. *Big Dick indeed.* The vice president had picked the perfect foil for Jan.

Pleasance said, "Run with it."

He laid out the ground rules. Secretaries and assistants could not be involved. Gabon would report to the interior secretary, who would brief Pleasance privately. The interior secretary beamed. Pleasance showed his gratitude with increased perks, access and budget.

When they broke up, as Pleasance anticipated, the commerce secretary was around to rideshare with Gabon. Pleasance trusted the IWC commissioner's discretion. Gabon was smitten by the thrill of proximity to an operation that could mean a promotion if Everett was re-elected.

Pleasance hurried to the Oval Office and caught Everett before he called it a day. Calling Lhea and Adrian in as well, Pleasance declared, "We just may be able to put fears of a trade war on hold and give your poll numbers an overnight boost."

He'd made copies of Sitka's report and handed them out. The three men read the one sheet and looked up with identical expressions.

"How?" asked Everett.

Collecting the copies, Pleasance explained.

Everett felt an icy hand close around his throat.

BOOK TWO

"Those who celebrated the end of whaling in 1982," said Sidney Holt, a thirty-year member of the International Whaling Commission's Scientific Committee and, as a member of the Seychelles delegation in 1982, one of the architects of the moratorium, "and who believed there would be no more whaling, have been living in a fool's paradise... The battle we thought we had won drags on. It is no longer being fought on the high seas; it is political warfare, where once again—as nations of the world struggle for a beneficial balance of trade, a balance of power, gross national product, military superiority, autonomy, or whatever it is that nations are willing to fight for—the whales die."

Richard Ellis
Audubon, November-December, 1992.

Tokyo, Japan

The Deputy Speaker, a fifty-eight-year-old veteran serving his seventh consecutive term in the Lower House of Representatives as a member of the ousted Liberal Democratic Party, got off the phone with the US ambassador to Japan. An hour before dawn, the city was far from awake, but in the outlying middle-class suburbs, people were up and about, preparing for their long commute to work on the overcrowded subway and bullet trains. The weather service predicted another day of sunshine and moderate temperatures.

Even though the New Frontier Party was in power, it wasn't uncommon to appoint a member of the opposition to the number two slot of the Japanese Diet. Called *hakuchu,* or close balance of power, it promoted, in theory at least, smooth functioning of the parliament. On the floor of the House, the Deputy Speaker designated himself as being *mushozoku,* or unaffiliated. Privately, he suffered from no such delusion. He wanted his LDP back in power.

"Go back to sleep," the Deputy Speaker told his wife. She'd hurried in with a concerned look on her face. They had a daughter in college in Osaka and the early morning call had set her pulse racing with apprehension. "It's just work."

"Oh." Relief washed over her plain face. She looked at the wall clock and said, "It's almost time to get up anyway. Do you want tea?"

"Okay."

She left the room and he made his next call without hesitation, even though he realized he would be waking the seventy-year-old man at the other end of the line. "Tomitasen?"

❊

"Yes?" growled Nobuo Tomita, sounding as old and grizzled as he was.

He awoke quickly, propping himself higher against the pillows as the Deputy Speaker recounted the conversation with the US ambassador. The first lady had caught the *Kagoshima*, a Japanese merchantman belonging to Kaiyou, buying whale meat from a pirate whaler in the North Pacific, which was outside their appointed region. Tomita's craggy face was rarely known to smile. One cracked it now. He thanked the Deputy Speaker for calling so promptly and offered him a few obtuse words of praise, in effect ensuring he would not go unrewarded.

Alert and charged with fresh energy, Tomita got out of bed. A widower for a year now, after a brief period of mourning he'd brought his longtime mistress into the house. Thirty-five years his junior, she barely stirred. He walked out of the room, punching numbers on his phone.

Nobuo Tomita had been a top graduate from the prestigious law faculty of the University of Tokyo, making him an atypical Japanese politician in a system where the brightest became civilian bureaucrats within government think tanks and the academically less distinguished ran for office. Educational credentials, social status and attitudes then worked in an indefinable way beneath the struggles of the various political factions—the heart and soul of Japanese politics—deciding who became prime minister, then controlling his authority.

For the past five years, none exerted more clout than the fifty-one-member fishing faction. In 1982, following the conservationists' 25-7 victory in the Metropole Hotel on the Regency waterfront at Brighton, England, ending commercial whaling, international pressure mounted on Japan to quit hunting altogether. But the Obata family, owners of Kaiyou, ensured that politicians remained defiant, organizing Diet representatives and councilors from the coastal fishing districts into a conservative *koenkai,* or support group, to endorse only that candidate for prime minister who would respond to their interests. The *koenkai* had strengthened into a powerful fishing faction.

Nobuo Tomita had been the front-runner to become prime minister five years ago. The LDP had 206 votes in the 511-seat lower house and was guaranteed the support of the fishing faction to put him over the top by one. At six PM, an hour after every political pundit went home declaring Tomita the next prime minister, Kaiyou was indicted for "whale meat laundering." The announcement concluded a three-month investigation triggered by none other than Tomita's son, Isamu, who exposed an illegal whale meat pipeline from Taiwan through Seoul, South Korea's Fish International to the Shokuryo Kabushiki Gaishi in Tsukiji, the huge Tokyo fish market. By some cruel twist of fate, the boy had grown up to become an active member of CITES, the 119-nation Convention on International Trade in Endangered Species.

Nobuo Tomita had never been an environmentalist. In fact, he was groomed under conservation's most formidable backroom opponents in Japan. Tomita had earned a reputation as a master *nemawashi,* or skilled fixer. His twenty-odd years in politics had been spent rewarding the whaling industry, which was instrumental in his rise. But within minutes of the indictment, the Obata family called out Tomita as a risky choice. How could he be trusted to keep secrets when his son would always have unimpeded access to the affairs of his father? The family muscled the fishing faction to ally themselves with the pro-whaling, anti-American Socialists.

Tomita reached his study when his call was answered. "Hattorisen?"

"Tomitasen?" The surprise in Yasuji Hattori's voice was music to the ears of the veteran politician.

They had not spoken since that fateful evening, when Hattori, as the Obata family's handpicked leader of the fishing faction, had spearheaded the biggest coup in Japanese politics. "I just heard this bit of news which I thought you might like to be aware of at once," said Tomita. *What goes around comes around, you son of a bitch.*

"What time is it?" asked Hattori.

"Early. Very early."

"So it must be bad news."

"You can be the judge of that."

Following the expansion of the Southern Oceans sanctuary, many members of the Whalers League of Japan turned to dolphin and tuna hunting to sustain their payroll. But Kaiyou refused to turn away from the quick and enormous profits whaling offered, hiring pirates and fly-by-night entrepreneurs from the Philippines, Taiwan and Korea.

Tomita did not hide his satisfaction when he repeated the Deputy Speaker's information. *If infighting breaks out in the Whalers League of Japan boardroom, the fishing faction will disintegrate,* was the clear implication of Tomita's words. WLJ's shareholders, who claimed the North Pacific as their territory, supported sixteen representatives of the fishing faction.

"Will this change our position at Friday's IWC meeting?" asked Tomita, throwing a little concern into his voice.

"I don't know."

"Well, good luck."

"Thank you."

Aiko, Tomita's young mistress, hurried back to bed and pretended to be asleep when he returned. She had been eavesdropping. He nuzzled and she stretched luxuriantly as if awakening from a pleasant dream.

"Ironical, is it not?" he whispered into her ear, tracing the curve of her breast. "Whaling, which took the ultimate prize in Japanese politics away from me, will now drop it right back into my hands."

Feeling his bony fingers reach between her legs, Aiko kissed him and straddled him gently. He had a bad hip and so she raised herself on her knees and rocked slowly. She prolonged their intimacy as much as she could.

A Kabuki dancer of marginal talent, she loved the gifts and comforts Tomita lavished upon her. Twice a week she saw Tomita's son, Isamu, to satiate her sexually. Isamu hadn't spoken or seen his father since costing him the prime ministership. Wealthy on his own, thanks to an inheritance from his maternal grandparents, Isamu could afford to be a full time activist. Aiko held his attention and fancy by being an invaluable source of inside information.

What are you up to, you old snake? wondered Hattori, pacing the plush living room of his penthouse in the exclusive Tokyo residential district across town. Tough and unscrupulous, this sixth offspring of a large whaling family from Yamada, on the poorer Pacific side of the island of Honshu, was the minister for Agriculture, Forestry and Fishery. He glanced at his Rolex, debating whether it might be too early to make the next phone call. But time was of the essence.

He dialed the prime minister of Japan.

What are you up to? wondered Hattori. [decorative separator]

Prime Minister Shigesaburo Maeo, seventy-six years old and heavyset, had *worker* written all over him. He did not belong to the educational elite, nor was he a member of the national government's bureaucracy, a qualification mandated by the Liberal Democratic Party for all who sought the prime ministership. Maeo didn't even make it through middle school. He'd spent his youth as a deck hand on Japanese pelagic whaling fleets. A flenser with an easy charm and a natural talent for public speaking, he rose to become the sailors' spokesman. Soon, Maeo transitioned into the ranks of the General Council of Japanese Trade Unions, the primary supporters of the Japan Socialist Party. Four years later, he was elected to the Diet's House of Representatives. At the time, the JSP membership consisted of idealists and misguided academicians caught up in petty squabbles, extreme militancy and narrow public appeal.

The 1982 US-backed moratorium on whaling provided him the platform to broaden the JSP's power base beyond the trade unions. Calling the West "invaders of Japan's culture, tradition and internal politics," Maeo gradually consolidated the JSP into an influential anti-American faction. His own hatred for the United States was rooted in his parents' gruesome death in Hiroshima by the atomic bomb. At the turn of millennium, approval ratings for the LDP had reached an unprecedented low. Maeo exploited the discontent in the elections that followed, uniting the splintered opposition by promising the leaders ministerships—coveted rewards in Japan—if they usurped power, a long shot that needed fifty-one defectors, which came in the form of the fishing faction.

Once in power, Maeo consolidated the fragile coalition into the New Frontier Party. Come time to be re-elected, he led the NFP to win 209 seats. For the first time in Japan's political history, the Liberal Democratic Party came in second. Hattori's fifty-one strong fishing faction once again decided who became prime minister.

Maeo knew that his long time archrival and nemesis, Nobuo Tomita, was at this very moment playing the mathematical game of finding 256 members in the 511-seat lower house to usurp power. Tomita could not scavenge the support of all sixty-six independents because there were not enough ministerships to go around. He had to prey upon the sixteen representatives supported by the shareholders of the Whalers League of Japan who had been violated by Kaiyou in the North Pacific.

"Have you talked with anybody at Kaiyou?" asked Maeo.

As dawn broke over the capital, top advisors of the Inner Council had gathered at the official residence of the Japanese prime minister. One of Maeo's nine *hisho-kan*, or political secretaries, took notes.

"I called the Obata House," began Hattori. "They assured me that they will settle this among themselves within the WLJ."

"We still have to make an outward show of condemning Kaiyou," said the chairman of Policy Research, whose council replicated government ministries and agencies. Staffed with sharp bureaucrats, they formulated policies that Diet members presented on the floor of the House.

"Why is it we have a crisis before every IWC meeting?" muttered Hattori irritably.

The telephone rang.

"That must be Isodasen from Washington," said the cabinet secretary, nicknamed "wife" in Japanese politics because Maeo saw more of him than his wife.

Indeed, it was Shayo Isoda. Japan's whaling commissioner had been involved in the dead-end negotiations at the White House this past weekend. A chubby bureaucrat who'd also risen from the trade union ranks like Maeo, Isoda had grown up in Taiji, the birthplace of Japan's whaling industry. He met Maeo, stumping in town as the JSP candidate. The future prime minister was taken by the young man's zeal to return the luster to the two whales sculptured over the arched gateway into Taiji.

The cabinet secretary put Isoda on the speaker phone. He apologized for joining the meeting late. "Is our position going to change at the IWC on Friday?"

"We have not got that far yet," said Maeo. "What is the latest?"

"Still no official word. I spoke with a US State Department source. He told me he was under the impression the first lady was still in Los Angeles working the phones for votes. Clearly, nobody even knows she is in the North Pacific."

"What about the *Kagoshima*? Where is the ship now?" asked Maeo.

"There is very little information," replied Isoda, "but Paul Worthy's submarine may have been involved."

Maeo turned on Hattori. "You assured me it would never put to sea."

Hattori shrugged helplessly. "We haven't been able to do anything because it's been at the naval shipyard in Pearl Harbor."

Maeo shook his head in resignation. "The first lady probably has proof incriminating Kaiyou. We have to assume she has the *Kagoshima*'s captain in her custody as well. But why isn't all this on the news. That bitch lives for headlines."

"Have you spoken to Dale Gabon?" asked Hattori.

"He has not returned my call," replied Isoda.

Maeo became wary. "He's a sly fox."

"I don't see how we can vote against the president's wife now," said the Policy Research chairman.

"Are you suggesting we change our vote to yes?" Hattori looked at the prime minister.

Maeo glowered. He was keenly aware, without the fishing faction leader pointing it out, that the unity of Hattori's faction would splinter if their hard-line stance changed.

"We can abstain," suggested Isoda.

"Then so will our whaling allies," said Hattori.

"You're right," Maeo agreed with Hattori. "They are not going to vote no on their own. They depend on the US for military support. We are the only ones who can challenge the Americans."

"We must handle this situation with tact," cautioned the Policy Research chairman. "We have immense economic interests in the

United States, Europe and Asia, where whaling is an emotional issue."

"Whose side are you on?" asked Hattori irritably. "The IWC has become more an organization about anti-whaling than whaling. It's ridiculous that countries like India have votes when they don't even eat meat."

"Retaliation will be short-lived," Maeo snorted. "We have the cash surplus to withstand any worldwide boycott of our products."

"What if the Americans invoke Packwood-Magnusson?" asked the finance minister, breaking his silence for the first time. In 1979, during the two-faced presidency of Jimmy Carter, who made voluble public statements against whaling while privately doing nothing to enforce sanctions against Japan, Senators Packwood and Magnusson passed an amendment to the International Fishery Conservation and Management Act that slapped any nation flouting IWC rules with a ban on fishing within US territorial waters. "For ten million dollars of whaling, do we want to sacrifice more than a billion dollars of fishing?"

Maeo glared at him. "It cannot be about money anymore if we have to take the next step."

The finance minister averted his eyes.

"Confrontation is not the answer either," said the Policy Research chairman bravely.

"They have thrown the first stone," snapped Maeo.

"Exactly," agreed Hattori.

Everyone in this room not only shared Maeo's anti-American bias, albeit with varying degrees of intensity, but also a deep belief in Yamatoism, the doctrine of Japanese superiority. At its best, Yamatoism was a unifying force, and at its worst, a racist philosophy propagating "dominant financial and economic roles ... and a new Japanese order erected in its place." From his first day in office, Maeo had made it a priority to dethrone China, whose growth into a manufacturing behemoth had shoved Japan to an afterthought in Asia. So he began Yamatoism's surreptitious revival by increasing funding to the Japanology Institute to study and report the uniqueness of the Japanese people. Maeo also made the Yasukuni Shrine, the memorial to World War II soldiers, a national monument and declared December 7 a day of mourning. America had been outraged, but the emotion-charged issue in Japan won wide public support and the holiday passed unanimously in both Houses. Last month, he openly credited Yamatoism when Japanese investment worldwide surpassed China.

Isoda continued, "Our allies and I tried for a negotiated settlement when we met with the president in the Oval Office. His wife attended and openly defied her husband. This is a woman who does not know her place and is dictating US policy."

"Everett will not threaten us with the amendment," declared Maeo confidently. "He knows we will threaten right back with a trade war."

"Which," smirked Hattori, "we have for all intents and purposes already won."

"I would caution against an attitude like that," ventured the finance minister tentatively. "America is our biggest customer."

"America is our biggest *debtor*," spat Maeo with sudden venom. "This whaling vote presents us with an opportunity to draw the line in the sand. It can also complete the final piece of our economic expansion plan to elevate Japan to the summit and replace the dollar with the yen as the world's benchmark currency!"

Honolulu

Jan watched the headlands of Oahu hove in sight under a starlit sky. It was an hour before midnight. She hadn't been able to sleep, still feeling the rush, twelve hours later, of a mission that began with the modest objective of grabbing a ship's manifest incriminating Japan. Instead, it had culminated with perhaps the biggest coup ever for the anti-whaling cause. By directly linking Kaiyou to the pirates, she could indict the entire government in Tokyo, whose rise to power was inextricably married to the Obata family. Throw in videotape that Worthy had recorded of the slaughter of endangered sperms, especially Vesprhein and the hooker killing a calf, and world sympathy would rise like a tidal wave.

Jan stood on the bridgewing of a Navy gunboat, flanked by Raquel, Boycott and Knight. As US waters approached, the *Earthforce* and the *Stavenger* had been surrounded by three Navy gunboats. She wasn't surprised, and neither was the commander of the lead boat, when Jan informed him that she was dropping the *Stavenger*'s anchor in international waters. Worthy's data banks showed none of his pirates had any outstanding arrest warrants in the United States, but some were wanted in countries with extradition treaties. Worthy's crew replaced Jan and her friends. His submarine stayed with the *Stavenger,* hovering astern.

The tender chugged into the passage. The early hour had emptied all traffic. Smells and sounds of habitation replaced the pure odors of the ocean. She planned to call a press conference right away, before news leaks diluted the shock and awe of what she'd done and discovered. To elicit the greatest pressure from the PR nightmare for Japan and the axis of pro-whaling allies, this exposé had to drop like a bombshell. Jan smirked at the ironic coincidence. They were passing the sugarcane, pineapple and lush green tropical vegetation through which Japanese planes had swept into Pearl Harbor for the most famous shock-and-awe attack in modern history.

"Have you figured it out?" asked Raquel, jarring Jan out of her thoughts.

Vesprhein and the *Kagoshima*'s skipper were unforeseen boons. Suddenly, the euphoria of their capture receded. Jan faced an unfamiliar challenge. Getting them admitted into the US. She needed Everett.

Jan shook her head. "I've been asking myself, why would Carsten help? A win for me could be disastrous for him."

"Uh-huh. But you have come up with something," Raquel smiled.

"Of course," Jan grinned, hiding her deep anxiety. She had only one move to play.

Washington DC

"Hello?" the president answered the direct line at his bedside after two rings. Dawn was breaking over the capital.

"Hi, honey." Neutral voice.

"Jan?" he tried to sound surprised. He was expecting the call and had been up and waiting. "Are you all right? Where are you?"

He realized she was aware he knew exactly what she'd been up to, but to her credit she played nice. "Pearl Harbor."

I can kill this story, he'd assured his economic advisors. Now the plate beckoned. He picked up the proverbial bat and stepped up, confident of the exact pitch she was going to throw at him.

"I want two temporary visas."

And there it was. He needed to strike out a couple of times so that he did not tip her off that he was here to play. "That's State Department jurisdiction. I'll ask George to call you with the number."

"No," replied Jan. "There's no time for that. I want them at the IWC meeting on Friday."

"Who are they?" asked Everett innocently.

Jan told him about Vesprhein and the *Kagoshima's* skipper.

Everett was already familiar with their bios. It hadn't been hard to figure out who she'd want to parade to the world. He feigned shock, "One of them is a pirate? Are you nuts? That's political suicide."

"Neither man is wanted in the US."

"One's a criminal, Jan."

"You authorized a visa for the head of Hezbollah," snapped Jan, "a wanted terrorist with an FBI bounty of ten million dollars on his head."

"Yeah," Everett threw irritation and sarcasm into his voice, "this is in the same league as his address to the UN about a treaty for peace in the Middle East."

"Fine," Jan snapped.

Here it comes. Everett waited.

"Consider my days campaigning alongside you over."

On cue. Her only curve ball. And she'd thrown it. Everett waited until he heard her draw her breath as a prelude to hanging up, then jumped, "Wait!"

He envisioned Jan smiling, as if she were ahead in the count. It was time to swing and connect. But first a little plate ritual. "Can you assure me the pirate will be off US soil the morning after?"

"Yes."

"They must stay in your custody for the duration."

"Okay."

"The press doesn't know you're in Hawaii or that you sank a ship. The blackout continues. We control how this whole thing leaks out." *Whack!* Contact in the meat of the bat. The ball was in the air. Sailing. Had he put enough behind it?

"Fuck, no!" erupted Jan, as he'd expected.

"We cannot have shock waves, Jan. Too much is at stake." Sailing, sailing.

"No deal," said Jan firmly.

He pushed her to the wall. "Wall Street is on edge. It will be a bloodbath with no winners. Not you, for triggering it. Not me, for allowing it. Innocent people will lose money." He could hear her frustration. "It's the only way those two are getting on US soil."

"Okay," she said finally and hung up.

She probably slammed the phone down. Everett knew he could count on the fact that when Jan balanced emotion against practicality, she always went with common sense. Everett dialed again and announced triumphantly, "She went for it, George.

＊

Pleasance was on his way to work, coming around Dupont Circle along Connecticut Avenue just a few blocks from the White House. The capital was up and about. Traffic thickened at every intersection as he wound closer to the heart of the nation's government.

"Excellent," replied Pleasance. "I'll take it from here."

He always suspected Everett had a dark side, full of cunning— after all, he did win the senate seat from an entrenched Democrat. Lhea had even made a comment about it when, after his economic advisors left, Everett had shared how he intended to shut Jan down. Everett had quipped, "Still, I'm no George." It elicited mutual admiration. Pleasance caught their reflection on the glass across the fireplace and felt a chill. In that moment, they could've been the White House of Nixon, Haldeman and Ehrlichman at the height of their power, pre-Watergate.

Pleasance waited for the president to disconnect, then voice commanded his next call over his Bluetooth. The sun broke through the gap between buildings and struck his face at an angle that added a cruel glint to his eyes. With this fire squelched, they would next blindside the first lady with the outcome at the IWC fall session this Friday and silence her for the rest of the campaign.

Honolulu

The slender lukewarm jets cascaded down the sensuous curves of Jan's sculpted yet utterly feminine figure. She chased the soap bubbles down her flat stomach and over her arms and legs. She saved her conceit for when she was in the shower, examining her body daily for even the slightest touch of age or a hint of flab. Her muscles were as fit and firm as in her twenties, but her skin had softened. She was careful never to allow her body fat to exceed 5 percent.

She'd slept well. Her blue eyes shone brightly as she stared back at herself in the full-length mirror. She felt refreshed and invigorated.

Banding her hair into a ponytail, she slipped on a white T-shirt and denim shorts to combat the full force of the Hawaiian heat and humidity. It was just past eleven when Jan emerged from the bedroom, ready for the challenging day ahead: eliciting testimony from Vesprhein and the Captain of the *Kagoshima*.

Local State Department officials, led by a bespectacled undersecretary who embodied the image of the pencil pusher, had descended within an hour of her concession to Everett. Vesprhein and the Japanese skipper received a forty-eight-hour Special Status visa. The undersecretary reiterated all the restrictions Everett had laid out. Around three AM, they pulled into a sprawling estate that Worthy had rented on the outskirts of Honolulu for the duration of the refitting and trials. The two prisoners retired to separate bedrooms.

As Jan passed by, she knocked on them. Neither man answered. Knight appeared, dressed for a run along the beach.

"Patrick, good morning."

"Hey."

She asked him to check inside. The prisoners were both asleep. Knight jogged off. Jan walked toward the kitchen. She heard a sharp clatter, then a mournful wail. She hurried in. Raquel was crying.

"Raq! What's the matter?"

"There was a message. Must have come in when we were at sea." Raquel replayed the message on her cell phone.

"Oh, honey, I'm so sorry," said Jan and took Raquel in her arms.

Jan and Raquel had met at a Green rally in San Diego State College. They were paired to make signs. There could not be two more opposite women. Jan was the product of upper middle class suburbia and Raquel grew up in the gang-infested streets of South Central Los Angeles. Her story was typical of black families there. She was raised by a strict grandmother. Her mom couldn't shake a crack habit or stay out of jail, eventually dying in a knife fight behind bars. She never knew her father. Somehow, she inherited her grandmother's decency and work ethic. Growing up and maturing faster than her years, she stayed out of trouble and made it to college.

These two teens from either side of the tracks became fast friends. With her long hair always in braids and a flashy ring in her nose, Raquel seemed the likely firecracker, but she played the rock to Jan's impetuous risk taker. Jan spewed profanity, was quick to anger, spoke plainly and wore her emotions on her sleeve. Raquel rarely, if ever, lost her composure. A highly regarded professor at the Marine Research Lab in San Diego, she was a thinker and a philosopher, which fit Jan's own love of knowledge and explained their deep friendship. On the one hand, Raquel believed in the philosophies of Martin Luther King Jr. and Gandhi; on the other hand, like Malcolm X, Raquel believed violent acts were sometimes necessary to save lives, though she didn't think she could personally ever take a life to save one.

"I'll book you on the next flight," said Jan.

After Boycott left with Raquel to the airport, Jan called Everett. She found him in the Oval Office, signing a couple of Bills before hitting the campaign trail this afternoon. Realizing the name would mean nothing, she told him Raquel's boyfriend had been killed in a plane crash. Everett liked Raquel and was genuinely saddened. The tragedy softened the first couple's own acrimony—for the duration of the phone call, at least. Jan wanted to send flowers from the White House and their condolences.

"Fax the details to George," said Everett. "Then you know it's going to get done."

As much as Jan disliked Pleasance, she admired his diligence. "Will do. Thanks."

"Bye. See you Saturday?" he asked.

"Yeah."

They planned to spend it at Camp David. On Sunday, Everett was having the Committee to Re-elect the President over. She'd already told him she'd come in only when it was time to lay out her itinerary on the campaign trail. After they hung up, Jan wondered when they had stopped saying, "I love you."

She found a sheet of paper and handwrote the name of Raquel's boyfriend: *Dan Sitka*.

Washington DC

All documents for the president's attention were received and stamped by the assistant to the White House chief of staff, a forty-six-year-old Hispanic mother of five with an unshakable expression of worry on her face. She placed Jan's handwritten fax containing the Seattle address on Pleasance's desk. He insisted on scrutinizing every document, even routine authorizations. His desk was immaculate, with no trace of the incredible amount of paperwork that received his perusal every day.

Pleasance arrived a few moments later, forewarned by the president about the condolences and flowers that needed to be sent to Raquel Ruppert's deceased boyfriend. Distantly acquainted with her, he considered the African-American marine biologist as much a nuisance as Jan. He picked up the fax.

Reading Dan Sitka's name, he went still. Raquel and Sitka? Pleasance recalled a remark by Gabon that one of the nurses on duty told the Mineral Management Service director that Sitka gave her a letter to mail. She couldn't say who it was addressed to. *Raquel.*

Had Sitka repeated the details that were in the report? He could not take the chance Sitka had not. He called the Federal Bureau of Investigation on Ninth Street and Pennsylvania Avenue.

"George?" The FBI director, a White House appointee, wasn't expecting the call.

"I want a letter intercepted." Since 9/11, the FBI had enjoyed unlimited access into virtually every facet of an American's life. If Raquel shared its contents with Jan, the first lady's reaction would be extreme. Such was the nature of Sitka's discovery. It would derail the unstoppable chain of events of the Sitka scenario carefully set in motion by two discreet calls made by the president.

New York

The recipient of Everett's first call was Delta Harris, the photogenic, tough talking, US ambassador to the United Nations. Following the rape incident involving the US Marine and a local girl in Seoul, which triggered widespread unrest across South Korea, Delta had emerged as a clear and steady voice of an administration that seemed completely out of its depth in foreign policy. Delta was on her way to John F. Kennedy airport to get on a plane for the routine 'look-ahead' Thursday night meeting at the White House, an innovation she'd instituted. It forewarned the president of potential crises based on reports from his war-gamers in the Pentagon, a team of economists, historians, political scientists, psychologists and military strategists who met everyday in a tightly guarded basement. These "classrooms of the US war college" had never been used as the foundation for an administration's foreign policy, but they provided Everett a welcome surefootedness and he had Delta to thank for it. A Beltway insider who enjoyed proximity to power, she had transformed her passive UN appointment from messenger to Kissinger-style superdiplomat.

"Delta, hi," said Everett.

"Mr. President?" Surprised, Delta took him off the speakerphone.

"Don't worry about the look-ahead. I need you back at the UN." Everett went on to explain why.

"Turn around," she told the driver.

Minutes later, the limousine drew into the basement of the distinctive vertical slab that was the United Nations. The Marine guard smartly saluted her. Another employee of the gigantic

1800-strong bureaucracy, whose job it was to memorize offices and floors, pushed the button in the elevator. Her staff was surprised to see her back and hurriedly lost their lethargy and relaxation. She ran her office with an iron fist.

"Get me the secretary general," she said tersely to her twenty-six-year old Hispanic assistant. "Fix your tie." The assistant gulped. She did not care he'd loosened it thinking she was gone for the day.

Delta's office contained the usual staple of flags, an autographed picture of the first couple in a gold frame and mementos from other administrations she'd served. She rounded her large desk and dropped into the leather chair. On cue, the intercom buzzed. Her assistant reported in a crisp voice, "The secretary general is on the line."

While the UN propagated democracy around the world, internally it subscribed to military junta-like sycophancy to the United States, though a shift in power and attitude had been occurring. Third World countries wanted to be part of the new global economy, rendering America's military superpower stature obsolete. Japan and China, with their vast cash reserves, stepped in and changed the rules for global leadership from weapons to money.

"Good morning, sir," greeted Delta.

"Good morning, Delta," replied the secretary general with a thick Indian accent. He was supposed to act without prejudice, but it was common knowledge his stint had been abbreviated due to heart trouble. He was angling for a political position when he returned to New Delhi, so he had promised his discreet cooperation when contacted by the prime minister of India in Washington, the recipient of Everett's second telephone call.

"It's set," the secretary general said cryptically. "Nine o'clock tomorrow morning."

Honolulu

Vesprhein grinned. "Looking hot, m'lady."

If he hoped to make her self-conscious, he didn't succeed. Jan kept her long, bare legs crossed and didn't miss a beat, "I know."

"I like you," Vesprhein said.

She ignored him and looked over to Boycott. The red light over his camera blinked. Boycott nodded, "Speed."

Jan turned back to Vesprhein. "You can start."

Vesprhein cleared his throat and spoke directly into Boycott's camera, "My name is Arlov Vesprhein."

The pirate sat in a rattan chair. A couple of studio lights filled in the details on his face predominantly lit by the morning sun slanting through the window from a clear blue sky. Leaves on the trees outside brushed against each other with a friendly rustle. A dog barked somewhere above the distantly audible traffic. Jan sat across from Vesprhein. Boycott watched a compact flatscreen displaying what the camera recorded. Knight hovered in the background, pen poised over pad.

"I was born in Reine," continued Vesprhein. "It's the capital of Mosken, one of the remote Lofoten islands above the Arctic Circle in Norway. The town is a shell of what it used to be. Most of the houses and fishing huts are empty. There are less than fourteen hundred people. Maybe only five family-owned boats, if that, operating." He glared at Jan, "If you win the ban on coastal whaling tomorrow, they'll be wiped out too."

"Why did you go into whaling?" asked Jan.

"My father, grandfather and great-grandfather were whalers. Like them, I went to sea almost as soon as I could walk. We did well. I went to private school. That should end the burning curiosity you arrogant, shit-brained Americans have toward anyone other than yourselves who speak English fluently."

Jan refused to be provoked. Vesprhein continued, "My father

started to see the good times end. Every season, Japan and Russia—the Soviet Union then—got better ships and newer equipment and priced us out of the Antarctic. The Norwegian Crew Law prevented my father from joining his boats with them or even taking a job with a foreign fleet. To make matters worse, the fucking IWC began to issue quotas. Our government took over all whaling. You know what that meant?" He snorted, "Small whalers like my father got fucked out of work, even though our family had given more than a hundred years to this business." He shook his head. "My father drank himself to death. I was sixteen."

"Is that when you got into pirate whaling?"

Vesprhein nodded. "I was a trained gunner. Fuck, I was the goddamn best, I don't mind saying. I had what you might call a natural *flair* for killing whales." Vesprhein smiled. That comment had gotten to Jan. "Anyway, I had to support my dear old ma because my father was too drunk and too frail to do it by that time, so I found work in the Canaries on the *Tonna 2*."

Jan recognized the name. The *Tonna 2* was one of the early killer-factory ships that ironically went down chasing a whale in the 1980s, a time when pirate whaling, in anticipation of the moratorium that was to take effect in '85, became so lucrative, an armada operated up and down the Atlantic.

"Then I joined as the first officer on the *Irish Rum*." Another familiar name to the eco-warriors. These pirates operated out of South Africa. "We were doing great until we found out the skipper had decided to switch sides, copping a deal just for himself. He didn't know we knew. When he showed up on the bridge, I didn't waste time to find out the details. I shot the motherfucker fair and square after giving him an opportunity to defend himself, then promoted my helmsman to first officer for, you know, having the courage to hold the skipper down while I pumped in the rest of the bullets." Vesprhein shrugged. "Two years ago I had to kill him too because he wouldn't call me Captain. Don't forget that next time you address me."

"I'll try, Arlov." Jan knew what he was trying to do and smiled. Vesprhein grinned right back. Jan became serious. "Let's talk about the Japanese."

"We had a great deal going with Kaiyou. They didn't care that I took over the *Irish Rum* as long as we delivered whale meat. Since I barely trust myself, I kept every production contract, bill of sale and also took pictures."

"Where are they?"

Vesprhein nodded to the tattered satchel leaning against his chair leg. "The past decade has been gold. IWC kept reducing quotas, so demand soared. Kaiyou gave me a ship to operate out of Taiwan, a non-member. From there it was shipped off to Japan. You Americans found out, threatened to cut off aid, so we routed it through South Korea, Hong Kong and the Philippines. The US was on our ass again. Kaiyou shut down the entire Asian operation and opened one in Chile. Gotta hand it to the Obata family, they always found a way around. The Japanese were already taking the maximum allotment, then buying every ounce of meat that Iceland, Norway, Korea and Russia had to sell. It was still not enough. Five years ago, I invested in the *Stavenger*. Paid it off in a year, thanks to Kaiyou."

Jan gestured to his satchel. "Let's look at what you have."

Vesprhein made no move. "The immunity extends to my crew, yes?"

"What's with this loyalty?"

"It's called honor among thieves, *Mrs. President.*"

"You're a fascinating guy, Arlov."

"Women around the world have said that," winked Vesprhein.

"All whores." Jan observed anger mount then quickly dissipate like the shadow of a large fish vanishing into the ocean.

He smiled. "All except one."

There's something redeeming about this ruthless bastard, Jan thought and tried to pinpoint when and how the possibility entered her mind. Was it something he said? His total commitment to his own code, which he set for himself and lived by no matter what the cost? His irresistible combination of ruthlessness and charm? No, it was deeper and more complex, an oblique feeling that swirled out of her subconscious, created by intangible fragments of perception that shaped opinions and would never stand the test of rational thought. An unreal, oh-wow-what-if hope nagged her despite the repulsion and outrage.

That was it! Oh, wow. What if?

Jan stopped herself. It was a ridiculous thought.

Washington DC

Friday dawned unseasonably warm. Everett awoke as the all-news station came on his bedside radio at five precisely. He never lazed in bed. Jan usually slept in until seven or eight. One of the last tasks for the Secret Service agent going off the night shift was to put on a fresh pot of coffee. Everett poured a cup, flipped through the stack of major newspapers, all painting apocalyptic scenarios from a vindictive, capital-rich Japan if Jan won the vote. He picked up the remote for the flat-screen on the wall.

"It is incredible that seemingly unconnected events can intertwine and become defining moments in history," the familiar anchor said. "The single most important global resource for the first time since World War II is not the military but money. At present, nobody has more of it than Japan, while the United States, architect of the post-war economic system, is the largest debtor nation ever. A victory for the first lady at the International Whaling Commission meeting in Los Angeles, while a triumph for conservation, could very well see Japan, the world's largest creditor, throw down the economic gauntlet."

Everett switched channels. They all led with the IWC vote. "The slaughter of whales has always been a contentious issue.

Today more people know about whaling than ever before because of its spokeswoman and her podium, First Lady Jan Everett. The sad reality is that this debate, somewhere, somehow, ceased to be about whaling. It is now about power, and three months from now in November, the American people will cast their ballot to express whether they hold President Everett responsible for losing it, if he does, to Japan."

Everett turned off the television, shaved, showered and dressed in a conservative blue suit. He informed Whacko—the White House Communications Office underneath the Oval Office—that he was on his way so that they could page Pleasance.

"Good morning, George," greeted Everett. Pleasance waited outside the elevator. It was a daily ritual with them to walk together to the Oval Office, covering items that needed to be kept between them.

Pleasance smiled thinly, "Prime Minister Maeo should be getting the bad news right about now."

Tokyo

Maeo turned in around midnight, glad this tense, exhausting day was over. Half an hour later, the phone rang. The cabinet secretary at the other end of the line said he'd been contacted by Japan's permanent representative to the United Nations. "America has called an emergency UN Security Council meeting for nine AM tomorrow."

Maeo lay back down. Ignoring his wife mumbling in her sleep, he stared at the ceiling. He had badly underestimated American guile.

Los Angeles

The first lady's limousine pulled past the media circus. No IWC meeting had ever drawn so much attention. Downtown was gridlocked with First Street closed at either end of the five-star Vista Hotel, whose modern tower stole the attention from the historic steeple of city hall. Four Secret Service agents swarmed the car. A barrage of questions erupted when Jan's long, stockinged legs scissored out of the limousine. She rode alone deliberately, so nobody would pay any heed to Boycott, Knight and two other agents hustling Vesprhein and the Japanese skipper out of the second limousine.

"Are you worried the president may be hurt if you win today?"

"What about Wall Street?"

She talked to the reporters, none of whom mentioned her high seas adventure because the White House had kept the incident out of the news, engineering a bland leak that "the first lady was planning to corroborate her case in the strongest manner possible." She tried not to be discouraged. The two men would still cause a buzz of curiosity by sitting at her table, and she planned to present them as surprise witnesses. But without a lead-up of damaging headlines, she had not been able to muster the outrage needed to overcome her one vote deficit.

Walking into the large banquet hall, Jan found it packed, a far cry from the early days, when the International Whaling Commission had been an exclusive club. Fourteen members, with one vote each, decided the fate of thousands of whales. They authorized the killing of more whales than in all previous unregulated years. Japan was inducted into the IWC on the insistence of General MacArthur for the purely humanitarian reason of alleviating national hunger in the aftermath of World War II. That crisis passed, but Japanese taste for whale meat never did. Neither did their defiance, even as the makeup and attitude within the IWC shifted, beginning with the social change in the US in the 1960s. Anti-whaling sentiment spread and culminated with a moratorium on all commercial whaling in 1985.

One month before the ban took effect, the fisheries minister responded to skyrocketing whale meat prices with an assurance that

Japan would find another way to continue whaling, a $60-million industry at the time. It was not an empty promise. Ronald Reagan's Treasury secretary was in Tokyo pleading with the government to recycle its trade surplus and purchase US Treasury long bonds to fund the Reagonomic deficit spending. In return, Japan was permitted to ease into the moratorium by 1988, when a different set of economic and political circumstances left the US completely powerless to enforce the pact.

Reagan's short-term solution of halving the dollar against the yen to erase the trade deficit had backfired. The deficit had doubled. Congress resorted to Japan bashing. On October 19, 1987, six months before Japan had agreed to halt whaling, Tokyo decided to serve notice they had America by the balls. Japanese securities firms glutted Wall Street with the government bonds they'd been accumulating since 1985. Between business hours of a single trading session—remembered to this day as Black Monday—the New York Stock Exchange lost 30 percent of its peak value. America became a conciliatory voice at IWC meetings from then on until Jan Everett arrived at the White House and propelled the United States to the forefront of conservation again.

But the damage was done. When Cetacean Bay, the newly expanding whale sanctuary in the Southern Ocean below the fortieth parallel, was finally created, there remained only 21 percent of the original 500,000 fin whales, 19 percent of seis, 2 percent of humpbacks, less than 1 percent of the biggest and most productive blue whales.

Jan sat down between Boycott and Knight to one side and Vesprhein and the Japanese skipper on the other side. Eyes swung. Whispers began. Curiosity mounted.

The IWC chairman stood up. "Good morning. I call the meeting to order."

For the first time, the entire membership was present. The session was also carried live on TV. Another first.

The mayor of Los Angeles delivered a brief welcome. When opening statements from the members, non-members and observers were passed out as meeting documents, every eye turned in surprise to Jan's table, specifically to Vesprhein and the Japanese skipper. They were mentioned in the GreenPlanet papers.

The chairman slapped his gavel once. "This plenary session of an extraordinary meeting of the International Whaling Commission has been called to vote on amendments in the schedule relating to aboriginal and coastal whaling. The floor is now open."

Jan raised her hand. GreenPlanet had been allowed to participate as a nonvoting member. Per IWC procedure, the chair recognized her organization.

"GreenPlanet."

Jan stood up. "Thank you, Mr. Chairman. I am happy to see every member of the IWC present today.

"Once again it is a time of crisis. The moratorium has failed. *Utterly!* In 1982, when we voted to ban commercial whaling for ten years, those of us who thought the whale war had ended were deluding ourselves. Canada simply quit the IWC to do what it pleased with its marine resources. Korea did the same. When the moratorium came up for review in 1992 at the Glasgow session, it was upheld again 18-6. Iceland left the IWC to resume whaling. Instead of ceasing to hunt, the government-supported Institute for Cetacean Research in Japan exploited a loophole in the IWC Schedule to announce a sixteen-year program of whaling for 'scientific and research' purposes. They set unilateral quotas. Japan silenced voices of opposition from St. Lucia, St. Vincent and Trinidad with promises of financial aid. Last year, we successfully closed that loophole. The killing still hasn't stopped! Why?

"Another loophole in the IWC Schedule called 'coastal and aboriginal' whaling, which was created with the intention of supporting remote, sparsely populated coastal communities suffering a shortage of other types of fishing. What we encountered in the

Norwegian Sea this past June was a million-dollar slaughterfest. Two members of the scientific committee will attest to this charge. If whale meat consumption is this centuries-old tradition, as Norway so piously claims, how is it that eighty percent of her harvest—and we have DNA tests on whale meat purchased by GreenPlanet undercover agents to prove it—finds its way to Japan, a nation which has never made even a pretence of obeying the moratorium. They openly celebrate the ninth of every month as 'Whale Eating Day.' They even put out a PR brochure extolling the necessity for whale meat." Jan waved the glossy, blue brochure.

"Ladies and gentlemen, like scientific and research whaling, coastal and aboriginal whaling are nothing but alternative names for commercial whaling. If we do not plug this loophole, the pendulum will swing back into a new era of killing. Since 1972, twenty international pacts have been signed to uphold the moratorium, yet few are followed and almost none are enforced. Earlier this year, the IWC allotted whaling nations two hundred and twelve minkes each." Jan looked directly into the Norwegian commissioner's eyes and raised her voice, "I ask you, sir, *how much is enough?*"

The blue-eyed man with blond hair looked away uncomfortably.

"But I suppose we must be thankful Norway's defiance is at least open." Jan swung her gaze across the room to the Japanese table. "Japan's violations, on the other hand, are cloaked in subterfuge."

Shayo Isoda, the Japanese commissioner, stared back undaunted.

"This is Arlov Vesprhein, captain of the pirate whaler, the *Stavenger.*" He raised a bored face. "And this is the captain of the *Kagoshima*, a merchantman belonging to Kaiyou." Jan pointed to the Japanese skipper, squirming on the other side of her, "the world's largest fishing company and the biggest shareholder of the Whalers League of Japan. We caught them red-handed a couple of days ago on the high seas." Surprise rippled across the room. Jan punched in, "Mr. Vesprhein's clandestine pacts with Japan go back fifteen years. We have documented proof and both men have confessed to bloody harvests of all types of whales, including the critically endangered blues just this past summer below the fortieth parallel in Cetacean Bay." Men and women straightened. "Between these two alone, I was sickened to discover the number of endangered blue, sei, fin, humpback, sperm and gray whales taken exceeds fifteen thousand!"

A shocked silence fell over the room. A couple of reporters edged out the door. "We rely on the honor system from whaling nations to supply catch information. Now we know the numbers from them are deliberate lies. So it follows that population projections by the scientific committee are grossly inaccurate."

Jan held up *The Report*. "Making this document, our bible in deciding quotas, worthless." Jan dropped it. The impact made a resounding *boom*! "It's time to end the lies and deceit! Make your vote a historic vote—one that future generations will look back and point to as a defining moment and a turning point in the whale war. Vote no! Save the whales! Please!"

She sat down. Thunderous applause exploded across the huge standing room only, auditorium. When the clapping finally subsided, Isoda raised his hand.

"Japan," recognized the chair, to some hissing and booing.

Isoda spoke through a translator. "In what was a nice history lesson, GreenPlanet exemplifies the current state of mind in the IWC. Emotion more than scientific fact governs this body, which has become a voice for protection of whales' rights rather than an objective forum for the sustainable development of marine resources. There are 760,000 minkes. Several hundred can be taken without even the slightest effect on the species. We oppose the resolution to ban aboriginal and coastal whaling."

"GreenPlanet," recognized the Chairman.

Jan stood up. "Whaling is a matter of ethics and ecology. Japan has slaughtered almost a thousand minkes every year for the past two decades for 'scientific research,' yet they cannot tell us even today simple aspects of the whales' life cycle such as breeding habits, calving, or migration."

"Japan."

"We have used research whaling to dispel misinformation and show conclusively that whales are no more complex than a herd of cows. This GreenPlanet resolution will close the door on all whaling."

Jan stood up and spoke before she was recognized. "Only because Japan hopes to begin commercial whaling again."

"We want it since 1988," Isoda responded sharply in broken English, not waiting for the chairman either.

Jan shot back. "So you confirm my charge that your research, coastal and aboriginal harvests have really been for commercial purposes."

"I not say that."

"You didn't have to."

Isoda blinked. The room went completely quiet. Jan knew she'd nailed him.

The chair pounded the gavel. "I must intervene and insist we follow procedure."

And so the debate raged. Passions ran high, as they always did. Even though everyone's position was already set and every vote pre-determined, both sides traded punches with more drama than ever before because of the media coverage. The chairman finally ended the debate. Jan wondered if she'd been able to change just one more mind in the room. *More likely, too little, too late.* The chairman announced that voting would commence immediately after lunch. Jan noticed that not a single pro-slaughter member left the banquet hall, no doubt hoping to avoid protestors, media questions and public pressure from her revelations about Vesprhein and the Japanese skipper. They could cast their ballots in a vacuum and the outrage would be after the fact. The sinking of the *Kagoshima* and capture of the *Stavenger* had been for naught. Jan second-guessed herself.

She should have called Everett's bluff—left the two captains parked in international waters and just gone for the headlines. The media would have surrounded the pirate ship, as they were probably doing right now. *Damnit!* Always right on when it came to strategy, she'd outsmarted herself by fixating on putting the two men on display.

"Nine o'clock," Boycott nudged Jan.

She flicked her eyes. Dale Gabon, the IWC commissioner for the US, was speaking to Shayo Isoda. Gabon and she had shaken hands for a photo op earlier. It made her skin crawl just to stand next to him. Isoda stood up and the two commissioners exited the dining room.

Jan's eyes narrowed suspiciously. "Carsten is up to something."

❃

"All these TV cameras," said Isoda, preceding Gabon into the elevator, "for first time makes me worry how I look."

Gabon guffawed. "By the end of the day you'll have more marriage proposals than you can handle."

"I don't think my wife like that very much."

"Is she here?"

"No. Tokyo. My son has school. You married?"

"Happily for twenty years," nodded Gabon. "I have a teenage daughter."

The elevator deposited them on the twentieth floor. A private security guard, hired by the IWC to keep the media away from the members staying on the two blocked-off floors, glanced at the picture IDs clipped over their breast pockets and nodded them on their way. Gabon fished out the keys to his room. Stepping aside, he ushered Isoda in and locked the door.

Gabon showed Isoda Sitka's report.

Tokyo

Prime Minister Maeo had watched Jan's fiery speech. TV stations had promoted the IWC vote all week long. While there wasn't much interest in the cities, he was certain that fishing communities along the coasts would be watching with deep interest. Maeo called in his cabinet secretary, dictating a brief statement to preempt the media blitz. In it, he distanced his government from Kaiyou. The text had been approved by the Obata family.

The phone rang. It was Isoda from LA.

He told Maeo about Sitka's report.

That's why the sinking of the Kagoshima *never made the news.* Maeo also guessed the White House had advised financial traders on Wall Street, explaining why there wasn't even a dip in the stock market following the first lady's startling revelations.

"It will counter any revolt from Hattori's fifty-one," said Isoda.

"Do they expect us to change our vote?" asked Maeo angrily.

"Yes," replied Isoda.

"Nobody puts a gun to my head." The defiance sounded hollow. He couldn't escape silently acknowledging that Everett had masterfully sidestepped a disastrous campaign-ending crisis. *The US president is quite the wolf.*

Los Angeles

"GreenPlanet has proposed a ban on coastal and aboriginal whaling," the IWC chairman began after he returned to the dais and called the session to order. "Such a ban would constitute a Schedule change of the International Whaling Commission's charter drawn up in 1946. Thus it requires a three-fourth's majority, or sixty votes, to be implemented. Twenty-one votes of opposition will defeat the amendment." He paused. He'd been full of dramatic lulls and impassioned calls all day. "Those for the ban will vote yes and those against will vote no."

"The cameras bring out the ham in just about everybody, don't they?" joked Jan.

"It's LA," quipped Boycott. "Maybe he's auditioning."

"Our roll call," went on the chairman, "starts with Antigua and Barbados."

The West Indian delegate stood up. "Yes."

"Argentina."

"No."

"Australia."

Jan looked into Boycott's pocket TV, which picked up a local live broadcast. The vote tally updated at the bottom. After a series of Yes votes came a bunch of No's from Brazil, Chile, China and Denmark. The tally stood at 12 under Yes and went up to 8 under No.

"Dominica."

"Yes."

"Finland."

"Yes."

"France."

"Yes."

"Germany."

"Yes."

"Grenada."

"Yes."

"India."

"Yes."

"Ireland."

"Yes."

A flood of anti-whaling nations propelled the Yes number to 25.

"Japan."

❋

Everett, Pleasance, Lhea and Adrian sat around the horseshoe in the Situation Room watching the vote live. Tokyo had given no indication whether they had rejected or accepted the White House ultimatum.

"No," responded Isoda.

Everett looked at Pleasance. Maeo had refused to bow to US pressure. Had their plan backfired?

※

Jan bit her lower lip. The number of votes against her motion added up to twelve. Korea, Norway and a split in Eastern Europe—former Soviet allies—quickly raised the No's to eighteen. *Three more votes and it'll be all over.* But she refused to give up.

"Oman."

"Yes."

"Peru."

"No."

Jan dug her nails into Knight's arm. Defeat approached to within two votes.

"Russia."

"No."

The tally of No's on Boycott's TV screen changed to 20. *Just a formality now,* Jan knew, even though countries S-T had voted yes.

"United States."

Gabon stood up and nodded. "Yes."

Fifty-nine for, twenty against. *Here it comes.* Isoda, at the Japanese table, remained stolid. Jan watched pro-whaling delegates energize because the country which would put them over the top was next.

"Venezuela," she said aloud, looking over.

The South American oil power was led by an eccentric and vitriolic anti-American dictator. The leader of the delegation was a dark skinned Latino in a crisp grey suit, with slicked back hair. He met Jan's eyes. She knew his country earned in excess of $50 million from pirate whaling sales to Japan and acted as a warehouse for Norwegians, who dumped minke whale meat for pickup by Japanese merchantmen.

"I just remembered," Knight whispered, "Japan and Venezuela signed some sort of financial aid package a couple of weeks ago."

It's over, mouthed Jan dejectedly. She felt her sentiment sweep across the room. The reporter on Boycott's little TV even said so.

The Venezuelan stood up. "Yes."

Jan blinked. She wasn't alone. It took everyone in the room a moment for his answer to register. Jan shot to her feet clapping. Applause thundered across the room. Chandeliers tinkled and the banquet room rocked. The pro-whalers looked dazed. Victory had been theirs. Now it was gone. Boycott elbowed Jan and pointed to Isoda. The Japanese delegation slipped out of the hall.

Before she could draw any conclusion, Gabon congratulated her. She shook so many hands, the US commissioner's slipped in and out unnoticed.

She had ended *all* whaling.

Washington DC

Everett agreed with Pleasance there should be no press conference. That would play right into the hype and confirm the gravity the media had been according the IWC vote. Instead, the president issued a brief statement through Zoe Zurich's Communications Office. "The United States, which has always been committed to conservation, is extremely pleased by the outcome. The president called the first lady and congratulated her. They are planning a quiet weekend at Camp David."

In the Oval Office, Everett smiled tightly. "The ball's rolling now, George."

Everett telephoned the Indian prime minister and expressed gratitude for his cooperation in influencing the UN secretary general. The State Department would be considering his request for arms and aid favorably.

The gloom and doom scenarios of Japanese retaliation ceased when what had transpired unraveled throughout the rest of the news cycle. It went back to September 13, 1994, when the Japanese

Foreign Minister Yohei Kono used a speech at the United Nations general assembly to express Japan's desire for a permanent seat on the UN Security Council. This was their first public admission, after a decade of discreet but strenuous canvassing, but the effort stalled. When Prime Minister Maeo took office, he resurrected the issue, forcing every country seeking financial aid into declaring support for Japan's inclusion.

The UN Security Council consisted of five permanent members, all victors of World War II. The other ten members were chosen on a rotating basis for two years. The P5 had been inching toward bringing in Japan, whose money they needed to bankroll UN missions. This year, Japan surpassed the United States as the number one contributor. But the Security Council wanted to keep the overall number unchanged. Intense diplomatic wrangling finally found consensus. France and Britain would be replaced by Japan and the European Union. The EU would fill its seat with a member nation on a rotating basis. But to change the make up, the general assembly needed to revise the UN charter. A single veto from one P5 member could undo the years of negotiations and keep Japan out for another decade, if not forever. Everett threatened to do just that, *neutralizing* any retaliation from Maeo. In fact, the Japanese prime minister was forced to condemn the Obata family and say nothing about the sinking of the *Kagoshima*.

The next morning, when he came downstairs to make his routine Saturday morning radio address, he found Pleasance beaming. His approval ratings had risen five points overnight.

Everett shared his optimism. "I guess the Sitka scenario is off to a perfect start."

Los Angeles

Jan awoke with a headache. GreenPlanet volunteers had thrown together a quick victory party with cheap booze that flowed plentifully. Non-whaling countries attended in full force. GreenPlanet President John Chambers unabashedly shook hands as if he had something to do with the win. Raquel reached Jan from Seattle with congratulations. Jan had spoken with Everett to gloat as well. Boycott and Knight left early to board a red-eye back to Vancouver. The party broke around one in the morning.

"You realize your total ban is only gonna increase my business," said Vesprhein, sitting in her kitchen when she walked in rubbing her eyes. He'd been at the party too and almost charmed a pretty redhead into coming home with them.

"Lower your voice," Jan whispered, clutching her temple with her thumb and forefinger. "I haven't had a hangover like this since college."

A Secret Service agent stood at the door. He nodded, "Good morning, ma'am."

Jan poured a cup of strong coffee and stepped over Vesprhein's packed duffel bag to a drawer. "I thought you'd be gone."

"Flight's delayed," said Vesprhein. "Coffee's not so good. I'd shoot my cook if he served sludge like that on my ship."

"Can we not talk?" Jan popped a couple of aspirins from the drawer.

"Why not? I'm thanking you. You just doubled my business."

"If you still have a ship," Jan smiled blandly.

"You gave me your word," Vesprhein raised his voice accusingly.

"Shh. Don't yell. I promised your men would not be prosecuted. They won't be. I promised to return you to your ship. You will be."

Vesprhein squinted. "What's the catch?" He answered his own question, "Worthy! He's parked right beside the *Stavenger*. The instant I lift anchor the sonofabitch's gonna sink me. You set me up!"

Jan winced, "Lower your voice."

"Like hell!"

"I hope you have a backup career. This one's over." She left.

"Hey!" Vesprhein started after her.

The agent leveled his gun between Vesprhein's eyes.

Jan turned at the doorway. "If it's open season on whales, it's open season on you."

"Bitch!" he spat.

"And to think, I was just starting to fall for your charm."

"Cunt." And in that moment he looked menacing, dangerous and every bit the cold-blooded killer Jan knew him to be.

Seattle, Washington

Dan Sitka's body lay in a crude, handmade coffin. The mortuary had covered up the multitude of facial lacerations. An ornate shroud of beads, expensive blankets and ribbons effectively concealed the amputated arm and leg. The Sitkas were Native Americans and the funeral ceremonies followed tradition. After the last mourner left, Raquel and the Sitkas returned home and relaxed, drinking coffee in silence. Mrs. Sitka sifted through the few dozen condolence letters that had arrived over the past two days. Suddenly she caught her breath and her hand trembled.

"A letter from Dan. To you, Raquel."

Raquel took it. It was postmarked the day before he died. Raquel figured Sitka must have been confused, addressing the letter to Seattle instead of San Diego. Sitka's unsteady handwriting made his agony real. The ink was smudged in circles, where droplets of sweat had fallen, and now Raquel's tears crinkled the paper too. As she read further, the lump in Raquel's throat gave way to incredulity.

It can't be. She should know. What he wrote fell into her area of expertise. *If true, it could spell extinction.*

Camp David, Maryland

Everett teed off toward the eighteenth. His bodyguard, Anthony Trent, drew level and informed him the first lady had landed. Everett completed the hole and headed back to the retreat built in the Catoctin range by Franklin D. Roosevelt, who called it Shangri-La. The president's convoy passed the log guardhouse. He waved to the saluting Marine. The yellowing afternoon sun showered the cluster of wooden structures with slats of light that rippled each time a gust disturbed the towering firs. The limousine pulled up in front of the largest building. Everett climbed out, whistling. For the first time in months, the press and public were on his side.

"I doubt if Jan and I are going out again," he informed Trent.

"Very good, Mr. President," nodded the bodyguard.

Everett trotted up the steps and let himself in. Trent and the agents remained on the grounds outside, honoring the complete privacy that first couples came here to enjoy.

"Jan." Everett shut the door and stripped off his jacket. The pellet furnace, which had replaced the old fireplace in these energy-efficient times, filled the low, rough-beamed house with welcome warmth. The curtains of the huge picture window were drawn tight. Everett threaded between the sofas and rocking armchair for the kitchen. He stopped in the doorway.

"Congratulations," said Jan, turning. She was naked and dripping wet from a shower.

"To you too," responded Everett. Both got what they wanted from the IWC vote, and at that moment, their marital problems vanished.

"I'm in a mood to celebrate," said Jan. She raised her left foot and rested the arch lightly on the edge of the chair. He marveled at her conditioning, which allowed that simple move to carry the supple, sexy grace of a ballet dancer.

They may have stopped talking and listening to each other, but he could not deny the physical attraction. He stepped forward and kissed her. The cool wet surface of her body drenched the front of his shirt. Her tongue coiled around his. She unzipped him. He lifted her on to the kitchen table. Jan took charge, as always. Their breathing, sounds and movements fell into sync. He abandoned himself to their sexual synergy.

As he lay content, breathless, the phone rang. Jan asked, "Are you expecting a call?"

"No." Everett leaned for the wall phone and answered brusquely, "Yeah? Raquel?"

Jan straightened. And just like that, the intimacy evaporated.

Jan took the phone from Everett. "Hey, Raq, what's going on?"

"Sorry to intrude," apologized Raquel. "But this couldn't wait."

Everett left the room.

"I got a letter Dan wrote and mailed the day before he died." Raquel read the letter verbatim. "Dearest Raq, You're not going to believe what I saw when I was drifting in the Bering Sea. Whales. All around me. Blue whales! I thought this had to be a dream. I blinked, shook my head, blinked again and these great big things were still there. There had to be hundreds of them, more than a thousand easily. That's right, more than a thousand whales in one spot! I even reached out and touched one. I am going to make an official report. Don't worry about me, I'm fine. I'm not calling you because you'll probably take the next flight out and miss the IWC meeting. See you if I don't talk to you first." Raquel's voice cracked. "I love you. Dan."

"First, are you okay?" Jan asked.

Raquel collected herself with a sniff. "I'm fine. Thanks. But what do you think? I mean, this is *huge*."

"Is there any way to confirm it?"

"Blues are the loudest whales. Someone must have heard something." Raquel thought for a moment. "I know. Oliver Welling. Remember him? The NOAA scientist at Hatfield who introduced me to Dan?" The National Oceanic and Atmospheric Administration conducted research out of the Ocean Science Center in Oregon. "I can go down there right away. It's a short flight."

"Are you sure? I don't want you to leave Dan's parents if—"

"It may work out better, actually. My flight to San Diego is super early tomorrow and Dan's parents are insisting they want to drop me off at the airport, something the ex-wife was not even offered, if I might point out."

"Mee-ow."

"If I head out this afternoon, they can sleep in. Oh, thanks for the flowers. The Sitkas were honored by condolences from the White House."

Hanging up, Jan hurried into the bedroom. Everett was flipping through news channels. She excitedly narrated the gist of Sitka's letter.

❄

Shit! Everett felt a snap of anxiety choke his breath off for an instant. Despite his alarm, he did not show it. "What are you going to do?"

"Nothing. Leave them be. This may be the first conclusive proof they are really making a comeback."

"How so?"

She explained. In 1968, after an estimated 338,000 blue whales were slaughtered, marine mammal specialists stopped short of declaring the leviathans extinct. They were placed on the list of the US Endangered Species Act when a census put their number in the entire North Pacific at a paltry 1,600. Recently, the National Marine Fisheries Service Office of Protected Resources speculated that the blue population may be about two thousand. Sitka's sighting was terrific news. The NMFS's census was accurate.

"This has been a great week so far," Jan exulted.

"I can't complain either." Everett sounded upbeat. "My approval ratings are at 33 percent."

"Pleasance must be jerking off with joy."

"Oh, stop it. We're doing great. Enjoy it." He swung off the bed and started for the bathroom. "Excuse me. I gotta go."

"On the subject of shit, you're full of it."

Everett glanced at her sharply. His forehead moistened and he covered his discomfiture with a poor joke, "Hence my visit to the bathroom."

"I jumpstarted your poll numbers. I didn't hear a thank you from the White House."

"You know it. I know it. That's all that matters."

"Guess you're going to be in there a long time."

Everett laughed, closed the door and turned the lock. *That was close.* Jan usually caught on pretty quickly because he was a bad liar and she knew him too well. He picked up the telephone and punched a single digit code. A series of memory-dialing beeps sounded as he pressed the instrument to his ear.

The phone rang twice. The voice at the other end answered, "Pleasance."

"She knows, George."

Corvallis, Oregon

Raquel looked out the window of the tiny, propeller-driven aircraft fighting the menacing dark clouds that growled, flashed and pelted rain upon them. Bad weather had dogged the flight all the way from Seattle. Raquel hadn't let go of her nervous grip on the handles and the welcome bump of the wheels on the runway could not come soon enough.

An hour later, she crossed the Yaquina Bay Bridge in a rented Honda Accord. The downpour obliterated what was, under moonlight and stars, a spectacular view of the Pacific Ocean barely a mile away from the estuary. Raquel made the final turn toward the Ocean Science Center. She knew her way around, having worked as a research assistant at the Marine Experiment Station. She pulled into the parking lot beside the Marine Resource Studies Institute. Inside, she hung her raincoat next to another one, oriented herself and squelched noisily toward the door marked: Oliver Welling, NOAA.

Raquel knocked, entered and greeted the mild-mannered scientist, "Ollie!"

"Raq." Dr. Oliver Welling embraced her. "Sorry about Dan."

"He died doing what he loved." They held each other for a moment. She looked around at the shelves filled to capacity, the untidy scatter of papers on his desk and stacks of books on the floor. "I see you haven't cleaned up your office since—"

"You can leave now."

"Can I get some coffee at least?"

He poured some into a Styrofoam cup. "It's Saturday evening. It's raining. I'd be home ironing my best suit for church tomorrow if you hadn't dragged me here."

"Yeah, right." Welling was an atheist. She took the steaming cup he held out. "Thank you." They had met when he was researching his thesis down in San Diego. After graduating as a geologist from Caltech and stinting at Global Petroleum for five years, he'd joined NOAA as an ocean seismologist, specializing in oil exploration. Sitka flew him on several scientific missions. Welling became fascinated with the reaction of bowhead whales to oil exploration in the Canadian Beaufort Sea. He made it the focus of his postgraduate work.

Armed with a Ph.D., he signed on as an ocean acoustic analyst in Whales '93, a Navy sponsored test program to discuss alternative uses of its Integrated Undersea Surveillance System, the anti-submarine sonar array installed during the Cold War. Until this experiment, the US military had made no effort to archive any marine mammal sounds. Bored operators occasionally recorded a few tapes of humpbacks singing because they were pleasing to the ear, but otherwise their computers were programmed to disregard seismic and marine life sounds. The Department of Defense once thought the blips—slow, measured, low frequency sequences later attributed to fin whales—were part of an ingenious Soviet sound surveillance system to expose US submarines.

One November morning, Welling heard a long, low rumble that he initially dismissed as an electronic anomaly. But the analysis machine came alive, putting the sound on paper in the form of regular, comma-shaped strokes. It was not just a whale call, but a blue whale call. The world's largest mammals communicated almost entirely out of human hearing. Only a handful of people could claim the privilege of hearing them. He excitedly ripped off his headphones. The label on it placed the sonar array that he was monitoring along the southern edge of the continental shelf around Newfoundland. The calls filled twenty-five feet of paper that morning alone.

In the first six weeks of Whales '93, more whales were detected than in all the years prior. At one point, the massive defense department computers overloaded and crashed. In 1994, the Navy released access to other arrays of listening devices near Monterey Bay, San Nicholas and Hawaii. Welling quickly became the leading expert in underwater whale acoustics, specializing in blues.

"So what's up?" he inquired. "You were very cryptic on the phone."

Raquel handed him Sitka's letter. "While you read that, can I set up a conference call and put Jan on the speaker phone so she can listen in?"

"Jan as in Jan Everett? The first lady?" He began to clear his desk and straighten his hair.

"She's going to be on the phone, Ollie."

Welling stopped abruptly. "I know that. I wanted to sound neat."

"Read the letter."

Jan answered the phone.

"Hi," greeted Raquel crisply. "I'm here with Oliver Welling."

"Hello, Madam, uh, First Lady?" stammered Welling.

"Call me Jan. So is it possible? What Dan saw?"

"It's a fact," Welling said solemnly, his fingers flying across the keyboard.

"But more than a thousand *blue* whales?"

Welling's computer came up with spectrographic images that Raquel immediately recognized as blue whale vocalizations. "That's them? How many are there exactly?"

"Eighteen seventy-two," replied Welling. Acoustics had evolved as the tool of choice to census whale populations.

"One thousand eight hundred and seventy-two?" The disbelief in Jan's voice came through over the speaker phone.

"Yes, ma'am."

"That's the entire Pacific population," exclaimed Raquel. Off Welling's nod, she reacted, "How's that possible? Most of them don't go that far north."

Before Welling could respond, Jan asked, "When did you record these?"

"I started hearing them about two weeks ago," said Welling. He had appropriate clearance to use the Aleutian Trench SOSUS devices. "It started with about a dozen but multiplied rapidly."

"And you didn't tell anyone?" said Raquel.

"I figured it must be an array malfunction. I'd never heard more than six at one time. Max." There were only a dozen known blue whale breeding populations in the whole world and the count never exceeded twenty in each. His voice deepened sadly, "I was going to ask Dan to overfly these coordinates and give me a visual confirmation before I shot off an email to the NMFS."

Raquel reached over to his keyboard and converted the spectrographs into real sound over his speakers.

"Aren't they in the wrong hemisphere for this time of year?" asked Jan. Whales wintered in the tropics where they bred and summered at the poles, feeding. Blues waited all year for the polar food pulse, or explosion of plant and animal life in the Antarctic.

"Are these real-time live calls we're hearing?" asked Raquel, turning up the volume.

"Yup. Why?" Welling frowned seeing Raquel straighten with concern.

"I hope I'm wrong." Raquel pulled out her laptop. "I have to hook into my office desktop."

"Plug in," said Welling. His recording continued to wail over the speakers.

"Wrong about what?" asked Jan.

While she waited to connect online, Raquel explained. In the months immediately prior to the Norwegian Sea incident, she had been working from a federal grant to record and analyze blue whale vocalizations of a cow and a calf in nearshore waters off Sri Lanka. The result was an extensive database of call signatures she had matched to specific behavior, such as mating, playing or danger.

"I'm in." Raquel brought up the spectrographic images on the hard drive of her office computer back in San Diego, rolled through them and stopped. This one matched the spectrograph he was playing.

Welling read the heading under which she'd filed this call. "Distress."

"So why are they not getting out of there?" asked Jan.

"I have a theory." Welling kicked his office door shut. "Remember last year? All that uproar about the Navy blasting undersea sounds to measure global warming?" Public notice of a plan to bombard sound every four hours for ten years from two giant loudspeakers 2,800 feet under the ocean off Point Sur in the Monterey Bay Marine Sanctuary and off the Hawaiian island of Kauai appeared in an obscure item on page 5177 of the Federal Register.

"Of course," said Raquel.

"Raq and I led the protests," added Jan. "The Pentagon scrapped the experiment."

"Not really," said Welling. "The Navy covertly moved it to the Marshall Islands." This US territory of atolls in the Pacific conducted classified Department of Defense missions. "About a month ago, I ran into a seismologist who'd just spent two weeks in the *Aquarius II* at Kingman Reef off the Palmyra Atoll, south of Hawaii." The *Aquarius II* was the National Oceanic and Atmospheric Administration's newest underwater habitat, allowing scientists to live and work on the seafloor for days, weeks and even months. "He mentioned picking up twenty-minute sonic booms around 200 db. That's identical to what was proposed in the earlier experiment."

"They scared the blues north," said Jan.

Raquel looked at the world map on Welling's wall. "And the experiment is slam in the middle of their migration route."

"Yup," Welling nodded. "Another friend of mine at the Navy office—he was quite drunk at the time—he told me about sperms increasingly running into US submarines and surface ships and, what do you know? The timing coincides with the start of this Navy experiment."

"They're losing their hearing," Raquel surmised bluntly.

"A deaf whale is a dead whale," nodded Welling. Whale acoustics were not in the least arbitrary, but carefully patterned sequences of modulated tones evolved over thirty million years into a sophisticated means of communication. They lived and died by sound.

Jan agreed. "The loss of the entire Pacific population will doom them to extinction."

"Of course," said Raquel. "They have made the most robust comeback. North Atlantic blues number six hundred, if that."

"That's not even the worst part," said Welling. "Winter's coming early to the Bering Sea this year."

"Shit," sighed Jan.

"North of them the sea is already frozen solid, blocking off any escape. East and west are Russian and Alaskan landmasses. South is the only way out, which they are afraid to take."

"Won't hunger and the cold trigger their survival instincts to leave?"

Warm blooded animals needed food to generate heat through metabolism. Whales overcame this dilemma with their immense size, allowing them to starve, sometimes for as long as eight months. Their cells thrived at a much slower pace because of a curious but simple mathematical fact—a whale's surface area to volume ratio was 175 times greater than that of a mouse. This minimized heat loss, which occurred primarily through the skin. Contrary to popular belief, blubber was not a thick warm coat, rather it contained the fuel to maintain a minimum level of metabolism when there was no food.

"Blues are not the brightest in the class," said Raquel.

"How long before they become ice-locked?"

"Let's see," said Welling, pulling up the latest National Weather Service bulletins for the Bering Sea with a couple of keystrokes. "The freeze is moving south from the North Pole at the rate of eighteen miles a day." He did some quick mental math. "Two weeks? Three, max, before the water ices up solid at the whales' current coordinates."

"We are going to have to mount some sort of rescue," Jan declared grimly.

"Like what?" asked Raquel.

"A whale drive."

BOOK THREE

"I don't think we are going to change the Japanese attitudes toward wildlife for another hundred years," says Dorene Bolsze of National Audubon's Science Division…" First they decimated striped dolphins, then pilot whales, then Baird's beaked whales and now Dall's porpoises…That's one thing the Japanese are not guilty of — discrimination. They kill everything."

Ted Williams
Japan Bashing Reconsidered
Audubon, September-October, 1991.

Camp David

"A what?" Everett asked.

Jan and he cleared the table after a breakfast catered by a local restaurant. "A whale drive to Cetacean Bay."

"You're kidding."

"I am not. Wipe the table, or we'll have flies all day."

Everett caught the sponge she threw to him. Jan and he dispensed with all help at Camp David because they treasured this seclusion. He grabbed several paper towels from the roll standing by the sink. "When did all this come about?"

"Last night when I spoke with Raq."

"Then I guess you didn't sleep on it enough." He sprayed the tabletop with cleaner and began a slow circular scrub. "Think about it, Jan."

"I have thought about it."

"Then think harder! This is an election year. Your antics—"

"Antics!"

"—are taking you all over the map. You're a loose canon." Then suddenly, "Was this Raq's idea?"

Jan walked to the sink, sealed the drain and opened the faucets.

"I suggested it."

"Why am I not surprised?"

Jan faced him. "What's that supposed to mean?"

"Reacting without thinking—about *me* is what you do best."

"I get things done, something 53 percent of Americans think you don't." Jan dumped food into the trash.

"Oh, come on, Jan, don't bring George into this."

"Why not?"

"Because it's about us. Why couldn't you tell me this yesterday when you made the decision? Why did you wait until now, half an hour before the CRP is scheduled to arrive, to drop this bombshell?"

Jan had grappled all night with how she was going to break the news to him. She dropped the plates into the soapy water. "Because we'd have fought all night and neither would have gotten any sleep."

"How practical of you," Everett responded sarcastically.

"I should be back a week before election day. Everyone knows that's when most voters make their decision."

"You're not canceling a date to the movies, Jan. This is a campaign for the presidency."

"Which is more important than the survival of the biggest mammals on earth?"

"I mean there are no second chances."

"At least you'll be alive if you lose."

"Is that what you want?"

"We'd be happier."

"You'd be happier."

"We wouldn't be having this argument, for one thing."

"You're being selfish."

"If that's what you call rescuing the most critically endangered species, thank you."

"After a million years, I'm sure they know how to survive."

"They would if the Navy wasn't booming underwater sounds at

them. Did you know that the Pentagon experiment I stopped just moved coordinates?"

"It's a big ocean out there, Jan. Most of it still untraveled. The whales can swim somewhere else."

"Their migration patterns are *fixed*. If we don't put the whales back on course, they will *die*."

"What makes you think you'll be able to save those whales? They could be in international waters by the time—" Everett broke off.

"How do you know that?" Jan interrupted.

"What?" Everett looked away, caught.

"That the whales are in American waters?" Jan's eyes widened when Everett squirreled his away. "I never said they were." Jan blinked once. "You knew?"

Everett dropped the pretense. "Okay, I did. Before he died, Sitka told his boss, the MMS Director. He wrote up a report and forwarded it to the interior secretary."

"When?"

"Thursday."

"That explains my IWC victory, doesn't it?"

"You got what you wanted. An end to whaling. I got a trade war averted and a boost in the polls."

"What was the deal?"

Everett took a deep breath. "Japan can harvest those blues."

Jan slammed the cabinet door under the sink, rattling the dishes on the counter. Her eyes caught fire. "Those whales represent the entire Pacific population. Do you realize what you have done?" She clenched her fist so tightly her nails broke the skin of her palm. She ignored the pain. "You've sentenced the biggest mammal on this planet to death! To extinction! Who do you think you are? God? Fuck you, Carsten! Fuck your campaign and everything you love so much about being fucking president." She picked up a plate and smashed it into the sink. "Fuck you!"

Jan stormed out, slamming the door behind her. It shook the

entire cabin. The Committee to Re-elect the President was climbing out of two cars when she emerged.

"Hi, Jan," greeted Adrian.

She ignored him. Her eyes sought and found Pleasance, burning him with a glare so hostile he took a step back. "I won't be campaigning any more."

She stalked off toward the woods.

Los Angeles

A circle of high pressure pushed down on the tail end of a powerful storm rolling across the Northwest. Thunderstorms moved further south than anticipated, drenching California. Thick cloud cover and a blanket of heavy rain permitted nothing more than a dull gray to start off Sunday in Los Angeles. John Chambers slept soundly. He was flying back to Vancouver this morning.

"The phone. It's ringing. Answer it," said the gorgeous, twenty-something woman, unspooning herself from him in the hotel bed. As a long time corporate powerbroker, he kept a top-level, super-discreet escort in almost every major city. He loved his wife and they had three children, all grown up now, but he felt being a "player" added to his stature as a high roller.

Chambers irritably squinted at the bedside clock and picked up the phone. His mouth was dry, his grunt almost incoherent. "Yeah?"

"This is Jan."

The first lady's voice had an immediate waking effect. He was expecting her call. Still, it was six AM in LA and nine where she was, Camp David. "Are you familiar with the concept of time zones?"

"It's urgent." Jan ignored his sarcasm as he guessed she would.

"What is?" He remained testy to keep up the act her call was unexpected. Jan told him about the blue whales. He knew about them. She then told him her idea of a whale drive. He knew about that too. Pleasance and he had spoken yesterday.

"I need *Lifeline*." The 155-foot vessel GreenPlanet had purchased to combat driftnet fishermen.

"And a few hundred thousand dollars," added Chambers shortly.

"A drive like this is unprecedented," Jan insisted. "The media hype will generate enough donations to cover our expenses and more."

"The media hype will be around the presidential race, Jan. It's more up Worthy's alley and his Earthforce group."

"Bullshit. It fits right into the GP agenda and you know it. Come on, John, you can play out your vendetta another time."

"Not everybody is petty."

"I deserved that," she retreated.

"Humility and Jan Everett? That's refreshing." Not that he bought it. She needed him.

"I was tense about the IWC vote. I lost my temper and overreacted. I'm sorry."

"An apology too. No wonder it's raining down here in SoCal." Chambers could hear Jan biting her tongue to remain civil. "The answer is still no. The expense does not justify—"

"We are a non-profit, John. We do not raise money to pay out dividends."

"No, Jan, we raise money for causes with a chance."

"We don't win every environmental battle we take on."

"Exactly why we should not get into one that we know we won't. Whales are not cattle that can be gathered and herded."

"You're a car salesman. How the hell would you know?" Jan was referring to his previous tenure as the CEO of a multinational automaker.

"Ah, there's the Jan we all know." *Just keep pushing her buttons.* "Do you recall how much trouble they had herding two humpback whales down the San Francisco-Joaquin River last year? That was a narrow river delta. You're talking about two thousand whales in the open ocean. The variables—currents, sharks, weather, to name a few—are limitless."

"Pleasance got to you, didn't he?" Jan asked suddenly.

"We did talk yesterday. And don't threaten me. If you do, I'll order a highly publicized audit of your GP account. The president won't be too happy to begin this grueling home stretch with a scandal about the first lady treating GreenPlanet coffers like her own piggy bank, spending money at will for her pet causes and depriving other environmental battles of funds. Oh, if you have any ideas about upping and leaving with *Lifeline*, the harbormaster has been forewarned. Try anything funny and you'll be arrested. Have a nice day."

Chambers hung up and dialed quickly, unaware that at Camp David so did Jan. The calls set two separate telephones, seven miles from each other, ringing simultaneously north of the US border.

Vancouver, British Columbia

Knight waited in the lobby when Boycott strode in with a backpack slung over his shoulder. Jan had conferenced them and told them about Sitka's report and her idea for a whale drive. Boycott called it "kickass cool."

GreenPlanet's headquarters was a sheer glass tower, six stories tall, on Third Avenue. Designed by renowned French architect Pierre Kahn, it had been featured in every prestigious architectural magazine and become a tourist stop. Being Sunday, there wasn't a soul. The two men's voices echoed.

"A whale drive, that's pretty awesome, don't you think?" said Boycott chattily. The doors opened and they climbed into the elevator.

"It's unusual," nodded Knight.

"Can you be a little more concise?" Boycott ribbed, "How come you have a diarrhea of words when you write, but you're so frigging stingy when you speak?" He was the outgoing jokester, while Knight defined taciturn.

"The former pays and the latter doesn't."

"Touché."

Boycott and Knight went back a decade. They'd started out as co-workers and grown into good friends. Boycott was married. His wife—a patron of the arts, older than him by five years—administered the city's biggest gallery. They knew Knight was gay and wondered why he chose to remain in the closet. He couldn't be among more progressive friends. But they all respected his decision and the subject never came up. Boycott thought Knight and he yin-yanged each other like Raquel did Jan, and the men complemented the women, explaining why their foursome had survived the egos, differences, tensions, tempers, personal upheavals and ideological wars that the heat of battle evoked when fighting on the frontline as much and as often as they did. Watching each other's back came without even a second thought.

The doors opened. Knight used the light spilling out of the elevator to flip the switch for the overhead fluorescent. They ambled to the door marked AUDIO-VISUAL, unlocked it and walked in.

"Manny?" Boycott was surprised to see Mandrake Mileu, the chief of security, and two guards lounging in the chairs.

"Is everything all right?" asked Knight.

"The Grand Poohbah," said Mileu, "called me this morning. Said you two might be taking off with Jan Everett on a mission."

"Yes, so?" shrugged Knight.

"He asked me to stop you."

"Like hell," retorted Boycott.

"In that case, Chambers wants me to check your bags, take your keys and passes and," Mileu paused, "inform you that you're fired."

San Diego, Southern California

Raquel followed the curve of the narrow walkway between two magnolia trees. Clearing the trunks, she came upon an embankment. Dean Nathan Usry, president of the Oceanography Institute, was on the flat below teeing off toward the sixth hole. He was hard to miss in a T-shirt with a striking horizontal pattern that enhanced his corpulence. Raquel had never met him on the golf course, but his clothes seemed a natural spillover from his normal school attire—bold ties and colorful suits. The ball fell well short of the green. So the rumors were true. He golfed as badly as he dressed.

Turning to replace his club in his bag, he saw her walking down the steps and his eyes lit up. He hollered over in his usual loud and gregarious manner, "Raq! Good morning."

She embraced him and kissed his cheek. She was dead tired. Her eyes drooped. She'd flown from Corvallis to Portland last night, spent the night at the airport and taken the first flight back to San Diego. Then she'd driven straight here.

"Want to join me?"

"I can't play."

"Hasn't stopped me."

Raquel laughed. "I'll walk with you."

They strolled in the direction of the ball. He whispered, "Not a word to anyone how many strokes I take."

"My lips are sealed."

"No, no. Absolute silence is absolutely damning. Reply 'always under par' to all inquiries about my game."

"Nathan, something's come up that's really exciting." She told him about the whale drive. "I'll need the rest of this semester off. Cumins and Olsen have agreed to fill in for me. I'll set it all up."

They reached the ball. Usry fussed over his next club. "Can it be done?"

"A whale drive? I don't see why not." Raquel told him about

experiments to shepherd migrating grays off the California coast and who she'd tapped for the mission.

"Wow! That's a veritable who's who of robotics and marine science," said Usry.

"They're all in."

Usry's next swing landed him on the green. "You know that federal funding runs this place. I received a call yesterday from the White House chief of staff, no less."

"George Pleasance?"

"You know him? Of course you do. His name belies his character." They reached the green. "Oh, boy, I've never holed in three in the twenty-six years I've been golfing."

"What did Pleasance say?"

Usry did not answer at once, pulling out his putter instead. He stood squinting behind the ball for a long time. Finally, he tapped it gingerly. He waved his arms. "Turn, turn, turn." It curved away from the hole. "The other way!"

Raquel shrugged. "Maybe the next hole."

"Out of the question. It's across a lake whose fish owe their lumps to my inability to hit the ball across."

Raquel chuckled. He holed on his next putt. She became serious again. "Did Pleasance threaten to cut off funding if we went ahead with the drive?"

"Not directly, of course." Usry readied himself to tee off again. He executed a few practice swings. "Everett has been very good to us. If he wins and owes us a favor, it could mean a bonanza."

"Bottom line, Nathan?"

"You can't go." He struck the ball, punctuating his pronouncement.

Raquel took her eyes off the ball arcing high in the air. "I'll take an unpaid leave of absence."

"I'm sorry, no." He picked up his golf bag.

"Then I have to quit, I guess."

He looked at her helplessly. "Yes."

Raquel turned toward the clubhouse in a daze. The flippant tone of the conversation contradicted its grim outcome. Always lining up her next job before she quit the previous one, she was unemployed for the first time since high school. She got home and dialed Jan, who was on the phone with Boycott and Knight, apologizing for getting them fired from GreenPlanet. Jan conferenced Raquel in, heard what happened and became furious.

"I'll figure something out for you guys," Jan assured them. "About the drive—"

"Maybe we can call Paul Worthy again," suggested Raquel.

"I already did," said Jan. "*Earthforce*'s maiden voyage showed up some problems. Minor stuff, but it adds up to at least a month in repairs."

"Anyone else owe you a favor?" asked Boycott.

"Nope."

Honolulu, Hawaii

Unmindful of the drenching from the spray, Vesprhein stared ahead with unseeing eyes. He wore an expression of dour frustration behind the collar turned up around his ears. It had been a fucking nightmare of a day. He'd left Jan's home livid and his mood only worsened when his flight out of Los Angeles was delayed another two hours after he got to the terminal. The Secret Service shoved him into a holding cell with petty thieves. It was small and crowded and he found himself next to the stinking toilet. He finally landed in Honolulu at three AM. A couple of unfriendly cops deliberately roughed him into an unmarked car, then handed him over to the two Coast Guards at the helm of this speeding launch.

The *Stavenger* gradually solidified as a black arrowhead against the starlit sky. The topside was dark. Fewer than half a dozen lights were on, all in the Pig, indicating the pirates were below. He figured the media must have swooped in like vultures after Jan's speech at the IWC. There were no news-copters now. Mist and darkness had grounded them, but the men couldn't risk being photographed.

Vesprhein had no idea how he was going to get away from Worthy without losing his ship. Barely did the thought cross his mind, when a searchlight atop the *Earthforce*'s sail about half a mile to port sprang alive and tracked the launch.

Vesprhein shielded his eyes. He recognized Worthy's silhouette hurry outside. Both Coast Guards at the helm threw up a friendly wave. The engine of the launch faded just in time for Worthy's muffled voice to reach Vesprhein after a split second delay. "He's back."

The launch pulled up beside the *Stavenger*'s long accommodation ladder. Snatching his passport, Vesprhein scaled the ladder without a word to the Coast Guards, who showed no desire to talk to him either. Quvango and Iron Lady appeared on the bridge when Vesprhein walked in.

The radio operator, relaxing in front of his console, straightened nervously. "Captain, Worthy on the open frequency."

"Put him on speaker." Vesprhein wanted all hands to hear the eco-legend's intentions so there was no talk of betrayal later. The operator fumbled the switch.

"Hello, Arlov." Worthy didn't hide the laughter in his voice. "Goodbye, Arlov."

❄

"Ready on torpedoes," Rorque Jr. reported from the *Earthforce*'s control.

"Recommend bearing!" Worthy shouted back.

Rorque's reply was eager. "1-6-5."

"Make it so!"

"Aye, aye."

"Open outer doors!"

"Open. Flooding tubes."

"Stand by!" He turned on the bullhorn. "Captain and crew of the *Stavenger!* You have five minutes to abandon ship!" He lowered the visor of the Crusader II helmet and saw cryptic green images of commotion.

The *Earthforce*'s radioman interrupted, "Paul, Jan on the phone. She wants to speak with you, pronto!"

"Don't sink the *Stavenger*," were the first words out of her mouth.

❇

"Good morning, Arlov."

Vesprhein jerked his head around, recognizing Jan's voice on the *Stavenger*'s speaker.

"Order on all decks!" he barked over the intercom. The panic-stricken exodus froze. He took the first lady off the speakers and picked up the phone. "What do you want now?"

"Your ship."

Washington DC

The flight into Dulles International from Los Angeles landed on time. IWC Commissioner Dale Gabon, the first one off the plane, was snappily attired, as usual. Below a calfskin coat, he sported a thin-lapelled wool-and-linen suit over an expensive Italian shirt. His silk tie from Gordon's, England, had drawn a compliment from the attractive stewardess.

Gabon hailed a cab and settled into the back seat, feeling quite smug. He had been instrumental in triggering the praise being showered on Everett over the past thirty-six hours. Reaching home, he found a note from his wife. She'd taken their daughter to the mall. After shaving, showering and microwaving a plate of leftover food, Gabon settled in front of the TV and channel-surfed to a baseball game. He pulled the Rolodex onto the cushion beside him and picked up the telephone to call the US ambassador in Japan.

The Sitka scenario had only just begun to unfold.

Camp David

"We need a spokesperson for the daily spin," said Pleasance, glancing down at his dog-eared, notes-filled legal pad, to kick off this meeting of the Committee to Re-Elect the President.

"Delta Harris," responded Everett almost reflexively.

He liked her. More than that, they'd clicked on a personal level during their Thursday look-ahead meetings, which were one-on-one in the Oval Office study over dinner and drinks. They enjoyed discussing government and politics. Like Jan and he used to. He sometimes caught himself staring. Delta wasn't drop-dead beautiful like Jan, but she possessed dark, striking features and her eyes sparkled with intelligence. Born and raised in old-money Savannah, Georgia, she was schooled in the etiquette of Southern grace, but she was tough as hickory. As Jan became less and less a part of his life, he thought more and more about Delta. Psychoanalyzing himself, he realized his need for the company of strong, compassionate women probably came from growing up with a tyrannical father.

The president's pollster, an Arkansan full of nervous twitches, bolstered her choice. "She's pulling extraordinary numbers."

"That's settled then," Pleasance said. "The math says we need at least four Midwest states, but first we have to resurrect your presidency as an office that matters."

The room became silent. Uncomfortable. Just the way the meeting had kicked off following Jan's outburst. Everett had quickly put everybody at ease—he could do that; his people skills had been called Clintonesque—dismissing the first lady's announcement as a flash of temper carried over from an early morning squabble. Only Pleasance, Lhea and Adrian knew that it was more serious.

"Subtle, George," smiled Everett.

Laughter broke the tension.

Everett was dogged by a public perception of irrelevance. But the IWC coup had started to turn that around. "What are the latest numbers?"

The pollster spread out his perceptual map, which was continuously updated from the campaign's research department. Answers to carefully constructed questions asked over telephone, fax, e-mail, TV and radio call-in talk shows all over the country, charted the strengths and weaknesses of each presidential candidate. Everett occupied the center. Color-coded dots identified his support base: entrepreneurs, white suburbia, environmentalists and women across the board. Leeds and Todd, left and right of the president, were almost level with him in popularity.

"You're at thirty-three, Leeds twenty-eight and Todd twenty-six," the pollster read off the numbers. "Margin of error, plus or minus four."

"We have to go back to what got you to the White House," said Pleasance. "The Washington outsider."

"If there's one thing that still impresses the hell out of people," revealed the pollster, "it's the bullshit bubble." Beltway jargon for the trimmings around the president—Air Force One, sleek black cars, Secret Service.

"We have to spin Jan's absence to our advantage," said Pleasance.

"Drum up the rescue as a sacrifice for a cause that's above and beyond politics," suggested Everett.

"I may have something to say about that," interrupted Jan, leaning back against the door until the latch clicked. Everyone jumped to their feet. Jan picked out Pleasance. "George, when did you start wiretapping my calls?"

The color left Pleasance's face.

"You advised John Chambers and Dean Usry about my whale drive *yesterday*. I didn't even tell Carsten about it until *this morning*. You got my friends fired, you son of a bitch!"

"Jan!" Everett said, then asked Pleasance, "Is this true, George?"

"You have to ask him? Don't you trust me?" Jan shook her head. "You two fucking deserve each other."

"Jan!"

"I can end your run for four more years right here, right now. As much as I would like to do that and expose your hypocrisy, I'm not going to because I need the clout of the presidency to pull off this rescue. The deal's simple. My silence for your cooperation. Make my drive happen or you can kiss a second term goodbye."

Tokyo

The Japanese Diet, derived from the Westminster parliament, concentrated executive power within the cabinet. The prime minister represented the pinnacle of power. He presided over two political pyramids: his party and the government. But every post-war occupant of Japan's highest office had been hamstrung by the tenuous alliance of the factions supporting him. No one illustrated this constraint better than Prime Minister Shigesaburo Maeo.

He paced circles around his minimalist office. He could not blame the US or use the president and the first lady as punching bags to raise public ire. When Everett played the UN card, Maeo knew he'd been outmaneuvered. Making Venezuela change its vote fooled nobody. The sinking of the *Kagoshima* rippled in and out of the news, which was saturated with the increasing possibility his government might collapse, thanks to the escalating dissent within the fishing faction—the most critical of his government. The press attributed it to the IWC vote. They had no inkling of the Sitka report and the greedy dissent it had triggered. Minster of Agriculture, Forestry and Fishery, Yasuji Hattori, the fishing faction leader, could not sway the three shareholders of the Whalers League of Japan, who claimed the North Pacific as their territory, into sharing the

Sitka whales with Kaiyou. They saw the fishing giant's exclusion as fit punishment for encroaching. In response, the powerful Obata family threatened to pull out, along with their twenty representatives or almost half the faction.

Anxiety always brought Maeo to his feet, but his aging joints couldn't support his desire to walk around. He sat down, absently rubbing his kneecaps with his gnarled fingers. No solution presented itself. He clung to power by one single thread of certainty: even the Obatas knew better than to jeopardize the potential bonanza harvest.

❄

Across town, Maeo's seventy-year-old rival, Nobuo Tomita, had been sharpening his claws all weekend by successfully rounding up the support of independents. By Sunday evening, he was just nineteen votes shy of the 251 he needed to vault into power. He made no overture toward the Obata family, anticipating their support after he introduced a no-confidence motion when the Diet convened on Monday morning. He lay awake in bed. Butterflies in his stomach gave him the runs and he used the toilet four times in the hours leading up to dawn on Monday. The phone rang moments after the sun cleared the horizon.

"Tomitasen?" It was the Deputy Speaker. "I just got off the telephone with the US ambassador."

"Is something wrong?" asked Tomita. The Deputy Speaker told Tomita about Sitka's report.

"I see."

The LDP leader's stomach settled immediately, mirroring the dip in his excitement. Tomita returned to bed and confided in his mistress, Aiko. She listened carefully and asked questions. She hugged him sympathetically. That's why he liked her. She was always genuinely engaged.

Later, he made a call to Taiji, the whaling village from which Japan's IWC Commissioner Shayo Isoda hailed. Liberal Democratic

Party underlings reported a line outside the office of the Whalers League of Japan. With diminishing hope, Tomita called Kobe harbor. There was activity around the last surviving factory ship of Japan's once mighty pelagic whaling fleet, Kaiyou's *Rising Sun*.

"The no-confidence vote will have to wait," he confessed despondently to Aiko. Maeo had succeeded in working in the Obata family with the use of their ships and a processing contract. One thousand eight hundred and seventy two blue whales were equivalent to almost 11,000 minkes or fifty-five years' catch under the present IWC annual quota of 200 minkes. A staggering $160 billion yen!

"So exposing the hunt is not an option." Then he wondered aloud, "Why is Washington feeding me information?"

❋

On the pretext of making tea, Aiko hurried into the kitchen, called Isamu, Tomita's son, and told him everything. He seemed interested only in the *Rising Sun*.

Camp David

"Christ Almighty, Jan," exclaimed Everett, "what were you thinking when you decided to join with pirates on this whale drive? Have you seen their record? They're the worst thieves, rapists, murderers—the chief engineer is a pedophile."

"Blame George." Jan disappeared into the bedroom. Her announcement that she would use the *Stavenger* and the pirates for the drive had effectively terminated the CRP session. "Hey, you want to forgive him and forget he might have a bug up your ass to hear you fart, it's your call. But not me. I meant what I said. He fucks with me one more time, it's over." She began to undress.

Everett followed her in. "Okay, he was wrong." But he understood his most trusted aide's motives. Jan's drive could completely unravel the Sitka scenario. Still, Pleasance should have cleared any wiretapping with him first. "Big picture. All whaling is banned."

"Not at the price of wiping out an entire species." Jan's eyes blazed. "I could have lived with coastal and aboriginal whaling that at least we can keep tabs on."

Everett peeled off his pants. "I did what I thought was best. I did it for you."

"Bullshit. You did it to salvage your campaign." Jan moisturized her arms. "According to Wall Street, if you'd lost the IWC vote, you'd still have come out ahead."

"But the perception of who wielded power in global issues would have irreversibly shifted in Japan's favor."

"So what if it did?"

"We would lose international credibility. The world's perception of us as the most powerful nation on earth would diminish. Why can't you use a National Marine Fisheries vessel?"

"I need someone ruthless like Vesprhein, not a federal employee worrying about his pension, in case I have to ram a catcher boat to get there first."

Everett slipped on his robe. "What you're doing is sabotage, both of our marriage and my presidency. Have you no limits?"

"It's not about limits, it's about taking chances. You're so immersed in your polls and numbers and playing it safe that you've lost sight of what really matters. Don't you get it? This drive will determine more than whether the whales survive. It's about whether *we* can survive because neither one of us is going to give up what we do."

Everett said nothing. The silence lengthened and deepened, adding on implications. The possibility of truce through concession receded. When the telephone rang, any hope of compromise disappeared. Jan left. Everett answered.

Vice President Adrian informed him that the Sitka scenario had passed the point of no return.

Kobe, Japan

Women, mostly wives, sweethearts and whores, stood on the docks to see their men sail away before dawn. Ten catchers, belonging to the different entities of the Whalers League of Japan, were tied up against each other. Their harpoon guns were shrouded under canvas and their decrepit hulls wore a freshly painted numeral from *1* to *10*. Every catcher would be identified by number until its return. Anchored beyond them, closest to the harbor exit, though she would be the last to hit the swells of the open ocean, was the centerpiece of the fleet, *Rising Sun*, a giant silhouette riddled with lights. Fumes rising from her aft funnels hollowed a chimney of black all the way to the sky through the dripping white, opaque mist, which erased her outermost lines, suggesting she was bigger than she appeared.

All night Sunday and all day Monday, men and material poured in. Carrying suitcases, sacks, shoulder bags and boxes, hurriedly packed sailors from the constituencies of the fishing faction reported to the league office. The men had been pre-screened at their points of origin. The remorseless Bering Sea would be waiting with treacherous weather, making this hunt grueling work. Only able-bodied youngsters were picked to crew the catchers. The factory ship relied on experienced old-timers to marshal the army of youth with the dictum of this voyage: stealth and speed.

Nostalgia gripped the piers while giant cranes swung back and forth, ceaselessly feeding the cargo holds of the eleven vessels with provisions. No one was privy to the date and time of departure, but rumors that castoff would be sometime after dark kept alive a sense of urgency. There was a lot of fucking in rooms, cars, alleys, toilets and other imaginative nooks around Kobe harbor. Every bar and tavern was standing room only. Whores, overworked and in short supply for the first time anyone could remember, were glad when word finally came at five PM that the fleet would put to sea around midnight.

The catchers cast off one by one. The women on the dock moved with them. The biggest surge of loved ones came when the *Rising Sun*'s fore and aft deckies singled up the lines. Her tugs throttled forward. Water erupted at their sterns, bringing the *Rising Sun* around well away from the quay without the happy *whoopwhoopwhoop* of foghorns. The awesome monolith disappeared behind the white curtain.

Loudspeakers blared no farewell songs. No men lined the ships' rails to wave and shout. No wives or drunken whores wailed or fell off the dock into the water. There was none of the cacophony associated with the sailing of a mighty pelagic fleet. The factory ship and catchers could have been ghosts, so silently they melted into the heavy mist.

The only evidence that a fleet had been here came from images captured on a Camcorder by Isamu Tomita, CITES activist and son of the Liberal Democratic Party Chief, Nobuo Tomita.

Washington DC

The usual media circus awaited the president and first lady when Marine One put down on the South Lawn. Ducking outside to a beautiful day, Everett saluted the Marine standing to attention at the foot of the stepladder and gave Jan a hand. Everett tightened his grip around Jan's shoulder and she hugged him for the cameras. They smiled their way to the White House. Everett's unqualified success, defusing what had seemed like an impossible situation with Japan, dramatically softened the questions shouted at him.

Jan leaned into his ear. "Seems like a good photo-op to announce the drive."

Everett ignored her. They reached the colonnade, turned around, waved and passed inside, where they immediately separated and moved off in different directions. She headed for the elevator. Her friends were already in Honolulu, getting a head start on the logistics of the voyage. Everett started for the West Wing.

Pleasance appeared out of his office and tentatively followed the president into the Oval Office. Trent took up his usual position outside the door.

"About yesterday," said Pleasance, "you've every right to be angry. I am sorry, I really am. It won't happen again. I promise. That is, if you want me to stay on."

"Of course I want you to stay on." Everett could not think of another strategist in the same league who could combat the daily pincer moves of his rivals. "Now, to damage control." Everett wasn't looking forward to informing the Japanese prime minister that the first lady was coming for the blues as well. The intercom buzzed. The digital display identified the caller. Everett left the speakerphone on. "Jan?"

"Paul Worthy's contact in Japan said a Kaiyou factory ship, *Rising Sun*, and ten catchers left Kobe three hours ago." Everett knew that, thanks to Adrian's call to Camp David last night, but he'd kept it from Jan. "I'm leaving in an hour."

Everett went upstairs and found Jan packing.

"Hi," she smiled distantly and turned away to rifle through her closet. "Don't you have a national security briefing?"

"I moved it back fifteen minutes." Everett stretched a hand toward her back.

"Did Pleasance send you upstairs to find out if we can outrace the Japanese fleet to the whales?"

He dropped his hand and his lips thinned angrily. "No."

She turned around. "You can tell him that the *Stavenger* is faster than their fastest catchers. Also, the tail end of an Arctic storm has slowed in front of the pelagic fleet. If that storm should stop, we think it'll neutralize their one day lead."

Jan disappeared into the bathroom.

Heading back downstairs, Everett wondered why he had gone up to see Jan. He had no answer and was glad that he did not. Right now he had to remain focused, which wasn't hard along the home stretch of a campaign. There would be time later to mend fences.

All the participants of the Oval Office briefing were waiting when he strode in.

"A news leak after the first lady puts to sea will be the way to go," said Pleasance.

"How much of the drive can we monitor?" asked Everett.

"The Bering Sea part should be no problem," replied National Reconnaissance Office Director Robert Random. "We have a KH-14. But when they head south of the Aleutians, we're going to lose them all the way to the fortieth parallel."

The chairman, Joint Chiefs of Staff, quashed any notion of moving the satellite over Korea. He reported that this past weekend anti-American demonstrations in Seoul had turned violent again, which classified the region as a flashpoint. To enact all potential scenarios, war-gamers needed twenty-four hour supervision.

"We can use recon planes to overfly the drive."

Murmurs of agreement rippled.

"That sounds good," said Everett and stood up. "Anything else?" Negative head shakes. "Great." Everyone filed out. Everett stopped the National Security Advisor. "I need to speak with you alone."

The NSA returned to the couch.

"I know you've endorsed Leeds," Everett began, "and I respect your position." *I bet you can't wait to tell your pal, Leeds, that the first lady won't be campaigning with me.*

"Do you want my resignation?" offered the NSA.

"No. Just the opposite." During the campaign, Everett and his aides had schemed, the NSA could be baited with tidbits of apparently increasing importance. When they entered the final leg in October, if the race remained close, they could hurt and embarrass Leeds by exposing the NSA's leaks to him. "Your political preference has not interfered with your job performance and that's all I care about. Any leaks of this whale drive could endanger Jan's life, so I'm going to trust your judgment." *I've zipped the NSA's lips with that.* It would be obvious how the press, if they did, got wind before Jan set sail.

"I understand." The NSA nodded.

"One more thing." This was not discussed at the CRP yesterday. In fact, Everett was acting entirely on his own. "Jan is going to be on board a pirate ship. I want an increased level of intelligence about all aspects of her security. Daily reports for my eyes only."

"Okay," nodded the NSA.

"When I say for my eyes only, I mean nobody else is privy to that intelligence. Not Lhea, not Adrian, not Pleasance, not Random."

Everett was certain that the omission of rival Leeds' name was not lost on the NSA. As Washington's rival keeper of secrets, the NSA was the perfect choice to keep tabs on Pleasance keeping tabs on Jan. Since Pleasance suggested Everett speak with the NSA alone after the Oval Office briefing, the White House chief of staff would never discover that the president had slipped in his own private agenda.

Honolulu, Hawaii

Air Force Two put down at Hickam AFB. Jan pulled into Pearl Harbor half an hour later. Two Secret Service agents climbed out after her. Raquel, Boycott and Knight waited on the pier.

"Looks like you guys have been running around like crazy," said Jan and hugged them all. "Let me reward you with good news. Raq, you'll have your job back if you want it. Patrick, David, I'm sorry, I …"

"Oh, well," drooped Boycott.

"But NatGeo wants both of you." A global multi-media giant with a dedicated TV channel, the largest-selling nature magazine and an interactive website that boasted a million hits daily. "David, NatGeo will pick up the entire cost of your equipment rentals." Jan had earlier told him to put it on her card. "I'm not done yet. They want to air the drive as a series. You and Patrick have final cut." Or, total creative control.

Knight's face lit up like a thousand-watt bulb. "To hell with Vancouver."

Jan's eyebrows lifted and she smiled. "That's about as animated as I've seen you, Patrick."

"Ohh!" Boycott teased, "Our boy is finally talking."

Jan laughed. She told them about Pleasance's wiretapping. "In a way, it was a good thing. Raq, I ran down your wish list and didn't hear any protest."

Welling and the dream team that Jan and Raquel had assembled were putting the list together in Corvallis.

"You look like you're having way too much fun," intruded Worthy's familiar voice. He was behind the wheel of a tender. Throwing the painter toward Jan, Worthy wobbled the little launch to a stop.

Jan embraced the eco-maverick. "How's Vesprhein doing?"

"I haven't been aboard," said Worthy. "Matter of principle."

"What about you guys?" Jan asked her eco-warriors.

Raquel shook her head. "No way. News cameras everywhere. They'll recognize us, make the connection with you and know something's up."

"One of Worthy's men rigged up a phone link and I spoke with Vesprhein," said Knight. "He wasn't shy about what he wanted."

"We divvied up his list among ourselves," said Raquel. "Of course, I got food. I called the Pearl Harbor mess. The food will be ready for pick-up at five."

Knight went next. "I'm handling the *Stavenger*'s fuel needs. The Navy's on it."

Boycott raised his hand. "Spares and miscellany. All available at the refitting yard."

"I suggested we begin loading after dark," said Worthy.

"Can we sail by midnight?" Jan asked.

"Absolutely."

❄

Sunset rolled in thick fog from the ocean, forcing the news-copters back to land. A tanker set out from Pearl Harbor at once. Two Coast Guard launches commenced running Vesprhein's shopping list to the *Stavenger*. Electronics experts from the Navy arrived. They dismantled the *Stavenger*'s radio, installing one that scrambled all communications. Then they set up a "versatile" satellite dish capable of grabbing TV signals anywhere on earth.

Boycott went aboard the first boat with his videocamera and hitched a ride back to shore on the last one so he could tape Worthy approaching the pier. The eco-maverick had insisted on sailing Jan out to the killer-factory ship. Jan was on the phone with Everett. He was working late with Pleasance, Lhea and Adrian. They were headed back on the campaign trail at daybreak. Everett took the call in the study adjoining the Oval Office.

"Run up a big tab?" he asked.

"It'll be covered by donations to the Rescue Fund in the first hour, don't worry."

"Your chief of staff will make it public after you sail. Random is setting up a satellite phone link so we can keep in touch."

"Thanks."

"Happy hunting."

Jan answered with a stony silence.

Everett apologized quickly, "Slip of the tongue. Be careful."

"I'm through being careful. I'm playing to win. I suggest you do the same." Jan emerged onto the pier. "I'm ready. Let's go."

"You too?" Worthy inquired of Jan's Secret Service agents, who crammed into the tender.

"No, sir, we will be replaced prior to departure."

"Everett's putting four SEALs aboard with me," informed Jan.

"See you in a bit," waved Raquel. Knight and she were going to stay behind to put out any last-minute fires.

The *Stavenger* appeared suddenly through the fog. Supplies were being hauled up the rear slipway under the watch of four armed men from the *Earthforce*. Worthy groped the tender alongside and refused to go aboard. "I'll happily explore her wreck. As for meeting Vesprhein, I will—when I spit on his grave."

Jan hugged and kissed Worthy on the cheek. "Thanks again for everything."

"My pleasure. I'll join you on your final leg to Cetacean Bay, I promise."

"I'm going to hold you to it."

Boycott went up first to capture the arrival of the first lady aboard the *Stavenger*. The foredeck was empty. Jan swung on to the catwalk.

"Well, well, well, m'lady," growled Vesprhein when she walked onto the bridge.

"Arlov—"

"Captain."

"You've got to earn that."

"I'm doing this for nothing."

Jan smiled. "Only because you can't put a price on freedom."

"This whale drive is crazy. You can't do it."

"I say we can. That's all that matters."

The work never stopped. Jan was amazed at the logistics for a long voyage. Crates of food, meat, tinned milk, jam, juice, soda, beer, hard liquor and more were taken down to the kitchen. Paint, hawsers, canvas, tools and spares to fix just about everything, from sewing a button to complex repairs, were sorted and stowed. Fuel throbbed through lines from the tanker under the supervision of a stoker, wanted in China for murdering his wife when she bore him a stillborn son. Raquel and Knight came aboard the launch with the last load. Around eleven, the slipway was closed.

Worthy's armed men and two Secret Service agents handed over to the four Navy SEALs, big, typically military, who introduced themselves to Jan with just their last names. Napoli, Owens, Larkin and Prophet from Team Dam Neck, Virginia, with training specifically to combat terrorists. They organized the living quarters after a security recon.

Since only the *Stavenger*'s captain enjoyed the luxury of an attached bathroom, Jan and Raquel moved into Vesprhein's quarters. Boycott and Knight bunked next door in the day cabin. The SEALs took the office right across from the first lady's door. Vesprhein argued loudly, unhappy to be escorted into Alfonso's old room around the corner, one of a series housing the rest of the bridge crew, who slept two to a cabin. SEAL team leader Napoli advised the pirate that he did not have much choice and Jan affirmed it when she sat in the bolted down wooden chair on portside of the bridge.

"Nobody sits in the captain's chair but me," hissed Vesprhein.

"Nothing is yours on this voyage unless I give it to you. Get used to that."

Quvango came up the companionway. His stride faltered when he saw Jan in the chair. He nodded a respectful greeting toward the ladies.

"Quvango, right?" inquired Raquel and deliberately lowered down on to the armrest.

"Yes, ma'am." The Angolan helmsman took the wheel and snickered, his whisper carrying to Jan. "Y'can never stop a bitch from takin' charge, Cap'n."

"Fuck you."

"He's right." Jan said. "You should listen to him." Raquel and she couldn't help smiling when they drew a startled look from every thug who crossed the bridge.

"Anchor's up," reported Iron Lady. "Engine room standing by."

"Slow ahead," said Vesprhein.

Iron Lady rang the telegraph. The screws engaged. The bridge vibrated. A pencil rolled across the chart table and fell. The *Stavenger* picked up speed to twelve knots and moved out of the fog into a beam sea. The ship leaned uncomfortably, hung for long seconds and slid her pitted flanks up again. Rollers marched under the pale blue moonlight and improving visibility.

"Half speed," said Vesprhein, striding aft.

A rat-faced Frenchman arrived with a mug of steaming coffee. Vesprhein took it wordlessly.

"Will you get me one, please?" Jan asked. "Raq?"

"No, thanks. I'm turning in."

"Good night," smiled Jan. Raquel disappeared down the companionway.

"I asked for coffee."

The Frenchman looked to Vesprhein.

"Now!" Jan shouted. He jumped, then vanished downstairs.

"You know, m'lady," Vesprhein said with exaggerated courtesy, "the men, they aren't used to taking orders from a woman."

"They will be."

He grinned. "You gotta earn that."

Jan held no illusions about the morale on the boat. She was riding a powder keg. The men were clearly unhappy with this unpaid excursion. They would obey orders all right, like the Frenchman, but she was fully aware that treachery lurked just beneath the surface.

Tokyo

Maeo listened in stony silence to Everett's narration of the unexpected relationship between Sitka and Raquel that had led to Jan's discovery of the blue whales. Dawn brightened over the east coast, while twilight darkened toward night in Tokyo.

"But she is a full day behind," said Everett.

The Japanese prime minister found no consolation in the president's assurance that the first lady would not expose the pelagic fleet or the secret hunt. After disconnecting, Maeo clutched his hair in a fit of anger. Then he pulled himself together and called Hattori.

❄

Raised voices emanated from the plush boardroom of the Obata Tower, the nation's tallest skyscraper. The Whalers League of Japan was meeting and every member was on his feet. They hurled their rage at Hattori for going along with Maeo and taking Everett at his word. Now they were left with a bill of several million dollars for the biggest pelagic expedition since the heyday of whaling.

"I have a solution," the prime minister said, calling Hattori again a few minutes later. "Put me on the speaker phone."

Hattori rapped his hand on the table and brought silence to the board room.

"*Seiji no sekai wa issun saki wa yami,*" Maeo began, quoting the late Shojiro Kawashima, vice president of the Liberal Democratic Party. *In politics, an inch ahead is darkness.* Maeo came to the point at once. "In exchange for Venezuela's vote, the US president promised us the stranded blues, yes?"

The WLF members nodded and Hattori answered for the boardroom, "Yes."

"So those whales are yours," said Maeo, and as he spoke, Hattori noted how carefully the prime minister chose his words. "The fleet captain should be free to use any means at his disposal to harvest them." He said nothing more because everything else was understood.

North Pacific

The *Stavenger* blazed forward at forty-eight knots. Dawn brightened into a beautiful day all around. The sea was friendly, the swells gentle. A whisper of a wind blew across her deck, where four pirates loitered, brushing their teeth, gargling into the ocean. The engines beneath their feet pounded faultlessly, vibrating every rivet and plate, lifting the bows out of the water and digging the stern in like a hydroplane. Water stirred up almost fifteen feet above the poop deck. By the time her seething white wake dissipated, the killer-factory ship was miles in front.

Jan woke up to the sound of water. She walked into the bathroom, knuckling her eyes. Raquel was in the shower. "'Morning."

"Hey," Raquel greeted back. "What's the plan for today?"

"Get some sun. Relax. Irritate Vesprhein." They had nothing to do until their dream team joined them with the equipment. Jan gargled and rinsed her mouth.

Raquel stepped out and squeezed by to towel herself in the cabin. "Maybe this time apart will resolve things with Carsten."

"I won't hold my breath."

"You really think it's over between you two?"

Jan rolled down her thermal underwear and stepped across to the can. "Let me put it this way, neither of us is going to be surprised if we don't get back together."

Half an hour later, they surrendered the bathroom to Boycott and Knight. When the men were done, the quartet headed down, accompanied by Napoli and Larkin. They paused in the doorway to the Pig.

It was crowded and noisy. Cigarette smoke rose to the ceiling and hung in static curls, dispensing a thick odor that replaced the stale smells from the previous day. A buffet counter, separating the Pig from the kitchen beyond, consisted of a row of metal buckets, which fit into clamps over a hot plate. The contents this morning were scrambled eggs suspended in oil, hash browns suspended in oil and strips of bacon suspended in oil. A mound of toast filled a plastic crate. A two-gallon can of ketchup, an industrial coffee maker, water cooler, salt and pepper shakers, dented mugs, forks, knives and spoons lay at the end of the counter.

The Pig subsided.

"If you're looking for healthy, grab some fresh air," growled Vesprhein, appearing behind them. He plowed past, deliberately shoving Jan. She grabbed Boycott for balance.

"Watch it," Napoli said.

"Get fucked." Vesprhein kept walking.

Napoli started after him. Jan stopped him, "Let it go."

The captain's arrival loosened the silence. Greetings hollered across. Vesprhein ignored them and grabbed a plate.

"You have an interesting collection of literature in your room," said Jan, drawing level with Vesprhein.

"I like to keep up," he answered shortly, slopping running eggs onto his plate.

"It's a miracle your heart is even beating," remarked Raquel.

"You're welcome to take over the kitchen," Vesprhein said. "It could use a lady's touch." Vesprhein looked at the Turkish cook, "Mr. Assad, would you like a lady's touch?"

Assad showed a toothless grin. "Oh, yes sir!"

Jan strained the eggs before putting them on her plate. "You don't seem like the reading type."

Vesprhein shoveled hash browns onto his plate. "My tattoos don't fit your stereotype of the well-read man? Or could it be you believe that people who don't give a flying fuck about an animal's right to life are illiterate?"

"I saw a copy of *The Case for Animal Rights* by Tom Regan," said Jan, passing on the hash browns.

"Are you a closet conservationist?" asked Boycott.

"Ha!" snorted Vesprhein. "Regan embodies the hypocrisy of your entire movement."

"You mean, not using animals for science experiments, eliminating hunting, trapping, even eating meat?" said Jan. "I'm for it."

"Is that why you just helped yourself to a second strip of bacon? How come the pig does not qualify for an absolute right to life? Or is that reserved only for whales? Could it be that pork, beef and chicken are a huge part of the US economy?"

Jan continued to press the oil out of the bacon strip. "The pigs and cattle and chicken are born and raised in captivity, specifically for consumption. We are not decimating a species in the wild. On the other hand, the whale—"

"The whale is a myth," interrupted Vesprhein, dumping ketchup from the half empty can. "There are about seventy-seven species of whales, not all endangered."

"Maybe so—"

Vesprhein cut her off again. "But it's convenient to reduce them to the singular. Then the propaganda can be all inclusive and more compelling." He strutted off, grandstanding to the Pig all the way to the captain's table. "*The whale* is almost extinct. *The whale* is man's intelligent counterpart in the water. *The whale* is a gentle giant who feels pain. *The whale* is a friendly human of the oceans who chooses a partner for life. *The whale* travels in family groups, has a childcare system and speaks in a language that's mathematical poetry. Is any of that true? No! By playing fast and loose with facts, you green fuckers combine different traits of popular cuddly species, living, endangered and extinct and package them into this mythical Superwhale. Why? It's good marketing to sell a single product that meets the entire animal rights agenda."

Jan took the bench across from Vesprhein. Raquel and Knight sat down on either side of Jan. Boycott and Napoli flanked Vesprhein, who spoke with his mouth full, jabbing a fork toward Jan. "Environmentalists—fuck, why go any further than you? You jumped on my Norway over those minkes. But wasn't it Norway that enacted the first Whaling Act of 1929 to regulate hunting? Norway in 1934 adopted the first national legislation to restrict when, where and how whales could be harvested. Norway in 1938 initiated a move to preserve stocks. There is no evidence to suggest sustainable harvests have any effect on the ecology of oceans."

"Why kill them at all," argued Jan, "when they have a bigger market alive? Case in point, whale watching brings in seventy-five million dollars."

Knight spoke for the first time. "Doesn't hunting reflect that whaling nations kill for killing's sake? A state of mind similar to accepting the genocide of inferior human beings."

"D'Amato and Chopra, 1985," Vesprhein annotated. "*American Journal of International Law*, 'Whales: Their Emerging Right To Life.' If there ever was a people who were convinced their farts don't smell, it's you Americans. Take the 1982 ban, or the 1990 renewal of the ban. The US downplayed the fact you voted yes only after you got the IWC to adopt a distinction between aboriginal and commercial catches, so your Eskimos can hunt."

"Not any more," retorted Jan.

"Really?" He stood up and walked over to refill his coffee. "Let's review your win on Friday. It came only because the president, to save his political ass, handed almost two thousand of the most endangered whales to the Japs. The hypocrisy continues, yes?"

Jan got up and dumped her plate into a crate full of dirty ones. "Do you see me in the White House looking the other way? Don't judge me by my husband's actions." She stopped in front of him. "I'm not the compromising type."

"No?" Vesprhein pointed to his crotch. "I guess you haven't felt this."

Without missing a beat, Jan reached and grabbed his balls. She tilted her head. "Nothing special there."

Everyone in the Pig caught their breath. Jan withdrew her hand and the pirates erupted with calls and whistles. Vesprhein covered his astonishment with a tight smile.

Afterwards, Jan nudged Raquel with a wink. "God, is he big."

Washington DC

More than two million dollars flooded into the Rescue Fund by the end of the first day. Significant wasn't the amount, which surpassed all expectations, but the small denominations, conclusively indicating the sources were middle class. Pledges came from all fifty states, even from the East and South, Democratic and Republican strongholds, respectively.

I might actually bring myself to like Jan if this positive trend continues, thought Pleasance. He arranged for Everett to make a thirty-second statement to the nation between prime time's two hottest sitcoms. The Neilsens estimated fifty million people heard him thank Americans on behalf of the first lady. His poll numbers inched up two points, but the election stayed a tossup: Leeds 28, Todd 28 and Everett 35 percent.

North Pacific

At dinner, Jan and Vesprhein argued about the IWC's New Management Procedure. He defended it and she attacked it. The NMP calculated the maximum sustainable yield of whales without depleting them below 54 percent of their original stock size. Vesprhein called it one of the few scientific advances within the IWC.

"Scientific?" Jan rebuffed. "NMP assumes whale populations are being reported accurately by whaling nations."

Jan felt rejuvenated, realizing how much she missed good, intelligent debate. She'd been in two in one day. Vesprhein was the last person she imagined she'd be sparring with. He was very sharp, with facts at his fingertips she'd known only one other man to possess: Everett. And she'd fallen in love with him. There was something about the ability of men to counter her, point for point, which she found attractive. She did not allow her admiration to overshadow caution, though the line blurred with each successive debate.

Like her and the eco-warriors, the rest of the pirates sat around with nothing to do. They played cards in the Pig and in their aft quarters. They lazed on the deck, and when they passed a pod of grays, they watched the whales instead of slaughtering them. Conversations inevitably steered to their uncertain future. The first fight broke out between the Jamaican meat handler and one of the engineers, a Russian navy deserter.

"Aren't you going to stop them?" asked Jan, when Vesprhein strolled on to the upper gangway overlooking the slaughter deck, where the two men were going at each other viciously.

"Fuck, no," Vesprhein scoffed and hollered his wager to the red-bearded chief engineer. The captain put his money on the Jamaican. "They'll knock each other up and then it'll be all right. Takes pressure off the kettle."

The Jamaican landed a stunning blow. The men dragged the unconscious Russian off the deck.

"The really good fights," grinned Vesprhein, catching the tightly rolled banknotes tossed up by the chief engineer, "will come after a few more weeks at sea. That's when the broken bottles come out."

"Jesus."

❀

Three days out of Hawaii, Jan received her first call of the voyage from Everett.

"How's it going?" she asked.

"George calls it focus-impact strategy," said Everett enthusiastically. He was stumping in the South. "Go in, impress the hell out of the folks by looking presidential to the hilt, then hit them with the failure of Congress and leave an ad blitz that my rivals represent that failure."

They spoke cordially for half an hour. The Defense Department's latest SVS — Secure Voice Program — scrambled their conversation. They hung up with no talk of reconciliation.

Yaquina Bay, Oregon

The *Stavenger* arrived off the intertidal flats of the open Oregon coast in the dead of night. Media on the ground had been banished outside the Ocean Science Center compound and a steady downpour over Newport grounded the news-copters keeping vigil over the campus. The killer-factory ship slipped into the estuary unseen. Lights from campus buildings barely penetrated the rain. Guided by a male voice from the watchtower, the *Stavenger* crawled toward the illuminated single-berth pier. A crowd of policemen and federal and Secret Service agents milled about the fenced-in yard and structures that comprised OSC's ship support facility.

Oliver Welling, animatedly waving, became immediately recognizable. He half-ran and half-walked aboard as soon as the gangplank was lowered.

"Hello, hello, hello." He embraced Raquel and shook Jan's hand. Welling pointed to four figures draped in heavy raincoats. "That's them."

"Ah, the dream team," she smiled before Welling began the introductions. Jan had read the bios and now faces and personalities went with those names.

Alex Fallon and Gene Taggart, in their late twenties, postgraduates in Marine Robotics from MIT, looked like they were full of youthful exuberance. Trevor Smith, a forty-one-year-old serious-faced professor, taught oceanography at Woods Hole, Massachusetts. Brian Yale, also from WH, appeared outwardly colorless, but at thirty-eight he was renowned among his peers as the first marine mammal expert allowed aboard a nuclear submarine on one of the US Navy's secret tours of duty in the North Atlantic. They all shook Jan's hand.

Welling excitedly described what he'd been able to procure. It made Raquel's wish list seem obsolete. Four ten-foot-tall waterproof crates marked THIS SIDE UP FRAGILE HANDLE WITH CARE were lowered onto the slaughter deck and arranged one behind the other. For reasons of security, the five new arrivals took up residence in the storage cabins off the same corridor as the eco-warriors and the SEALs.

The *Stavenger* departed as quietly as she'd arrived.

North Pacific

Vermilion suffused the gathering storm clouds with a menacing bloodiness that wisped to rich pinks over the *Rising Sun* and her ten catchers. Crimson swells reared angrily where the sky touched the ocean and turned to a dark blue, cold, rising sea upon reaching the fleet. The whalers had sailed every mile out of Kobe at full speed over little choppiness. Today was going to be rougher, feared the captain of the fleet, ShinjiroYamamura, fifty years old, stocky and powerfully built. He spoke little and smiled even less. This unwavering sternness commanded authority.

The first weather bulletin of the morning quashed the optimistic forecasts he'd been receiving all night that they might skirt the tail of that Arctic storm. The weaving, stumbling system had come to a dead stop ahead. The red dawn quickly turned into a gray day. Yamamura put all the vessels under storm watch. The seas ran harder. The catchers poised higher and higher atop the ridges and plunged deeper and deeper into the troughs, disappearing for long seconds behind surging swells. The bows rode and crashed rhythmically. Up and down, up and down. Soon, the hands were timing their tasks. Then the skies went black.

The wind howled in explosive gusts, lopping the tops off waves into a blinding spray. Yamamura knew they'd entered the storm when they came upon rain, an icy, blinding sheet that frequently turned to hail. Thunder echoed the lightning's flash. The sea ran so high at times it drew level with the *Rising Sun*'s lofty bridge. Hail became snow. Wind became gale. Swells became incredible waves.

Caught between the wrath of storm against sea, even the imperturbable factory ship shuddered and shook all the way to the lower hull. The crazy pitching invited water into the alleyways.

Pumps chattered without respite, the ships lost their rhythmic rise and fall and the sea roared in from all sides. The ten catchers vanished. Occasionally, Yamamura saw lights. The absence of distress signals assured him he'd lost none.

Having been a catcher captain for a decade, he could imagine the small boats heeling madly. The crow's nests brushed the ocean. Screws shot clear out of the water, grasping air. The sailors wore life jackets and nobody slept or played or read or chatted. Though it was dry inside, the perception of moisture was everywhere. They couldn't keep their balance and the compass would not stop spinning. Yamamura did not worry. There would be little panic. The men had grown up working in open boats and combated worse weather.

Watching the *Rising Sun*'s bow dip in front of him, he clutched the chart table absently. His thoughts drifted to Vesprhein. They'd met a few times on the high seas to transfer illegal whale meat. So he knew the *Stavenger* well. She was fast. The fastest. After all, she was designed for escape.

The angry white sea heaved under him. Water enveloped the factory ship. Decks, fore and aft, disappeared. The windows rattled. If fate had deliberately set this storm upon the fleet to level the playing field of time, Yamamura resentfully realized this voyage could very well depend on the pirate's plans.

Foul play was farthest from Vesprhein's mind when he awoke and stepped from his cabin toward the hatchway. The Pig was half full. None of the eco-warriors and scientists joined him at his table. It would be the first time Jan and he would not be locked in a verbal battle since setting sail. Arriving on the bridge, he found Iron Lady and Jan bent over the chart table beneath its canvas hood.

"Good morning, Arlov," she greeted him, straightening, lolling with the ship's motion.

Vesprhein snorted disinterestedly and went outside. Holding her course steady against the fetch of a firm wind, the *Stavenger* clove through the northwesterly swell at a brisk fifty-knot clip. The sun lay halfway up the eastern quadrant. Vesprhein's eyes darted and furrows of curiosity wrinkled his brow. Ignoring the ice-cold handrail scalding his palm the instant he gripped it, he leaned forward. Led by Raquel, the Hatfield scientists prowled about the slaughter deck below. Boycott trailed them with his camera.

"What are they up to?" he asked Jan, leaning in through the bridge window.

"Getting ready to build a prefabricated scientific station," she replied. Vesprhein, Quvango and Iron Lady roared with a loud guffaw.

"Are you crazy?" said Vesprhein, unable to separate the chuckles from the words. "The first fucking squall will wash it overboard."

"Not this one. It's made from the same materials they use to live year round on the polar ice cap."

Vesprhein skeptically watched the scientists open the first crate. Jan and Knight played gofers, while Boycott used the pretext of videotaping the construction to duck working. None of the pirates helped. At lunch time, Vesprhein found the Pig empty. Assad, the cook, told him Jan and Knight had wheeled out trays of food. The captain carried his plate outside too. The nerds were bolting down the roof and sidings over a framework of high-tensile tubes that spanned the forward third of the slaughter deck. The middle was occupied by the remaining three crates, then another thirty feet of vacant space to the rear slipway.

A sixth sense for the sea distracted him.

The ocean was shifting subtly.

As were his thoughts.

Murder entered his mind.

Vesprhein trickled his plan to the crew throughout the afternoon via his stoolies, who passed it on via mumbled conversations during breaks as they crossed each other in the corridors and while they crapped and pissed in the bathrooms.

Darkness arrived by late afternoon, along with lengthening swells and stiffer winds. The sky remained without a trace of cloud. Seemingly disinterested, Vesprhein made another of his infrequent appearances on the catwalk. The scientists were weatherproofing the joints under the bright work lamps that the pirates used to cut up their illegal harvests. Raquel and the MIT postgraduates tapped into the ship's power, creating multiple outlets for the electronics they intended to set up tomorrow. The scientists assembled a pellet stove that would heat the station.

"Done for the day?" he asked Jan.

The whole team looked beat. They hardly noticed that the waves approached in a wide crescent. Even if they had, Vesprhein was confident they would not have known what to make of it. In the open ocean, occasionally the seas worsened while the weather remained fair. An experienced seaman, Vesprhein had instinctively sensed the symptoms this afternoon: perfect skies high above, trailing bands of vapor at mast-top level and shortening seas.

He waited on the bridge until he heard them come out of their cabins and took the companionway down to the officers' deck. The eco-warriors and the scientists had showered and changed. He followed them into the Pig. The killer-factory ship rolled, causing Jan and her friends to grab each other and the bulkhead. The sound of the sea took the *Stavenger* on her beam and carried inside like rolling thunder as water immersed the deck, swept across the shack, pounded the crates and drained out of the scuppers below.

"Are we headed into a storm?" Jan asked Vesprhein, nodding to the fiddle battens on the mess deck tables, which prevented the food from being thrown about. Bottles and other breakables were laid flat or wedged in.

"Not that I know of," lied Vesprhein easily and glared at Assad the cook. *You fucking fool!* By rigging the mess deck, Assad almost forewarned the eco-warriors and scientists of rough sailing. He wanted them to go to bed oblivious of the circle of danger tightening around them.

"Should we check the lashings of the crates?" Raquel asked, when he came to the table.

"Nah," dismissed Vesprhein. He didn't want them down there just yet and quickly changed the subject. "If you got all that gear, how come you didn't get the research vessel I saw parked in that college harbor."

"She's not armed," answered Jan.

"You think the Japs are going to pick a fight?" asked Vesprhein.

"We are taking away fifty years supply of whale meat."

"Have you animal rights crazies ever considered outbidding the hunters?"

"What do you mean?" asked Boycott.

"The dockside value for each minke in Japan and Norway is about forty thousand dollars. All you do is buy up the IWC quota before the hunt begins."

"That's thirty-two million dollars." She calculated for eight hundred whales, the previous season's total allowable catch.

"So? Put your money where your mouth is," challenged Vesprhein. "We'll see then how badly you want to keep the fuckers alive. My guess is you'll let them be served up, even take a bite or two."

"It doesn't matter anymore," shrugged Jan.

"I still say getting a total ban was a big mistake. You'd have been better off making the IWC auction the annual catch. Green groups and governments, eager to save whales, can buy them all up and not hunt 'em."

"Washington is paying Mexican fishermen not to engage in dolphin-unfriendly tuna driftnetting," said Knight.

"What would prevent pirates like you from making up the score illegally for the losers?" asked Jan.

Vesprhein shrugged with a grin. "Nothing."

❄

"He's probably got the clap," said Raquel the moment Jan and she walked into their cabin.

"What are you talking about?'

"You know what I'm talking about."

"I'm not going to sleep with him."

"What if you weren't first lady?"

"But I am."

"What if you weren't married?"

"Moot again."

"What if you and Everett separated?"

"I don't know."

"Oh, really?"

"Okay, he's got everything on my wish list. Brains, brawn and ink all over."

"It's the danger that excites you, doesn't it?"

"Hardly."

"He is charming in his own way, I suppose," Raquel mused aloud and teased, "Handsome. Cavalier. I can just picture it. The two of you on the high seas, one adventure after another. Open ocean. No limits."

"Oh, God." Jan dismissed.

"Quite a change from that stuffy life in the Oval Office."

Jan did not respond.

"Is it the freedom or the man that really excites you?" asked Raquel.

Again Jan did not answer.

❄

Vesprhein looked out of his porthole around midnight. As he had anticipated, the ocean had turned completely white and ran in a confused swell. Even though her screws turned at full speed, the *Stavenger* slowed against waves attacking her with a force of six thousand pounds per square foot.

The speaker in his cabin rattled with static around the night watch's urgent voice, "Crates movin' like crazy!"

Vesprhein jabbed the intercom, "Sound the alarm!"

Bells rang. Vesprhein hurried out into the passageway. The eco-warriors and scientists groggily stumbled out. Napoli and Larkin appeared, holstering their guns. They rushed on to the upper gangway overlooking the slaughter deck. A rabble of pirates were already there. The lashings held, but each time the floor angled from side to side, the three crates slithered a little more aft.

"You better tie them down tighter," yelled Vesprhein above the roaring sea that threw a wave over and across the ship.

"It's too dangerous to go down there, ma'am," cautioned Napoli, after the *Stavenger* finally settled to even keel and water stopped raining down.

"If those mothers break loose, they'll smash the ramp open and dump down the slipway into the ocean."

The seas got shorter and steeper. The *Stavenger*'s bows sank under the shoulder of a trough. Hundreds of thousands of gallons of water hurtled across deck. Everyone grabbed the railing, and for several seconds afterwards, they crouched under a freezing gush. The scientific station survived, but the crates slid dangerously.

"We've got to get down there," said Jan, "and fast."

Vesprhein looked at her. "You can't do this by yourselves."

"Are you offering to help?"

"There's no need for the first lady and her friends to go down there if your men can handle it," intervened Napoli firmly.

Vesprhein's eyes went cold. He laughed it off. "I couldn't give a shit about your stuff. I just care about my ship."

"Nice try, Arlov," Jan said. "We'll do it ourselves. Come on, guys."

"We'll shoot to kill anyone who even thinks of going down there," added Napoli. He ordered Owens and Larkin to remain outside and keep an eye, dispatched Prophet to lock the radio room and followed Vesprhein to the bridge.

Vesprhein settled into a wide-legged stance beside Quvango at the wheel. The Angolan helmsman looked straight ahead through the clearview glass. Iron Lady stood tensely by the telegraph. Prophet leaned against the aft windows, with a view of the bridge. Napoli gripped the captain's chair. Vesprhein deliberately looked over his shoulder at the SEAL team leader.

"Half ahead, port," said Vesprhein. He kept the *Stavenger* plunging evenly through the confused seas. When the time came, he'd have her shaking like there was no way else he could keep her afloat.

The dumb bastards had played right into his hands.

"Turn on the lights," Jan called out.

She led her team down the ladder after the work lamps blazed alive. It was five degrees below zero. The cold penetrated the scarves wrapped around their faces and stung through the dripping oilskins. In stark, macabre contrast to the wild, uncouth sea, the star-studded sky remained serene. It was hard to believe there wasn't even the hint of a storm above this berserk ocean. The moon kept a dispassionate eye on the mountainous waves run amok.

The crates scraped and groaned menacingly each time the *Stavenger* reared and crashed.

"Yikes," muttered Boycott and synopsized everyone's sentiment. He'd brought his camera down. Naturally.

The three ten-foot-tall crates stood in a single file along the center of the slaughter deck, lashed down by two chains passing over the top of each crate and inserted into S-shaped hooks evenly spaced along either edge of the deck, where the floor met the wall. The chains and hooks were usually used to hold down whales for cutting. They had to pull the chains down a few extra links, tightening the lashings over each crate. During the brief moments when the chain was disengaged from the S-hook, only the strength of the persons clutching the chain would immobilize the crate. The minutest let-up could release the crate and crush them to death.

"Ready?" asked Jan. The team stood on either side of the first chain holding down the crate farthest from the slipway. Boycott rolled the camera. "On three."

They nodded and waited. The *Stavenger*'s forward progress was a cycle of seesaw motions. First the bow dipped, then her stern settled. A brief window of even keel followed, before the bow climbed again to begin a fresh cycle.

"One, two, three!" yelled Jan.

Grunting, they tugged and pushed the chain toward the floor, disengaging it from the S-hook. The crate stood still of its own weight. Yale released the chain prematurely.

"Don't let go!" cried Jan.

The link slipped away before the tip of the hook could engage it. The *Stavenger* commenced a new cycle. The slaughter deck sloped forward. The crate scraped ominously. The bow cut into the sea.

"Oh, shit!" Yale put his weight back on the chain.

The *Stavenger* leaned forward faster and faster.

"Almost there!" yelled Jan between clenched teeth. Their feet pressed down on the deck plate, seeking traction, but the weight of the crate mounted exponentially. Their feet began to slip, as did their grip on the chain. "Got it!"

A heartbeat later, the slaughter deck, lifted by a wicked sea passing under her stern, sloped sharply forward.

"Now you know what nick of time means," joked Boycott with a nervous smile.

A wind erupted. Water and air combined in a cacophony of violence. The *Stavenger* returned to even keel. The team pressed into the narrow space between the crate and the wall and lashed down the second chain. The box didn't budge when the next sea crashed through and the satisfaction of accomplishment quelled their fears.

They commenced work on the second crate, securing it moments before the ship glanced a huge comber. Once again, water curled on deck, smothering everyone and everything. The hammer blows from this set of seas went on for several minutes. Just when Jan felt they'd never escape the press of water, the Pacific subsided. The wind died away. Swirling water stopped tugging at their feet.

They moved to the third crate, which stood closest to the slipway.

❄

Seeing the eco-warriors grab the first chain, the eyes of the Russian Navy deserter, who had been involved in the brawl with the Jamaican meat handler, retreated from a porthole looking into the cutting deck. He hurried down a passageway and waved. Five seconds and two thugs later, the signal reached the Korean lookout and the rat-faced French steward.

They duckwalked outside, pressed themselves against the bulkhead and peered up at the bridge. It glowed a bright yellow behind the heavily misted windows. The two small men darted across toward the platform overhanging the poop, where a rack of depth charges were stowed. The Korean undid the ties that held the explosive globes on a miniature railway. The Frenchman set the charges for shallow detonation. It took all of a minute to accomplish and return inside unseen.

❄

On the bridge, an unmarked red light beside the wheel came on dimly. The tiny plastic hemisphere was so filthy, the glow wasn't seen by anyone but Vesprhein. The depth charges were live. Time now to use his uncanny ability to read the sea. He nodded imperceptibly to Iron Lady, then disrupted the few seconds of even keel that he knew the eco-warriors were counting on by barking suddenly, "Full ahead, port!"

Engine revolutions went to maximum. The *Stavenger* surged, leaning left.

❄

"Watch out!" yelled Jan.

The third crate slid away sharply. The disengaged chain ripped through the eco-warriors' gloves. They barked out in pain. Raquel flew backward. The free end of the chain swung in a sharp arc. Everyone ducked.

The sharp turn at full speed sent the unharnessed forward edge of the third crate careening toward the eco-warriors. They were at the bottom of the steepening incline of the slaughter deck.

"Jesus, no!" Welling cried.

Everyone was on his own. They dived beyond the destructive arc of the crate. Boycott didn't react.

"David!" shrieked Jan, realizing his field of vision was restricted by the viewfinder of his camera.

The chain cut his feet from under him. He cried out and fell hard on his back, shifting the camera protectively onto his chest. Jan grabbed his legs and began to pull him out of harm's way. A wave passed underneath, wobbling the *Stavenger* violently. Jan slipped, fell and lost her hold on Boycott. His head remained in the path of the crate, which advanced with an ear-rending screech against the deckplates. The videographer squeezed his eyes shut without a ready quip for the first time. Jan held her breath. Inches from his cheek, the crate's massive waterproof surface slammed to an abrupt halt.

The second chain holding the rear half had stopped the sweeping forward section a yard shy of the wall. Recovering, Jan muscled him to safety before the full impact of the undercurrent, which swung the *Stavenger*'s masts crazily back and forth. The lee rails went under completely. For nearly half a minute, the water overwhelmed the ship. Miraculously, the single chain held the third crate. The team barely sputtered to their feet.

BoomBoomBoomBoom!

❄

Four explosions detonated in as many seconds.

"What was that?" asked Napoli.

Lights died and blinked back on.

"Explosions!" said Vesprhein, acting surprised. "The depth charges must have knocked loose!"

Napoli looked at Vesprhein with narrow, suspicious eyes, but the pirate knew where the SEAL team leader's priorities lay. Napoli called Owens and Larkin on the upper gangway. "Status on the first lady!"

Static was his response. Napoli glanced outside.

Vesprhein held back a smile. Right aft of the poop deck, the *Stavenger*'s stern lifted out of the water.

※

Jan and her friends flung about like dice in a rocking cup. Nothing was stable. Cross currents finally settled the *Stavenger*. Jan waved up to the SEALs on the catwalk, signaling everyone on the slaughter deck was okay.

The freed chain came swinging back over the third crate.

Jan yelled, "Hook that back up when the crate straightens out!"

Knight, Welling and Yale grabbed it and hung on, aware the rear lashing would protect them from being crushed against the bulkhead. Raquel clutched the S-hook, ready. The crate scraped back.

"Now!" shouted Jan.

They re-engaged the chain to the S-hook and stopped the crate from swinging back and forth.

※

Vesprhein saw that the rear slipway light was not on. *Where's that goddman Russian?* He should have thrown the switch by now. Vesprhein studied the ocean and sensed another sea in the forward port quarter. "Starboard twenty!"

"Starboard twenty!" repeated Quvango.

The ship slewed beside a wall of water climbing out of the ocean. The sea rose until it towered above the bridge. Vesprhein timed the *Stavenger* to parallel the wave just when it dropped, broadsiding her entire length. The ship heeled over, enveloped in a raging swirl of white. The inclinometer danced over thirty-five degrees. Prophet lost his balance.

Iron Lady skated toward him in a flash.

Napoli, fighting his own battle to stay erect, lost his feet and his gun.

Vesprhein jumped him.

❆

"Grab a partner!" yelled Jan and took Boycott's hand.

It took the strength of two to fight off the assault of water that leapt over the bridge structure and thundered down like an avalanche. The *Stavenger* seemed several degrees away from starting back, if she ever could. The sea buried the ship. Jan helplessly watched Welling's hand tear loose. He bellowed in panic, inaudible in the tumbling sea. To Jan's dismay, he slammed into Knight, prying loose the reporter's grip on a door handle. The roaring gush carried the two men. They dislodged the others and the entire team tumbled into Jan, prying her grip off a bulkhead pipe. In a mess of flailing arms they swept toward the rear slipway.

Indianapolis, Indiana

Everett napped between rallies behind the closed doors of his suite aboard Air Force One. Lhea, Zoe Zurich, Delta Harris and the CRP dozed in their seats. Not George Pleasance. He stayed awake, alert and energized.

Every aspect of the tight race was taking on a sense of urgency. Pleasance loved this pressure-cooker. Voluminous data swirled in his head and out through his pen as precise strategy ideas on to his legal pad at the rate of a page a minute. Reacting to the sound piping in through his headsets, he looked up suddenly at Democrat Keith Leeds on TV. Pleasance's lips compressed into a thin line.

North Pacific

Jan repeatedly tried to grab someone's hand, but she couldn't find one. The combined noise of the powerful flood, the *Stavenger*'s screws, the deathly metallic rattle of all rigging aboard and the defiant groans of the three crates overwhelmed the shouts of the eco-warriors and scientists. They were buffeted back and forth between the bulkheads in the thirty feet of open slaughter deck between the end of the third crate and the slipway.

Jan slid past Trevor Smith, holding on to a pipe. Before she could clutch something, the ramp dropped open and the ship lurched back. A torrent seeking the Pacific Ocean lifted her. Suddenly, the gaping hole of the slipway rushed toward her, a dancing, lopsided frame around an inky black ocean laced in boiling white.

"Raq!" shouted Jan, stretching as she shot past her best friend atop the trapped water.

"Jan!" Raquel shouted back.

The high wind shrieked again. As the ship leveled off, the forward plunging bows of the *Stavenger* crashed into the sea with a thunderclap, lifting the stern screws out of the water. The exiting deluge teetered into a confused whirlpool, giving Jan a chance of survival if she could wade close enough to one of the others. Everyone reached out. No sooner did hope surge within her, when the stern collapsed back into the ocean.

The river within the slaughter deck emptied in one roaring gush.

Carrying Jan with it.

✻

Vesprhein anticipated the ship to heel a lot further and longer. He lost Napoli when the reverse tilt gathered momentum. Napoli pounced on Vesprhein, pummeling his skull into a row of deck rivets. Vesprhein tasted his own blood, groaned and lost the focus in his eyes. He was only vaguely aware of Iron Lady being turned around by Prophet, who matched Napoli in fighting skills. Prophet followed the *Stavenger*'s tilt the other way and slammed the Englishman onto the chart table. Vesprhein heard violent punches and Iron Lady going down with a series of grunts.

Quvango turned to help. Vesprhein felt Napoli's weight lift off him. The SEAL team leader ran the helmsman into the bridgescreen. Vesprhein heard breaking glass, then breaking water.

The *Stavenger* slanted sharply again. Vesprhein tumbled against the bulkhead. Napoli lost Quvango, vulnerable for an instant. Vesprhein crawled to his knees just as the bridge island leaned well over the port side gunwale, forcing him to use both hands to stop himself from dropping into the ocean. After a split-second pause, the *Stavenger* sprang back the other way again. Simultaneously, her bows dug into the sea.

Vesprhein regained his balance to find Napoli in his face. "Steady this ship, you fucking bastard!"

Napoli fired his gun into Vesprhein's thigh. The bullet hacked off a chunk of flesh. It was as if someone plunged in a red-hot rod.

Vesprhein threw his head back and cried out.

Napoli tightened his finger on the trigger again. "Next one will take out your kneecap!"

Vesprhein bellowed through clenched teeth. "Slow ahead both, midships!"

Prophet flung Iron Lady by the hair to the Telegraph. The Englishman gasped, "Slow ahead both, midships!"

"Steady as she go," stammered Quvango, weaving back to the wheel, his lips swollen and one eye shut.

❄

The lowered ramp shot upward with the climbing stern. The large flat surface, scarred with the blood of thousands of whales dragged up and heartlessly plundered, slammed Jan, knocking her back onto the slaughter deck just as she was about to be tossed overboard. Jan found the rusting hydraulic shaft that opened and closed the ramp.

"Link up!" Raquel ordered.

Smith took up the anchor position.

The *Stavenger*'s rhythmic rise and fall smashed down the stern.

"Jan! Don't let go!" yelled Raquel. The flooding water and grease on the shaft were stealing Jan's grip slowly but surely. "Hang on!" Raquel glanced from Jan to the men locking arms. The shrieking wind and tossing ship kept them off balance. "Come on, guys, come on, hurry!"

For the first time in her life, Raquel felt a rush of panic, perhaps because for as long as she'd known Jan, the first lady had shown an innate survival instinct. Jan always found that opportune hold, or the life-saving grip, then turned around and saved everybody else. Raquel would never forgive herself if she could not rescue Jan *once*.

"Raq! Go!" shouted Boycott.

Raquel came out of her anxiety, feeling his grip on her wrist. She fearlessly advanced as the last link of the human chain. A smile cracked Jan's face. Raquel felt a surge of relief.

"Grab my hand!" shouted Raquel.

Jan loosened her hold to obey. The *Stavenger*'s bow rebounded skyward. The stern sank, the ramp flopped back into the ocean, tearing Jan away from Raquel's outstretched hand. Raquel blindly, desperately, pulled at the human chain and found another foot. Enough to grab the first lady's long, blonde hair. A gasp wrenched out of Jan's throat then a prolonged cry!

As the stern angled down. Raquel fought gravity and the hungry ocean. Strands of Jan's hair ripped loose, roots and all. Blood spritzed onto her hand. Finally, the *Stavenger* began its forward dip.

Jan slid into Raquel, who let go of the hair only when she felt the first lady hug her securely. Raquel shouted, "She's safe!"

The human chain swung the women into the safety of the ship.

"Close one, eh?" winked Boycott and grabbed his camera, which he had wedged safely.

Seattle, Washington

Democratic presidential candidate Keith Leeds addressed independent fishermen who operated small, family boats in the Pacific Northwest. "Following the IWC vote to ban aboriginal and coastal whaling entirely, and particularly in light of the first lady's startling revelations about Japan, it has become necessary to address the livelihood concerns of our fishermen." He waited for the loud clapping to die down. "Japan's association with pirates is reprehensible, unforgivable and unfair to honest, god-fearing Americans like you, upon whom we impose strict adherence to the law. As president, I promise to introduce a bill in Congress that will ban Japan, the biggest harvester of marine life inside our territorial waters, from fishing within our 200-nautical-mile EEZ until American fishermen have harvested their full quota!"

Applause rang out. In 1976, Congress extended American territorial waters from twelve to two hundred nautical miles. This 200-nautical-mile limit was called the Exclusive Economic Zone, or EEZ. Nations had to follow preset guidelines based on UN mandates and US law in order to fish within the EEZ. Leeds invited a Coast Guard, flown in from the Aleutian Islands, to the microphone. His beat, the Bering Sea, saw daily competition between American and Japanese fishermen.

"Most of the Bering Sea," read the Coast Guard from a prepared statement, "is claimed by the United States and Russia. But there is an unregulated donut of international waters in the middle that can be reached only by passing through our waters. Fishing fleets from Japan, China, South Korea and other countries not only over-harvest the donut hole, they help themselves illegally as they sail to and from it across the more productive American EEZ. Last year, we logged thirteen mayday calls in a single hour as a result of confrontations between American fishermen like you, operating small, family boats, and Japan's large factory trawlers. Fellow fishermen in the vicinity don't respond because a rescue means losing their livelihood to the trawlers. Congressman Keith Leeds's bill will give us the authority to shut the gates, so to speak. Not only will it help fishermen like you, but the Coast Guard as well. Twelve of my men have died in the past five years trying to mediate the fishing wars."

The head of the North Pacific Fishery Management Council, one of the eight management councils overseeing enforcement of the 1976 EEZ law, stepped up next. "The Bering Sea is America's greatest seafood larder, stocked with thirty-six billion pounds of bottom dwelling cod, sole, flounder, perch, mackerel and walleye pollock. In 1980, your small, family boats took about a hundred thousand metric tons, worth over a million dollars. If not rich, you could at least grow old working the sea." The rally moved with unanimous nods. "Today, you have to work sixteen hours, often around the clock, or you will lose your catch to the illegal foreign raiders. Yellowfin sole was a year round fishery. Now it lasts two and a half months. The black cod season has gone from being two hundred days long to fifteen. The average herring season currently lasts twenty minutes! Elect Mr. Leeds. He represents a secure future for us and a step in the right direction."

"What is he trying to pull?" demanded Everett. Pleasance had awakened him and the rest of the Committee to Re-elect the President to watch the telecast. "The Japanese buy every goddamn ton of fish those small family boats harvest. They'd be out of business if it weren't for the Japanese."

Pleasance turned down the TV. "He's just stirring up controversy to occupy us in our own backyard, mending the damage, while he slips off to the swing states and tries to get ahead."

"We should have seen this coming," Everett growled.

Neither he nor his two rivals had been able to make significant inroads into each other's strongholds. Republican Will Todd owned the South. Most of the East was with Leeds. The West belonged entirely to Everett. All three candidates had long since given up on a broad mandate. The goal became winning 270 electoral votes, nothing more. As the numbers stood, the victor would be the man who carried five of the Big Eight: California, Texas, Illinois, Indiana, Michigan, Ohio, Pennsylvania and New York. In California, Everett was insurmountable. Leeds claimed New York. Will Todd controlled Texas. So the three men relentlessly stumped the other swing states, where they were running even.

"How do we respond?" asked Lhea.

"Taking a position contrary to Leeds will come off as defending the Japanese," warned Delta Harris, now the Campaign Chairman and the daily spin doctor in front of TV cameras.

"And protectionist," added Lhea.

"It will also rekindle speculation about a marital rift between Jan and you. No way." Pleasance firmly shook his head from side to side.

Everett looked out the window. *Fishing would not be an issue if Jan hadn't gotten mixed up in this whale drive.*

Air Force One's shadow rippled across the wooded hill country north of the Ohio River. Though Central Indiana was the richest agricultural region in the United States, industry dominated the Calumet District in the northwest and Japanese auto makers were the biggest employers. Kaiyou had a huge ship parts factory too.

Everett looked away. "Plus, we cannot afford even a whisper of a trade war with Japan here in Indiana."

The phone rang. Pleasance jabbed the speaker button, "I said no interruptions!"

"I-It's Mr. Random from the NRO," stammered the operator from the communications' cubicle in Air Force One. "He said it's need to know."

Pleasance curtly nodded those who did not belong to the inner circle out of the room. Then said, "Put him on."

Random came to the point at once. "Jan has drawn even with the Japanese fleet."

Everett frowned. The secret slaughter of the blues by the Japanese was imperative to launch the next phase of the Sitka scenario.

Northwest Pacific Basin

An early morning snow had laid a white quilt on the deck of the *Stavenger*. She raced under a cold, damp and gloomy morning. The ocean ran a heavy swell. Freezing wind blew in from the north carrying spicules of ice. Bigger chunks disintegrated noisily under the crashing keel.

Unable to sleep much after their harrowing escape, Jan and her friends decided to get an early start setting up their gear. In spite of all that water, the shack, to their relief, was dry within.

"Good morning," said Vesprhein cheerfully, filling the doorway.

Jan wasn't surprised he'd gotten over the disappointment of last night's failed attempt to sabotage her. She did not expect him to harbor any regret. He'd probably told his men that this was a long trip and there'd be other opportunities.

On the other hand, the sight of him sent a shudder through her. Stumbling on to the bridge last night, still shaking after the nerve-wracking brush with death, she'd discovered that the SEALs had come even closer when she saw Vesprhein's flesh wound, Iron Lady's bruises, Quvango's broken nose and the shattered bridge window.

"How's your leg?" Jan pointed to Vesprhein's thigh. He wore jeans and the bandage wasn't visible.

"Fucking hurts," he winced, glaring at Napoli, who had conspicuously cocked and leveled his gun when the pirate appeared. "What are you guys doing?"

"You'll see," said Jan.

Vesprhein shrugged, turned on his heel and walked away.

"We have to be very watchful, ma'am," said Napoli. "You're setting up sophisticated tracking equipment that Vesprhein will *really* kill for."

Last night, in the privacy of her quarters, Napoli had revealed that events could have been premeditated. Vesprhein was an excellent seaman and the crew ruthless and tight-knit enough to have staged it all under the guise of rough sailing. For Jan, it served as another reality check. She should never forget that Vesprhein's knowledge and intelligence, which she found almost seductive, also made him dangerous. He was a calculating criminal who could turn from charming to deadly without notice. She'd seen it up close the morning after the IWC vote when she told him Worthy planned to sink his ship.

Boycott broke the silence. "In video parlance, this is called dead air." Nervous laughter. "Let's unpack those goodies."

Jan suggested they maintain a presence, night and day, inside the scientific shack. They agreed to rotate in pairs along with a SEAL. Then they got down to work, splitting up to erect their individual workstations. Jan and Knight shuttled between Raquel and the scientists whenever one hollered for menial help.

Trevor Smith set up a twin-screen Intergraph Workstation, upon which converged an international data net from NOAA and INMARSAT satellites, Navy Fleet Numerical Oceanographic Center in Monterey, California, International Ice Patrol planes and merchant ships. Entrusted with the task of iceberg prediction on their way up, he'd assume the duties of trail scout and tracker for the drive down to Cetacean Bay.

Brian Yale unraveled a stack of acoustic gear to overcome the obstacles that physics posed below the ocean surface. Sound waves tended to scatter, fuzz and limit the view. To make water transparent, he used a combination of vertical sonar that looked straight down, a sidescan Towed Ocean Bottom Instrument and satellite-based infrared sensors, radar altimeters and scatterometers. A computer program integrated all this data into a sharp, high resolution composite image, allowing Yale to play the equivalent of a flanker in a cattle drive. It would be his job to ensure no whales straggled from the pod.

Oliver Welling's station was delegated the task of keeping an acoustic census of the blues during the drive. In addition to being hooked into Yale's sonar gadgetry, multiple screens displayed data from his own tracking devices, including temporary hydrophones and expendable sonobuoys. Since he had requisite security clearance, Jan had arranged for him to tap into the Navy's classified sea floor arrays to keep tabs on the progress of the Japanese fleet.

The most important workstation in the shack belonged to Raquel, Taggart and Fallon. It was their responsibility to start the whales moving, and when they did, to restrict them to a single herd. Jan anticipated the Japanese fleet would shadow the drive like rustlers and pick off blues that strayed.

Alex Fallon busily set up three rows of nine-inch screens, six per row. They would display pictures from tiny cameras on eighteen tail-driven, fully autonomous, remote controlled robotic tuna. Gene Taggart unveiled two dozen of these complex mechanical fish, which had evolved from Charlie, a prototype that first swam in a test tank hooked to an overhead guide, to SuperCharlie, an advanced underwater vehicle featuring sixty ribs, a motor-driven segmented spine, tendons and foam-tissue with Lycra skin cover that could easily be mistaken for a real bluefin tuna. Complex, highly sophisticated software mimicked this most versatile fish in the ocean down to its speed and hairpin moves. Taggart and Fallon tested every SuperCharlie, manipulating them from a mouse-driven screen. The sound emanating from the tiny but powerful speakers on each vehicle, critical to the success or failure of this drive, was fed via a radio microphone by Raquel from the voluminous library in her computer.

To simplify security, the SEALs stripped all the communications gear from the *Stavenger*'s radio room and set it up in the shack. By nightfall, when Jan and Knight arrived carrying trays stacked with dinner, cords and connectors covered the floor. The LEDs displayed esoteric messages. The screens were alive with graphs and images. Technical jargon exchanged rapidly between the scientists above the nonstop *clack-clack* of keyboards. Eating as they worked, the scientists brought all aspects of the scientific station together.

With bad news.

"The ice is closing in a horseshoe from the north, east and west," said Smith, nodding to the right screen of his Intergraph Workstation. A multitude of circles intersected over a map of the Arctic Ocean between the North American and Asian continents all the way down to the Bering Strait. A red dotted line marked the 200-nautical-mile EEZ. He imported the whales from Welling's screen markers into his. "The blues are being forced into a smaller and smaller area."

"Making them easier targets and a quicker harvest," Jan concluded anxiously "Any Japanese lead over us can become critical."

Welling made contact with an undersea habitat off Acapulco, Mexico and they confirmed the booms from the Navy experiments in the Antarctic had been silent this past week. Before leaving Washington, Jan told Everett to sign an executive order canceling the tests as part of their deal.

"So why aren't they moving south?" asked Jan.

"They're still afraid," said Raquel, drawing everyone's eyes to her laptop. She moved it beside Welling's monitor displaying SOSUS reads of the whales' calls. His spectrographs matched the distress ones she pulled from her library.

"In a way that's working to our advantage, isn't it?" said Jan. "It's keeping them within American waters."

"Not for long." Smith clicked on the whales. The ice attributes scrolled up. He plucked off the variables necessary to make a forecast. They included ocean currents, prevailing temperature, wind chill and other environmental data. The Iceberg Data Management and Prediction System was good up to five or six days. Animating the predicted freeze as a solid line at the end of every twenty-four-hour period, he explained, "On Monday night, the ice will overrun the whales' present coordinates. By midday, Tuesday, it will reach the EEZ."

Welling moved the markers representing the blues to follow Smith's projected freeze. "Our whales will have no place else to go but into the approaching pelagic fleet."

Knight drew a sharp breath. "The Japanese won't need to enter the EEZ at all."

"And in international waters they can do what they please," said Jan. "There will be the usual condemnations, threats of boycotts and our presidential election politics will let them get away with the slaughter." She straightened, determined. "We have to get to the blues by dawn Tuesday."

"The latest," asserted Smith.

Today was Friday, eleven days since they'd set sail.

"What is our ETA?" asked Boycott.

"Monday evening," replied Jan.

"Then what are we worried about?" asked Boycott. "We're running even with the Japanese fleet. So they are not going to get there any sooner."

"Before you start toasting, consider this," intervened Vesprhein, stepping through the door. He first took a moment to whistle at the millions of dollars of technology crammed into the scientific shack. "A storm system moves out of Siberia every forty-eight to seventy-two hours. The Japs could slip by one and we may not. It's all a matter of luck from here on out."

Vesprhein's words became prophetic. The *Rising Sun* and her fleet slipped ahead of an erratic, low-pressure system that zigzagged in too swiftly for the *Stavenger* to avoid.

Jan arrived on the bridge to an unfriendly sky emptying rain and ice. Temperatures sank below freezing. Snow squalls swirled blindingly, all but blotting out the *Stavenger*'s shadowy hulk and blinking riding lights. The fury reduced visibility to half a mile. The merciless sea pounced on the killer-factory ship with twenty-five-foot combers.

All hands were recalled to stations.

Jan agonized. With each hour they spent in the storm, they fell twice as far behind the Japanese whalers. All afternoon, the *Stavenger* rolled twenty, thirty, even forty degrees. Tons of water shipped over and across the slaughter deck. The gray afternoon skipped directly to a black, stormy night.

"The *Rising Sun* has pulled ahead of us by about four hours," reported Welling from the shack.

"What's the status on the freeze?"

"Moving in just like I forecast," answered Smith.

"By the time we shake free of this weather," opined Vesprhein, "we'll be about six hours behind them." When they sat down for supper in the Pig, Vesprhein chuckled with his mouth full, spitting up morsels of food.

Saturday dawned dully. The *Stavenger* pushed slowly across a steep beam sea which was hers alone. Jan walked out on deck. Napoli followed at a discreet distance. Emerald foam danced along the rail and the ocean washed as far back as the quarterdeck. During the brief moment that Jan pressed her feet down for balance, the soles of her shoes froze to the metal. The temperature dropped sharply with every degree of latitude north they traversed. Jan hugged her arms about her and stared melancholically across the ocean.

Japan's tenacity in the face of international criticism had long since ceased to puzzle her. Minority opinion was responsible for all policy making in Japan, where representative democracy was most powerful. The fifty-one members from the fishing districts fiercely protected the continuation of whaling in spite of the fact that it generated little income, created few jobs, hardly augmented nutrition and evoked a minimal sense of tradition. The seaweed industry was worth three times as much as whaling. For this ten percent of the Diet, the motive was not some intense prejudice against conservation, but cold mathematics. Any shutdown would initiate the implementation of the Japanese severance pay system, which mandated that every laid off worker be compensated more than sixty thousand dollars. On the other hand, the government covered losses with subsidies and loans. As long as the ensuing kickbacks funded their campaigns, the politicians from the fishing districts opened a conduit to the highest echelons of government for corporate giants like Kaiyou. The mutual gains far outweighed any humane considerations toward the largest, most amazing animals on earth.

Jan sensed movement out of the corner of her eye. Napoli sharpened, his hand tightening around his gun.

"Easy, cowboy," sneered Vesprhein's familiar voice. He limped from the bullet wound. Jan nodded. Napoli retreated. The deck gave a nervous tremble when a tall graybeard crumbled and broke inboard.

"Good morning, Arlov," said Jan, stamping her feet until the water washed off the deck to prevent her soles from freezing to the metal again. "Isn't it early for you to be up and about?"

"Yeah." He leaned his elbows on the railing to the right of her. "But I figured it'd be worth the inconvenience if I can ruin the rest of your day."

"What is it?"

"We are now eight hours behind. With ten catchers, the Japs will mop up those fuckers before we can get within sighting distance. They'll tow whatever whales they haven't processed into Russian waters, where you can't go and where they probably have a deal to blow your ass out of the water if you do."

"You're probably right, but I've never conceded anything without a fight."

"I'll bet you used to beat up the boys in your school."

"I didn't have to. I outwitted them."

"Well, you'll need to fight this time. They're not going to hand those whales to you."

"I'll do what I have to."

"I'm sure you will." Vesprhein smiled. "Still, if you're in for a fight, you're lucky to've found me."

"Putting aside your shameless lack of modesty, I suppose so."

"You're married to a man who couldn't have gotten his present job being shy about himself."

Jan threw him an inquiring glance. "Is there a point to this conversation?"

"I want to clear the air. You think I tried to kill you the other night."

"Didn't you?"

Vesprhein shrugged. "Of course not."

Jan's silence effectively conveyed her disbelief. The wind twisted a brief snow flurry. Despite all the layers of clothing, they shivered in silence.

"We're more alike than you think."

Jan laughed. "How so?"

"We don't take shit from nobody and we don't give a shit how we get what we want."

"Only I'm good and you're evil."

"Different sides. Same coin."

"So we'll never see eye to eye."

"But we cover each other's asses."

"Don't you forget it. You and your crew will be the most wanted men if something should happen to me."

He cracked an easy smile. "You and me, we have chemistry. I think we'll fuck sooner or later."

Jan grimaced. "Just when we're getting along, you have to ruin it by opening your mouth."

"Not enough polish for you? Or do you have a problem with someone who speaks plainly?"

"Plainly? Or just plain crude."

Vesprhein smiled, looked around. "You are on a ship, m'lady."

"I'll give you this much, your audacity might be a valuable asset to me."

"You think we could make it, don't you?" Vesprhein persisted. "Under different circumstances."

"Under different circumstances?" Jan shrugged coolly, then let a twinkle enter her eye. "Maybe."

Vesprhein' grin froze. He recovered, laughed. "Now who's fooling who!"

Vesprhein made a gun out of his finger, retreated and swung on to the catwalk. Reaching the bridge, he looked over his shoulder. Jan stared straight up at him. He disappeared inside.

Had it worked? Jan thought smugly. From here on out, he was going to be nagged by whether she'd been serious. Hell, she didn't know herself. He was so goddamn good looking and dangerous— and honest, in his own way. She felt warm around her neck. *Is it the freedom or the man that really excites you?* Raquel had asked. A smile twitched at the corner of her lips and a faint blush rose into her face.

Northeast Pacific

The *Rising Sun* and her ten catchers went flat out, up and down, spray smacking over. Loud explosive reports filled the air. The gunners, hair flapping in the wind, water running off their oilskins, crouched over their cannons and fired practice harpoons toward coordinates being barked into their headset radios.

A gunner had to react instantly and accurately because he did not have more than a minute when the whale surfaced. It was his decision then to aim and fire, or hold back. This morning, the gunners were being timed with a stopwatch and their accuracy monitored. The practice harpoons were reeled back and the gunners drilled over and over for the upcoming slaughter.

Each catcher was equipped with satellite navigation and sonar equipment, but the Japanese traditionally relied on the naked eye. Lookouts on this hunt were blessed with perfect 20/20 vision. The best could spot a whale a few seconds before it surfaced and communicated it with a single syllable, "Whale!" Then he evaluated its speed and diving pattern. The art and skill lay in predicting where the leviathan would surface the next time, enabling the captain to slow or hasten the catcher's speed. Changing engine revs, acquired only through experience, was critical. The whine within certain frequencies alarmed and warned off whales.

Shinjiro Yamamura, captain of the fleet, laid down his binoculars on the ledge of the *Rising Sun*'s bridge window with a satisfied expression. The cooperation between the lookout, helmsman and gunner, so essential to expedient killing, was improving steadily. He expected them to be ready when they crossed the 200-nautical-mile EEZ into US territorial waters on Monday evening.

As he walked to the officers' mess that night, where he was hosting his ten catcher captains, he heard the sounds of celebration from the crew dining room. The line outside the pantry hatch wound all the way to the alleyway. He had ordered the release of a bonus ration of hard liquor. The crew, whose pay was tied to the size of the harvest, had been on the same will-they-won't-they-beat-the-eco-warriors roller coaster. Now that the slaughter seemed a certainty, he wanted to exorcise the tensions of the past ten days and boost morale going into the hunt.

The ten catcher captains came to their feet in a smart salute when Yamamura walked in. He nodded them to sit down. "I will not return with empty freezers," he announced flatly, sweeping his eyes over their faces. "We have only a twelve-hour lead over the *Stavenger*. To harvest those whales in so little time will require a hundred percent of effort. Any one of you who feels he is not up to the task and the pressure, speak now."

None of them moved. They knew the legend of Yamamura. His

stony demeanor belied a ruthless determination that went beyond frightening. A few years ago, the story went, Yamamura was returning from a whaling voyage in the Antarctic that had been interrupted when he viciously rammed an eco-ship which would not stop harassing his fleet. The incident created an international furor. Kaiyou ordered him back. For the first time in his career, Yamamura was short of the five hundred-ton mission objective by a hundred tons. On the third day, they sighted a sleek, severely endangered, male fin whale that would exactly fill the shortfall. Finding his catcher captains reluctant to disobey the Obata family's directive which banned taking any more whales, Yamamura boarded one of the catcher boats, discharged the captain and ordered the engines to full power.

The gunner nailed a harpoon into the bull. The steel line reeled off the powerful winch. The whale, known as the greyhound of the sea, sounded a death cry and ran. The boat pitched dangerously from side to side as she became wrapped with the bull in a deadly embrace, one captive of the other. When he dived, he dragged her below the water line. When he came up for air, so did the crew. The battle went on for two hours. The ship pitched dangerously from side to side. Water crashed about everywhere. Electrical shorting all but crippled the ship. Yamamura dismissed cutting the fin loose as an option. The story of the beast's victory would be repeated, embellished and exaggerated, until it became a joke along the wharfs.

While fighting the deepest swell yet, the flailing whale dove in a last bid to survive. The catcher pitched sharply. The rails submerged. The scuppers overflowed. The sea invaded. The engine room went under. The bull died in mid-dive and became a 150-ton anchor, keeling the laden vessel. Before the ship overturned completely, the men panicked and jumped overboard to save themselves.

Not Yamamura. He decided he'd rather die than face the ignominy of defeat at the hands of a prey he'd been killing since he was fifteen. But the whale came to rest on an undersea plateau. The line went slack suddenly. The boat tilted back up. When his crew sheepishly crawled back on board, Yamamura was calmly sitting in the Captain's chair on the bridge, sipping beer.

"To a successful hunt!" he raised his glass.

He loved to plunder whales. Chasing and then slaying these magnificent giants in cold blood filled him with a sense of conquest. Every year, he waited with rabid anticipation to lead Japan's "scientific and research" hunt of 900 minkes in the Southern Oceans. When Jan got it banned, Yamamura had been devastated. Revenge consumed him. Their history of hate and hostility toward each other coincided with the story of the fin. It was she, Senator Everett's wife at the time, who'd led the torchbearers. The Obata family made an outward show of condemnation, demoting him to a tugboat. Though they restored his rank the next season, Yamamura felt slighted. He thought he should be above punishment. After all, he was the most experienced and accomplished whaling captain in all of Japan. This past week, when Jan got all whaling banned, Yamamura could not contain his rage. He visited one of Tokyo's several sadomasochistic dungeons. He'd frequented them before to vent unbridled fits of fury with violence against women. He whipped a whore unconscious, imagining she was Jan.

Returning home, he found a message from his bosses at Kaiyou that he found impossible to believe at first. Then Yasuji Hattori showed him American satellite pictures of Sitka's blue whales. A day after leaving Kobe, when he received news about Jan's whale drive, he was pleased. Nothing would be more satisfying than plundering what the first lady held so dear. His obsession mounted with each passing hour, until all he felt was hate.

❋

On the other side of the international date line, there was no quitting in Jan either. "If we're losing the race for the blues, then we just have to stop the Japanese from crossing the EEZ until we get there on Tuesday."

"How?" Vesprhein guffawed. The first lady had caught him off balance again, sitting beside him in the Pig rather than across, as she always did. She knew he was acutely aware of the press of her thigh against his. "You're fuck in the middle of the North Pacific."

Boycott nodded. "And we can't reveal there's a pelagic fleet on a secret whale hunt."

Jan's eyes sparkled with optimism. "I know."

San Francisco

Gerard Leblanc was paralyzed from the waist down. Confined to a wheelchair, he had still made class valedictorian and graduated from law school near the top of his class.

After a brief stint at Washington's prestigious Delmar & Porter, Leblanc returned to the Bay Area. He teamed up with his law school classmate, Stanley Perle, and they set up a firm. For a whole month, nobody walked through the door of their tiny office in San Francisco. Then a friend referred Jan, their first client, who felt the proposed oil drilling off the California coast threatened the migration of gray whales. Even though his partner opposed kicking off their fledgling law firm with pro bono representation, Leblanc took the case and won a highly publicized injunction against the state government in Sacramento.

Today, Leblanc & Perle was the largest law firm on the west coast.

Tonight, nobody got any sleep.

Every light burned on both floors of the sprawling office. Despite the hour, Leblanc wheeled energetically between three associates, two secretaries and an intern. Jan had called him from the *Stavenger*. After eliciting a promise of silence, she told him about the Japanese fleet, the blue whales and Everett's clandestine deal. But Leblanc could not mention any of it. It would end her husband's reelection bid. She wanted Leblanc to find some other legal recourse to ban the

Japanese from entering the EEZ.

"The *Kagoshima* affair is the only thing we have," mused Leblanc.

"But the Supreme Court ruled in '84 that the commerce secretary can refuse to certify Japan," said an associate. Such a certification was necessary to invoke the Packwood-Magnusson Amendment and stop the Japanese from entering American waters. In 1984, when Japan hunted sperms in violation of the moratorium, the United States District Court for the District of Columbia ordered the commerce secretary to certify Japan for conducting whaling operations that "diminished the effectiveness" of the IWC. But President Ronald Reagan arm-twisted the Supreme Court into reversing the ruling by a narrow five-four margin.

"We are presenting the same question, yes," nodded Leblanc, "under an entirely new set of circumstances."

"Pirate whaling?"

"Exactly." Leblanc clapped his hands. "Look into the 1984 filing. Pull up everything on their table of authorities. Case laws, treaties, statutes, legislative materials."

The associate hurried off.

Leblanc summoned his secretary and dictated the plaintiff's statement of the case. "The ultimate issue here is whether Japan shall be allowed to go unpunished. From the very outset, the International Whaling Commission has been entrusted to set and monitor harvest limits. To provide enforcement leverage, the United States Congress enacted Section 8(a) of the Fishermen's Protective Act, called the Pelly Amendment, which threatened trade sanctions if fishing quotas were violated by any nation. But every sitting president has exercised the discretion he enjoys under the Pelly Amendment not to take action simply on nonbinding assurances from the guilty governments. Congress decided this was unacceptable."

He flipped the pages of the US Code. "In 1979, Congress adopted the Packwood-Magnusson Amendment to impose nondiscretionary sanctions against nations that diminish the effectiveness of the Convention of International Whaling Regulations. Congress also placed an obligation of compliance with all international treaties upon nations to fish in US territorial waters, marked by the 200-nautical-mile Extended Economic Zone." Leblanc broke off and buzzed the intern. "Call every news outlet. Leak the gist of our filing and tell them to be outside the courthouse tomorrow if they want a copy of this injunction."

He returned to his dictation.

Washington DC

Everett learned of the anticipated filing from the news when he woke up in the morning. As he hurried to the phone, it rang. Pleasance was already on it. He conferenced in Lhea, Adrian and Delta.

"An injunction, if one is handed down, plays right into Leeds's hands," said the vice president.

"Worse," warned Lhea, "it completely disrupts the Sitka scenario at its most critical juncture."

Everett was more concerned that the fallout was purely political when Congress overrode the president, but it was fucking embarrassing when his own wife's actions concurred with his rival's speech just days ago in Seattle. Pleasance informed him the media were gleefully resurrecting rumors of a marital rift.

"What can we do, George?" asked Everett.

His chief of staff always had an answer, but it was Delta who surprised everyone on the call, suggesting, "Can we squeeze the judge?"

Aleutian Trench

Jan emerged from her cabin after a sleepless night to a bitter cold

Monday morning. She realized the tension knotting her stomach would not unravel until she heard from Leblanc. She pressed against the wall and waited for the ship to stagger over the top and corkscrew down the other side of a wave.

The *Stavenger* dodged long seas, two, three, four thousand feet long, deceivingly sloped on the lee and near vertical on the side chasing her. Occasionally, they caught up and shook the speeding vessel, wildly swinging the lofty crow's nest, shuddering the deeply submerged keel and rattling everything in between.

Jan resumed walking. The floor tilted back and forth for several seconds, searching for even keel. Jan had not showered because it was too cold to strip down. The hot air system barely maintained the temperature a few degrees above freezing. Condensation left thousands of drops of water clinging to the deckheads like bees on a hive. It was dank all the way to the bridge. She came up the companionway and shivered. The temperature was pretty much the same as on the rest of the ship, but it felt colder, probably because the unobstructed three-sixty view of the forbidding sea did not provide the psychological barrier available below, where the windowless corridors imparted a sense of enclosure and distance from the merciless elements outside.

The skeletal night shift stamped around clothed in cocoons of jerseys, overcoats, oilskins, scarves and caps. Still their teeth chattered. They wrapped one hand across their chest and rubbed the other from shoulder to elbow. Jan, muffled in four layers of clothing, with only a narrow slit for the eyes, nodded to Larkin, who paced to keep the chill out of his bones. She was reluctant to mutter a greeting as it entailed opening her mouth and that might admit the cold inside. Larkin said nothing either and smiled with his eyes.

Jan leaned over the chart table. The GPS marker blinked the *Stavenger*'s current position south of the Aleutian Islands. Flung like stepping-stones in an 1100-mile arc, they demarcated the Bering Sea from the North Pacific. She walked to the port side bridge window and wiped a circular peephole in the misty glass. The snow lifted, revealing a vague brightness that was supposed to be dawn. A brief six to eight hours of bleak grayness differentiated day from night.

At fifty knots, the *Stavenger* etched her bows into the ocean every ten seconds. It became second nature to instinctively lean with the seesaw motion. Jan barely noticed the creaming smother of cold water washing over the scientific shack and draining out of the slaughter deck. Chunks of ice thudded noisily across. At all times now, to a person, they wore neoprene Gumby suits as the first layer of clothing and life jackets as their last.

Leblanc's call about the outcome of his meeting with the judge was expected any time. The lawyer had to succeed. He had to get a hearing scheduled for today. Then he had to win an injunction. They hadn't fallen any further behind the *Rising Sun*. But twelve hours was enough time for the fleet to slaughter all the blues and leave American waters.

Jan knew Shinjiro Yamamura was the most dedicated whaler alive. Nobody better represented Japanese defiance against western bias against slaughter. Even if the eco-warriors reached the blues first, the danger, far from being over, would be just beginning. Yamamura would not sail away disappointed from half a century's supply of meat. He would pursue the drive relentlessly all the way to Cetacean Bay, rustling to fill his holds.

Jan sought Pacific Time on her multi-dial watch, which also showed Eastern and Zulu Time. The digital display also read off local time, its chronometer constantly being corrected by a versatile GPS chip.

"I'll be in the shack," she said, daring to open her mouth and speak through the scarf. She paused, preparing herself for the short, bone-chilling walk to the scientific shack. Her eyes teared up the instant she emerged outside on the upper gangway overlooking the slaughter deck. It was impossible to breathe without turning away from the frigid, near solid gusts. Even then, every inhalation seared the respiratory passages all the way to her lungs.

Welling swiveled when a cold blast accompanied Jan inside. "Good morning."

The entire team had gathered. No one else had had been able to sleep either. Everything hinged on Leblanc's success or failure in San Francisco. Yale and Raquel came awake with a start. They'd worked the graveyard shift.

"Did he call?" asked Raquel, straightening sharply.

Jan shook her head.

Taggart and Fallon, the MIT postgraduates, by virtue of their youth looked enviably well rested in spite of having slept the least. They kept themselves nervously occupied by fine tuning individual SuperCharlies. Trevor Smith fidgeted in front of his Intergraph Workstation. Knight typed his chronicle. Boycott sat on the floor and drank coffee.

"What's the latest?" asked Jan and only half listened to the responses. She freed the wool around her face and unbuttoned her oilskins. The pellet stove heated the shack to about 20ºC, Indian summer conditions in comparison to the rest of the ship.

"No change in freeze projections," said Smith.

"Ditto with the whales," said Welling.

Both men put up the pictures on their screens.

"And the fleet?" asked Jan

"They crossed into the Bering Sea."

San Francisco

US District Judge James Cimarron stood at the window of his chambers, which overlooked the front of the courthouse, watching a throng of reporters chase Leblanc, who was being wheeled across by a junior associate. He lost them when they passed behind the colonnade.

Cimarron could not help but shake his head again. He had just received a call from the US Department of Justice. The Attorney General himself was at the other end of the line. Entirely unexpected, he informed Cimarron of an opening in the Justice Department. Referring to Jan's injunction in passing, the Attorney General mentioned that the judge was number two on a short list of five.

A knock sounded on the door.

"Come in," he said and returned to his chair.

His clerk entered. "'Morning, Your Honor."

He placed courtesy copies of Leblanc's *ex parte* papers on the judge's desk. Cimarron sat down and donned his reading glasses. Leblanc had requested what Cimarron anticipated: an immediate, or an emergency, hearing on the motion.

The judge realized what he must do to rise to number one.

Bering Sea

Dawn filtered weakly through the snow blown by the tail end of a dying storm. The hammering wind stripped great gouts of spray off the towering ice-laden seas. The air was a translucent pink and yellow haze that hung thickly over the ocean. Sunlight reflected off the treacherous litter of icebergs, big and small, in rainbows of violet to red, sometimes bright enough to be blinding. The monotonous, all- pervasive shriek of air across the wild waters gradually acquired a new sound, barely perceptible at first, then mounted quickly into a metallic thunder.

Eleven ominous silhouettes materialized through the mottled spectrum.

The *Rising Sun* and her ten catchers roared by at breakneck speed, black and white ghosts bathed in a patchwork of low beams, long glares and stormy colors. The proximity of the impending harvest was evident everywhere. Aboard the catchers, the lookouts wiped their binoculars, the bridge crew checked their sonar and radar equipment and the gunners oiled their harpoons. On the factory ship, men and women cleaned the towering gray boiling pots that would steam the meat dropped into them from the open cutting deck above. Even the veteran hands were excited.

Once again, this great ship would reek with the thick wet stench of fatty blood. Huge jawbones and yards of hide would swing through the air from the derricks. The pipes, dials and ladders would disappear behind a mist of fatty fumes. Floor to ceiling, bulkhead to bulkhead, every surface would glisten with oil. Within an hour of the first whale being dragged up the slipway, the bloody, oily gravy would shoot out pungent odors, enabling the *Rising Sun* to be smelt from miles away across the open ocean before she was sighted.

A pair of middle-aged women laid out rows of thigh boots outside the cabins. Clean and shining now, they would become so bloody and drag in so much gore once the slaughter began, the alleyways would turn slippery like ice. Therefore, a pair of sailors slung ropes along the bulkhead from the crew's accommodations, wrapped them around the balustrade of the steel companionway down aft and on either side of the narrow avenue between the vats, all the way to the cutting deck. The coarse fibers of a rope would lend the grip that a smooth, bleeding handrail could not.

Blood would be carried into the toilets, and the commodes would be coated with it. The smells of the carnage combined with feces and urine made these closet-sized spaces, ventilated only by a weak fan, into stinking hellholes. Women had been hired to do nothing else but scrub every surface with caustic soda and hot water all day. By the end of the voyage they would have cleaned acres upon acres of floor, bulkhead and lavatories.

In his quarters, Shinjiro Yamamura buttoned his uniform with a flutter in his stomach. He had never killed a great blue whale. All night he'd dreamed of nothing else. There was a knock on the door.

"Enter."

The assistant operator from the radio room hurried in, wearing an expression that did not bode well. Yamamura snatched the message from his hand. He flicked his wrist and fingers, dismissing the lad and read the message. Yamamura's eyes reduced to slits. When he arrived on the bridge, he realized the contents of the message had already reached the officers and crew, but they made sure to look busy.

Yamamura strode to the chart table. "What's our position?"

The navigation officer pointed out they were southwest of the Commander Islands on the Russian side of the Bering Sea. He plotted their course with his finger, running it toward a broken black line marking the boundary between Russia and the United States. "We should be crossing into American waters in about four hours."

Yamamura looked at the message. In about three hours, a California court would hear arguments on whether all Japanese fishing vessels should be banned from American waters.

San Francisco

Judge Cimarron accepted Leblanc's plea for expediency and ordered a hearing after lunch so that the assistant attorney general, lawyers from the Office of the Legal Advisor and general counsel of the National Oceanic and Atmospheric Administration had adequate time to prepare a response. Cimarron's integrity precluded him from even considering the implied return favor the Attorney General expected.

When arguments began at one PM sharp, the Japanese pelagic fleet was an hour away from US territorial waters and another four from the whales. The *Stavenger* had only just begun to cross the Aleutian Islands into the Bering Sea, hopelessly behind by half a day.

Attu Island, The Aleutians

On May 11, 1943, sixteen thousand US troops stormed ashore

at Massacre Bay. Signs of that bloody eighteen-day battle, which killed 549 Americans and 2,350 Japanese, remained intact all across this westernmost Aleutian island. Old military buildings lay in the same state in which they were abandoned five decades ago. On a windswept hilltop stood a titanium starburst monument, marking the dead that the Japanese left behind. The collapsing remnants were undisturbed and unrepaired. Set against the harsh weather with few signs of habitation, the ruins stood like tombstones, carrying epitaphs of blackened bombardment and creating an impression of desolation. This bleak end of the earth, where the US fought one of its fiercest battles of World War II, was once again the nerve center for another kind of war against Japan.

Twenty-two Coast Guards, the only inhabitants of Attu today, maintained a Long Range Navigation—Loran—Station. They monitored the Bering Sea, where fishing armadas from the two countries scrapped every day for a piece of the three-billion-dollar gourmet catch. Legislation by successive administrations, Everett's White House included, had effectively sold off the world's most productive waters to Japan.

Kaiyou, which owned all the biggest shore-based processing plants in Alaska, was guaranteed 45 percent of the US quota, 85 percent of which was taken by giant, high-tech, multimillion-dollar Japanese-owned factory ships. Smaller Alaskan family boats, which ironically delivered their catch to the Japanese, found themselves scavenging a living. The Coast Guards saw the injustice and, realizing Washington had long ago turned their backs, used their authority to regulate the movement of Japanese vessels, assuring that Americans were not completely edged out of business in their own waters.

USCG Navigator Barry Zedler was one of half a dozen on duty this morning. Drawing the envy of others, who were hunched over their busy radar screens, Zedler stretched and yawned. "Coffee, anybody?"

A couple raised their hands without averting their eyes. Zedler scraped his chair back and stood up. His area of responsibility was north of the donut hole—the circle of international waters between American and Russian borders. Terrible weather, roving snow squalls and the fast descending freeze had emptied his sector of all boats. It got really hectic, at times nerve-racking, during spring and summer, when warm subtropical weather swept dense fog banks 3,000 feet high across the Bering Sea. The zero visibility made for dangerous fishing, since hundreds of vessels competed fiercely for the depleted stocks of some three hundred species of fish. Even south of the donut hole, where all the activity was now concentrated, the Bering Sea packed a lethal combination of twenty-foot waves, forty-knot winds and breakaway chunks of ice.

The Loran station had already received three distress signals this morning. The last one, an hour ago, was a scream for help on high-frequency radio from a boat going down somewhere in the 12,000-foot deep Aleutian Basin. Like most, the boat sailed in violation of the Commercial Fishing Industry Vessel Safety Act of 1988, which required all vessels to carry life rafts and an EPIRB—emergency position indicating radio beacon. Unable to obtain a pinpoint for rescue, the navigators helplessly listened to the cry for help die into another casualty statistic, which added up to about twenty-five to thirty every year.

Zedler placed the steaming mugs in front of the two men who'd requested coffee. "How's it going?"

On this Monday morning, the navigators' attention was also directed to identifying and warning all Japanese vessels. They'd received a memo from Commander Stosz at Kodiak Air Station about the first lady's injunction being litigated in San Francisco. The TV was on. They kept an eye on the scrolling news ticker for updates because cameras were prohibited inside federal courts.

The telephone rang at Zedler's station. He hurried over and picked it up. "Zedler."

It was the base commander from Adak Island, midway along the Aleutian chain. Amidst the suburban setting of a McDonald's, a shopping mall, a school and modern housing, servicemen and their families completed two-year tours on the US Naval Air Station, which had been activated for the first time since the Cold War. America's latest high-altitude, ultrasecret stealth spy plane, the Cormorant, which looked like something straight out of a science fiction novel, took off for daily recon missions following the rise of nationalism in Russia.

"One of my boys saw eleven ships," said the base commander, "one large and ten small boats, clipping north of the donut hole. They were flying Japanese colors."

"I picked them up too," said Zedler. "But they're in Russian waters."

"Heading east into ours."

"Nothing wrong with that until the court says they can't. Thanks for the info, anyway." Zedler glanced idly at the eleven blips.

One of the men shouted, "Zee!" Zedler looked over. "The first lady's in the basin. Everyone's going crazy out there, chasing after her to get a glimpse." He grabbed on to a strong dot. "That's her. She's ripping through."

Zedler suddenly went still. *Could it be?* He looked from the blip representing the *Stavenger* to the *Rising Sun* and her ten catchers. He placed a thumb over the first lady's position, a forefinger over the Japanese fleet and drew them together.

Shit. He grabbed the phone. Before he could dial, conversation ceased abruptly.

News was breaking on TV.

Unimak Pass, The Aleutians

Jan was back on the bridge. She'd felt a tremendous boost when Leblanc prevailed in his effort to get a court hearing. That was the easy part. Now, could he obtain an injunction? Everyone in the shack fidgeted nervously, their eyes constantly searching the news ticker at the bottom of the TV for breaking news. Jan couldn't sit still. Finally, the frustrating lack of live coverage got to her and she had to escape the oppressive tension in the scientific shack.

The *Stavenger* caught a break in the weather. After several days of the ocean dominating the ship, the role reversal translated into a steady course, monotonous vibration and a boiling wake. The bow plate divided the racing sea with a force that could be felt all the way up on the bridge. The wind was dead astern and the scudding mist too high to be worrisome. Far away to the southeast, the sun ascended behind thousands of feet of cloud as a dull white spot. Even though the air was crisp and clear, the temperature remained stuck around freezing.

The Aleutian Range rose majestically to the east, a slice of sheer, snow-covered cliffs marking the tip of the Alaska peninsula, widening inland like a wedge that opened the way to the broad and endless expanse of the forty-ninth state of the Union. To the west was Unalaska Island, a world dedicated to seafood. Kaiyou owned four processing plants here.

"The ecosystem cannot withstand that kind of harvest, day after day, year after year," she pointed outside to bait Vesprhein into an argument as a way of untying the knots in her stomach.

Dozens of Japanese refrigerator ships, called trampers, moved in and out of Dutch Harbor continuously. Boats big and small dropped anchor long enough to unload their frozen product and raced back out into the storm-tossed seas until it was too dark to see. But nightfall did not stop the factory ships, which were self-sufficient floating cities. Aboard them, scores of men and women worked rotating shifts around the clock. High-tech machines beheaded, sliced, ground and processed almost twenty-three tons of fish an hour.

"Blame it on American greed," said Vesprhein. "Shortage has raised fish prices, attracting everyone with a paddle and a net."

Jan nodded. "It's an industry that got too successful for its own good. Now politics of investment and boat ownership have spun it out of control."

"Hey," realized Vesprhein, "for once, we agree."

Jan caught his look. He expected a return compliment. She wasn't paying one. "Thank God it's not something I can boast about."

"Echo forward and port," crackled Trevor Smith's voice. A small, luminous pinpoint, like a candle flame struggling against a puff of air, flickered.

"Ship traffic is getting thicker," said Vesprhein. "We have to slow down."

Jan shook her head firmly. "No way."

Smith's voice came on again, "We have two detached echoes away to the starboard."

Vesprhein looked at Jan. "These crazy bastards sail blind."

"I'll take my chances," Jan said firmly.

He pointed to cat's paws of woolly wisps wandering in from the north. "That means fog."

"Do what you have to do," shrugged Jan. "But don't slow down."

"Lookouts to stations!"

At first, the mist came in transparent tendrils. The *Stavenger* blazed past ship after ship. Then the mist thickened into swirling clouds, reducing visibility for the brief stretches the ship was trapped in them. Before they knew it, it turned into a gray world of shadows. Distances became deceptive. Only the half dozen factory ships had radar. The rest, and there were at least twenty contacts on the *Stavenger*'s radar at any given instant, groped their way by floating fog buoys and sounding their foghorns and sirens incessantly. One sounded dangerously close. A break in the mist revealed a family boat fleeing in front of the *Stavenger*.

"Jesus," exclaimed Jan and grabbed a fistful of Vesprhein's sleeve.

"Port ten!" yelled Vesprhein, but not before he took a moment to look down. Jan self-consciously dropped her hand.

"Port ten," repeated Quvango.

For fifteen, thirty seconds the *Stavenger* held her course, arrowing straight toward the boat, tiny by comparison. The huge killer-factory ship slewed in a racing turn, but her towering bows seemed intent on devouring the little vessel. At the last moment, the *Stavenger* sheered by the family boat with less than thirty feet to spare. Instead of white faces of fear, they grinned and waved up at Jan. To them she was a hero, fighting to get the Japanese banned from American waters. Jan weakly returned the gesture.

Iron Lady mopped the sweat off his brow. Quvango eased his grip on the wheel. Vesprhein remained calm, almost callous. "Around here, size matters." He winked, leaned over and whispered to her, "But you know that."

"Processing ship, starboard," sang Smith.

Now the *Stavenger* looked miniscule.

The bridge speaker crackled with Raquel's voice. "The verdict's in."

San Francisco

Arguments lasted about an hour. Judge Cimarron took off his glasses, rubbed the bridge of his nose and almost absently recounted, "The plaintiffs contend that the commerce secretary violated a clear non-discretionary duty when he did not certify to the president that Japanese nationals were engaged in purchasing the protected sperm whales illegally killed by pirates on the high seas, who, the plaintiffs go on to allege, were indirectly financed by Japan. The defendants, on the other hand, argue that the Supreme Court ruling of 1985 upheld the discretionary powers of the commerce secretary, pursuant to which he may or may not make a certification to the president. Since he has thirty days to do so, this injunction is premature, if not entirely without ground."

Cimarron noticed Leblanc's shoulders sag.

"The plaintiffs seek a ban on all Japanese fishing within US territorial waters, marked by the 200-nautical-mile Extended Economic Zone. But the defendants insist that the Packwood-Magnusson sanction cannot be invoked without the commerce secretary first certifying that Japan diminished the effectiveness of the International Convention for the Regulation of Whaling."

Cimarron coughed. He folded his glasses and laid them down on the mess of papers before him. Turning over one of several hourglasses on his desk, he stared at the trickling sand, keenly aware of the penetrating stares from both attorneys. Cimarron was an old dog at this and did not let on which way he was going to lean. Hell, he wasn't even ready to hand down his ruling yet.

"Congress passed the Pelly and Packwood Magnusson Amendments to give teeth to fishing regulations, including whaling. When the Supreme Court defined the parameters of enforcement in 1985, it was only in that particular instance of Japan's violation with regard to sperm whaling. The ruling is public record and I will not go into it beyond the fact that the Japanese filed an objection with the IWC to insulate themselves from any enforcement of US amendments. Not so, in the present instance, which involves an illegal purchase of whale meat from pirates. So the circumstances are as distinct as apples and oranges. But should Japan's entire fishing industry be penalized for actions of a private enterprise?"

The government lawyers brightened. Leblanc leaned back in his chair, his defeat plain to see. But Cimarron could not ignore the facts and the law. He had to drop the hammer.

"I find that the commerce secretary has ignored the plain intent of Congress. He enjoys discretion—very limited discretion—but not authority. I also cannot ignore the history of the current administration not to certify violators," a veiled reference to Norway's minke hunt, "and I do not see that attitude changing toward Japan for its violation of the IWC mandate banning illegal whale meat trade, a mandate, I might remind the Executive Branch in Washington, that the United States has sworn to uphold. So, I not only feel an overwhelming obligation to act, but the law demands I do."

He enjoyed the best view of the lifting shoulders and brightening smiles on Leblanc's side of the table, a stark contrast to the sudden disappointment on the government side. Some reporters scrambled out of the visitors' chairs.

Cimarron snapped, "Order in the court!"

The reporters settled back and pin-drop silence returned.

"The court grants the plaintiff's motion for an injunction and directs the commerce secretary and the secretary of state to certify to the president that Japan is in violation of the IWC regulations. Effective immediately, this court directs all appropriate federal and state government agencies to prohibit all Japanese and Japanese-owned vessels from entering and or operating within the 200-nautical-mile Extended Economic Zone of US territorial waters for the purposes of fishing, including whaling.

"My written ruling will be available in a week." Judge Cimarron pounded the gavel. "Court is adjourned."

Cimarron stood up feeling smug, not for the damn good theater but for payback two decades in the making. The White House should have researched him as Leblanc shrewdly had, specifically seeking his court to file the motion. They would have discovered he was the godson of Charles Richey, the former US District Court judge, whose decision in favor of the conservationists in 1984 had been corruptly overturned by Ronald Reagan's cronies in the Supreme Court.

Ayakulik River, Kodiak Island, The Aleutians

Coast Guard Commander Ross Stosz hated this part of his job. He raised his flare gun while keeping an eye on the tick of his wristwatch. Around him, eighty-three boats revved their engines like race cars at the starting grid, but there was none of a race track's lane discipline. Skippers of these vessels jostled each other for position, while the sockeye salmon unsuspectingly jumped in and out of the water, looking to spawn upstream at the mouth, where the Ayakulik River emptied into the North Pacific.

The second hand of Stosz's watch passed the top of the hour. He pulled the trigger and a red flare shot into the sky. There wasn't even a pause after the report of the gun. Engines blasted to Full Ahead. Diesel smoke blanketed the air. Hulls scraped against each other explosively. The boats roared forward to circle seine nets around the sockeye salmon worth seven dollars apiece. The frenzied harvest would continue for four days, when Stosz would call a halt to allow the Alaska Fish and Game to assess the stock.

Unable to watch the frantic, free-for-all, no-holds-barred fishing, Stosz retreated into the wheelhouse. He was the commander of the US Coast Guard base in Kodiak, the second largest commercial fishing port located on the other side of the island, where in excess of three thousand vessels were registered.

The radio operator's voice crackled. "Zedler on the phone."

"Bad news, Zee?" Stosz asked Zedler immediately.

The Coast Guard in the Loran station at Attu had already advised Stosz about the fleet and his suspicions that they might be headed for the first lady's blue whales. Stosz had still not received a call from Jan, though he knew one was coming. The verdict was only a few minutes old.

"They are within shouting distance of our waters," said Zedler. The eleven blips inched toward the US-Russia border clearly demarcated on his radar screen.

"What do we have in the area?"

Zedler braced himself before he said, "Nothing."

The Coast Guards were already spread thin with fishery patrols. Six C-130 Hercules from Kodiak provided intelligence for four vessels patrolling three million square miles. Since darkness came early, foreign boats had begun to line up inside the southern edge of the donut hole with the US boundary, crowding those sections under siege from severe weather since they were the most likely to be ignored by the Coast Guard.

"The first lady won't give a damn about my lack of manpower," Stosz thought aloud. Zedler agreed by saying nothing. Stosz knew Jan only by reputation. "She'll have my ass if I don't find a way to enforce the judge's order."

Continental Shelf, Bering Sea

The smash of eleven plummeting bows came like a series of explosions. A leak from the radio room had informed all hands about the court ruling. Preparations for the slaughter slowed.

His eyes flat and angry, Yamamura stood alone in the sheltering of the forecastle. He gripped a davit with hands enclosed in two layers of gloves. A mandatory order required every member of the crew to be similarly attired. Under conditions as severe as these, even brief exposure caused frostbite. Yamamura had made it clear that medical attention would be denied to anyone who willfully disobeyed. Faced with a task as formidable as theirs, the services of every single crew person were indispensable. Fear was the simplest way to elicit compliance.

He stared impassively at the tremendous seas being delivered by the wicked weather. A catcher disappeared behind a gigantic trough. Engines were at maximum revolutions but the fleet moved at considerably less than half speed. The twelve-hour lead he'd enjoyed over the eco-warriors was down to nine and shrinking with every passing minute.

Yamamura sensed the talk on all levels of the factory ship subside to tense anticipation. It was his decision—his alone—to proceed or turn back. He felt the pressure of exercising the free hand Tokyo had given him to do what was necessary to harvest those blues.

He came out of his reverie. So engrossed had he been in thought, he noticed for the first time that he was shivering violently in the cold. Snow freckled his lashes and brows. Yamamura groped for the handle of the bridge gate and walked past his shuffling XO— executive officer—who did not dare ask Yamamura what he'd decided.

"Radar," he snapped into the intercom. "Are there any Coast Guard ships?"

"No, sir."

"Keep careful watch."

The navigation officer straightened sharply. "We are less than two miles from American waters."

Yamamura strode to the chart table, stared down for a second and then raised his head with a crisp order, "Maintain course and speed. We are going in."

Aleutian Basin, Bering Sea

Darkness crept across like a stealthy shadow. The wind came from the northwest in stinging blasts that carried a smell peculiar to the Arctic. A noisy flock of sea gulls winged hurriedly home, staying below the low clouds that pelted down sudden, short flurries of snow. With an enormous, creaming bow wave, the *Stavenger* dodged through the crowded waters.

Jan and her friends celebrated Leblanc's triumph but they sobered quickly. The freeze continued to advance. They needed to pick up speed. Jan returned to the bridge and continued her subtle seduction of Vesprhein, telling him that she knew he could be swift and safe. After all, he was a pirate who'd perfected the art of escape through tighter, more hostile traffic.

Vesprhein became a proper show-off, signaling frequently in three directions at once. Like a schoolyard bully, he fed off the angry foghorns and sirens protesting his close passing. Jan fed off the excitement too. The *Stavenger* darted through the close-knit traffic. Vesprhein commanded the ship with impeccable authority, brazenly intensifying his erratic zigzags at full-throttle. *Is it the freedom? Or the man?*

"Jan!" Raquel called from the scientific station, snapping Jan out of it. "You better come down here."

Jan entered the scientific station to a prickling silence that distanced the cacophony of ships outside.

"The Japanese fleet hasn't stopped," said Raquel.

"Are you sure?" asked Jan.

"Positive," replied Welling and he pointed to the eleven signatures picked up by the St. Matthew underwater sonar array just west of the whales.

"Raq, get me the Coast Guard."

"They can't do much," said Smith.

"Why not? It's their fucking job."

"They have government mandated weather criteria before they will deploy." Smith plucked off raw weather data from the National Weather Service's downlink station in Gillmore Creek, Alaska. "It's an icy mess up there. The numbers are way over the safety scale."

"How far are we from the blues?" asked Jan.

Welling clicked on his computer. "About eleven hours."

"And Yamamura is?"

"About three."

"To outrun us," ventured Boycott, "he has to quit hunting after six hours. In rough weather, that's not enough time to take all the blues."

"There was never the possibility he was going to harvest all the whales," said Knight. "Without interruption, it would take them at least two days to kill all 1,872 whales."

"If the forecast stands," said Raquel, rubbing her bloodshot eyes, "they should consider themselves fortunate if they kill a hundred blues, at best, in the dark."

"I'm not fucking ready to let him have even one!" snapped Jan. She could call Everett, but he would merely start the wheels of bureaucracy spinning. *Who else is out there who can stop a fleet?* She had no idea. Neither did the others.

Resignation cast a pall in the shack.

Continental Shelf

Shinjiro Yamamura hadn't left the bridge since his decision to ignore Judge Cimarron's order. He paced port to starboard, front to back, peering outside into the driving wind. The air was colder than the sea. Vitrified water hung like amorphous black glass. The wind slammed and retreated in gusts of thirty knots, creating a cruel symphony of force with the heavy-running swells that smashed across the deck.

Yamamura sensed fear and tension among the officers and crew. On the other hand, it heightened alertness. From the navigation officer to the lookouts, everyone kept a wary, jumpy eye.

"See anything?" Yamamura snapped into the intercom.

The eleven ships looked like cotton balls bouncing forward at three knots. Spread out in an uneven arc, the snow-covered silhouettes picked their way through an endless litter of ice so heavily laden upon the sea, the towering waves became sluggish, pendulous cliffs. Spray froze on the underside of rails in a myriad of serrated patterns. Shafts from the massive floodlights danced into the deepening blackness. The beams illuminated an incongruously still landscape to the north, where the Bering Sea was frozen solid. Roaring, corkscrewing gusts of wind hurled out of there, driving little bullets of ice. Starboard, a tumultuous sea crumbled house-sized bergs into fist-sized chunks in the blink of an eye. The falling snow would cement these into a lid of ice as the freeze descended south.

Radar and sonar reported no contacts. Eleven lookouts shivered atop the sugar candy masts. Men on the icy decks in wide-legged stances battled to find purchase. Stilettos of ice filled their lungs, making breathing painful. Peering through night vision goggles, they saw nothing either.

The navigation officer shook his head with a nonplused expression. "They should be here, sir."

Yamamura returned to the bridgewing. They were only seven hours ahead of the *Stavenger*. He'd instructed the gunners on the ten catchers to double the explosives in their harpoons. With no time to let the whales sound and run, he ordered those that did not die at once be cut loose. He intended to continue the slaughter until the first lady showed up at the scene. *Why not?* The bitch would not abandon the surviving blues to chase him. *Where are those damn beasts?*

The catcher farthest ahead, *7,* rose from the hollows of a wild trough. The lookout straightened, his shout preceding an identical report from the *Rising Sun*'s sonar operator by less than an instant.

"Whales!"

BOOK FOUR

Whale Steak with Green Peas

One 2 lb joint of whale meat
4 dl red wine
2 dl water
15 juniper berries
2 dessert spoons of black currant
cordial, cream, cornflower.

Brown the joint on all sides in a stewpan, add the red wine, water and mashed juniper berries. Simmer under lid for about 30 minutes. Place a weight on the lid. Remove the meat and wrap it in aluminum foil while finishing making the gravy.

Gravy:

Add the black currant cordial to the juices in the pan. Add cream to taste and thicken with cornflower. Cut the meat into thin slices and serve with potatoes, green peas, sprouts and mountain cranberries.

"Minke Whaling in the North East Atlantic"
Living off the Sea

Galena, Alaska

"Slim, ready to play the fox?" inquired Bubba.

"Roj."

"Stay under Mach One," requested a new metallic voice.

Slim laughed. "I remember the ROE, Sandy." Rules of Engagement.

"I know you do, Slim, but you always seem to forget them," said Sandy, who rode along as an observer in Bubba's back seat.

"It will illustrate how fast everything happens up here."

"Enough chatter," snapped Bubba. "Maneuvers begin as soon as you roll out. I'll give you ten seconds and then come after you."

"Roj." Reaching the entry point marked on the sectional map

in front of him, Slim started a hard left. Afterburners blazing, he screamed his single seat F-15 out of there.

"One Mississippi, two Mississippi, three Mississippi. Here we go!" Bubba rolled inverted and pulled on the stick. His F-15E made a tight turn and blasted off in pursuit.

"Shiit!" exclaimed Sandy. "You told him ten seconds." The G-forces slammed Sandy into his seat.

When Bubba leveled off, the tightly cinched straps and leg restraints eased the pull. He looked out through the canopy. They were at thirty thousand feet and the dense clouds righted themselves beneath, while the stars returned to their rightful place above.

"Just following the dictum of unpredictability," Bubba chuckled behind the oxygen mask and visor of his fiberglass-composite helmet.

The two F-15s on this night run belonged to the 21st Tactical Fighter Wing out of Galena Air Force Base. As guardians of the forwardmost point of US air defense, the Arctic Warriors of the Alaska Air Command were the tripwire to the lower forty-eight states. Low population and vast expanses of uninhabited terrain allowed extensive practice runs to train the pilots for two roles: air sovereignty and air superiority. Recent intelligence showed serious cracks in Moscow's command and control over strategic bombers stationed in the eastern republics, where the nationalists enjoyed their strongest support. The threat of a rogue pilot making a hostile run into US air space became increasingly real.

Lieutenant Commander "Bubba" MacVicar was the acerbic instructor, "Slim" Handler his cocky student.

"Heads up display." Bubba oriented himself behind the numbers and symbols filling glass plates that reflected the instrument panel.

Tonight, the exercise was a dogfight, one on one.

Slim dropped to eighteen thousand feet, disappearing into the thick clouds. Bubba screamed in after him. The two jets crossed the coast on to the open Bering Sea. Lightning flashes jumped at them sporadically. Slim picked up Bubba when the instructor's radar emissions got close. Now each had icons of the other.

At that moment, the controller's voice interrupted, "Warrior One, Warrior One?"

Bubba clicked on his radio. "Loud and clear, ATC." Air Traffic Controller.

"Your priorities have changed."

"Repeat that ATC."

"Your priorities have changed." ATC then explained the amended ROE. "Advise Warrior Two."

"Roj." Bubba raised Slim on the radio. "Slim, the dogfight is off." He relayed the new priorities.

To impress his instructor, Slim timed and executed his 3G split-S descent flawlessly.

"Nice," conceded Bubba, then one-upped his student with even less stick, rudder and throttle.

Both pilots leveled off two hundred feet above the frozen Bering Sea. The night was pitch black. Their helmets projected infrared imagery on their visor screens. Snow squalls furiously punched at them but the F-15s eluded the turbulence. The airspeed indicator steadied at five hundred knots. Side by side, they thundered across.

Sonic blasts opened the ice with cracks that sprouted fast growing branches. Fissures noisily proliferated in the wake of the deafening jets, whose searing tailstreams condensed the air into twin corkscrews of fluttering white haze. The velocity vector cued them to pull up just enough to clear a line of bergs. The hundreds of hours of practice and pre-briefing showed in the way they crisply rolled and leveled their wings.

"Surface contacts," said Slim.

"I see them," confirmed Bubba, reading his radar.

Continental Shelf

The pregnant cow's internal clock was in disarray. She had never given birth in the Arctic. From the frequency of her contractions she was mere moments away. Her other calves had been born in the warmth of the low latitudes on her way to the Southern Ocean, where the young found plenty of krill to supplement their mothers' milk. Krill was a Norwegian word that translated simply to whale food. These small, ten-legged, shrimplike crustaceans inhabited the Southern Seas in groups called rafts.

The calves had to grow strong quickly and fatten their coats of blubber. In adults, it became almost a foot thick. Blue whales did not eat again until they returned to the Antarctic. Through minimal metabolism, blubber provided all the nourishment during their long, lean months.

Every whale in this horseshoe had been fasting for at least six months in anticipation of the migration south to Cetacean Bay. They had received calls of enormous food blooms this year from their elders, who stayed all year round in the Antarctic. This was a remarkable, evolutionary mechanism to prolong life among old whales. Once past their sexual prime, they were of little use to the tribe, so they did not waste energy on migration, contributing instead by scouting krill, which gathered in hundreds of millions to mate at this time of year. Using their very low frequency sound, designed to carry clear across to the other side of the planet, they guided their kin toward the best feeding grounds.

Another painful contraction gripped the cow's eighty-foot long body. The sub-zero temperatures did not allow her to dilate fully. A sharp movement rocked her belly and the contractions came at closer intervals. Two females swam over to nurse her through labor. The pregnant cow thrashed and rolled, slipping beneath the water to push, and resurfaced with tremendous blows to catch her breath. She thrashed and rolled, shrieking in phonation beyond the range of human hearing. She thrashed and rolled, drawing closest to approaching danger when she ventured toward the mouth of the horseshoe. She thrashed and rolled.

A sitting target.

"Whales!"

❄

The lookout in 7's crow's nest became the first human ever to see a blue whale in labor. All the natal details about these rare mammals were based upon studies of fetuses laid out on cutting decks of whaling vessels.

7's floodlights put the three blues in full blazed view.

The other catchers, trailing a mile behind 7, battled the choppy seas and staggered over the horizon. The crisscrossing beams of the advancing ships exposed clumps of startled blows everywhere in the glassy darkness. The crew, to a man, found themselves involuntarily going still. Their eyes went wide. Exclamations of disbelief gasped out. Gunners, particularly, started down the catwalks on a determined run and slowed to a stumbling, astounded halt. A new kind of chill — excitement — surpassed the bitter cold momentarily. How puny their harpoons seemed. After a lifetime of hunting diminutive minkes, none of them were prepared for the extraordinary sight presented by one thousand eight hundred and seventy-two closely packed blue whales, *each* weighing more than forty elephants and occupying as much space as sixteen hundred men. Their boat barely measured half the length of the beast.

Hearing approaching engines, the whales disappeared below the surface. Bubbles filled the sonar screens with a green splatter, indicating they also began to exhale below the water. Keel mounted speakers on the catchers came alive with a nonstop blast at 3000 Hz.

Tremendous blows! A flurry of flukes!

Nobody knew why, but whales reacted adversely to that frequency. The leviathans, who until then had stayed separated by tribe, ran helter-skelter and created a scene of spectacular congestion. Taking quick breaths, they dived, but panted right back to the surface. Their own sonic blasts added to the panic, overlapping, confusing and blinding them. The directionless stampede turned the water white with agitation.

"Nets!"

Yamamura's voice barked out of every loudspeaker of the fleet.

The *Rising Sun*'s towering gunnels loomed into view. The distinctive all-deck factory ship stood high above the sea, her bridge lights glinting like the eyes of some sea monster.

Yamamura dropped his binoculars. Magnification was unnecessary and only restricted his field of vision. He felt a quaking tremor of the deckplates under his feet, caused by a crush of men and women taking turns at the portholes. Like him, other veterans who tried to remain unimpressed, weren't able to keep up the charade. Not a soul remained untouched. He overheard an off-hand comment, "That's a lot of work."

Yamamura looked at his XO. "All stop."

The *Rising Sun* slowed to a halt behind the catchers, which took positions across the open end of the icebound, horseshoe shaped sanctuary. With a rending scrawl of winches that overwhelmed the lonely howl of the wind across the frigid Arctic, miles of driftnet splashed and unspooled into the water.

First on the scene and the first to drop nets, 7 was also the first into the horseshoe, now half a mile ahead of the rest of the catchers. Drawn by her size, the captain had locked on to the cow, unaware she was so big because she was pregnant. 7 pulled within two hundred yards.

The catcher jumped over a beam sea, exposing the deadly meshwork of driftnet dragging alongside to snare the cow if she tried to dart past the hunters. The cow panted back to the surface for air, emerging dead center into 7's cross hairs.

The catcher closed to within a hundred yards.

The whale would not be able to submerge. In about a minute, calculated the gunner, she'd be within range. Yamamura had ordered that all harpoons be fired from forty yards to ensure death with one shot. The gunner flicked his eyes toward the digital distance display atop his barrel. Numbers rolled.

98.96.94.92 …

Ice and water washed across the gun platform as he aimed for her backbone. The double penthrite charge had been set to explode after sixteen inches of penetration. The shock, more than injury, would kill her instantly. Nevertheless, a marksman stood on deck with a high caliber rifle to pump the cow with bullets if she did not die at once.

82.80.78 …

The gunner wrapped his finger around the trigger.

72.70.68.66 …

❄

At that moment, a stern American voice came over every radio of the pelagic fleet, "This is Lieutenant Commander Robert MacVicar, United States Air Force. Do you read?"

Tuned to the maritime frequency that ships were required to keep open at all times, the operator on the *Rising Sun* almost fell out of his chair. He grabbed the intercom and called the bridge, "Captain! The American Air Force is on the radio."

Yamamura straightened with a snap. "On bridge speaker only."

The American's voice crackled, repeating his admonition, "This is Lieutenant Commander Robert MacVicar, United States Air Force. You are in American waters in violation of a court order."

The intercom lit up with calls from the catcher captains.

"Proceed with the hunt," Yamamura said to the XO, who blinked, astonished, but upon meeting the fleet captain's hostile glare, passed on the order hesitantly.

Yamamura called down to Radar. "Do you see anything?"

"No, Cap—" He broke off and corrected himself with a stammer,

"T-two contacts. Airborne. East of us."

Yamamura became acutely conscious of the stillness, of the squeak of his shoes' rubber soles on the metal floor, which just moments ago, had rattled with a thunder of eager feet. He realized the American presence had leaked below. The ramp stopped lowering and the half open slipway left the stern of the factory ship seemingly gaping in surprise. Along the cutting deck, where flensers gathered in oilskins and rubber thigh boots, the bloodlust turned to anxiety.

Officers on the bridge shuffled nervously. Yamamura glanced out the window. An army of ice spicules, carried by a furious gust, invaded the sea in front of him, obliterating his line of sight.

"Cease operating in these waters or face hostile action," sounded the pilot's voice after a lengthy pause.

Yamamura spotted the wing lights of the two fighter-bombers.

❋

60.58.56 ...

"Steady as she goes!" yelled 7's gunner.

52.50.48 ...

Excitement wriggled like a worm in his guts. The hydraulics of the gun mount smoothed the rise and plunge of the bow.

42.40 ...

7's gunner began to squeeze the trigger when the F-15s materialized in the upper two quadrants of his cross hairs. The aircraft advanced in a flash. The gunner fell flat on his back with a startled cry. His hand slipped. His finger squeezed the trigger.

The harpoon sizzled toward the pregnant cow.

Water out of her blowhole sputtered, indicating the cow was sounding mid-breath. Instead of flying wide, her premature dive and the gunner's hasty shot combined to correct the harpoon's trajectory toward her. She was not submerging fast enough. The harpoon aimed relentlessly for the trunk leading up to her flukes. And then her frame bucked with an unexpected contraction as the tiny dorsal fin of her calf struggled outside. She flailed her tail sharply into the water.

The harpoon passed through the cutout between her leaf-like flukes.

Harmlessly striking the water, it detonated as it was designed to if the penthrite wasn't triggered by penetration into whale flesh within five seconds of being fired. The explosion sent the whales scattering north. They crowded against the jagged shore of ice. The cow ran into the net that 7 dragged alongside. She swung back and forth, and the high-tensile mesh wrapped around her completely, entangling and trapping her emerging calf.

❄

In the lead F-15, Bubba twisted his neck to look out of the canopy as they shot by. "Shit."

"He missed," reported Slim on the radio, a moment later.

"Shallow angle delivery," ordered Bubba, relieved.

"What if I miss and hit the fucker?" asked Slim.

"Our orders are to intimidate only," replied Bubba sternly. "Do you understand?"

"Oh, bah."

"Do you understand?" repeated Bubba, this time packing iron in his voice.

"Yes, sir," came the prompt and respectful reply.

❄

Yamamura stared at his immobile catchers. "The hunt proceeds!"

His outburst fell on deaf ears because the F-15s broke formation, rolling to either side of the factory ship. The jets dropped to the level of the windows and unloaded the missiles hanging on the side closest to the ship. Tornadoes of smoke spinning in their wake, the Unis slammed into the Bering Sea.

Water erupted and drenched the decks. Yamamura cringed, tripping into the arms of his helmsman.

"*Rising Sun*," MacVicar's voice returned on the speaker, "that was your final warning. Leave American waters or face direct action."

The F-15s circled in opposite directions and started back toward the big ship, flanking her with the other pair of Unis.

"Reverse full!" barked Yamamura suddenly, again taking his XO by surprise, who repeated the order to the engine room and all the catchers.

The ten skippers gladly cut loose their nets.

By the time the USAF jets did their third flyby, the pelagic fleet was in full retreat.

Kodiak

Coast Guard Commander Stosz sat down in relief when Galena Air Force Base relayed Bubba's terse message, "Mission accomplished."

Stosz had been at wits' end a few hours ago when he received the first of several calls from Jan. He prepared himself for the worst when he informed her of his inability to enforce Judge Cimarron's order due to a lack of manpower. Contrary to stories of her quick temper, Jan was anything but nasty. They methodically worked down a list of authorities who could stop the Japanese fleet. Alaska Fish and Game was short-handed too. There was momentary hope when they discovered a National Marine Fisheries Service icebreaker in the Bering Strait, but the freeze was so thick, it would take twice as long as the *Stavenger* to get there. Alaska Whaling Commission patrol boats were too small to survive the inclement seas. The Naval Air Station at Adak, midway along the Aleutians, which operated the Cormorant spy planes that had spotted the fleet for the Coast Guard, and Shemya Air Force Base, on the western tip of the chain, which flew RC-135 jets on top secret electronic and photographic missions over Russia, could not divert any aircraft for reasons of national security. But the Alaska Air Command, upon hearing the first lady's voice, offered to redirect a training mission underway to the coordinates, even to conduct a bombing run.

"Commander Stosz!" hollered a Coast Guard, clutching the phone to his chest. "The first lady."

Stosz picked up the extension.

Jan spoke before he could. "Thank you, Commander. Congratulate the pilots."

"I will, Ma'am." *Now for the bad news.* The seriousness of his tone alerted Jan because he heard the cheers behind the first lady subside. "The catchers cut loose driftnets. One whale seemed to be entangled. There may be others."

❉

If Stosz sobered the elation, Welling killed it. He pointed to a clutter of blips south of the Bering Strait. "Orcas."

Killer whales.

The *Stavenger* was passing through the international donut hole. In direct contrast to the cheers accompanying her across American waters, nothing but hostility greeted the first lady along this leg of the voyage. Angry foghorns shrieked at her. Empty bottles and garbage hurled at the speeding killer-factory ship.

"Will they get there before we do?" asked Jan.

"It's going to be close," replied Welling.

❉

Streamlined in a hydrodynamic body covered with skin as smooth as rubber, colored jet black on top to blend with the darkness of the deep ocean and counter-shadowed with white below to camouflage them against the light skies, orcas were the unchallenged kings of the oceanic food chain. Nicknamed "wolves of the sea," they hunted with the same stealth, organization and intelligence. Eighteen made up this tightly knit pod, which picked up the blue whales' terrified cries.

Led by a ten-ton veteran bull thirty-three feet long, they clocked thirty knots beneath the ice, expertly finding soft spots in the freeze to surface and breathe. Intermittently, they "spy-hopped," or shot straight out of the water, to visually survey for the next break. Propelled by their broad tail flukes, they steered using their paddle-shaped pectoral fins, which they used to signal one another when they stalked in silence.

Echolocation, the process by which orcas emitted sound to locate prey, was unnecessary. By incessantly screaming their distress, the blues gave away their size, number, distance and precise position. These killer whales had always confined themselves to the labyrinth of waterways between the islands of Canada's Northwest Territories. Increased beluga whale quotas, overfishing and an unusually thick polar ice cap had driven this pod west. They had come within hearing distance of the blues at precisely the same time as the arrival of the pelagic fleet. Subsisting on body fat for almost two weeks, the orcas advanced gluttonously, emboldened by the diminishing volume of a sound they'd come to fear.

Ships.

❄

The *Stavenger* exited the north border of the international donut hole with an abrupt curtsy to the waves. The wind freshened to twenty-six knots, stayed fine on the starboard, lifting the sea and pushing down the mercury. The tripods, yardarms, masts, cables, stays, halyards, turrets and other lofty surfaces held the snow longer and longer, until they became permanently caked in white. The continuous spray from the sea froze on top. Soon, the forepeak was buried under four feet of ice. Looking aft from the whaleback, the *Stavenger* could be easily mistaken for an iceberg. Larger surfaces, save the piping hot funnel, stopped melting off the snow, which moved indoors, dragged underfoot by the crew stamping in off the deck. It enveloped everything with an inescapable, miserable, cold wetness.

On her way down to the shack, Jan passed half a dozen unhappy pirates, working outside with pick axes, attacking the ice with a private fury. They glared at her from behind protective goggles. She'd ordered the cleanup after Vesprhein told her it was slowing them down. The snow increased the ship's resistance by almost twenty thousand pounds. She felt for them. The frigid wind thrust the breath back down her throat just inhaling normally.

"Icebergs," Trevor Smith informed Jan, when she walked in.

"You better tell the bridge."

"I can't make out anything from up here," replied Vesprhein.

Jan nodded to Smith. When she'd been up on the bridge, Iron Lady and Vesprhein constantly scrubbed the condensation off the glass to try to see ahead. The cylinders of illumination jutting forth from their floodlights could not separate the mist from the snow. Everything appeared white—uniform, depthless, blinding.

"I'll guide you through them," offered Smith.

"We'd be safer coming to a stop and letting them pass," cautioned Vesprhein.

"No," said Jan firmly.

"Starboard your helm!" snapped Smith, ending any debate.

"Starboard your helm!" roared Vesprhein's voice over the com without questioning the oceanographer.

The ship heeled right. Jan flew into the wall of the shack. The giant scrape of ice on the hull was followed by the sound of the berg exploding into fragments.

"All clear ahead," indicated Trevor Smith.

"How much further?" asked Jan.

"Less than a hundred miles," answered Yale. "Two hours."

"The killer whales?" asked Raquel.

"An hour," said Welling, then frowned. "But look. They've stopped."

"They probably heard us," said Jan.

"That's not it," said Trevor Smith, drawing attention to his Intergraph Workstation. "There is no break in the ice from their current position all the way to the blues."

"Thank you, God," reacted Jan with clenched fists.

But good news came with bad.

Welling isolated the entangled cow with a dedicated inset on his screen. The whale showed comparatively little movement.

"She's dying," Jan pronounced.

Washington DC

The National Security Advisor arrived in his office, as he always did, at seven AM. He filled his mug with steaming coffee and sat down, his eyes automatically going to the one-page intelligence report from the day before, placed on his desk by the special assistant to the president on national security affairs, who walked in precisely fifteen minutes later.

"Good morning," the men greeted each other.

Following the San Francisco District Court ruling yesterday, the White House had been on a defensive, damage control mode, while Keith Leeds did victory laps on the airwaves. Jan had undermined the Executive in a way that Congress never could have.

The special assistant sat down. He was the NSA's mole in the White House. "I just received word out of our listening station in Alaska that pilots from Galena Air Force Base were on the open frequency, warning off a Japanese vessel called the *Rising Sun*." Eavesdropping was a routine function of the National Security Agency, sentinels of domestic intelligence. He referred to his legal pad. "The request came from Commander Stosz. He was contacted by the first lady."

"The Japanese were probably getting too close to her precious whales," dismissed the NSA.

"Don't you think it's curious that the *Rising Sun* belongs to Kaiyou?"

The NSA arched his eyebrows in agreement.

The special assistant continued, "Why would they even be there after being exposed at the IWC meeting?"

"Request NPIC for pictures from the region."

❄

Across the banks of the Anacostia River, at the National Photographic Interpretation Center, on First and M Streets, Bruce Wilhelmson parked his car. He was the wiry, bespectacled threat analyst who had been watching over the first lady when she boarded the *Stavenger* and sank the *Kagoshima* prior to the IWC meeting. Thanks to his seniority, he had again drawn Jan's reconnaissance, classified EYES ONLY by Robert Random, director of the National Reconnaissance Office.

The special assistant's request did not reach his desk. He would never have known about it had he not been involved with Bianca Stevens, the assistant administrator.

"Didn't Random tell you nobody was privy to intelligence about the first lady and the drive?" asked Wilhelmson.

Within hours of the race for the blues, the couple had noticed there were no written memos. Also, the pelagic fleet seemed to know the "classified" whaling coordinates. They'd put an easy two and two together to surmise some sort of hush-hush White House deal with the Japanese.

"Leeds will give us bundles of money for what we know," chuckled Wilhelmson. The exclusion of the NSA, who supported Everett's Democratic rival, Keith Leeds, from the loop, implied ramifications that went beyond security to the nail-biting presidential race.

Bianca smiled crookedly. "That's not a bad idea."

Her tone caused Wilhelmson to glance toward her sharply. "I was just kidding."

He realized she was not when she said, "We can make a down payment on a house and get married. It's not like we're selling national secrets to a foreign government. This is obviously a game with taxpayers' money that Everett is playing to be reelected."

Wilhelmson had never done anything dishonest in his life. "Let's talk about it at home."

"Okay." From the tone of her voice, he knew she'd made up her mind.

Continental Shelf

On the bridge, Vesprhein took in the millions of dollars of meat lolling in front of him.

"All stop," he said absently, glancing over at the FishEye. He could not recall ever having seen the screen so cluttered.

"Holy crap," muttered Iron Lady, looking up from the blips to the whales.

Quvango whistled for perhaps the fifth time in as many minutes. Napoli stepped up beside him to the screen. Pirates mobbed the iced-over rails. Prophet, Owen and Larkin mingled with them. While everyone else broke down with awe, Vesprhein circled the bridge, studying the idiosyncrasies of these whales. *Just in case.*

To avoid breathing in water, the blues waited for a wave to attain its steepest angle, then plunged horizontally through it, grabbing air simultaneously. They timed their landing into its trough, where they exhaled and inhaled again quickly with such power, the noise superseded the elements.

Vesprhein lit a cigarette. "Quite a fucking sight, huh?"

He stood alongside Patrick Knight, whose fingers flew across the keyboard of his laptop. The pirate captain skimmed the reporter's screen. Letters popped and stretched into words that became quick sentences translating the indelible images to words. Knight wrote about the worsening weather, rising winds, climbing seas and plumes of blows, all combining to reduce visibility to a moist, snow-filled blur. His fingers suddenly stopped in midair.

The *Stavenger*'s lights found the entangled cow, thrashing feebly.

Jan and Raquel, wearing a belt full of assorted cutters, and Boycott, striking a familiar silhouette with the camera, backed off the slipway. In spite of their thermal scuba gear, they felt a jolt of cold when they hit the water. Catching their breath, they submerged.

Jan swam ahead of Raquel. She found the throw of their headlamps was shallow, almost pitifully so, amidst the mountains of hide fluidly moving all around them. Swimming with whales could be frightening. They were about six thousand times more powerful. Instead, it always turned out to be an exhilarating experience because whales never asserted their enormous advantage. Like disciplined railway trains in a crowded station, their massive bodies, each as long as a Boeing 737, zigzagged with poetic grace without colliding.

"He is never chased," Melville wrote of the blue whale, "he would run away with rope walks of line." Hence the leviathan's scientific name, Balaenoptera musculus, or the muscular winged whale. Even Raquel's research in the Indian Ocean had brought her no nearer than a couple of miles, which was as close as anybody got to a live blue. A 1928 black and white snapshot of a cow laid out on the factory ship had been the only evidence capturing the whale's entirety at close quarters until last year, when a dead blue mysteriously beached along the Northern California Coast.

Jan came upon the cow, followed by Raquel and Boycott. They enjoyed a moment, no more, of delightful surprise seeing the tiny tail flukes of the emerging calf. *A pregnant cow.* Then the hopelessness of her predicament hit them.

The skin of a whale was actually tender enough to be rubbed off with a finger, so the harsh strands of the driftnet imprinted her body with a mosaic of blood. Around her blow hole it was two layers thick. Her mouth was wrapped shut, allowing only a tenth, probably less, of her loosely hinged lower jaw to open. She hadn't breathed properly for hours. Most of one fluke was torn off. She rolled a sad, agonized eye toward the two women, whose arrival by her side came just as a contraction shuddered through her body.

Jan energized into action, directing Raquel to cut around the protruding tail of the newborn while she swam up on top of the cow and tackled the strands over the blowhole. Having freed dolphins and California grays in the past, she knew that this was slow work, but now they raced the clock. A blue whale's labor and delivery lasted about twelve hours. At this point the cow should have been wriggling out the calf's head.

Ten minutes later, Jan freed the blow hole and braced herself for the whale to grab a huge breath of air. Nothing happened. Jan swam around to the front. The cow's eyes were closed. *Oh, Jesus, she's lost consciousness.*

Jan hurried underneath and placed her ear against the blubber. A blue whale's heart weighed two tons and pumped in excess of sixty gallons with every beat through valves a foot across. Instead of the usually powerful, whooshing, twenty heartbeats per minute, Jan heard an irregular, barely audible throb.

She dashed to Raquel and signaled furiously to stop cutting and thumbed toward the surface. They swam up. Boycott remained with the cow, filming.

"She's gone into a coma," Jan announced breathlessly, when they broke out of the water. "But the flotation buoys attached to the driftnet will keep her floating."

"What about the baby?" asked Raquel.

"We have a choice. Take a chance the cow may regain consciousness or perform a caesarian now and save the calf."

"How?" asked Raquel. "The water is too rough to operate."

"We'll pull the mother onto the cutting deck."

"She'll suffocate."

Jan shook her head. "Probably won't ever regain consciousness."

They took their dilemma to the scientific shack, where Boycott, joining them soon afterwards, played back videotape of the other whales' behavior. Raquel identified their bleating as grief. Even they sensed the cow was dying and circled like mourners. The two nurses nudged the unborn calf, who could not emerge without thrusts from the mother. In the end, Jan and her friends concluded that the blue population could not afford the loss of two whales. Baleens had the slowest reproductive rate. Females took years to regain sexual maturity between births.

"Let's do it," Jan declared.

"Lash her by the tail," said Vesprhein into the mouthpiece of the headset radio Jan gave him. Nobody was better qualified to expedite the eco-warriors' intentions.

Jan watched Knight and Raquel, at the listening end of his instructions, tow a steel line from one of the *Stavenger*'s winches toward the pregnant cow. She stood in a doorway leading to the slaughter deck, perusing a book on whale anatomy with the Colombian flenser. He came highly recommended by Vesprhein as one who'd cut more whales than any other man aboard. She picked his brain about critical details of the womb of cows he'd slaughtered. Jan hadn't practiced veterinary medicine for over ten years. Her surgical skills were rusty at best and she'd never operated on a whale. But then, she didn't know anyone who had.

The wind continued to douse the ship with spray, which froze on top of the ice already there.

"Winch her in!" she heard Vesprhein on her headset.

The cranes screeched with the loud metallic scrawl of reversing gears. The line tightened with an earsplitting groan. The loop of steel around the cow's trunk leading up to the tail section tightened like a tourniquet, eating into the blubber. For a few moments it seemed as if it would cut right through. Finally, cartilage stopped the metal. The cow dragged toward the ship. The nurses leapt out and reached for the unborn calf. They crashed their tails upon the water with enormous thuds, almost taking out Knight and Raquel.

"Careful as you haul her in!" shouted Jan. "Don't bump the

baby!"

The cow remained unconscious all the way on to the cutting deck. Looking from her book to the whale, Jan raced up her tail with a spray can and began to mark the abdomen for the caesarian procedure.

"I can't hear her heart!" Raquel screamed.

The cow was dead.

"Begin the incision," Jan hollered urgently to the Colombian flenser. "Don't go more than an inch deep."

He fired up his chainsaw and touched the blade to the cow's skin. Gobs of flesh and blood erupted in an arc. He worked from bottom up.

Jan looked up at Vesprhein. He had joined the rest of the crew on the upper gangway to watch this incredible surgery. "I need another flenser."

Vesprhein sent down the Norwegian scrimshaw artist. He worked from the top down. Jan repeatedly looked at her watch, heedless of the blood drenching her. Raquel bit her nails. Boycott danced around with his camera. Knight brought his laptop down and transcribed the process. His fingers tapped the keys with the same urgency that strangled everyone else. Even the scientists were out of their shack. Fifteen minutes later, hooks peeled back the inch-thick blubber on either side of the twenty-foot-long incision.

"Now take the incision to the womb," gasped Jan, realizing she'd been holding her breath.

The Colombian flenser grabbed a swig of rum, returned to the bottom and started the chainsaw whirring again. The incision had to be precise since the space between the baby and the mother was about three inches. The operation slowed. Yet speed was of the essence.

Twice, the zipping blade came dangerously close to the infant's skull.

Then it was over.

The cow's womb lay open, exposing the calf, a female. Perfectly formed, her fins were folded flat against her sleek flank. Her mouth was wedged shut and her eyes were closed. The glistening blood and amniotic fluids immersing her showed hints of coagulation. A few more minutes, Jan realized, and it might have been too late.

The twenty-five-foot calf—as big as a minke whale—didn't have a breath in her body. Oxygen and nutrient transfer from cow to calf occurred through blood. Air never entered. This way, she escaped the tremendous changes in pressure when her mother dived and surfaced. The calf twitched. Her lids became unstuck and her eyes opened to take in her first sight.

Jan.

The first lady felt her heart skip, for an instant feeling as if she'd made an intangible connection with the whale. She felt a flood of emotion that was pure joy. The calf twitched again, more vigorously, the shudder of life extending all the way to the extremities of the flukes of her tail.

"We have to get her into the water," said Jan, breaking everyone out of their trance. "Fast!"

The twitches became convulsions. The eco-warriors struggled to wrap a pair of harnesses around the calf. She opened and closed her mouth with inaudible cries.

"Take her away," yelled Jan to the crane operator.

The winches scrawled again. The eco-warriors, scientists and pirates watched the calf lift toward the sea. Boycott ran off the slipway, an umbilical cord trailing from his camera to feed images live to the monitors in the scientific shack, where everyone hurriedly gathered.

The harness struck the water.

Boycott ducked beneath the surface, rolling tape. The calf wriggled free, then struggled violently, unable to climb to the surface. A collective gasp of dismay erupted.

"Of course," Jan slapped her forehead, "She doesn't know how to swim!"

The cow would have nuzzled her to the surface for her first breath of air. Without her, the calf would drown, her mouth open. Jan glanced over to Raquel's spectrograph, which recorded the tiny whale's wail of terror. Her eyes dilated, bewildered by her environment, a stark contrast to her mother's womb, where she enjoyed the sensation of depth without breathing. *Pressure must be clogging her ears and sinuses with blinding pain.* A lump rose in Jan's throat as she watched Boycott follow her plummeting to death.

Suddenly, the two nurses emerged from the opaque depths into the tiny flutter of illumination from the light atop the camera. One of them got her head under the calf and nudged her toward the surface.

"Yes!" Jan pumped her fist. They ran outside to see a tiny spout splutter a yard into the air.

"She's our baby," said Raquel. "We should give her a name."

"Miracle," suggested Jan.

Knight smiled. "It's appropriate."

"Isn't that sweet?" said Vesprhein. "Now, how the fuck are you going to herd those beasts outta here?" Raquel clapped her hands and led the scientists back into the shack. Vesprhein stopped Jan. "What about the dead whale? Can we cut her up for our holds?"

"No!"

"You want to dump fifty thousand dollars worth of meat?" He pulled Jan aside. "The beast is dead," Vesprhein argued. "Leaving her is wasting her. This way the crew'll feel they're being paid for this fucking circus."

Vesprhein had a point, though Jan's conscience was strongly opposed. But this drive, yet to begin, was going to last several weeks. The disgruntled pirates were only going to get unhappier. The whale was dead and another had taken her place. In the end, Jan was practical, choosing common sense over ethics. She granted Vesprhein's request. Upon hearing they could salvage the whale meat, the pirates' mood lifted sharply. It was an unquestionable victory for Vesprhein.

✻

"A squall line of wind and snow is moving in," said Trevor Smith. "It'll be upon us in a couple of hours."

"We should be out of here by then, right guys?" Jan looked at the MIT postgraduates and Raquel.

"If all goes well, yes," nodded Raquel.

"Do you want to do the honors, Jan?" asked Fallon, holding up a SuperCharlie.

"Sure." Jan took the robotic tuna and remarked, "It's really light."

Raquel and Taggart remained in the shack, while Fallon, Knight, Yale, Smith and Welling followed Jan with one SuperCharlie apiece.

The slaughter deck vibrated with a deafening blare of machines and men. Winches rattled, chainsaws buzzed and men shouted to be heard. The scientific shack, being sound proof, airtight and weatherproof, had cut out much of the noise and reek of gore. The scuppers overflowed with blood. The cow was an unrecognizable carcass, hacked, chopped and torn apart. Her stomach contents oozed every which way.

"Careful," shouted Vesprhein from the upper gangway. "It's slippery."

Jan noticed a softening in his tone, probably because his holds were starting to fill and a few more whales might die along the way to Cetacean Bay, filling them completely. Wading though ankle deep fat, the eco-warriors arrived at the slipway.

Jan spoke into her headset. "We're here, we're ready."

"Go ahead," said Taggart. "Release him."

Jan lowered herself on to the balls of her feet and dropped the robotic tuna into the water.

It sank.

❋

Raquel held her breath. The SuperCharlie dropped about twenty feet, then Taggart struck his keyboard. Nothing happened. Then it leveled off. Everyone exhaled, none more loudly than Raquel. He opened the robot's eyes, which contained two high-powered cameras that fed a pair of images to the first of the bank of eighteen screens. He wriggled the fish through a few test maneuvers, handed him over to Raquel and told Jan, "Release the next one."

Having practiced long hours on a simulator that the MIT postgraduates had rigged up during her shifts watching the scientific shack, Raquel guided the tuna expertly through the congested traffic and parked it under the ice behind the farthest whale north. The freeze had surreptitiously dropped down another half mile. With Smith updating the shack continuously about the deteriorating weather, she placed all the fish around and below the whales in the next hour—the time it took, Raquel realized when Jan opened the door and stamped into the shack, for the pirates to completely gut the cow. All that remained of the blue was a fleshy skeleton.

"Whiteout," reported Jan.

Before the first lady shut the door, Raquel caught a glimpse of the conditions. Nothing was visible through the wall of driving snow. A foaming sea washed continuously down the bridge windows. It didn't matter that the killer-factory ship wasn't even moving, the icy waters buried the bow with a wave and lifted it back up on the next. This was the worst weather yet, hardly an auspicious start, she thought. *But it's here now—my moment.* Her next keystroke would trigger the whale drive.

Or not.

The *Stavenger* rolled from port to starboard, forty degrees one way and fifty-five the other. Raquel poised her finger over the keyboard and took a deep breath. "Here goes."

Keeping her dignified demeanor, she gently tapped the space bar with her thumb. *Clack.* An anti-climactic kickoff to the biggest, most incredible and most unique rescue effort ever mounted in the history of conservation and mankind.

Silence ensued and stretched for an eternity.

Then, diverse vocalizations blasted out of the SuperCharlies.

Clicks, whistles, squeaks and screams.

Raquel, Fallon and Taggart plunged their joysticks. Synchronously, every head in the shack lifted to the live feed from the SuperCharlies' eye-cameras on the TV screens. The diminutive tuna darted forward, belching out sounds disproportional to their size. Raquel glanced at her spectrograph. Bulls closest to the mechanical fish sent out sonar blasts.

"What are they seeing?" asked Jan, riveted.

"Twenty-seven-foot orcas," replied Raquel absently. All simulated by an internal virtual reality module. *But were the bulls convinced?*

As one, the leviathans turned in fear.

The ecowarriors and scientists felt a liquid rumble beneath their feet.

Raquel pumped her fist. "It's working!"

"Ee-ha!" cried Boycott.

Jan grabbed the intercom to the bridge. "Let's go!"

"Slow ahead," ordered Vesprhein.

The flight of eighteen hundred and seventy-two blue whales displaced a rage of waves and shook the sea all the way to the ship. Heeling into the trough of one, the *Stavenger*'s screws engaged. Water engulfed the ship up to the crow's nest and thudded noisily upon the roof of the shack as wave after wave swept over the ship. The whales finally passed underneath them. The *Stavenger* picked up speed, plunging through foam and snow powered by a wind that could knock a man off his feet. In spite of a swell that never left the ship's beam, causing her stern to go under each time the bow propelled out of the water, and even though there was not a moment of even keel for the next several hours, nothing could dampen the jubilation in the scientific shack.

The whale drive was off and running.

Bloomington, Indiana

Rolling blockades cleared the freeway a mile ahead and behind the presidential motorcade. A helicopter followed watchfully. Everett stared dully out of the window toward the receding buildings of the Indiana University campus, where he'd just finished stumping. Around him, Pleasance, Lhea and Delta were littered in the back seat of the limousine in postures distinctly individual, unmistakably weary and overwhelmingly worried. By turning back the Japanese fleet, Jan had struck at the heart of the Sitka scenario, throwing all aspects of it into disarray. Now Maeo could do to Everett what Everett had intended to do to Maeo.

Damn Jan! Everett's face tightened. The future of his campaign, his very candidacy, hinged on how Tokyo reacted. *Damn her.*

Bering Sea

The sunlight filtered through thousands of feet of cloud, then emerged into the snow-flecked air over the Bering Sea as a gray day and finally refracted beneath the surface, where it created a brief panorama of blue that faded to infinite black amidst the slow turning icebergs hanging like inverted mountains from a choppy ceiling of water. The agitation diminished with depth. A couple of hundred feet below, the water was still.

Gradually an undercurrent began to build.

Powerful ripples pushed aside the seemingly imperturbable dreadnoughts of ice. Their glassy faces reflected streaks of light and riddled the fathomless depths with laser-like shafts. A low-pitched sound, like that of a birthing earthquake, became audible and grew louder. Smaller fish fled. The growl intensified, swelling, protracting, yet unbelievably still far from its peak. The Bering Sea went into complete disarray, from the pummeling weather on the surface, to this rocking disturbance beneath. The deafening, high-pitched scream of the elements above transformed without any clear demarcation into the rumbling howl below. The turmoil climaxed!

The source emerged dramatically out of the blue-black distance. A horde of great shadows.

Led by a bull, bucking his tail more than a hundred feet behind him, the blue whales solidified into view. As a pall of dust would a cattle drive, foam preceded, surrounded and trailed the leviathans. After clocking speeds of thirty miles per hour, the whales had settled down to twelve. This was twice their normal cruising speed. So calves rode on the backs of their mothers, who kept close to the surface. Young whales needed to breathe almost every five minutes.

Miracle straddled a nurse with her tiny flippers. During her short existence in this world, she'd learned that by lifting her flukes, she could raise her head above the water. Depressing them sent her down. They were not yet strong enough to let her generate forward thrust. The layers of skin filled with fibers would eventually fill out with muscles that could thrust her forward with incredible power.

❄

Jan stood in the shack, fascinated by the whales and the technology that drove them.

With ice no longer a threat, Trevor Smith donned the hat of trail scout. He used his Intergraph Workstation to ensure they remained inside the US 200-nautical-mile EEZ at all times. The decibel level of killer whale sounds from the SuperCharlies was lower, creating a sense of distance, but not enough to erase the danger. The blues believed that the orcas were still stalking. An advanced algorithm in the perception module of the robots matched the volume for corresponding changes in size.

Raquel and Fallon walked in, refreshed after a brief sleep and shower.

"Morning," Jan greeted them before the outgoing shift of Taggart and Welling went on a stats binge.

"The average difference in pressure from head to tail when one of them dives is three Gs," said Taggart. In layman's terms, if the tail of a blue whale protruded out of the water, the head was at a depth that would require even accomplished divers to stop and decompress at least six times before they reached the surface. It took the whale mere seconds.

Welling pointed to a schematic of the maneuver they had animated during their long shift. "They can do that because they are not breathing air under pressure like divers. In fact, I think they are not breathing at all. I think they empty their lungs before diving."

"How do they vocalize without air?" asked Raquel.

Welling and Taggart shrugged. There was so much that defied logic about these enigmatic giants. Like their sense of smell. Welling noticed that the lead bull always blew first, presumably establishing it was safe. Chemosensors on the SuperCharlies picked up secretions dripping out of his anal gland every time he did. This was some sort of scent marker, because the whales of his tribe surfaced one after the other in exactly the same spot. Yet scientists knew for a fact that the olfactory area in a whale's brain was grossly underdeveloped, opening the possibility that the pair of grooves below their upper lip might be a chemoreceptor. Images and data from this drive were going to keep scientists busy for decades.

"Several whales are lagging," reported Raquel, settling in.

"Let's rest them." Jan nodded to Smith, who got busy trying to locate calm waters within the EEZ.

The *Stavenger* dropped anchor under a rare, starlit night of calm. The SuperCharlies moved into positions around the drive. Soft, seemingly distant, killer whale sounds were restricted to the north, east and west of the drive. On the south side, the scientists simulated a school of thresher sharks, another mortal enemy of the blue whale. Aware that the former adversary hunted with sonar and the latter was motion sensitive, the blues were quiet and still, taking turns to sleep.

International Donut Hole, Bering Sea

The familiar hulking shapes of the *Rising Sun* and her ten catchers plodded south in a parallel course a hundred miles west of the eco-warriors. Their hulls rose, half-exposed screws beating up white patches of froth. Yamamura entered his cabin. An eighteen-year-old female scrubber he'd made eye contact with a few times during his rounds waited for him. She'd been offered her fifty thousand yen by his steward to keep him company.

He sat down. "Undress."

The girl coyly obliged. When she was naked, he stood up. She stepped forward toward him. Yamamura smashed a clenched fist into her face.

Most of the bridge knew about his sexual perversion but embraced a police-type code of silence out of fear. When he finished spending his hate on her, Yamamura called his long time steward, who took the woman to the infirmary. The medical report placed the blame for her bruises on a jealous brawl. To ensure her silence, she wouldn't be paid until they docked in Kobe at the end of the voyage, when she would also receive a dire warning she'd never work again if she named Yamamura.

A knock sounded on his door. He finished dressing. "Enter."

It was a bridge officer. "Sir, the *Stavenger* has stopped east of the donut."

A lopsided smile lit up Yamamura's face. He jaunted back on to the bridge, a stark contrast to the angry, spite-filled man who strode out of there a few hours before. He proceeded directly to the chart table.

"They are resting the whales," he concluded. The blues had to be exhausted. This was their first stop since leaving the horseshoe. They would be there until daybreak. "Instruct every catcher, except *9* and *10*, to change flags and paint over Japanese markings." They carried other whaling countries' colors to get around the IWC's quotas.

Yamamura ran his finger from their current position all the way east over the international waters to the US 200-nautical-mile EEZ. The *Stavenger* would not pick up the Japanese fleet's turn toward them until it was too late, because hundreds of vessels, engaged in their daily no-holds-barred fishing, crowded the screen with blips.

"Plot a course across the donut."

200-Nautical-Mile US EEZ, Bering Sea

Vesprhein stared at the first lady walking down the slipway. The scuba gear fit like a second skin. Boycott fell in step beside her with his camera.

"She be hot, eh, Cap'n?" grinned Quvango. "You reckon you got a shot?"

Vesprhein shrugged. He and Jan had spent the last few days almost entirely together. Jan was using Vesprhein's remarkable marksmanship to embed transmitters into every whale. Fired from a specially designed crossbow, these fist-sized tracking devices emitted barcoded signals, identifying each whale individually. The scientists then went about cataloging every animal's characteristics, like the tribe they belonged to, gender, all the way down to individual scars, identifying marks, behavior anomalies and other physical and psychological characteristics. This first-ever database would enable marine mammal experts to follow the entire Pacific population for years to come.

Larkin, the SEAL on duty behind them, snorted, "Yeah, right. Just 'cause they've been arguin' every day, doesn't make 'em a married couple."

"You're saying I can't bang her?" Vesprhein smirked.

"Not just me. Your chief engineer's odds. He has you at a hundred to one. I'd put it at less than that."

"That Limey turncoat." Vesprhein reached for the phone and punched up the engine room.

"Yuh?" grunted the bearded chief engineer.

"Hundred at a hundred."

The com went silent. Vesprhein knew the math was hitting home. Ten thousand dollars. He could picture the red-bearded man from Warwickshire, England, tugging at the tea cozy on his head. Ski masks did not properly fit that oblong skull. His nose poked though the spout and one ear protruded out of the hole meant for the handle. Finally, the chief engineer replied bluntly, "I can't cover that, Cap'n. You know it."

"Then get the fuck out of business, you unfaithful solitary sonofabitch!"

Any other crew member would be shaking at the knees. Not the CE. Vesprhein regarded him as an equal in ruthlessness. The engine room was second to the bridge in importance on a ship and that's why he'd hired this ogre who never came to the bridge and determined that outsiders had no authority to enter his domain, unless invited. On the rare occasions that even Vesprhein did, he was suffered more than welcomed. The chief engineer remained silent, waiting for the captain to change his bet.

"Twenty?" asked Vesprhein.

"Yuh."

"Put me down."

"Can't be open-ended. I gotta know by when."

"Before we cross the fortieth parallel into Cetacean Bay."

"I want a piece of that dream," said Larkin.

"Crew only." Vesprhein shook his head, then paused. "Ah, what the hell, we'll take yer money." Vesprhein threw the intercom to Larkin.

❇

Jan backed off the slipway into a blue, weightless world. Every breath she took roared in her ears with compressed air that she could taste. She kicked and dived down, her long legs scissoring between the swarming, magnificent dark shapes. Guarded by bulls, the whales remained divided by tribe and stayed in distinct, separate circles.

With the camera strapped to his shoulder, Boycott disappeared into one while Jan searched for Miracle through the constant, fluid movement of light and dark. Her eyes returned forward and she found herself on a collision course with a bull, looming so large she sized up smaller than roadkill. There was no way she could get out of his way. At the last moment, the whale cut away easily, almost condescending in his gracefulness. The tail flukes, as wide as the wingspan of a plane, beat past overhead gently. At full strength, he exerted the power of seven hundred and fifty horses.

An avid skydiver, Jan felt the same soaring freedom swimming underwater. Roaming amongst the planet's most awesome life forms just elevated the experience beyond expression. She allowed the cross currents created by the thick traffic to carry her laterally, drop her vertically and sometimes even angle her upwards.

How whales maintained the integrity of their herds became increasingly apparent. It wasn't vision, which was limited in the murky depths, or their chemoreceptors, which they utilized predominantly to taste food and follow a scent trail; neither did they seem to possess a keen electric sense, prevalent in several species of fish, to detect minute currents generated by muscle action. Rather, it was what scientists had suspected all along: acoustic imaging. The computers had isolated a pattern of asynchronous diving and surfacing, preceded by brief calls that obviously were signals to alert other members. This prevented the whales, now huddled even more closely than they usually were in this unnatural environment of the drive, from colliding.

Jan approached Boycott filming a pod led by a heavily scarred bull.

Suddenly, she felt a jolt! An enormous force shoved Jan from behind, shooting her up faster than her rising air bubbles. She fought her ascent, slowing and swirling around. A silhouette charged her. She darted left, thinking it was an attack, then relaxed abruptly.

Miracle.

The demands of the drive had taught Miracle to swim more quickly than normal. She rolled and used one flipper to slap Jan who slammed into the seventy-five-foot nurse. When Jan steadied, Miracle placed a twinkling young eye right up against her mask. Jan laughed, hugging the infant as much as her arms would go around. In these first days, the calf put on more than ten pounds an hour, or two hundred pounds daily. Miracle slithered away and stopped.

She wanted to play.

Her mother would have indulged, but the nurses did not. Jan reached out and grabbed a flipper. Miracle took off as soon as she did. The two nurses protectively flanked them while they cavorted within the confines of the tribe. Jan realized why. The calf had no skill avoiding collisions because she still saw with her eyes. Acoustic imaging was like language; she would learn to emit, receive and understand the use of sound over time. The brief playfulness ended as suddenly as it started.

Hungry again, Miracle nuzzled along a nurse's grooved belly. The cow contracted her mammary muscles. A pair of folds parted, two immense nipples sprang out and squirted a great, thick, overwhelmingly fatty jet of milk to pinpoint the location of her teat. The female compensated for wastage by producing nearly a hundred gallons, three times what the newborn consumed. Miracle formed a funnel out of her inflatable tongue. The nurse humped her flank above the surface so that the calf could suckle without drinking in water.

The oxygen warning light of their tanks blinked. Jan and Boycott reluctantly started back for the *Stavenger*.

International Donut Hole

Yamamura stared down at the repeater screen. His ten catchers slipped amongst the dozens of boats lined up at the US boundary, waiting for darkness. They reported just one US Coast Guard vessel on patrol. Outnumbered as usual, the USCG stayed around only for relief and rescue. But Yamamura knew Japanese vessels would be isolated and apprehended since the San Francisco court order was so high profile and recent.

He wasn't wrong. The instant *9* and *10,* the only two catchers flying Japanese colors, crossed into American waters, the Coast Guard blared a warning over the loudspeaker. The catchers fled north. The USCG cutter took up chase.

Yamamura smiled. "Send them in."

Engines of the catchers, disguised under Korean, Chilean and Polish flags, revved with the suddenness of detonating grenades. It wasn't dark yet, though the low-angle Alaska sun had rolled beneath the horizon. When the whalers catapulted out of the pack with a flurry of foam, pandemonium erupted. Skippers of the other boats barked out orders. Throttles roared. Dense smoke coughed up the countless funnels. While the boats jockeyed for position to circle seine nets around fish, the catchers surged over the waves in tight formation, deeper into US territorial waters.

200-Nautical-Mile US EEZ

The anchored *Stavenger* careened precipitously into a trough. A squall out of Siberia dropped snow and temperatures, whipped up twenty-foot waves and punched out forty-knot winds. Raquel and Fallon, immersed in ensuring the SuperCharlies stayed deep enough away from the angry waves, did not see the eight barely discernible blips leave the other raiders behind.

Sitting side by side, Jan and Vesprhein wound down another

polarized debate about whale-watching in a deserted Pig. A deck hand washed dishes. The cook, Assad and the day crew hit the sack, as did the other eco-warriors and scientists. Larkin, replacing Napoli as the first lady's bodyguard, stepped outside the door of the Pig to smoke, even though every pirate lit up inside.

"Americans brand anything and everything that doesn't fit into their own narrow view of morality as deviant," alleged Vesprhein, yawning.

"Oh, yeah," said Jan acidly, catching his yawn. She swung her leg, straddled the bench and faced him. "Upholding the sanctity of life is twisted."

"Are you twisted?" he asked with a sly grin. "I love kinky."

Jan shook her head. "You don't give up, do you?"

"I want to fuck you and you want to fuck me. What are we waiting for?"

"Hell to freeze over."

"According to Dante, it has."

Jan laughed. "If I were not who I am and you were not who you are, that might have done it."

It was Vesprhein's turn to shake his head and smile. "But we are who we are, no?"

"Eight contacts!" Raquel's voice exploded over the speakers.

Jan raced outside to take the ladder down to the shack. The wind blasted low across the waves and roared down the deck ventilators. The whales swam between the fast moving ice floes, which ground against each other like chainsaws against the hull. All the eco-warriors and scientists arrived within moments of Jan.

"They are coming at thirty-six knots," said Trevor Smith.

"How far away are they?" asked Jan.

"Fifteen minutes."

❄

Eight reinforced bows battled through the punishing waters of the Bering Sea at full speed. Two men were needed on the wheel to hold course. Aft, smoke poured toward the lightning-riddled clouds. The blizzard made it impossible to pick out the catchers. Like prowlers in the night, they kept their searchlights and sonar off to avoid detection, relying instead on the eyes of their best lookouts to spot the whales. Gunners waited tensely on the bridge, ready to race along the storm-besieged catwalks to their harpoons and commence the slaughter at a moment's notice.

On the *Rising Sun*, Yamamura stood still, his hands clasped behind his back, waiting for his catcher skippers to report they'd sighted the blues. The factory ship remained in the international donut hole. The weather outside continued to deteriorate. Visibility was less than a few cable lengths. He could not conceive how Jan could stop his men from killing at will. The *Stavenger* was armed, yes, but she was still one and they were eight.

The catchers came over the horizon.

The resting waters were dead ahead.

The gunners raced to the catwalks, bracing themselves against the guardrail all the way to the platforms, and snapped on safety harnesses. The lookouts clambered up the wildly swaying masts into their wobbling perches and fastened themselves in. Searchlights came on, setting the night ablaze with greedy beams.

The *Stavenger* wasn't there.

Neither were the whales.

"What do you mean?" demanded Yamamura, raising his voice.

The radar operator could not understand it either. His screen showed a blip consistent with the *Stavenger*.

"A decoy!" snapped Yamamura.

He should have known, he scolded himself, seeing as he was the father of a compuwiz son. At first, his fleet had been abuzz that the eco-warriors were using trained killer whales to shepherd the drive. Upon querying Tokyo, they were astonished to learn the sounds came from underwater robots. So this deception was probably a simple electronic sleight of hand for Jan's wunderkinds.

"Explosions!" yelled the factory ship's sonar operator.

Three flowers bloomed on his screen.

He identified *7, 3* and *8.* They'd struck depth charges. Yamamura heard the other catcher captains scream, "All Stop! Reverse Full! Crew to the rails! Report anything suspicious!"

Keeping a wary eye out for more explosives, they retreated and picked up survivors from the three vessels.

"Casualties?" inquired Yamamura tonelessly.

There were none. The eco-warriors had reduced the explosives, reported *7*'s Captain.

Damnit. Yamamura ground his teeth. If there had been fatalities, the first lady would have blood on her hands. "So, where are they?" screamed Yamamura at the sonar operator.

The operator shook his head fearfully. The circling scan on the radar came up empty.

The *Stavenger* and the drive had vanished.

❋

Jan, Taggart and Fallon exchanged jubilant high-fives. The MIT postgrads had mounted a decoy on a depth charge. Jan ordered Vesprhein to raise anchor and cut the *Stavenger*'s engines just as Fallon and Taggart activated the decoy. Except for a brief flicker, which the radar operator aboard the *Rising Sun* dismissed as disturbance, the blip representing the pirate ship never left his screen. The *Stavenger* drifted with the southbound currents. The MIT postgraduates masked the whale calls under an acoustic splatter, which they created to read like the rough weather and sounds of the other fishing boats.

Yamamura had lost a third of his fleet in a matter of minutes. Was that deterrent enough? Jan wondered. If he was anything like his bio, she had probably awakened the monster in him.

Bristol Bay, Aleutian Islands

Standing on the bridge of a Coast Guard cutter, Pleasance smiled smugly.

The searchlights picked up the first spout. Every camera swung toward it. Then a blue whale underneath surfaced in the full glare of intersecting beams, which darted off to pick one of their choosing, as dozens, then scores more whales blew. The bad weather prevailing throughout the day over the Bering Sea had cleared miraculously during the past hour. The freezing darkness was without even a veil of mist.

Most of the world stopped for what would be the most watched event on TV. Ever since the drive began a week ago, Jan had recaptured the headlines. Not by accident. It was part of Pleasance's ingenious damage control maneuvers following Judge Cimarron's order. Pleasance figured Jan had put Everett on the political map. *Why not use her again to resurrect him on the coattails of this whale drive?*

Pleasance tested public opinion by letting Robert Random release reconnaissance stills. Everett provided daily updates at prime time. People could not get enough. He impressed Jan with the closeness of the race and asked for videotapes of the whale drive. The *Stavenger*'s uplink gear had a built-in scrambling device. Only the National Reconnaissance Office could download the images. Carefully selecting the pictures, Lhea's White House media team manipulated public curiosity to a fever pitch leading up to this moment when the world got a live glimpse of the "first lady's heroic rescue." Pleasance asked Everett to suggest to Jan that the publicity could boost donation to her rescue fund and deter further bold attempts by the Japanese fleet.

As Pleasance stared out into the sea, he did not marvel at the beauty of these great beasts. Instead he thought, *this is a masterstroke.* With nonstop negative ads and daily news headlined by violence, it was hardly surprising that an entire planet's imagination was riveted by a celebration of life. About fifty boats, which included news crews from networks around the world and quick-thinking entrepreneurs who had organized tour groups, waited in the unusually dormant waters just north of the Aleutian Islands. A Coast Guard Sikorsky chopper and two cutters stood by to keep order. Despite a call for silence, an excited chatter went up amongst the reporters, researchers and whale-watchers alike. At home, the epic images were spectacular and heartwarming.

To subliminally connect the campaign and the drive, Pleasance had arranged for a press conference with Everett on the stump and Jan against a backdrop of the whales. He coached Everett to seize the opportunity and audience to quell the growing rumors of marital discord. "Jan has always been an outspoken animal rights activist. Like almost every husband and wife, we don't always agree. If it were not for this uniquely American tradition of individualism, personal initiative and free speech, this great rescue would not be happening."

Pleasance envisioned Everett's opponents, Democrat Keith Leeds and Republican Will Todd, watching helplessly as a Washington-wary nation lifted the president into that rarified place in politics where party lines dissolved. *They should worry,* gloated Pleasance. *This drive could successfully prolong the honeymoon through election day.* As he expected, polls released the next day shot Everett's support up to 40 percent, higher than the numbers that had vaulted him into the Oval Office. Leeds plummeted to 23 percent. Conservatives stood firm behind Will Todd at 30 percent.

North Pacific

Jan pensively strolled along the catwalk to the gun platform, put one foot over the lower guardrail and leaned forward. She wore a bright yellow oilskin, the hood drawn over her head. This morning, for the first time since leaving the Bering Sea, she'd discarded the ski mask from her attire. They'd left the Aleutian chain behind yesterday, finally escaping the cold swipes of the hard-hitting snowstorms out of Siberia, though stagnating water still froze on deck, and exterior vertical surfaces still gathered white moss. But the number of times the menace of ice had to be attacked with axes and steam hoses reduced from two times a day to one. Temperatures hovered around zero instead of several degrees below.

There were no clouds, but vapor masked the sky and sucked the light and heat out of the sun. The ocean rolled in long, even banks, a monotonous green glass that served to accentuate the vigorous beauty of the dark bodies all around Jan. Water parted with their great, slow, heaving surges. Every third or fourth time that they broke the surface, their flukes leaped clear out of the water.

Blues belonged to the kind of baleen whales called rorquals. They possessed a dorsal or back fin and were endowed with the most elegant bodies of the species. Their streamlined form allowed them to swim faster than most other whales. Jan and her team were permitting the blues to set their own pace. Their speed varied from 3.7 to 20 mph. The waters had been friendly so far, with fishing boats going out of their way to cut their engines and ensure a smooth, non-threatening passage for the whales.

A small, fluked tail straightened in front of her. Completely unafraid of the *Stavenger*'s screws, Miracle blew an unsteady spout of water, sounded, blew again and thrashed her tail enthusiastically at the first lady.

"Hi, Miracle," said Jan. It was a ritual with them. Whenever Jan stepped up to the railing along any part of the killer-factory ship, the calf surfaced within moments. Miracle was already one and a half times heavier than an adult hippopotamus. She would continue to grow at this astonishing rate for the next six months.

The calf looked shiny and clean, having sloughed off her barnacle-coated skin and grown another for the first time in her four-week life. Barnacles were parasitic shells that rooted themselves in the skin and accumulated rapidly to almost a thousand pounds on a large whale. Cetaceans fought back with rapid cell division. The eco-warriors and scientists actually saw the adults change their entire coats overnight. They first developed patches, then peeled away the skin entirely and replaced it by growing cells three hundred times faster than humans.

The scientists gathered the huge pieces and microscopically examined them, not unexpectedly finding toxins, mutagens and carcinogens. It triggered an animated blame game that found Jan at the wrong end of the captain's table during breakfast. She faulted developing countries for unregulated dumping, which, Vesprhein charged, the United States started. He was right. Congress reversed the Marine Protection, Research and Sanctuaries Act of 1972, declaring oceans had the "assimilative capacity" to absorb wastes. Today, the United States emptied, diluted, dispersed, sedimented and degraded fifteen billion gallons of toxic waste within its own 200-nautical-mile EEZ every day.

Vesprhein sauntered up. Napoli sharpened.

"Easy, cowboy," Vesprhein warned. Napoli closed his finger around the trigger anyway. Vesprhein settled against the railing beside Jan.

She smiled wanly. "You won an argument with me. No one's ever done that."

"Not even Mr. President?"

"You've never been married, have you? He knows better."

Vesprhein guffawed. "So, what have you decided?"

About an hour ago, the scientists presented Jan the examination results of Miracle's skin. There were almost seven hundred parts per million of toxins—3,500 times the level deemed safe. Blue whales had always tested low because they stayed so far away from land and human contact. This high contamination was clearly the result of their month-long captivity in the horseshoe close to the oil-polluted

Alaska coastline, and then being driven within the waste-ridden US EEZ.

"We didn't organize a rescue on this scale to lose them to pollution," said Jan.

"You want to leave US waters?"

"We have to."

"Then those whales become fair game."

Chicago, Illinois

Everett was riding high when he arrived in the windy city, but Pleasance refused to let the president rest on his lead. Illinois was a swing state that Everett had to carry and one of its university towns, Evanston, was the site of the first presidential debate. With all the momentum going in, he could land the knockout punch and vault ahead for good.

Everett worked under the direction of Lhea, who'd done such a remarkable job preparing him during his first run for the Oval Office. The president rehearsed his entry, took hostile questions from his staff and made mental notes about which questions required him to walk over to the audience. After lunch, Everett took a nap so he would be fresh for the debate scheduled to begin at six PM. He had been cramming facts and figures on the economy, defense, crime, everything, on the long drives and flights between rallies, at dinner, before he slept, when he woke up, in the bathroom and during all his free time.

Boston

While Everett slept, Leeds's war room in Boston received a phone call from an anonymous female caller. She wanted a half-million-dollar payoff, and when the Democrats heard what she had to offer, they knew the information was worth it. Everett's honeymoon was over. In fact, they could end it all at the first debate, or at the very least, cripple him beyond recovery.

North Pacific

A quarter sea washed against the hull. Jan, taking a turn on deck, leaned with the ship, which hung for a few seconds, then listed back to meet the next gentle onslaught of long rollers. Even though the morning air was cold enough to freeze the lungs, temperature and humidity rose at the rate of a unit every six hours. The ice that had bulked the *Stavenger*'s forepeak and other external features for much of the voyage, was melting away. A gust rushed by her, plucking the rigging discordantly and whistled around the superstructure through the cracks and gaps and holes.

She looked up and checked that the Korean was in his crow's nest. Two more pirates paced the bridgewing. Breath poured like steam from their pinched faces. Now that she'd decided to leave the security of the EEZ, Jan had asked Vesprhein to post lookouts around the clock to guard against any sudden, sneaky raids by the Japanese catchers. Boat traffic thinned away all night and all morning long. For the last hour, the *Stavenger* had been sailing alone.

Raquel joined Jan. "It's official. We just left US territorial waters."

Jan's stomach contracted tensely. "We are on our own the rest of the way. And it's a long, long way."

"Aren't you going to call Carsten and wish him luck?" asked Raquel.

Jan looked at her watch. The first presidential debate was a few hours away. "I guess."

They started back up the catwalk.

"You don't sound enthused," remarked Raquel.

"This drive has been—" Jan searched for the word and tilted her head when she found it"—clarifying. It's put my marriage, politics and all of that in perspective. They seem so trivial."

"What are you saying?"

"I don't want to go back to Washington."

Raquel looked at Jan. "Seriously?"

"You asked me if it was freedom or the man that excited me? I want to sail full time. Like Paul Worthy. I always envied him. No boundaries. No rules. After waking up every morning to open seas and open horizons, I realized I'll be miserable and I'll make Carsten miserable because I'll never be as happy as I am here and now."

"You're going to divorce the president of the United States?"

"You make it sound like treason."

"It's never happened."

"There's a first time for everything."

"Don't you embody that?" Raquel said, teasing.

"Oh, shuddap." Jan smiled and shoved Raquel on to the bridge.

A heavy swell caught the bow. The pulse of the engine faded. Quvango creaked the wheel-spokes back and forth. The *Stavenger* lay to with her head into the wind. Vesprhein and Iron Lady stood by the chart table.

"I'll wait until after he's re-elected," said Jan.

"What if he isn't?" asked Raquel.

"The tabloids won't pay nearly as much."

Raquel laughed.

"You could make a fortune if you slept with me," jumped in Vesprhein.

"True." Jan circled his waist, catching Napoli and the bridge crew by surprise. "You don't have the clap or anything, do you?"

"I'm clean," Vesprhein shot back. "Always use protection. Two condoms, in fact."

"Jan!" The overhead speaker crackled with Welling's frantic voice. "We have a problem. Hurry!"

The two women headed down the companionway at once. Raquel shook her head. "President to pirate. Imagine the media feeding frenzy."

Jan laughed and started down the ladder to the slaughter deck. Raquel followed.

Welling appeared in the doorway of the shack. "One of the tribes snuck away."

"How long ago?" Jan hurried in.

"Hard to say," replied Yale. "Fifteen minutes?"

"A SuperCharlie developed an audio malfunction which I should have caught," confessed Fallon, the MIT postgraduate.

"We got distracted." Welling nodded to the political commentaries leading up to the presidential debate on the TV.

Jan curbed a flash of temper. Raquel admonished them in a restrained voice. "Guys, we've been over this. Each tribe has a very specific migration route and will constantly try to escape toward it. So we cannot let our guard down for an instant. Don't let it happen again."

Unlike the straight-line course of this drive, circles and cycles dominated all aspects of a whale's existence. Migration routes were never just up and down, but east and west as well. Their distinctly curved paths were attributed to the whales' perspective at all times. Underwater, their acoustic horizon was a circle. Above the surface, the ocean was spherical.

"How many slipped through?" Jan asked evenly.

"Twenty-three," replied Welling. Jan did not even have to ask which way because Welling knew it was coming. "They are headed west toward the Japanese fleet shadowing the drive."

Raquel slipped into her chair. "How far away have they gotten?"

"Seven miles," said Yale.

"In fifteen minutes?" Jan's eyes widened with surprise.

Raquel's fingers flew across the sensor pad of her computer. "Feed me their calls."

Welling transferred the spectrographs of the fugitive blues to her laptop scrolling down her library of sounds. The comparison check stopped under: "Run!"

"We are so sorry, Jan," said Welling.

"We can put the SuperCharlies around the drive on autopilot and go after them, right?" asked Jan. Fallon swallowed nervously. She snapped, "What?"

"The SuperCharlies around the drive are up for a recharge."

Jan's eyes swiveled to the charge gauge. The LEDs were all the way down to 25 percent. Some were lower.

"Half an hour," said Yale. "Forty-five minutes tops."

Raquel was the only one who could even make the next suggestion. "Jan, we should let them go. Maybe they'll make it."

Jan knew that was the right thing to do. The drive was going so well—too well—she'd begun to believe they might not lose a single whale. She should have anticipated something was bound to go wrong. "What's the composition of the tribe?"

"Five bulls, seventeen cows and six calves," Welling read off the ID microchips that had been fired in the whales.

"Isn't that Miracle's—" Jan began. Welling nodded. She said resolutely, "We are getting them back." She left the shack for the bridge.

"Now we're going to chase after every fucking stray?" Vesprhein complained.

Jan nodded Iron Lady over to the chart table. "How far away is the Japanese fleet?"

The Englishman drew a ruler across the map between the magnets representing the *Stavenger* and the pelagic fleet. "About fifteen miles."

Vesprhein arrived beside her. "Even at full speed, we won't get to the whales before—"

"Shut up, Arlov," Jan raised her voice, taking her anger out on him. "And get us there!" Before he could say anything, she added, "Please! Just get us there."

Vesprhein held her gaze.

Jan's eyes pleaded.

He nodded. "Bring her around." After they'd scudded around ninety degrees, he ordered, "Full ahead!"

❊

"Contact!" echoed the radar operator's voice over the *Rising Sun*'s bridge speaker. "It is the *Stavenger*! Coming toward us."

Yamamura's stopped his cup of tea in midair.

Upon losing the eco-warriors in the Aleutian Basin, he had ordered all his officers outside. Standing them in the bitter cold, he'd proceeded to chew them out before the common crew in a rampage of wrath none had ever seen. The officers remained in his doghouse until last night, when they finally drew level with the drive and settled into a parallel course twelve miles west. Now, the faintest hint of the first smile since his outburst twitched at the corner of Yamamura's mouth.

He completed the arc of the cup to his lips and sipped the steaming tea. "Sonar. Check for submerged contacts."

His XO quickly repeated the order.

"Whales," came the reply moments afterwards. "I count twenty-three."

Like a trained army responding to a command, the pelagic fleet turned east and accelerated until the seven catchers were no longer riding the wavecrests but smashing through them, keeping perfect formation. The sluiced ocean rose in an unbroken curtain around every boat. Bridge screens rattled under the assault of spray. Only the crow's nests remained above the racing, frothing white. The *Rising Sun* brought up the rear, a giant fort shepherding the narrow, high-speed hulls.

❊

"Good news, bad news," informed Welling. He was the Boycott among the scientists—upbeat and quippy.

"Bad news," Jan selected distractedly. She wanted to be in two places at the same time. On the bridge, watching the open ocean whip by, she felt reassured they were going as fast as they could. While this kept her overwhelming sense of urgency under control, she couldn't lose the gnawing tension of not being able to see the monitors and screens, which provided an abstract, nevertheless comforting visual of the whales.

"The Japanese are going to be there about the same time as we are."

"Good news?"

"I just threw that in."

When Jan did not laugh, nobody dared to either. She left, saying, "I'll be in the wheelhouse."

After the door closed behind her, Welling grimaced nervously. "She's really pissed, isn't she?"

"Just pray we don't lose any whales," warned Raquel.

❈

The *Rising Sun*'s sonar reported the tribe about a mile away.

"All stop," instructed Yamamura quickly. "Quiet on sonar."

The diesels died on all eight vessels, ushering a sudden silence across the endless expanse. The thunderclaps caused by the bows slapping the water ebbed away. The catchers slowed in front of the factory ship. The crew sprinted to their stations. It was up to the lookouts now, who reached the crow's nests the same time their gunners unshrouded the harpoons. Skippers looked expectantly through binoculars.

The widely spaced troughs of the ocean were empty.

Yamamura, a wily, experienced whaler, realized that his order to drift silently would deceive the leviathans into a false sense of security.

❈

Raquel was monitoring the spectrographs when Jan called down from the bridge and asked, "How are they doing?"

"I have no idea," replied Raquel. None of the scientists knew how whales reacted in strange waters. They could only assume that the fear of the unknown filled the adults with a desperate need to get back to the familiar channels they and their ancestors had used in the annual migration from the Arctic to the Antarctic for eons.

The twenty-three fugitives swam about a hundred fathoms below the surface. It seemed as if the adults tolerated no playfulness from the youngsters, whose mothers stayed close. They paid little heed to the *Stavenger*'s pursuit, equating her screws with no danger. They should be hearing the Japanese fleet too, but Raquel figured their acoustic memory recalled the retreat of these ships, unaware obviously of the circumstances.

"How about Miracle?" asked Jan.

"Boxed in between the nurses," Raquel replied.

Sensors picked up nervous shimmies rippling their skins. Raquel heard the calf signal she needed air.

"No, don't," implored Raquel when the bull bleated back, indicating it was safe to blow.

"What?" Jan's anxious snap laced her voice in static.

❋

The lookouts saw the plumes and chorused, "Whales!"

Engines on the catchers fired. Throttles threw open simultaneously. The seven boats sprang forward just as the *Stavenger* leapt over the horizon at fifty knots, advancing from the opposite side. The whales were in the middle, equidistant from their hunters and rescuers.

Seeing the *Stavenger*, Yamamura took the microphone himself.

He did not want his skippers shirking from a confrontation. "Proceed with the hunt."

Evanston, Illinois

An unrelenting breeze from Lake Michigan swirled leaves, stripped by an early fall, in tight circles and took the wind chill factor down into the teens. Immediately north of Chicago, Evanston was established as an important lake port. The five institutions of higher learning provided an academic setting for the debate, part of a continuing effort by the Commission on Presidential Debates to involve youth in the political process.

Democrat Keith Leeds arrived first, wearing a blue suit and a red tie with a crooked knot. He did not pause to answer questions and the reporters attributed that to his lagging numbers. Republican Will Todd stepped out of his car a few minutes later. He wore a gray suit and a vest over a yellow tie. Todd, in stark contrast, shook hands and chatted his way in. Finally, Everett came, looking presidential to the hilt. He wore a dark blue suit, sober tie and a prominent Everett-Adrian button on his lapel. Vice President Adrian sat in Air Force Two. Treetop—the rules governing presidential succession—prevented him from being in the same place as the president outside the White House.

In the draw of names, Everett kicked off the three-way debate with the opening statement and would have the last word. Leeds' strategists were grinning. This was the Democrats' dream order of speakers.

Not surprisingly, from the get-go both Leeds and Todd slammed Everett, who retaliated by listing the campaign promises which got him elected and then asserted he'd been thwarted on all of them by the House and Senate. Closing statements began with clichéd Republican rhetoric from Will Todd: pro-life, pro-gun and the GOP's monopoly of the nation's moral compass. Leeds devoted the first fifteen seconds addressing traditional Democrats around the nation. Then, barely able to conceal his glee, he embarked on the final segment of his closing statement.

"A few weeks ago, following gross whaling violations by Japan on the high seas, we applauded the president for standing tall. But his threat to veto a permanent seat for the Japanese on the Security Council was his overt position. I thought we did not go far enough. Even the first lady agreed and secured a court order banning Japan from harvesting our marine resources within our territorial waters. Why then was a Japanese fleet allowed to brazenly cross into those waters just hours after Judge Cimarron's ruling? Quite simply because President Everett struck a covert backroom deal with Tokyo, giving them permission to harvest those blue whales that the first lady is driving to the safety of Cetacean Bay!"

Everett's lips parted in astonishment. He took one beat too long to compose himself.

North Pacific

At fifty knots, the *Stavenger* was the faster vessel. She moved closer to the whales quicker than the catchers.

"*Rising Sun* is pulling out," Smith informed Jan over the *Stavenger*'s bridge speaker.

The Japanese factory ship began a slow turn away from the impending hunt. The loss of a catcher, even two, was acceptable. Not the *Rising Sun*, guessed Jan.

"Fucking coward," she spat anyway.

The *Stavenger* rose and fell forward with the power and energy of a horse in full gallop. Towering waves excavated by her bow dashed up her flanks with a scraping roar and rained down on the bridge, already encased in the sound of maximum revolutions and the shaking of every rivet, strut and plate from keel to mast.

Confident she was far enough ahead, Jan shouted into Vesprhein's ear, "Put us between the whales and those boats."

Quvango leaned hard into the wheel. Without any reduction in speed, the *Stavenger* lurched into a sweeping turn. Immediately, she lost her fourteen-knot advantage because the catchers were sailing straight. The eco-warriors had only two thousand yards to cover while the Japanese were at least three thousand yards.

Out of harpoon range.

Welling's quavering voice came through the speaker. "The calves are breaking away toward the catchers!"

Jan's hopes sank. In a heartbeat, the race slipped away from the eco-warriors. The movement of the whales and hunters toward each other closed their linear distance disproportionately faster than the *Stavenger*'s curving approach to come in between.

"It's against IWC regulations to kill a blue whale," said Knight, breaking the stricken silence. That was as much angry defiance as the mild-mannered, taciturn reporter could muster.

"Maybe they don't know," Vesprhein shot back sarcastically.

Jan swiveled. "Maybe we should tell them."

"That'll scare them the fuck back to Japan," Vesprhein monotoned.

"Open the speakers!" Jan turned and grabbed the old Aldis lamp. Years of chasing driftnet fishers had taught her how to signal.

The *Rising Sun*, turned around completely, retreated from the hunt. Her frothy tail betrayed her acceleration.

Jan's voice on the loud hailer trailed the flashing lamp by a split second even though the order of transmission was the opposite. She spoke in Japanese. "It is a violation of IWC regulations to kill a blue whale! You are being videotaped! Pull away. Now!"

Jan called down to the shack. "Raq! What's going on with the other whales?"

The fourteen blips representing the rest of the tribe fled in the opposite direction to the seven on the surface. Raquel replied, "They have turned back toward the drive."

Jan clenched her fist triumphantly. That left just nine whales to rescue. But one of them was Miracle.

❋

The seven gunners had jerked away to a man when they heard the first lady. The digital distance-readout atop the harpoon gun put *10*, which coincidentally was nearest to the *Stavenger*, sixty yards from Miracle.

"They are going to dive!" barked his lookout, recognizing the body language of the whales.

10's gunner looked over at the other catchers. They were all at top speed. Twisters of thick black smoke blasted out of the piping hot funnels. Climbing white walls of water, displaced by the closely bunched vessels, collided violently in midair and fell back on deck. Gunners and marksmen, caught under the fierce downpours, trusted the harnesses anchoring them to their stations and pressed down the deeply corrugated soles of their shoes for balance. The crows' nests danced so far over they were within handshaking distance of each other. Pumps noisily drained the overflowing scuppers.

The gunner did not fear the elements, yet he looked nervously to the bridge. By ordering the bombing run and deploying depth charges to sink three catchers, Jan had made it clear that she would not hesitate to use deadly force against them.

10's skipper, like all the rest, held up his hands, stalling the harvest.

❁

On the *Rising Sun*, anger contorted Yamamura's face. He snatched the microphone. "Take the whales! That is an order! I will strip all officers of their rank in boats that disobey!"

As the American president's wife, Jan symbolized power that Yamamura was afraid might rank higher than his own and intimidate the skippers into cowardice. Centuries of Japanese feudal tradition placed deference to authority above all else. Yamamura glared around the bridge without actually registering a single face in his mind. At that moment, none of the officers around him would have traded places with the seven higher paid, profit-sharing catcher captains.

The suspense became almost a physical thing.

A nerve in Yamamura's cheek jumped.

The seconds of non-response by the skippers, each waiting for the other to make the first move, proved costly. Yamamura watched the *Stavenger* eat up the ocean ahead. She was now less than twenty yards from shielding the whales hurriedly emptying water out of their blow holes.

Yamamura's patience deserted him. "Fire!"

His voice fed directly into the gunners' headsets. He would deal with the skippers' disobedience later in a manner that would make the bastards rue the day they were born.

10's gunner saw the *Stavenger* loom inside the edge of his peripheral vision the same time Yamamura's furious order shattered his eardrums.

Without thinking, he squeezed the trigger. The sharp report catalyzed the other six into firing in quick succession. The staccato echoes multiplied endlessly across the open Pacific.

❄

"Miracle!" Jan gasped.

She clawed her fingers into Vesprhein's arm. He glanced down and casually closed a large palm over her white knuckles. Her other hand flew up in a futile gesture to stop the grenade-tipped shafts of rusting iron racing dully across. Even in their hasty dive, the whales looked awfully sluggish compared to the sleek swiftness of the harpoons.

The first lady's eyes riveted to the infant caesarean. Miracle seemed clumsy with dread, only a third into her dive. *10*'s grenade-tipped harpoon closed in a flash! A heartbeat before impact, a dark mound swelled under the calf. The replay of this save, captured by Boycott, who had the best, most chilling view at the forwardmost tip of the *Stavenger,* showed her nurse rise in one astonishingly agile, fluid movement. Miracle gripped her back with tiny flippers. The nurse and Miracle sank out of sight.

The harpoon missed the baby whale.

"Yes!" Jan exclaimed and without taking a breath sagged, "No."

Another calf blew directly in front of the harpoon. The youngster was struck from behind as he popped his head out of the water. The explosive arrow point entered with the ease of a knife through butter. The line went slack at once and sank below the *Stavenger*'s crashing keel, which passed every one of the next six.

The harpoons at the end of them all were dead on target.

Seven detonations!

Seven whales bucked violently.

The double charge of penthrite, assembled to kill an adult instantaneously, split open the calves. Clouds of blood and flesh erupted fifteen feet into the air. They died at once.

Jan's fingernails broke Vesprhein's skin through his sweater. His lips curled in a small smile. She did not know which way to look. To her right was the hypnotic spectacle of the slaughter, and to her left were the motherfuckers she wanted dead. The *Stavenger* thundered down the middle. The catchers, their screws winding down, cut across her swirling, white wake that extended all the way back to where the eco-warriors had begun their circular approach, a telling indication of how swiftly everything had happened.

Jan found her voice. It went from choking sad to gritty anger. "We are faster, we're bigger. Mow them down."

Vesprhein twirled his forefinger in a quick circle and signaled Iron Lady to bring them around.

"Stop port," ordered the Englishman.

The deck shuddered violently to the uneven shaft. Quvango took the wheel all the way over, then needed all his strength to keep it there. His mahogany skin stretched over his swelling, straining biceps. Jan felt the *Stavenger*'s angle change beneath her feet before she saw it through the stern scuttle.

"Port full!" Iron Lady counted seconds. "Midships, full ahead together!"

Spray lifted powerfully over the bows. The *Stavenger* engaged with a violent thrust of screws and rudder into a steep, fast, heeling turn. The floor tilted sharply. Jan slammed into Vesprhein, glanced down and caught her breath loudly. The trembling, groaning ship slanted so far, the bridge island looked directly down at the ocean. Waves shot straight up and pounded the screens. Thick smoke from her funnel choked the bridge windows to completely hide the foredeck.

Jan clutched Vesprhein tighter than before. She became aware of his breath on her cheek and his palm over her breast. But his massive arms felt safe and she stayed in them.

❀

"Tow the whales out of there!" exclaimed Yamamura shrilly. "Do not cut the lines. They can chase only one of you, and even if they do, it will not be for long. They won't want to go too far away from the drive."

"Begin pumping!" ordered the three captains who'd taken the calves.

Compressors roared air through the high-tensile lines into the mutilated corpses, making them buoyant, lighter and easier to tow.

"Tighten the lines!" ordered the four who'd fired upon the adults.

The hasty firing hadn't allowed the gunners to aim with fatal precision. Consequently, the three cows and the bull were all alive, staggering about in agony. The grenade had pulverized their insides. But they refused to sound, trying instead to swim toward their dead babies. The effort on a couple with shattered spines popped bones right through their inch-thick blubber. When the motor winches on the gun platforms started to spin up the slack in the lines, the leviathans' death cries, inaudible to their murderers, carried past the sixteen fleeing members of their tribe all the way to the drive itself. One thousand eight hundred and forty-nine whales responded with an instantaneous burst of speed.

❀

"Fuck," reacted Fallon.

Welling looked over anxiously. "What?"

"Increased speed is going to take down the charges on those SuperCharlies quicker."

"We have to start back right now," insisted Fallon over the

intercom to the bridge speaker.

"We can still take out at least one boat," said Vesprhein.

"Do it!" answered Jan.

Vesprhein tapped Quvango's shoulder. "Steady as she goes." Then he leaned into the mounted microphone. "Crane operator."

Jan looked at him suspiciously. "What are you doing?"

"You'll see," he smiled enigmatically.

Napoli flanked Jan and advised the other SEALs ranged around the ship at once. "Keep your eyes peeled."

❄

"Turn around!" the seven skippers ordered their helmsmen almost simultaneously.

None was more charged with nervousness than *I*'s captain, who ran through the bridge to the starboard wing. His catcher was nearest to the *Stavenger* after her turnaround.

"All ahead," he shouted.

The same words at almost the same moment echoed from bridge to engine room of every catcher. Two violent, opposite forces engaged simultaneously. The mortally wounded adults, thrashing blindly, wrenched one way. The catchers pulled in the other. The high-tensile lines snapped taut! This released a holdback mechanism along each harpoon shaft. Claws sprang outward and hooked into the dense flesh deep inside the whales, disembowelling them with tremendous force.

Strength and life, in that order, drained out.

I's captain and crew, whose pay was tied to the tonnage of their catch, had been jubilant to snag the biggest and heaviest of the whales. Now the 108-foot long, 168-ton sentinel bull was going to be the death of their ship. But they did not dare cut him loose. The skipper knew Yamamura meant every word of his threat to demote officers. *I*'s screw whirled at maximum revolutions and barely mustered twelve knots.

❄

Vesprhein waved to Iron Lady, "Take over the bridge. Keep us aimed to cut through him midships."

"Where are you going?" asked Napoli, snapping alert.

"Fishing." Vesprhein disappeared down the companionway, his feet banging against the rungs that he took two at time.

"What is he up to?" asked Knight.

Jan frowned with suspicion but didn't have time to dwell on it. She powered up the loud hailer with a scrawling whine and grabbed the Aldis lamp.

"Starboard ten," ordered Iron Lady.

Quvango cranked the wheel. The *Stavenger*'s bows edged over.

"We are going to ram you," Jan's voice boomed in Japanese, clicking the shuttered lamp. "All crew! Abandon stations! Abandon ship! Save yourselves!"

Jan swiveled, catching a movement at the corner of her eye. Breaking the clean, foreshortened lines of the *Stavenger*, the arm of her crane swung out from behind her superstructure. Vesprhein stood in a superhero stance inside the curve of its swaying hook!

Jan blinked and her eyes dawned with the clarification of her earlier suspicion. Knight articulated it. "He's going to try and take the bull."

"Like hell," retorted Jan firmly.

"The beast is dead," argued Quvango.

"I let you guys have one."

"The Japs will just come back for him once we leave," said Iron Lady. "Do you want them to have him?"

Jan saw his point. Iron Lady pressed the foghorn in an extended blast of final warning.

❅

With horrified eyes, *I*'s captain saw the pirate ship, wild waves slurping up her towering sides, advance with no reduction in speed.

"Lower away!" he yelled. *I*'s lifeboat broke free of the davits and splashed hard into the ocean, dropping the Japanese out of sight on the other side of the doomed catcher, whose vertical hull provided the evicted crew a few moments of security. That evaporated when their line of sight cleared and they were treated to an awesome, worm's-eye view of the *Stavenger* appearing on the other side, dead center of the catcher. Growing. Growing. Growing. Her massive bows dwarfed *I*'s wheelhouse. The *Stavenger*'s width midships outmeasured the catcher's length stem to stern.

I's Captain thrust the lifeboat away as fast the Yamaha outboard would go.

The other six catchers fled at speeds proportional to the size of their catch. Those towing the calves were well ahead of the three with the cows.

❊

Jan's heart pounded in sync with the engines. Like everyone else, her eyes stayed on Vesprhein. He waved like a child trying to impress. The crane operator completed the fast half circle of the hook to the front of the *Stavenger*'s thrashing bows.

"He's going to drop on deck," explained Iron Lady, "engage their harpoon line to our hook and swing out of there before we ram the catcher."

"Does he have the time?" asked Jan anxiously. The arm of the crane extended only thirty-five feet beyond the knife-point of the *Stavenger*'s curtsying bows.

"About fifteen seconds." At her current speed, the *Stavenger* covered almost two feet per second. Iron Lady tittered between his teeth. "So timing's everything."

Jan's eyes darted toward him. Iron Lady repulsed her—the scaly mosaic of his perennially dry skin, a mouth with barely visible lips, eyes that angled away just enough to recall those of a snake and a demeanor of convenience that he embraced with a chameleon's ease. But the Englishman thought so little of Vesprhein's chances, he did not even bother to hide his feelings. His expression was transparent. All he needed to become the *Stavenger*'s next master was for Vesprhein to miss a step or fumble the hook-up.

Jan's throat constricted. Goose bumps leapt out of her skin. Ruthless, conniving and never above murder, Vesprhein was still her best bet to complete this drive. Not because they'd developed a working relationship of predictable move, countermove, action and reaction, but because he elicited obedience from his men in a manner that even the Navy SEALs and her own stature as first lady never would.

❄

I's foredeck slid under Vesprhein's feet.

He let go of the chain. Dropping ten feet, he landed cleanly on the catwalk. That took a second. The *Stavenger* drew two feet closer. The crane operator retracted the arm of the crane to compensate for the shrinking distance and swept the hook after Vesprhein, who loped to the gun platform. When he got there, the *Stavenger* dipped into the ocean. Twenty-five feet away.

The displaced bow-wave surged toward *I*.

Vesprhein dropped to his knee too soon. The turnoff valve on the compressor noisily pumping air through the high-tensile line into the slain bull was just beyond arm's reach. He didn't have time to dash the trickle of sweat from his eyes.

The *Stavenger*'s bow-wave struck *I* like a breaker upon a jetty. Vesprhein reached for the railing around the gun platform, anticipated the sharp list and rolled with it. Four seconds ticked off before he was sure enough of his footing to let go.

The *Stavenger* drew inside twenty feet.

Vesprhein calmly shut off the air before disengaging the line. Otherwise, it would run amok like an inflated balloon released without securing the neck. The *Stavenger* slid within ten feet before he freed the line to the bull and stood up. "Fuck!"

The crane hook receded out of reach as the *Stavenger* started to climb one last time like an elephant lifting a gargantuan foot to crush an insect.

"Did he get out of there?" Jan rushed on to the bridgewing but the ascending bows put the catcher out of view. The crane operator couldn't tell either. The hook dangled below his line of sight. He decided to simply follow Vesprhein's orders precisely.

Iron Lady leaned into the microphone and shouted, "Brace for impact!"

The crane operator cranked the levers to retract the hook in a return half-circle a heartbeat before the *Stavenger*'s keel descended upon *1*.

Metal tore. Wood splintered. Wreckage blasted up the *Stavenger*'s pitted flanks. She carved through *1* like a chainsaw through balsa. The catcher's stem and stern shot clear of the ocean like a twig snapped down the middle. Small orange flashes rippled across the disintegrating catcher. Pieces of hull, deck, catwalk, bridge, mast, cabin and machine broke away and flew.

On the quaking bridge, Quvango danced to the ear-rending symphony with both hands on the wheel. Outside on the bridgewing, Jan clutched the railing and peered forward, her breath held in suspense.

Smoke from igniting fires within *1*'s collapsing bowels curled over the *Stavenger*'s sides and enveloped the bridge. Visibility became sporadic as she continued to stomp over *1*. Shockwave after shockwave went swiftly from a sullen rumble underkeel to a maelstrom of mangled remnants whirling skyward. The Japanese catcher ground directly beneath the killer-factory ship's superstructure with one resounding boom. The *Stavenger*'s screws smashed *1*'s derricks and foremast. Jan backed off the bridgewing, feeling heat and burning paint.

Finally, the smoke wisped clear. The crane arm became visible.

Vesprhein was hanging on!

Jan's shoulders sagged. Vesprhein dangled from the hook with one hand. The other grasped the line to the bull. He barely stayed ahead of the fiery shrapnel thrown up by the *Stavenger* violently bisecting *1*. His face cracked with a broad grin.

Then a thunderclap rocked him.

He pivoted around. *1*'s screw-shaft rocketed toward him.

"Arlov!" Jan waved from the bridgewing.

He met her eyes, his bravado grin fading.

There wasn't time to yell out her rescue plan. Even if she did, there was no way he'd hear her. Only a fortuitous, split-second break in sound had even allowed his name across.

She nodded to Napoli. He had one shot. It had to count. There wasn't time for another.

Tension curled Jan's fingers even tighter around the railing. Napoli aimed for one of several ropes and halyards that stretched tightly between tethers and pulleys on deck and atop the mast, and back to the top again.

The report was inaudible. Jan didn't realize Napoli had pulled the trigger until the bullet tore a two-inch thick tie-down rope along its second stretch up. The abrupt break turned the pulley with a rusty shriek, whipping the rope free with a powerful, lashing crack.

Shutting out *1*'s roaring annihilation, Vesprhein let go of the hook with a hope and a prayer. He fell directly toward the rocketing screw-shaft. A second away from being threaded by it, the frayed end of the rope reared out of nowhere and whipped within his reach.

Vesprhein grabbed it with one hand. The jute fibers cut his palm like a thousand razors. He held on. Tethered to the top of the mast, the rope snapped tight like a rod and stopped his fall. He swung aside and watched *1*'s screw-shaft sail past him.

The stench of oil and diesel burned Vesprhein's nostrils. Then he was off on a flight through the black, greasy vapor, between the exploding debris and over the top of the spindly columns of water that rushed up when the falling pieces struck the ocean.

Then silence burst his eardrums.

The *Stavenger* slid past *1*. A harsh sweep of wind dissipated the smoke, revealing what remained of the catcher. Matchwood.

Beyond the starboard beam, the other six catchers ran like fugitives, their half-exposed screws churning white patches of froth that turned crimson from the blood of the whales they towed. A blast of hot air struck Vesprhein's mouth with the familiar acrid taste of the *Stavenger*'s emissions. The poop deck whipped under his feet. Releasing the rope, he dropped onto it.

"Amazing," Jan said, arriving on the run, noticing that he still gripped the high-tensile line to the bull.

"You think I was going to let go of a quarter of a million dollars? He quipped

It was the kind of remark Jan never found amusing. This time, she laughed. He did not expect her to. She'd lost seven of her precious whales. But she hugged him impetuously, catching him by surprise. He tightened an arm around her waist and felt relief exhale out of her tensely knotted back. Then she pulled back with a wavering, self-conscious smile.

"You saved my life," Vesprhein said. "Thanks." Jan stared. He met her eyes. He guessed what she was thinking. *Was the gratitude sincere?*

Jan smiled, "I know you wouldn't have done the same for me."

And she meant it, he knew. If there was one thing he'd learned about the first lady, she did not have a false emotion. She deserved honesty back. He said seriously, "I owe you one."

Her expression changed. "In that case, I want your word that you'll see this drive to the end." She held out her hand.

Vesprhein took it without hesitation. "You got it."

Evanston

When Leeds dropped the bombshell about the secret hunt, Everett abandoned his closing statement to respond. "I know you are protectionist, Keith, but you still might want to acquaint yourself with the phrase international waters. There will be vessels ahead, beside and behind the whale drive that we can do nothing about. However, our satellites show none are cause for concern."

"Not according to the pictures my office is expecting," said Leeds.

Everett's lips fluttered. The president salvaged what he could with his closing statement.

Delta stayed behind to deny the allegation outright and spin the rest of the debate, while Pleasance and Lhea received the brunt of Everett's tongue lashing on their drive to the airport.

"It's not as bad as it seems," reassured Pleasance, adding that the instant-polling graphs had dipped but never nosedived. The president enjoyed the benefit of the doubt as Jan's husband.

"All that'll change when Leeds produces photographs," growled Everett.

"*If*," stressed Pleasance, "he can produce them."

The motorcade pulled up beside Air Force One. They were all heading back to Washington for a day. The car phone rang just as the agents opened the door.

"The first lady, Mr. President," said the operator.

Everett nodded Pleasance and Lhea out of the car. They closed the door.

"Those bastards killed seven whales," blurted Jan angrily.

"Hello, Jan," said Everett, in no mood to hear about her damn whales. "Thanks for asking how the first debate went."

"I'm sorry." Jan calmed down and asked almost rhetorically. "How did it go?"

"Quite well," replied Everett shortly, then added angrily, "until Leeds brought up the whale drive."

"What about it?"

"You know!" he snapped and didn't elaborate. They were on a secure line but he wasn't taking any chances.

"So what are you going to do?"

"We are denying it, of course."

"I mean about the Japanese. They aren't getting away with this slaughter."

"Have you been listening?" snarled Everett. "Any conversation with Japan will confirm Leeds' accusation."

"Well, it is true!" Jan's tone sharpened.

Everett bit down an angry retort.

Jan bristled, "As much as I'm rooting for you to win, I will blow your secret deal if their fleet captain makes another move toward the drive. Do you hear me? If we lose one more whale to those ships, it's over, Carsten. We're over."

The public outcry against Japan, while loud, would be lost in the tsunami of outrage at home and abroad toward his secret deal with Tokyo. Jan was the only one who could expose it, but out in the middle of the desolate Pacific, she was the farthest from being in any position to do it.

"I cannot get involved," Everett declared flatly.

North Pacific

Jan slammed the phone down without another word, turned around and witnessed the scientific shack disintegrate into a chaos of voices.

"Screen three is blacking out!"

"Identify the SuperCharlie."

"On the west flank."

"Charge level?"

"LED out."

"Squeeze a little more juice."

"Negative. I just lost contact with the robot."

"Probably sank."

"East flank is open."

"What's our ETA at the drive?"

"Computing."

"Screen five flickering!"

"That's the SuperCharlie on the west flank."

"ETA at the drive thirty-two minutes."

"Charge status on the remaining SuperCharlies?"

"Twelve to fifteen minutes."

"Screen five out."

"The west flank is now open!"

"Shit."

North Pacific

The pelagic fleet's course and speed continued to mirror that of the eco-warriors.

Yamamura walked deliberately alongside the bridge, his eyes fastened on the six catchers, matching speeds and lining up alongside the slipway to transfer their dead whales.

First was 2. She towed a male calf. He was bigger than the biggest minke Yamamura had ever caught. Giant pliers at the end of the *Rising Sun*'s big aft winch grabbed the tail. When a strained roar of steam indicated the winch had assumed the dead whale's weight, 2 pulled away, digging her stem into the ocean with a great surge of sea and spray.

Flensers on the factory deck plowed their knives into the calf as he was dragged past them up the slipway, slicing him from jaw to tail. A sharp odor of fatty blood wafted up. Other flensers in high spiked boots slit his hide into long skeins, dismembered his fins and hacked his developing jaw muscles. They attached the ribboned hide to cables of the winch amidships, which tore it off. Underneath he was red, white and raw. They hooked his jaw and upper mouth and tightened the cables in opposite directions.

With a loud crack of bone and blubber, the dead whale ripped apart.

Two rows of flensers, who could not see each other over him, worked from bottom up to slit the meat on his back. Swipes of flesh slid on deck. Blood rushed out from veins that were the girth of a human arm. Then they eviscerated him by crisscrossing over his belly with their knives plunged deep. His guts piled high in an avalanche of secretions, urine, feces and fatty blood.

Potmen appeared, sank their talons into the ragged chunks, dragged them across the gory deck and dropped them through the smoking holes into the towering boiling vats. The forward winch cables picked up his backbone and violently took his skeleton apart. Derricks hoisted the ribs and broken sections of spine into the air so the clinging remnants of flesh could be hacked off. The clean bones were shoveled off the deck, sawn, crushed, dried and bagged. The flensers climbed down the forward ladder to wash up and take a brief break.

Other flensers methodically devoured the second and third calves. A few minutes later, the initial gang reappeared up the aft ladder to start on the first cow. She was eighty feet long and a hundred tons. Yamamura unconsciously flicked his tongue over his lips, stirred at the deepest level by the same predatory thrill of conquest he'd felt in the immediate moments after he'd beaten the woman in his cabin.

The crew's apprehensions had dissipated when the tonnage from the three cows and calves reached them. Yamamura heard the brash talk to pursue the drive. Never one to mingle with the common crew, he decided he must capitalize on their high morale, alleviate their fears. He walked among them, interjecting that the American president could not and would not act—at least for another six weeks until the elections. Only the first lady stood in their way.

Seeing the fleet captain amidst them inspired more chatter and audacity. They greedily projected their earnings if they harvested the rest. They stood to make in one season what they would eke out in fifty.

The factory worked like a conveyor.

Yamamura took a deep breath of the wretched smells, unable to leave the deafening sights and sounds of carnage.

Washington DC

Robert Random, Director, National Reconnaissance Office, who had watched Leeds put the president on the spot, waited for Lhea to call. When he did, he knew the African-American senior counsel would be furious and he was, demanding Random pinpoint the source of the leak. After all, the pair had masterminded the consolidation of all surveillance and reconnaissance imagery. Random's first call was across town to the National Photographic Interpretation Center.

❈

NPIC Assistant Administrator Bianca Stevens replaced the receiver and summoned her boyfriend, Bruce Wilhelmson, into her office. "Close the door."

"What's wrong?" The threat analyst had been a nervous wreck ever since learning she'd called Keith Leeds's campaign to sell the photographs.

"Nothing. Relax." She kissed him long and hard then gloated, "I just got a call from Random. He wants me to investigate the leak. Just like I told you. We are home free, baby. And rich."

Wilhelmson twitched. "We haven't got the money yet."

"We will. You saw the debate."

Leeds's campaign had informed her they would not pay until the Congressman tested her tip in the debate, where he had promised pictures. The Democrats were now cornered to produce.

"We can even up the price," smirked Bianca.

"When are you going to call them?"

"Right now."

North Pacific

"They're breaking east!" exclaimed Welling and added, "but they're not scattering."

"Because," began Raquel and paused, rippling down her library to match the sounds from the drive, "the bulls along the unguarded east flank are still echo-ranging ultrasonically."

Ultrasonics were high frequency sounds with a range of a few hundred yards. They detected smaller objects. If the blues were going to run amok, they'd be imaging their environment with infrasonics, which was low frequency active sonar that picked out large scale bathymetric features like continental shelves, sea mounts and rising walls of islands.

"Bottom line, Raq?" asked Jan.

"They aren't convinced the killer whales are gone."

❄

The *Rising Sun*'s sonar operator opened his intercom to the bridge. "Orca sounds on the east side of the drive just stopped."

Yamamura raised his eyes slowly.

"A malfunction?" asked his XO.

"Let us hope so." Yamamura thought for a moment. "Order all vessels to lay off an intercept course."

The navigating officer reported from the compass platform at once. "Course to steer will be port ten."

"Sir," ventured his XO, "do you think it is wise to—I mean, so soon after we just took seven whales—"

"Six!" spat Yamamura. His eyes transformed into fathomless holes. "Did I seek an opinion from you, Number One? Port ten. All vessels to maximum revolutions."

❄

"Surface contacts!" called Smith. The pelagic fleet appeared in the upper left corner of his screen. "Doing thirty-six knots."

"That'll get them to the drive in fifteen minutes," calculated

Yale.

"That's the time we have left on the rest of the SuperCharlies around the drive, max," rapid-fired Taggart.

"Our ETA?" asked Jan.

"At our current speed of fourteen miles an hour," answered Yale, "about thirty-eight minutes."

Jan chewed on her thumbnail.

"This ship can do fifty knots," said Raquel. "That'll get us there in ten minutes. Way ahead of the fleet."

"We just need to reach the drive the same time as the Japanese, don't we?" asked Welling. "They won't want to lose another catcher. That means just doubling our speed to thirty miles an hour."

"Either way," said Jan, "it means leaving behind the sixteen whales in front of us."

Raquel shrugged. "We can come back for them."

"Not if Yamamura gets to them first. Don't you think he is figuring we'd probably try to salvage the drive?"

"Shouldn't we?"

Jan said nothing. Why did every eco-battle have to be heart wrenching? Victory was never clean. A mindless need to take life triggered the fight in the first place, which then always became about cutting losses. Once again she was forced to balance emotion against the practical thing to do.

Knight asked her gently, "Would you leave these whales behind if Miracle was not one of them?"

She looked at him. Sagging her shoulders, she reached for the intercom to the bridge.

"I have an idea," said Fallon.

Jan's hand froze in midair. When he stopped talking, he knew he'd redeemed himself.

"I'll be on the bridge," said Jan, giving the back of his neck a squeeze. "Good job."

The *Stavenger* pushed across rollers marching out of the low-lying mist. Her slow speed made the troughs seem deeper. She rolled in one with the intensity of a quarter sea. Ignoring the busy slaughter deck, Vesprhein trained his binoculars beyond the port bow. Two fugitive blues blew and sounded quickly.

"Can I ask Assad to serve whale steak for supper tonight?" he grinned. Jan spared him a bland smile. "There is no fucking way you can save the sixteen whales and the drive."

"As a matter of fact, there is a fucking way," retorted Jan. Fallon's idea was a simple and ingenious formula to reach thirty miles per hour without increasing their current speed.

❄

"Integrity of the drive?" asked Raquel.

Welling checked his screen. None of the tribes along the unguarded east and west flanks had yet dared to break away from their safety of numbers. He glanced over to the spectrographs. Cows continued to bleat *caution caution* noises, while the bulls showed no signs of letting down their guard. Studies speculated that adults carried memories. Maybe the blues remembered mates and offspring lost to killer whales, cunning hunters known to lull their prey with silence.

"Holding," he reported. "They are echo-locating ultrasonically. Shit! The Japanese ships cut their engines. They just went all quiet!"

Raquel straightened. Hearing the Japanese fleet fade, the blues lengthened their calls abruptly into songs, or repetitious vocalizations, that began at 19 Hertz and swept down to 17 Hertz. The lead bulls from the tribes on the edge of the east and west flanks thrust away in diverging paths, yelling *follow follow*. The cows shrieked *run run* to their calves.

"They have stopped perceiving danger," Raquel groaned.

"The Japanese have visual of the drive," said Smith, reading his scope.

❄

The sky shaded toward a glorious sunset with rich, changing hues. Seven rivulets of black lengthened upward like spilled dribbles of paint. Smokestack after smokestack slid silently over the pastel horizon. Finally, the hulking shape of the *Rising Sun* appeared, whispering across the heaving ocean.

"The drive is disintegrating!" reported the *Rising Sun*'s sonar operator to the bridge.

"What is the *Stavenger*'s position?" Yamamura asked radar.

"Still trailing the sixteen," crackled the reply at once.

Yamamura turned to his XO. "Order 2 to change course toward those whales if the *Stavenger* leaves them to pursue us. Everyone else, continue to drift in silence toward the whales." Seeing the stampede of plumes along the curved line separating the ocean from the sky, Yamamura smiled with the cold excitement of a hunter whose game just walked into his cross hairs.

❄

Raquel took charge. "Step on it!".

Fallon and Taggart worked their joysticks as far as they would go. The SuperCharlies zigzagged at twenty miles per hour, but a general stampede was taking hold. The mechanical fish could barely keep a steady course in the powerful undercurrents thrown every which way by the berserk giants. Whales stacked one below the other, seeking openings to break free along the east and west flanks. The infra-red camera eyes of two robots glowed bloodily into view along the eastern flank.

"My SuperCharlies are in place," said Taggart. "Ready to secure east flank."

Welling swiveled. "Raq?"

"Rear and bottom of the drive secure," she responded.

"Times five on all fish?"

"Yes," chorused Raquel, Taggart and Fallon.

"Speaker sequence, five seconds apart, east to west."

Her forefinger descended toward the keyboard. "Opening

speakers."

"Not yet!" yelled Fallon.

His SuperCharlies hadn't overtaken the three tribes leading the westward stampede. It would be disastrous if they came alive before they reached the open ocean. The whales might think the orcas were amidst them and run amok in every direction.

The drive would be over.

Raquel could not check herself.

Nothing sounded more dreadful than the soft *clack* of the space bar.

Washington DC

In the National Photographic Interpretation Center, Bianca Stevens and Bruce Wilhelmson watched two armed Federal Protection Service officers converge like the mouth of a poacher's bag. Wilhelmson swallowed hard and discovered his throat was suddenly dry.

The couple was handcuffed and led away through the main hall with the entire staff watching. The public humiliation was no accident. Random had deliberately ordered it to strike the fear of the consequences of disloyalty in every employee.

Ever since Random had usurped all control of the nation's vast, intricate, super-secret eyes and ears, he'd jealously guarded his immense power. It was obvious this leak was a transparent ploy to derail Everett's presidential campaign, but Random's paranoia also made him suspect it might be an attempt to undermine him. Reacting like a dictator on a purge, he had ordered a security clamp-down at all NRO facilities. Every phone was tapped and anyone entering and leaving was to be searched. No exceptions. Not even Bianca, the woman he'd placed in charge of the investigation at NPIC.

Random's distrust paid off.

"The leak came from the NPIC operator watching Jan and his

boss," the NRO director reported smugly to Air Force One, which turned into the runway for takeoff. "Both are in custody."

Air Force One

Everett waited until the plane leveled off, then nodded Pleasance and Lhea into the privacy of the conference room. They settled into swivel chairs around the table and fastened their seat belts. He recounted his conversation with Jan and declared, "We have to terminate the Sitka scenario and secure the loose ends."

Pleasance and Lhea agreed.

The plan, outlined by Dale Gabon, hinged on the Japanese taking the blues secretly. After the November polls, the White House would leak it to the public and put the heat on Prime Minister Maeo. Jan's reputation and record would neutralize any attempt by Tokyo to implicate the president as long as he kept her convinced of his innocence. If Maeo distanced himself from the hunt, the angry fishing faction would topple him from power. By keeping Nobuo Tomita abreast through the deputy speaker, the White House had the US-friendly, power-starved, Liberal Democratic Party veteran working overtime for the necessary support to take over.

Nobody on either side of the secret deal had anticipated the coincidence of events that led to Jan's discovery of the whales. Luckily for the White House, it happened after the IWC vote. Whaling had been banned, ironically thanks to Maeo, who'd bought Venezuela's vote with an assurance to the fishing faction that the Whalers League of Japan could harvest those blues. Then Jan won the race to the Bering Sea. Pleasance dreaded that an angry Maeo might reverse the Sitka scenario on them by leaking the secret hunt. Coupled with Judge Cimarron's court order, which had painted the president as pro-Japanese and placed him publicly at odds with the first lady, resurrecting rumors of marital discord, the scandal and uproar from the clandestine deal would have killed Everett's re-election bid. So it came as a huge relief when the pelagic fleet began to shadow the drive instead. Even after Jan sank three catchers, Tokyo remained silent, which was sweet music to the White House.

Now, by rustling whales, Yamamura had effectively married his prime minister to the same secrecy that the American president needed to ensure. Otherwise, public outrage would end both their careers.

"Jan went off our satellites when she sailed below the Aleutian chain," informed Pleasance. "We won't pick her up until she arrives off Hawaii a week before the elections."

"Let's nix aircraft reconnaissance over the drive," decided Everett.

Since the wiretapping, Pleasance had been walking on eggshells where Jan was concerned. He asked, "What about daily bulletins?"

"We'll make them up with photographs and videotape we didn't use earlier," answered Everett decisively.

"In that case, no more radio contact or phone calls to and from the drive."

"That's all right," Everett said. "We're not talking." He looked at Lhea. "Brief Robert."

Lhea nodded, then asked, "And the NSA?"

"Nothing needs to change," replied Pleasance. "Like we've always planned, we'll go for Leeds's jugular by exposing him as a two-timing son of a bitch who passed secret information to his friend. Until then, hammer Leeds in each rally and every press conference with the fact that he hasn't produced satellite photographs."

By taking Jan out of the equation for the rest of this campaign, Everett had affirmed his commitment to win.

Gallup released its post-debate poll: Todd, 33. Leeds 30. Everett, 28.

North Pacific

Raquel kept her eyes glued to the radar. The bull leading the charge came to a dead stop with astonishing swiftness. The frequency of his vocalization peaked. His echo-ranging went from infrasonic to ultrasonic in successive calls. The return revealed ten killer whales. A cloning algorithm in the perception module allowed Raquel to simulate multiple images: five per SuperCharlie. She inched up the volume of the SuperCharlies, which came on sequentially every five seconds. The blues saw orcas advancing behind, below and from the east—in that order.

The vertical stack of whales flattened in a hurry and scattered west.

Toward the Japanese fleet advancing silently.

Fallon's SuperCharlies hurried to overtake the three tribes leading this westward stampede. His robots were programmed to turn on the sound last—now just two seconds away from blaring. But they were caught in a massive traffic jam.

"Come on, come on," urged Raquel.

One screen dissolved into static.

"Fuck!" Fallon shouted a rare profanity.

The LED indicated the robot's battery was dead. Now there was only one SuperCharlie that could stop this exodus toward the Japanese fleet and its screen darkened without warning.

"Oh, no!" cried Raquel.

"Battery?" asked Knight.

"Uh-huh." Fallon shook his head from side to side.

The robot was trapped between two whales. Their hides were a moment away from brushing. Fallon fed the threatened robot forward with a burst of speed he did not think it had. The two dark mountains continued to collapse toward each other.

"Speakers on!" exclaimed Raquel fearfully.

The SuperCharlie vocalized too soon. The very next moment, the dark monitor brightened sharply with a thermal image of an open, empty ocean. It had squirted out from between the massive bodies.

Fallon shouted, "We're clear!"

The bulls, leading the breakaway, pulled up like horses reined in at full gallop. Cows and calves behind them thrashed around in a hurry, detecting the hunting cries of five orcas that seemed about as far away as the Japanese fleet.

"West flank secure!" shouted Fallon.

"Drive integrity re-established," Welling reported to Jan on the bridge.

The blues crowded together between the phosphorescent markers of the five SuperCharlies that cloned the sounds of a twenty-five-orca pod. All one thousand eight hundred and forty-nine animals surged south.

❋

"New intercept course is starboard fifteen!" hollered the *Rising Sun*'s navigation officer from the compass platform.

The XO reached for the handset.

"Wait," said Yamamura. His eyes darted to the repeater screen. "We will reach the whales at the same time as the *Stavenger*. How can that be?"

His navigation officer looked down for a few moments, then looked up. "I think I know how they did it, sir."

"Explain!"

"Simple mathematics." It was based on a theorem of motion called relative velocity. Two objects coming from opposite directions closed toward each other at the *sum* of their approaching speeds. When the five SuperCharlies howled forward with the simulated sounds of twenty-five killer whales, the harassed blues accelerated to sixteen miles an hour toward the *Stavenger*, which was herding the sixteen fugitives at fourteen miles an hour. The combined speed was thirty miles an hour.

Yamamura swiped his mug off the chart table with the back of his hand. The ceramic cup shattered. Hot coffee splattered. He marched aft. He had lost 40 percent of the fleet for about 1 percent of the catch. Should he risk more boats?

❄

Smith crackled the Japanese skipper's decision over the bridge speaker to Jan. "They've fallen back to their parallel course over the horizon."

"We'll reach the whales in time to swap in recharged SuperCharlies before we lose anymore," announced Taggart.

"Excellent job, guys," congratulated Jan.

"TV is down," said Raquel. "Snow on all channels."

"Check the radio."

"Nope."

"I'll be down." Jan left the bridge.

The transmission and receiving lights remained dark. UPLINK DOWNLINK UNAVAILABLE, flashed the LED. Jan's lips thinned with realization. *Sonofabitch.* She told them how her conversation with Everett had ended.

"So he cuts you off? What a bastard!"

"Fuck him," Jan shrugged.

Everyone looked over to Smith, the resident compuwiz. He answered right off, "This gear is Star Wars caliber. Way out of my league."

"There's no other radio on board?" asked Welling.

Jan shook her head. "Carsten had everything removed. What about the rest of this stuff?"

"Read only," replied Smith.

A hush descended.

They were alone and completely isolated.

Jan's despondency didn't last long. "We can use this blackout to drive the final stake into pelagic whaling."

Boycott grinned, "Always the fighter."

Jan went on, "We have the most eminently qualified people to help us with the planning and execution."

"With what?" asked Welling.

Jan raised a finger. *Wait.* She opened the door and summoned Napoli standing guard outside. She quickly got him current. The SEAL team leader tried to keep an impassive face but he could not. Jan could almost hear him asking himself how the president could abandon his wife to rejuvenate a political campaign.

"She's the last factory ship afloat," Jan reached the heart of her scheme. "With all whaling banned there's little or no chance the Japanese will build another one. Ever."

They began work on a plan to sink the *Rising Sun.*

Tokyo

With each passing day of the whale drive, which had not left the front page, anger mounted on the streets. The price of fish, as staple to the diet as rice, had doubled, thanks to Judge Cimarron's order banning the Japanese from American waters. Of course, the people knew nothing about the secret hunt. In hindsight, Maeo realized his unspoken permission to let Yamamura use force had been a knee-jerk reaction that now left him standing precariously on one foot with nobody but the Whalers League of Japan to lean on for support. Comforting was the fact that the League had little option but to stay on as his crutch.

Also, in spite of their losses, the WLJ was not ready to give up fifty years' supply of whale meat just yet. The $1.5 billion dollar catch could easily absorb the loss of the boats that had gone down and even pass it down to the consumers. The League's continuing greed helped Maeo stave off an immediate crisis. Also, the Americans could not sustain this ban on Japanese fleets entering the EEZ. Kaiyou and other giant fishing conglomerates, all Japan-owned, bought and processed 72 percent of all seafood consumed in the US.

Maeo called a meeting of the full cabinet. "This country has always had the best rapport with Republican presidents in the White House." There wasn't a whisper, a cough, even a rustle to break the ensuing silence. Everyone anticipated what he was going to say next. "Since we have become an issue in the American election, let us decide its outcome by electing one."

North Pacific

East of Hawaii, between the islands and the mainland, silver fangs of dawn appeared cautiously across the horizon. As the brightness yawned wider, rich colors streaked upward and across. An unobstructed sun ascended over the edge with a leisurely majesty, gilding the water and the clear sky. The *Stavenger* took shape in the growing light. She rose between the shimmering crests and hit the slow-climbing front swell dead-on. There wasn't a cloud in sight. It promised to be a glorious day. Necklaces of surf rolled across a placid ocean. The lookouts changed and the night shift went off all over the killer-factory ship.

Jan emerged out of the bridge and was struck by the heat and humidity. By noon it would be sizzling. She wore jeans and a T-shirt. Her untied blonde hair cascaded like a golden sail. Napoli trailed the first lady to her favorite spot, the gun platform, where she spent hours staring at the randomly erupting blows ahead.

Within moments, Miracle surfaced. The nurse appeared too, rolling lazily. Water washed over the sulfur colored diatoms covering her belly. This yellow coating deepened into gold when the sun's rays touched her.

"I heard you this morning," Jan shouted proudly to the calf.

Taggart and Yale, working the last few minutes of the swing shift, had recorded Miracle's call for the first time. As the calf was able to stay under water longer with each passing day, the scientists had noticed the nurses urging her into deeper, darker waters, where sunlight dissipated 10 percent every 240 feet. Miracle emitted clicks involuntarily and the returns gave her first acoustic image. It was blurred because the echolocating wasn't focused. Miracle called for several hours, mostly from just beneath the surface, where, the eco-warriors and scientists figured, brightness allowed her to visually confirm what her sonar picked out. Jan felt like a mother who'd heard her baby talk for the first time.

"You wanted to see me?" Vesprhein appeared outside the bridge. He was bare-chested, wearing only shorts, showing off his muscular, inked body. Jan was aware he'd caught her staring a few times.

Napoli and she met him halfway up the catwalk. Vesprhein was in the same great mood since he'd narrowly escaped with his life and the bull, which had yielded almost fifty tons of meat. Adding that to the pregnant cow that the pirates had chopped up at the start of the drive, their take so far was a third of the capacity of their holds. The closer they got to Cetacean Bay, she guessed, Vesprhein figured Yamamura might ambush them again and fill his holds to capacity. This hope had boosted crew morale too.

"We are going to sink the *Rising Sun*," said Jan with no preface.

"Your husband has stopped giving a shit about your whales to win the presidency," he said perceptively. "So you have stopped giving a shit about him to save your whales."

Jan ignored his allegation. "You will be coming aboard the *Rising Sun* with us. In fact, you and I are going to be a team."

Napoli nodded. "Owens and I will remain on the *Stavenger*. Just so you have the incentive to protect the first lady if you want to come back to a floating ship and your men want to sail free after this drive is over."

Vesprhein didn't argue. "What's the plan?"

"Objective one," said Napoli, "is to place explosives against the hull. We'll be rigging six of your depth charges with magnets and timers. Convert them into limpet mines of sorts. Objective two, evacuating the ship without going through her. We don't have enough people to get caught in a fight. So we must seize the bridge before they realize it."

"Easier said than done," remarked Vesprhein.

"Not really." Then Napoli elaborated.

Vesprhein arched his eyebrows and asked, "When?"

"As close to Cetacean Bay as possible," replied Jan. "If something goes wrong, we don't succeed, Yamamura will retaliate by going after the whales. If he follows them across the fortieth parallel, there are too many eco-sentinels who'll sink his ass."

Napoli nodded. "So we need to buy time."

Baton Rouge, Louisiana

Stepping off the paddleboat after a week-long sail down the Mississippi River from St. Louis, with stops along the way, Todd was greeted by his highest poll numbers. When Leeds was unable to substantiate his accusations about the secret deal with Japan, the president went after him at rallies and on the airwaves. The Democratic nominee blasted back and held steady in second place. Everett dropped another point to 27 percent.

The Doldrums, South Pacific

The drive descended into the Southern Hemisphere, where summer gathered with particular intensity this year. Temperatures climbed relentlessly during the day and dropped off negligibly at night. Everyone sported a sheen of perspiration. The men wore shorts and nothing else. Jan and Raquel, in tank-tops, inevitably elicited wolf whistles.

Visibility extended fifteen miles. The whales blew and sounded, breaking up the flat, blue sea into great white tosses of water. Plumes randomly shot into the air. Great bubbles burst around their massive dark shapes. The *Stavenger* divided the even swells in leisurely pursuit of the whales through the Doldrums, a belt of calm and light winds.

Prophet stood on the bridge. Quvango dozed at the wheel. Raquel manned the scientific shack with Welling and Fallon. Taggart, Yale and Smith slept. By the depth charge rails, Napoli, Knight and Boycott converted the second of the targeted half dozen explosives. The first one had taken almost four days, but once rigged, the remote detonator stayed inside Napoli's pocket at all times.

Since Vesprhein had promised to see this drive through in a manner that made Jan take him at his word, she'd called off the 24/7 guard. They found themselves spending more time alone, so much so the chief engineer's odds on the captain fucking the first lady were even. Jan and Vesprhein were in the Pig alone, except for Assad, who started lunch with a clash of pots and pans while they debated the right balance between economics, development and conservation.

"Take grizzlies," said Vesprhein. "Today, their population is four thousand and the acreage they need is enormous, shutting down drilling, grazing, logging, mining and roading to accommodate them."

"Are you saying we should stop protecting the grizzly?" asked Jan.

She had been trying to procure more budget money for the Endangered Species Act, a bill of rights for nonhumans, which had first been enacted in 1973. With each successive reauthorization of the act, Congress cut the annual funding a little more, fueling bitter debate about safeguarding the nation's 150,000 life forms. Of the five hundred species and subspecies to become extinct in the United States, only the New England marine snail was a victim to natural causes.

"You just need a population big enough to sustain itself from extinction. The species is saved and there's no need to expand wildlands. Besides," Vesprhein stood up and stretched, "these species are no pushovers. They've been through worse and survived. They'll learn to live in a shrinking habitat."

Arguing, they started out of the Pig. Jan plucked at the sleeveless top which clung to her sweaty skin. They veered into the corridor running outside her cabin.

"Why don't we ever talk about holding down the human population?" Jan wondered. "This planet was designed for about four billion people. We're past six."

"Hey, I'm all for that."

"Water covers three-fourths of the earth's surface," she continued. "Why should whales be limited to a few hundred. Or a few thousand? Why is it okay to limit other species to a survival minimum while human expansion goes unchecked?"

"You've won me over." Vesprhein grinned.

Jan's eyes flickered. She had been pondering a future for Vesprhein that even she had dismissed as impossible when it first occurred to her back in Hawaii while they were videotaping him for the IWC vote. Over the past few days, spending time alone with him, she began to feel more and more confident that she'd turned the corner of trust. What began as an unreal hope now seemed likely. She had run her idea by Raquel, arguing that Vesprhein's years on the opposite side of the whale war made him a perfect ally of the cause. With all whaling banned, conservationists had to reckon with increased illegal hunts. What better way to combat them than using a pirate to catch pirates?

Raquel thought it was a long shot, the longest, given Vesprhein's history and background. Then she slyly observed how this outrageous plan seemed to conveniently address both Jan's own longing for the open ocean and her growing fondness for Vesprhein. She had always teased Jan about her innocent crush on Paul Worthy; Vesprhein was Worthy, only on the wrong side of the eco-battle line. "But that makes him all the more attractive, doesn't it?" she asked Jan.

"Fifteen more days, Arlov," began Jan carefully, "we'll be at

Cetacean Bay."

"Gotta admit, I'll miss our daily talks."

Jan went for it. "Have you ever thought of quitting.

She caught him off guard. Vesprhein recovered, threw his head back and laughed.

She stopped in front of her door. "I'm serious."

Vesprhein looked at her. She was. He wiped the smile off his face and quickly looked up and down the corridor to make sure they were alone. He whispered fiercely, "Don't be!"

Jan backed into her cabin and gestured him inside. He locked the door. Jan said, "Your face was splashed around the globe during the IWC meeting. The drive is only making you more famous. After this is over, you won't be able to fade away. And you won't be able to hunt whales either. Even if they lift the ban, you'll be too recognizable. This drive has raised so much awareness that more and more green groups are probably going to be out there enforcing the zero quota. Then there's Worthy. He has a submarine now and he's hell bent on sinking the *Stavenger*. Face it. That part of your life is over."

"What are you offering?"

"Exploit the public interest and sympathy for this drive to wipe your criminal slate clean."

Vesprhein's eyes narrowed. "Why are you suddenly so interested in my fate?"

"Mine's tied to it," she admitted bluntly. "It's over with Carsten. We each love what we do too much and hate what the other does. But leaving him will also mean walking away from GreenPlanet, where I did what I pleased because of my clout as the first lady."

Vesprhein drew the logical implication. "You want to sail with me?"

"Full time," nodded Jan. He took a deep breath and stared out of the porthole. Jan stepped to his side. "I have friends who'll bankroll us. You won't be rich, but you won't starve either."

"What about my crew?"

"You own this ship. Tell them you're protecting your investment. Those who want to stay, will, and those who don't, won't. Knud Hansen did it. So can you." As creator, captain and gunner of the first single-vessel killer-factory ship, *M.V. Sierra*, Knud Hansen went on to kill seventeen thousand whales—more than any man alive. After his ship was rammed and sunk by eco-warriors, Jean-Paul Fortom-Gouin, a tiny French ecologist, succeeded in converting the giant six foot six Hansen to the cause of conservation.

"Let me tell you, being on the good guys' side of eco-wars can be just as dangerous and exciting, only you'll be chasing instead of running. It's your choice."

Vesprhein, rarely at a loss for words, was now. When he finally found his voice he said, "This is so … crazy. You're crazy, you know that?"

Jan smiled. "Same coin, different sides. Chemistry. We need each other. You said it."

"I was just coming on to you."

"And I told you, maybe."

❄

Outside the door, Iron Lady pulled his ear away. He had been on his way to the bridge crew lavatory, when he saw Vesprhein enter the first lady's cabin. Iron Lady wasn't surprised. The ship knew he'd fallen for her.

Also, of late, since they shared quarters, he found himself at the listening end of the captain's growing admiration for the first lady. Vesprhein went on too much about how she tackled every adversity thrown at her. He had schemed to kill her, yet she'd brushed it off. The race for the whales seemed lost. She never gave up. The Japanese tried to muscle in and she retaliated decisively. The president exiled her to the high seas. She found a way to use it to her advantage. He'd never met a woman so resourceful, so strong, so intelligent, so independent and of course, so beautiful. She was, in Vesprhein's words, a truly remarkable woman.

Tiptoeing away from the door, the Englishman couldn't forget that he'd come within a whisker of taking over as master of this ship, until Jan had stepped in and saved Vesprhein's life. Iron Lady's mind raced with seditious cunning. After all, Vesprhein had set the precedent, killing his captain for changing sides. Iron Lady realized he didn't have to go that far if he could inveigle the rest of the crew into recapturing the *Stavenger* when Vesprhein, Jan and the others left to sabotage the *Rising Sun*.

Washington, DC

Everett, Pleasance, Lhea, Adrian and Delta brainstormed in the sitting room of the president's private quarters upstairs. Everett finished his drink and topped off his glass again. They agreed he should drop out of the public eye and prepare for the second debate. Adrian would campaign in his place. They finished up around one in the morning.

Delta excused herself to go to the bathroom. She had emerged as the one Everett increasingly turned to for support since his break-up with Jan. As subtle as she was shrewd, Delta took full advantage of her constant physical presence beside the president, always ready with a word of comfort or quick praise, touching his arm, squeezing his shoulder. Pleasance noticed and did not discourage her. She shared his hunger for power.

When she reappeared, Everett was alone.

"Staying at your usual hotel?" Everett emptied the glass and stood up, staggering a little.

"Yes," she replied, steadying him with a quick arm around his waist. "Good night."

He found the tensions and the pressures of a failing campaign ebb in the kiss she intended for his cheek, but which landed on his lips as he turned at the last instant into her. He was ready to pull away, he knew he should, but her body responded and pressed against his. Involuntarily, he pressed himself forward and held his mouth to hers. Her body responded and their arms snaked around each other tightly.

Sober enough to realize what was happening, she pulled away. "Carsten, no—"

"It's over between Jan and me."

"What about the elections? It's too dangerous."

"You can stay in the guest bedroom."

Delta stared at him indecisively.

The Doldrums

Vesprhein pressed Jan's shoulders against the bulkhead. "How can I trust you?"

"What choice have you got?"

He moved close, lips inches from hers. "Are you really leaving him?"

She felt his hot breath on her neck. "Yes." His thighs pressed against hers. "Are you willing to change your life?"

Vesprhein looked her dead in the eye. "Yes."

Their eyes locked, the moment turned incendiary and their lips collided.

Vesprhein ripped open Jan's shirt. He snapped off her bra and roughly cupped her freckled breasts. Her nipples sprang erect. Feeling the edge of the bunkbed behind, she bent her knees and landed hard. Their mouths reluctantly tore apart. He went down on his knees and unbuckled her sandals. She'd already popped the buttons when he reached up and roughly yanked her jeans and panties down together.

She knew he was big, but realized how big only when he entered her. Jan grabbed his hair and caught her breath with a sharp moan. Her neck arched backward. Her legs jerked wider. Her ankles locked around his hips. His pelvis surged and ebbed. Ignited by pleasure, they gluttonously breathed in the tangy fragrance of their sex mixed with perspiration sheeting down their bodies. The torrid heat stuck and unstuck their skin noisily.

Jan had always enjoyed the physicality of sex and nobody was more physical than Vesprhein. She matched his audacity and raised him some. He wasn't surprised by her lack of inhibition. Their breath shortened to staccato gasps full of electric ecstasy as they trembled, convulsed and sought every inch of each other.

Washington DC

As much as Jan and Vesprhein were bold, sure and demanding, Everett and Delta were shy, tentative and complementary to each other's needs. They started with half kisses, their encircling arms gradually pressing each other closer. Everett felt no urgency, no rush. Jan always had dictated the pace and positions, and as they'd drifted apart, their sex became purely physical, lacking intimacy. Tonight, he rediscovered the sensuousness of foreplay. Delta and he were still dressed when they lay down in bed, enjoying their caresses, their smells and the taste and feel of their lips against each other. When they were finally naked, they made tender, gentle love.

In the morning, before the Secret Service agent arrived to turn on the coffee maker, Delta returned to the guest bedroom, deliberately leaving the door ajar so he could see her sleeping under the covers. She stayed in the White House on the pretext of helping the president cram for his second debate, which was lackluster. He surrendered another 2 percentage points to Will Todd.

Tropic of Capricorn, South Pacific

On the *Rising Sun*, Yamamura cleared the radio room to receive a person-to-person radio transmission from Tokyo informing him that the American president and the first lady had parted ways acrimoniously. So, she was on her own, unwatched and unprotected.

Twenty degrees below the equator, summer mounted with a vengeance. The fans did little but circulate air already hot, wet and heavy. Now a boiling rain of heavy droplets fell from the low, black clouds. For more than two days, the Japanese fleet plunged through a pewter haze of searing temperatures, squalls and seas. To keep the water out, the doors and windows were shut, releasing a stench of sweat into every level.

Yamamura knew he could not take the *Rising Sun* to the *Stavenger*, as Jan had done to *1*. The eco-warriors carried depth charges, which they would set off if they saw the factory ship bearing down. Sitting on his steel chair, then pacing in the confines of the bridge, Yamamura contemplated his options.

A head-on wind slashed across the bows, moaning through the lattices and lines. The sea broke into a turmoil of torn whitecaps and deep troughs. The six catchers strung around the *Rising Sun* like watchful dogs. Yamamura idly observed the bows climb toward the hidden sky, challenging the ocean thundering down and across. All levels simmered like a kiln. Since he permitted no laxity in dress code, every uniform was soaking wet, which could have been attributed to the downpour were it not for the overpowering smell.

As the afternoon passed, so did the careering water and swooping cloud banks. Evening showcased a spectacular red sunset. Nightfall drew a velvet darkness across the sky with high, bright stars and a sliver of a moon.

Just when Yamamura was about to turn in, the radio operator came running up. "Sir, the captain of *5* just sent this message."

Yamamura read it. His lips twitched ever so slightly in a smile. He'd realized he needed Vesprhein's cooperation for any plan to succeed. The pirate captain seemed to have read his thoughts because he had flashed a recognition signal that was actually gibberish, but *5*'s captain had recognized it. It was used only by Japanese cargo ships before every illegal whale meat transfer on the high seas. Then Vesprhein had flashed a quick message seeking to speak with Yamamura around midnight.

The *Rising Sun* slid over the black horizon punctually. With all her lights off, she became one with the night. Officers and crew, ordered indoors, crowded the portholes.

"Can you read me?" flashed Vesprhein from the *Stavenger*.

Yamamura took the signal lamp himself. "Yes. I want to move on whales."

"So do I. Need your help to retake ship."

"How?" asked Yamamura.

"US Navy SEALs on board. I will convince first lady to meet with you as if to discuss a deal."

Yamamura asked eagerly, "When?"

"Two, three weeks. Closer to Cetacean Bay."

"Why so late?"

"They will be tense. Afraid you have to make a move now or never. Thus will be more open to negotiate safe passage of the whales."

"Of course." Yamamura was delighted.

"Will confirm in two weeks. Same time. Out."

The *Rising Sun* melted back over the curve of the ocean.

Tokyo

Secrecy was paramount, so the finance minister rode the crowded train alone, incognito, alighted at the Nihonbashi Station, and took the exit marked A1. Faceless office buildings jostled next to stunning neoclassical architecture in Tokyo's number one business district. He sauntered on to the bridge underneath the expressway, crossed the street again and turned at the Currency Museum.

The sidewalk was deserted all the way to the Central Bank of Japan, whose chairman emerged as the finance minister approached.

The two men greeted each other with quick bows and strolled on together. The finance minister and chairman were two of the country's three economic czars, yet never once did the conversation touch on anything remotely monetary or fiscal. Each briefly inquired about the other's family and speculated on the weather ahead. September through October, called typhoon season, had cooler temperatures. They disagreed vigorously on the outcome of the sumo tournament final at the Kokugikan, then changed the subject to the upcoming Tokyo Festival.

This encounter alone, if discovered, could trigger volatility on Wall Street. But markets the world over would have reacted in greater panic had anyone seen them enter Takara headquarters to meet the president and CEO of Takara Securities, the third man in the triumvirate of power behind Japan's economic policies.

Takara, whose Japanese characters translated to "treasure," was the biggest, most powerful financial house in the world, a global supermarket, transacting three times the dollar amount of the annual US national budget daily. Last year, Takara's pre-tax profits matched those of the entire US brokerage industry. Its share of the Tokyo Stock Exchange was greater than the combined share of the top ten US firms in the New York Stock Exchange.

The guard at the door escorted them to the elevator but did not ride up. For all the enormous clout that Takara wielded on global finance, its headquarters boasted none of the extravagance found in Wall Street firms a fraction of its size. The executive level showed some affluence, with soft carpeting and a few high priced oils. The president's office, though, looked like the bridge of a starship. A digital atlas dotted Takara's network of branches worldwide with electronic displays indicating activity in every stock market. Other screens continuously updated the yen against different currencies, gold fixes and other economic indicators.

"When Takara talks, people listen," began the finance minister after pleasantries.

"What do you want us to say?" asked Takara's president.

The finance minister explained.

"That is a noble cause," responded the president, showing no emotion, "but Takara has a board of directors and millions of shareholders. Our fortunes are intricately tied with the US economy."

"After this, it will be the other way around," said the chairman of the Central Bank of Japan.

"True." The president looked from one man to another with a thin, lizard-like smile slithering across his face. Like Maeo, he supported Yamatoism and hated kowtowing to the Americans, especially now that they were in debt to Japan. He nodded once.

He was in.

Reine i Lofoten, Norway

As a young man, Kristof Jonsgard had led Onassis's unregulated whaling atrocities. Now eighty-one years old and jowly, he methodically set up the coffee machine to brew a pot and hobbled between the desks. It was still early and the staff wasn't in.

Sun slatted through the blinds. During these few weeks, the town enjoyed normal days and nights. Lying as far north as Siberia, the Lofoten Islands otherwise endured twenty-four hours of daylight during summer. In winter the sun did not break the horizon at all.

For more than a century, whaling had constituted half the town's income. What remained today was this office that stubbornly fought to keep sustainable harvests alive: the Marine Hunters Alliance. Jonsgard was its current secretary.

The MHA published a quarterly newsletter, *The Harpoon*, with essays opposing the anti-whaling movement and comics that made jokes in support of slaughter. Until three years ago, the MHA had restricted itself to voicing the needs of the local Nordic communities. When Jan entered the White House and brought whaling under siege, all the pro-slaughter nations united behind the MHA to counterattack. Money poured in. Newsletter circulation multiplied. The staff went from one to ten. But following Jan's stunning victory at the IWC, contributions to the MHA dried up overnight.

Jonsgard did not know how he was going to make next week's payroll. The loss resonated all the way to Oslo, inside the Norwegian parliament, where even the powerful fishing lobby could not exert their muscle. By holding Japan's UN Security Council seat hostage, President Everett had effectively annulled Tokyo's verbal assurance to finance Norwegian takeover of the advance warning radars. Europeans refused to step in since Norway had voted to stay out of the EU. With Russian nationalism getting more worrisome by the day, Oslo was ready to hand Everett a foreign policy success in these critical, final weeks leading up to the election.

A long beep signaled coffee was ready. Jonsgard shuffled over. The phone rang. He poured himself a cup first, then answered in Samnorsk, a kind of hybrid Norwegian, "Good morning. MHA. This is Kristoff Jonsgard."

The split second delay in the response indicated an overseas call. The voice at the other end, which he recognized as American, startled Jonsgard with a detailed knowledge of MHA's unspoken bounty for the deaths of eco-warriors around the world.

"What do you want?" asked Jonsgard nervously.

The American offered an amount so generous, in full and in advance, it would take care of next week's payroll as well as MHA's long-term cash flow. In return, the caller wanted Jan Everett assassinated on the Thursday before Americans went to the polls.

BOOK FIVE

It is unclear what the opportunity to see huge whales in the Antarctic would be worth, but operators of tour boats to the Antarctic are well aware that the sighting of a whale is often the most memorable event of a trip ...The current receipts of the Antarctic tourist industry are between fifty and seventy-five million dollars a year—money which is made, of course, by a business that is currently conducted without any reasonable chance of seeing a blue whale ... Though I don't know what an accessible group of extra large blue whales would earn for the tourist industry in today's dollars, it would undoubtedly be more than those who killed the largest blue whale realized for oil in her blubber. I imagine the figure might be between a hundred and thousand times more.

Roger Payne,
Among Whales

Cetacean Bay, South Pacific

Paul Worthy couldn't raise the *Stavenger* on the radio. The eco-maverick had been roaming the Antarctic sanctuary, where he played sentinel every summer, from October through March, stalking pirates who illegally slaughtered about a thousand whales. This year, he'd arrived with his newest weapon, his submarine, *Earthforce,* and the most watched video on the Web—his torpedo attack on the *Kagoshima.* Instrumental in getting all whaling banned, the sinking had also served to forewarn the hunters of the deadly consequences they risked. He'd reiterated the technology and firepower he packed in blogs and publications in culprit nations. The intimidation worked.

Green intelligence reported pirates were staying away in droves from the Southern Oceans, where the first attempt to protect whales predated even the IWC. Whaling nations agreed in 1938 to create an area called "the sanctuary," stretching from the bottom tip of South America to the Ross Sea and from 40°S to the ice edge. In 1955, reduced catches forced the sanctuary to be opened for three years only. It was never closed. Biomass, or total body weight of a species, calculated as a rough measure of the significance of a species in the ecosystem, depleted from one hundred to ten million tons. Conservationists and scientists demanded a moratorium to restore the marine ecosystem. But Antarctica was entwined in international pacts that specifically excluded whales, since Agenda 21 of the UN Conference on Environment and Development recognized the IWC as the responsible body to limit or prohibit the exploitation of marine mammals.

Pressure mounted on the IWC to act. An inter-sessional working group met in February, 1994, on Norfolk Island in the South Pacific, to study protecting whales below the fortieth parallel. They unanimously recommended "establishing a sanctuary in conformity with Article V of the 1946 Convention … and that a sanctuary can be created by the Commission if its members so decide." There was only one voice of opposition, Japan, which not only fought it but strong-armed enough support to shrink the sanctuary by moving down the latitude to 55°S in the Indian Ocean and 60°S in their backwaters, the South Pacific. Then the Japanese thumbed their nose by using the "research and scientific whaling" loophole to consistently take 900 minkes a year from inside the sanctuary.

Five years ago, Jan launched an effort to expand the sanctuary up to the fortieth parallel in all the southern oceans. Japan retaliated, mobilizing a massive effort to abolish the sanctuary altogether. It was war. IWC sessions turned contentious. Iceland quit. Korea and Russia walked out. Last year, Jan finally forced a vote and won by a decisive majority.

Cetacean Bay, a name she proposed, became reality.

To offset losses claimed by whaling nations, Jan suggested

regulating the sanctuary as a tourist attraction with entry fees. The idea was turning out to be a goldmine. This summer, visitors were expected to surpass five million, doubling the number of whale watchers who came last—the inaugural—year. Still, Cetacean Bay was so vast, pirate vessels snuck into remote regions. To combat them, as first lady Jan marshaled aid for volunteer Green groups, who not only policed and enforced the zero slaughter, they developed an intelligence arm, whose spies had exposed Japan's secret hunt last year and Norway's violation of the minke quota this past summer. One of the big recipients of this funding was *Earthforce*, Paul Worthy's militant environmental group, who also received a submarine as a gift from the first lady.

So he owed Jan big time. When he failed to reach her, he telephoned Everett. He knew the president reasonably well and was rudely stonewalled. At first, Worthy dismissed this to preoccupation, what with Everett sinking in the polls. Then he spotted White House lies in recent daily bulletins on TV. Worthy, who'd crisscrossed the Pacific countless times, recognized the waters as much further north. He became convinced the first lady had been thrown under wraps and isolated. *But why?*

Good old-fashioned guilt born out of gratitude, friendship, loyalty and his promise to join the last leg of the drive, precluded Worthy from giving up. Working round the clock, the *Earthforce*'s radio operators roamed the airwaves, hoping to luck into a transmission from the *Rising Sun* and her catchers. Worthy knew the Japanese broke radio silence only when absolutely necessary, and even then, they hopped frequencies to guard against eavesdropping. The chance of being tuned in at the right time to the right bandwidth was a long shot at best.

Worthy blindly started north. Just when they needed fair weather to continue monitoring the radio, the *Earthforce* ran into the opposite. Cetacean Bay encompassed all the notorious latitudes of the Southern Hemisphere—the Roaring Forties, Frantic Fifties and

Screaming Sixties. The sun streaked through occasional breaks in the black clouds, which swirled low with cyclonic rage. For every eight hours of tranquility below the surface, the crew was forced to spend another eight on the surface recharging the submarine's batteries under assault from running hills of pulverizing seas and screaming attacks of gale force winds.

The crew wore life jackets at all times, even when they slept. Worthy feared the rudder might snap. They frequently heard the screws, yanked clear out of the water, clawing thin air. The sea reared up and smashed the bows from sight, or opened up huge chasms and dropped the submarine between collapsing walls of water.

The *Earthforce* shook and shuddered, pitched and rolled, rose and fell, without a moment of even keel. Worthy cut lookouts to two-hour turns, most of which they spent mesmerized by fear. Icebergs, cut loose from the frozen continent by the sun's annual migration south of the equator, jumped and skidded off the giant swells. They collided against the hull and each other with shattering tides of sound waves.

For three days, the hours on the surface became a countdown to when they could dive again. Finally this morning, the *Earthforce* surfaced to calm dawn, sweet sunshine and lullaby seas. They were still inside Cetacean Bay, continuing north between towering castles of ice. Sunlight glanced off their different, beautifully lethal facets.

Rorque Jr. entered the Control Room and found Worthy over the chart table. "Hey, Paul."

"Good morning." Worthy turned around toward the former officer of Her Majesty's navy. "We located the drive."

They had made contact with NOAA scientists in an ocean-floor habitat off Hawaii, who'd pinpointed the SuperCharlies' orca and thresher shark sounds below the thirtieth parallel. Concern for Jan aside, they wanted to catch a glimpse of nineteen hundred blues together. The TV images hardly did justice to the magnificence of the real thing.

Worthy slanted the ruler across the chart, plotting an intercept course. "We aren't going to be much of an escort."

"Let's go anyway," said Rorque Jr.

"Absolutely."

The red line that Worthy drew met the advancing whale drive right at the fortieth parallel.

Washington DC

"We have eleven days to go and twelve points to make up," said Pleasance, addressing the Committee to Re-elect the President. Glum faces stared back. The third and final debate over the weekend in Denver did nothing to boost the president's numbers: Todd, 37. Leeds, 30. Everett, 25.

"Nobody's ever come back from behind a double-digit lead," said the pollster.

"So you want to give up?" Pleasance shouted. "Pack up and go home?" Eyes averted as Pleasance glared around the War Room. "The next person who thinks we are fighting a losing battle is off this team." He waited a moment, nodded once and outlined a strategy called geodemographic targeting.

It tapped into his formidable database of critical districts for such factors as turnouts, ticket splitting, party-switches, attitude polls and life-style analyses. Motorcade One pulled in and Everett hit on just the specific concerns most likely to sway the voters in that district. Then campaign ads saturated the airwaves. After a week of crisscrossing as much ground as the other two candidates combined, the president gained four points.

Todd's lead shrank to 8 percent, with eight days to go.

Southern Ocean, South Pacific

The watch changed all over the *Stavenger*, which slipped in and out of columns of mist. The sun was a distant, unfocused spot of light behind a thick white gauze. Iron Lady slid on to the bridge. Quvango lounged against the wheel, his dark features framed in the upturned hood of his coat. Around them, the night shift handed over with a chatter of tired voices and scraping boots.

"Did you find someone who can pick the gun room lock?" asked Iron Lady softly. He had emerged as the ringleader of the impending mutiny.

The Angolan helmsman nodded.

The *Stavenger* sluiced down into a roller, flaying the deck with balls of spume that rattled across like lead shot. Her passage in and out of the mist lent to the conspiratorial mood aboard. The enveloping white tendrils gloomed the bridge, softening the lines and graying people to moving shadows. Prophet, the SEAL assigned the day watch on the bridge, sauntered up with a steaming cup of coffee.

Under the sound of a lashing spray storm, Iron Lady murmured, "Set it up for tonight."

❄

"Sir," coughed Yamamura's first officer. "Kristof Jonsgard is on the radio from Svolvær. He would like to speak with you, person to person."

Yamamura crinkled his forehead curiously. He'd never met Jonsgard, the general secretary of the Marine Hunters Alliance, knowing him only as a voice who coordinated clandestine whale meat transfers on the high seas. Jonsgard always used a secluded radio bandwidth known exclusively to Japanese whaling vessels. When Yamamura strode into the radio room, the operator left, closing the door.

Yamamura picked up the microphone, clicked it on and said in English, "Yes?"

"This is for your ears only. Share it with nobody. There is a bounty of three million US dollars for the first lady." He paused. "Dead."

The imperturbable Yamamura caught his breath audibly. "Who is offering it?"

"An American. I don't know his identity. The money has been transferred. Do you want to claim it?"

Suddenly the inboard creaks and groans, the rhythmic dashing of water against the hull and every other sound and movement became magnified and intrusive. Whatever deal Jan planned to strike, pondered Yamamura, the ban on all whaling was an inescapable reality. This pelagic voyage could very well be the last. Jonsgard's reward made for a very, very substantial nest egg.

Furthermore, circumstances would never be so fortuitous to silence the loudest, most effective voice for animal rights. Cut off from any help, Jan was a free target, vulnerable to murder without consequences.

"Yes," replied Yamamura.

Every minute of the rest of this day seemed to stretch longer than usual. Finally, the sun dropped below the horizon and night brought a jeweled sky. At the precise hour, Yamamura slid the *Rising Sun* over the horizon. He nodded to his XO, who flashed the recognition signal.

❄

Jan stood beside Vesprhein on the *Stavenger*'s bridge. She signaled him to respond. He worked the Aldis lamp to answer, "The first lady is here with me."

The *Rising Sun*'s bridge and other lights blinked on. The darkness of the hull below left the bright pinpoints suspended in midair. The factory ship lay in a trough, pushed along by a slow roller.

"She would like to meet you on Thursday morning," continued Vesprhein.

They would be within shouting distance of Cetacean Bay, where Trevor Smith had shown Jan on his Intergraph Workstation dreadnoughts drifted in crowded packs. These icebergs could provide the ideal refuge for the whales in an emergency. The catcher captains would never risk venturing into this deadly jungle of ice.

"It has to be on the *Rising Sun*," Yamamura specified.

Jan was counting on it.

Vesprhein flashed, "Accepted."

Tokyo

Thursday, October 29, arrived at the Japanese capital before anywhere else that mattered in the world. Ten young men, living in different outlying suburbs, woke up at almost the same time. Daylight was still several hours away. A late October chill gripped the city. The wives of those who were married rose as well, readying breakfast, packing lunch and laying out ironed shirts, ties and suits. These women used to be part of the staff where their husbands worked and had been matched by the company so they would understand the early mornings and late nights. Dawn trickled in when the ten men crammed into the crowded trains and subways that would deliver them downtown. A few traveled as long as two hours, yet none showed any weariness when they all arrived punctually for the 7:45 meeting at the Shinjuku branch of Takara Securities.

These men were *kachos*, or section chiefs. Up and down the four major islands of Japan, in Takara's 148 offices, identical meetings were being called to order. Young women, wearing striped uniforms, passed out reports of the previous day's activity in major markets around the world. There were coy eye contacts. The bachelors would eventually marry one of these girls. The unwed few ended up as mistresses. The general manager of each branch, or *bucho*, strode in.

An air of urgency prevailed this morning, the third and final day of the US Treasury auction. Short-term bills and notes were bought and sold on Tuesday and Wednesday. Today, Thursday, climaxed with the drama of the world's most reliable and best-guaranteed investment: the benchmark US thirty-year "long" bond. It was issued to raise money to pay for the US national debt, which stood at a daunting $15 trillion, the combined currency of all the nations in the world put together. For the last decade, Congress had been selling more and more of these bonds. This was much like paying one credit card with another, except that Washington issued itself the next card, raising the limit every time.

The Federal Reserve did not sell the bonds directly, but delegated that to the biggest, most elite brokers. In 1986, Takara became one, and was today the biggest buyer and seller of US government securities. Be it war or peace, good times or bad, the US Treasury never defaulted on paying up when they came due. So countries, banks, pension funds and insurance companies sought US long bonds—none more so than Japan under Prime Minister Maeo for exactly the kind of financial Armageddon he was planning to unleash today.

"Good morning," boomed a voice on the speakers. The *buchos* and *kachos* in the 148 branches stared up expectantly at the live video-teleconference link to Takara's head office in Nihonbashi. They recognized the senior investment executive

"Congratulations to everyone for surpassing yesterday's target, but today is a new day with new challenges."

The words, forcefully delivered, were hardly sufficient prologue for the strategy that he went on to outline. Pencils faltered to a stop because there were no notes to take. Eyes lifted to the TV screen in astonishment. A few gasped loudly.

"Any questions?" The executive was being rhetorical. Decisions made at the top were not challenged. He signed off.

The conference room at every branch remained still for a full moment, then erupted. The *kachos* hurriedly convened table meetings with subordinates, who realized that after two days of bullish bidding on the US bills and notes, traders on the floor of the New York Stock Exchange were going to be blindsided. Takara's action would end careers, trigger suicides, shut down brokerages, bankrupt every state in the US, annihilate the dollar, start riots and cause a meltdown Americans dismissed as impossible.

Southern Ocean

The *Rising Sun* crawled over the brightening horizon on minimum screws. Foam dashed on to the bridgescreen. Yamamura, his head and shoulders outlined against the dull copper sky, shivered in the morning cold. Activity throbbed under his feet. On the other side of the floor plates, every man and woman had been up at first light, firing up the factory.

The six catchers, flanking the *Rising Sun*, rolled in an uneven line over the endless ranks of whitecaps. A strong wind blew in from the west, bending the steady trail of greasy smoke streaming out of the catchers' single funnels. Slender strips of cloud, tinged with the color of the early sun, floated in distantly spaced zigzags. Yamamura warned his six captains that the drive would be across the fortieth parallel by midday and expected a swift, efficient hunt when he ordered it.

Yesterday at sundown, they'd seen their first big iceberg, a square, glassy mountain, sweating water from top down. This morning, the faraway horizon was studded with more. The radar operator reported dense ice beyond this line. Staring at the low sun dancing off in breathtaking pinks and golds, Yamamura realized proximity to Cetacean Bay had little to do with why Jan delayed their meeting until today. She knew his catchers could never hunt among those jostling bergs, giving her whales a chance to escape.

The Japanese fleet captain raised his binoculars. The *Stavenger*'s silhouette solidified against the backdrop of icebergs at the intersection of sea and sky. The water took on a dark blue shade and the clear, cold air made for sharp visibility. As the sun inched higher, washing away the colors, details filled into the black outline of the killer-factory ship amidst the multitude of blows of gamboling whales.

Last night, Yamamura had announced over the ship's speakers that the American first lady was coming aboard the ship to make a deal. It came cloaked in a clever speech, delivered with Hitlerian hate and motive. He'd railed against the first lady, shrewdly linking years of anti-American propaganda and the crew's firsthand experiences on this voyage, specifically the loss of four boats, particularly *1*, cut in half by the *Stavenger* for all to see, to entrench Jan as the demon of Western cultural bias who had ended a livelihood that was their birthright. It worked.

All morning, resentful and defiant anticipation mounted aboard the seven vessels.

❄

The *Stavenger* took a slow roll starboard in a shallow, dragging trough. Her bow lifted, her stern cocked and water broke in white breakers along either beam. A crescent foam marked her lethargic course.

Jan emerged to the smell of coffee pervading every level of the catcher. Filtering to their stations two hours before they usually did, the day crew carried steaming mugs. Pungent vapors wafted out of the kitchen chimney to the slaughter deck, where she observed Napoli going over the deployment of the depth charges with Raquel, Boycott and Knight one more time. Owens stood over the gratings at the back of the bridge. He kept Iron Lady, Quvango and the two lookouts on the wings in front of him.

Finally, it came time to go.

She accompanied Raquel, Boycott and Knight into the shack. They huddled with the scientists, hand over hand, for a moment of solidarity and good wishes. Jan led the boarding party back outside. She wore jeans and a flannel shirt over a first layer Gumby survival suit. Her long, blonde hair was knotted and stuffed into the collar of the oilskin jacket. Raquel, Boycott and Knight, in thermal wetsuits, sat down and hugged on their flippers. When they stood up, Napoli,

Prophet and Larkin, helped them don the rest of their scuba gear, including a waterproof belt pouch containing tear gas canisters that the SEALs had brought on board

"Synchronize your watches," said Napoli. "I've set the depth charges for nine AM precisely."

Everyone's wrist came up, adjusting the minute and second hands to 7:33.

The pelagic fleet, visible through the open slipway, straddled the horizon line. Jan and the three SEALs emerged onto the ramp and formed a human wall, allowing Raquel, Boycott and Knight to back into the water unseen. Vesprhein pulled around with the lifeboat and cut the motor. Accustomed to severe Norwegian winters, he had only a life jacket over his bare upper torso, loose khaki Dockers and a pair of Timberlands. Jan, Prophet and Larkin climbed in. She settled on the bench beside Vesprhein. He throttled the outboard. The motor revved and the lifeboat pressed toward the Japanese factory ship.

It took fifteen minutes to get across.

The *Rising Sun*'s near empty holds caused the intimidating all-deck factory ship to ride high in the water. Jan had been surprised that Yamamura did not object to any of Napoli's preconditions before she came aboard, the most important being that none of the crew be allowed on deck. Faces pressed against the glass in all accommodation portholes below the forward superstructure, gawking at the approaching first lady.

Vesprhein eased on the throttle, turning in a wide circle toward the *Rising Sun*'s stern slipway. The sloping tunnel, large enough to accommodate a locomotive, dwarfed the approaching lifeboat. Vesprhein leaned backward and freed the three lines pulling the eco-warriors and explosives.

Vesprhein moored the boat alongside the slipway ramp. The two SEALs jumped out, unslung their guns and waited for Jan. Preceded by Vesprhein and flanked by the SEALs, she started forward on the factory deck. They passed between the big circular openings of the steel cooking vats deep enough to swallow a person. The lips were stained dark brown with the blood of whales. Oily steam, squeezed out of the blubber still cooking from the slaughter weeks ago, climbed through the evenly spaced gratings. A muffled roar, underlined by a churning, hissing noise, became audible.

Jan looked up, saw Yamamura on the aft bridgewing and almost smiled at his audacity to gear up his factory for a hunt.

"Sir!" the XO beckoned Yamamura into the wheelhouse.

Yamamura turned away and disappeared inside. He followed his XO's finger toward the *Stavenger*. A light flashed from an engine room porthole low to the water. The flashed message was succinct.

"It's a trap."

The XO reacted nervously. Yamamura posted a cold smile. So, Jan had no intention of giving up any whales. She needed an excuse to come aboard the *Rising Sun*. He didn't doubt she planned nothing less than the destruction of the last factory ship afloat.

Raquel pulled up by the *Rising Sun*'s drive shaft, moved a few feet behind and placed the first charge. The magnets grabbed the caked steel. She dove under the keel. From that vantage, the hull burst outward in a bulge so wide she couldn't fit the port and starboard extremities in a single field of view. The *Rising Sun*'s massive size caused her to wonder if the charges would be effective. She reeled in the line, released the second charge and clamped it to the other stern tube.

In the distance, Boycott affixed the first charge to the keel on the port side and proceeded forward. Knight did the same starboard and reached the bows. The charges, all planted in a straight line on either side of the ship, would rip the bottom out if they detonated at exactly the same time.

Prophet, Jan, Vesprhein and Larkin climbed the forward ladder to the *Rising Sun*'s officers' deck. The XO appeared around the giant winch. He bowed deeper than etiquette mandated. Only Jan bowed back.

He led the way up the bridge ladder. Jan noticed apprehensive twitches and thought nothing of them. The officers and crew came to attention and bowed. They looked nervous too. Yamamura did not, standing in front of them, his hands casually thrust into the front pockets of his tunic. Jan responded to the others' show of respect, but even as she bent at the waist, her eyes never left Yamamura, whose gaze focused unblinkingly on her as well.

In impeccable English, he said, "I'm Shinjiro Yamamura, captain of the fleet."

His right hand emerged. Prophet and Larkin stiffened their machine guns. Yamamura smiled gently, extending his hand. Jan shook it. The SEALs kept their muzzles level. Even that did not prepare them for Yamamura's next move. He smoothly brought his left hand out of his pocket with a revolver that he pressed between Jan's eyes.

His own officers looked shocked.

"Drop your weapons to the floor," Yamamura said with quiet venom.

The SEALs obeyed and stepped away. Yamamura snapped his fingers toward the microphone. His XO unfroze and fumbled it over to him.

"All boats!" Yamamura ordered in Japanese. "We have permission to take all the whales we can before they enter Cetacean Bay. Full speed forward. Begin your hunt!"

Vesprhein stepped away from Jan's side, cracking an easy, treacherous smile. "Good work, Captain."

Wall Street, New York

The crisis began slowly, first as a nagging discomfort when the

New York Stock Exchange opened. Traders on the floor nervously held their ground, while their highly paid superiors frantically tried to figure out if Takara's move could be tactical. When Takara's position did not change, the first cracks in confidence appeared and proliferated. Within minutes, shockwaves consumed Wall Street.

The Dow Jones fell 582 points instantly.

Takara was dumping Japan's entire inventory of long bonds and making no move to buy new ones. The bloodletting commenced.

It was Black Monday all over again.

Southern Ocean

Six throttles opened and shattered the tranquility of Cetacean Bay. The three catchers on each side of the *Rising Sun* surged forward. Clearing her bows, they fell in line and accelerated away.

"What the fuck?" Napoli jerked his binoculars toward the six advancing boats, leaping spray, gathering speed. He swung toward the *Rising Sun*'s bridge. Unable to see past the glass glare, he adjusted the mouthpiece of his headset radio. "This is SEAL team leader. Come in."

Prophet and Larkin did not respond, tipping off Napoli that they were in trouble.

"Probably have a gun on them," said Quvango. "Like this." He cocked an automatic next to Napoli's ear.

The SEAL team leader snapped his eyes toward Owens. Iron Lady had him covered. The pirates disarmed the SEALs.

"Since the captain—" the Englishman broke off to correct himself, "ex-captain took the only lifeboat, you have no choice but to get the scientists out of the shack and jump overboard before Quvango here releases the rest of the crew." Pirates, on and off duty, were under a lock-down at their stations or in their quarters. "They'll be coming after you with everything we got in the gun room." He ripped off Owens's headset radio and dropped it in the captain's chair. "Keep yours on, Napoli, so you can hear the first lady die."

He motioned them off the bridge with a dismissive flick of the wrist.

Outside, Napoli and Owens broke into a run as Iron Lady and Quvango burst into laughter. The SEALs vaulted over the guardrail and raced along the gangway overlooking the slaughter deck. They grabbed the handles of the ladder and slid down fireman style just as the door to the scientific shack opened and Welling emerged anxiously.

"What's happening?" he asked, seeing the SEALs. "We saw the catchers—"

"Get everyone out of the shack!"

"What?"

Napoli shoved Welling inside and addressed the others. "We no longer control this ship."

"Is Jan okay?" asked Yale.

Napoli shrugged. "I don't know."

"Jan said to set the whales free if there was any trouble," said Taggart, turning to his computer.

"We don't have time for that."

"This won't take a second," assured Taggart and flew his fingers over his keyboard.

Armed pirates burst on to the *Stavenger*'s deck, firing guns exultantly into the air.

"We gotta go! Come on, come on!" Napoli raised his voice.

Owens and he quickly shepherded the scientists toward the rear slipway. Iron Lady grinned down from the bridge. The SEALs and scientists ran off the ramp into the water. Bullets riddled up a crowd of spouts around them.

"That's enough!" Iron Lady shouted. "Stations everyone! We have fucking holds to fill!"

The *Stavenger*'s screws whined to maximum revolutions. The SEALs and scientists swam desperately out of their path.

Taggart gasped out of the water. "Look!"

"They're all sounding!" Fallon grinned.

The multitude of spouts disappeared as if someone turned off the tap. Tail flukes straightened and descended. In seconds, all that remained of the drive were whirlpools. Napoli guessed Taggart had darted the SuperCharlies into the heart of the drive. The blues thought the orcas and thresher sharks were among them and bolted in a stampede. Even as they thrashed about in the water, the scientists eagerly discussed the whales alternating ultrasonics, to spot the SuperCharlies' virtual threat, with infrasonics, to map an escape south into the open ocean. Huddling into tightly knit tribes, males would enclose the calves and females.

Scientific jargon aside, Napoli wondered if the first lady's blues could outrun the *Stavenger* and the six Japanese catchers to the southern horizon line crammed with icebergs?

Behind the bridge glass of the *Rising Sun*, Jan glared at Vesprhein. *How could I have been so wrong about him?*

"Three of her friends are underwater, planting explosives on your ship, set to go off at the top of the hour."

Jan looked toward Vesprhein, while the eyes of the XO and other bridge crew swiveled simultaneously to the clock over the wheel. 8:01 AM.

Yamamura calmly touched Jan's cheek with his gun. "You're making it so easy for me."

"Isn't she?" said Vesprhein. Without breaking his smile or stride, he wrenched the gun out of Yamamura's hand!

The Japanese fleet captain was caught with the same flatfooted surprise as the SEALs when he'd pulled the gun on Jan.

Yamamura blustered, "Don't be a fool. Your MHA general secretary is offering a reward of three million dollars for her. Dead."

"Really?" Vesprhein swung the gun toward Jan, Prophet and

Larkin. "Steady, mates. That's a fine pot of money." The caution in his voice stopped them from picking up their guns. "I know Jonsgard. He's like a father to me."

Vesprhein swung the gun back on Yamamura. "Never did like my father much."

"You sonofabitch!" Jan punched Vesprhein's arm.

Vesprhein grinned. "Or Jonsgard for that matter. But I sure could use the money ..." He began to swing the gun back toward her.

"Knock it off!" Jan said.

Vesprhein kept the gun trained on Yamamura. "I guess it's going to be like the lady says."

Jan shook her head. "Where are Raq and the rest?"

The SEALs swept up their guns. Larkin moved to the screen. "I see them."

Raquel, Boycott and Knight broke out of the water beside the *Rising Sun*'s accommodation ladder, a series of rungs welded into the side of the ship from keel to deck. Their heads twisted together to see the catchers speeding away. Stricken by the same thought, all three looked back in the direction of the bridge. Jan waved, signaling them to hurry up.

She looked at her watch. They were back on schedule. Raquel and Boycott made for the bridge on the double, while Knight scampered aft to guard their boat. The Japanese might unwittingly seize it during the next phase of their plan, which Jan kicked off now by turning to Yamamura, "Order your men and women to abandon ship."

He glared at her for a moment, then took the microphone. "Attention all levels. This is your captain. Our ship has been captured by eco-terrorists." Jan did not waste a reaction. "Bombs have been set to explode at nine AM. Evacuate to the lifeboats immediately in an orderly fashion. I will be the last to leave, after everyone is saved. Coxswains, take a head count. Make certain all are off this ship."

"Now," instructed Jan, "order your catchers back."

Yamamura looked at her, made a move as if to obey, but ripped the microphone, cords and all. "No."

"Motherfucker in hell!" exploded Vesprhein, seeing the *Stavenger* pulling away at full speed.

Raquel and Boycott rushed in at that moment. She exclaimed, "Problem. Our guys are in the water!"

Jan's eyes descended to the SEALs and scientists thrashing about in the sea.

"SEAL team leader, come in please," said Prophet into his headset radio.

"This is SEAL team leader," answered Napoli. "We are safe and can hold out until your rescue."

"Ask him about my ship," shouted Vesprhein.

"The first mate is in control," reported Napoli. "Clearly a planned takeover."

"Fuck, fuck, fuck," raged Vesprhein and dashed to the repeater screen. The six blips, representing the catchers, swarmed alongside the *Stavenger*'s dot.

Jan hurried to his side. "Where are the whales?"

"I don't know," dismissed Vesprhein. He jabbed the sonar overlay. They dusted onscreen in clumps, each clump representing a tribe, helter-skletering away from the SuperCharlies.

Yamamura smiled coldly, "You cannot save them. Most of them will die."

"We'll see about that," Jan said, then turned to Vesprhein. "We have this boat."

Vesprhein was one step ahead, grabbing Yamamura's scruff. "Order full ahead ..."

As he spoke the *Rising Sun*'s screws wound down to silence, indicating the engine room crew had abandoned their stations. The first men and women from the factory rushed out of the crew hatch, heading for the lifeboats. The giant factory ship decelerated rapidly. Jan could not find words. All was lost.

Cleveland, Ohio

Air Force One banked into its landing run. Ohio was a vital swing state and Everett had a day of rallies planned. This morning, polls showed the president had cut Will Todd's eight-point lead in half, even pulling into a dead heat in several battleground states. Optimism brimmed. Everett kissed Delta in his private quarters. They might just be able to pull this election out and make history, coming from a double-digit deficit with two weeks to go.

Then the telephones went crazy with news of the collapse on Wall Street. Pleasance and Lhea conferenced in from the War Room in Washington. Vice President Adrian, between rallies in the Pacific Northwest, came on the line. Air Force One stood parked on the tarmac. Everett stayed inside, avoiding the media frenzy in the terminal.

Everett looked at Delta. "Get me the Japanese prime minister."

"If we go down, we take him with us," said Adrian vindictively.

"How?" asked Pleasance with an undertone of irritation." By revealing the secret whale hunt and confirming that Japanese vessels are shadowing the first lady's drive? Right now, the one constituency we still hold is women. That'll evaporate and the president will become public enemy number one."

"George is right," said Everett. "We cannot expose Maeo."

"What can we do?" asked Lhea tensely.

"We can suspend all trading," suggested Pleasance.

"That's not going to help," said Everett. "The fix has to come from the Japanese. I just have to beg Maeo—"

"He is unavailable," interrupted Delta.

Everett closed his eyes. He felt Delta's comforting hand on his thigh

"Motherfucker!" cursed Pleasance.

"We're going back to Washington," said Everett. When Air Force One took off, an hour had elapsed since the market opened. The

Dow was down 1500 points.

Southern Ocean

"Three blue!" the Korean lookout's nasal voice crackled over the speakers and the gunner's headsets. "Two cow, one calf."

The Russian deserter had taken Vesprhein's place on the gun platform. The *Stavenger* and the six Japanese catchers, evenly spaced, smashed forward in a dead heat, scattering toward the widespread blows of the dispersing tribes. All seven ships were at maximum revolutions. His rangefinder read 200 yards. Out of range. The *Stavenger*'s superior speed closed the gap fast. His LED jumped to 150 yards ...135 ... 120 ...

The Russian's eyes squinted, then widened. He abruptly pulled away from the crosshairs. "What's that?"

Iron Lady croaked over his headset an instant later. "Shit."

Like a shark, fin first, the *Earthforce*'s sail sliced out of the water between the whales and the seven speeding vessels.

❄

"Yes!" Jan shouted, punched Vesprhein, high-fived Raquel and asked Boycott, "Did you get it?"

"Like magic!" he hollered back without moving his eyes from the viewfinder of his camera.

The submarine emerged like an undersea behemoth and galloped toward the advancing ships. Worthy appeared on the hurtling sail with a loud hailer and tuned into the open radio frequencies as well, "Stop or we'll sink you! Stop now!"

The southern seas exploded in a deafening clash of turbines as every engine went into Reverse Full!

❄

Jan wasn't surprised. The pirates and the catcher captains knew the eco-maverick was an even bigger kamikaze legend than her. He chased, boarded and rammed ships on the high seas with no concern for his own safety. They were all probably reluctant hunters even before Worthy showed up. Hunting whales illegally was one thing; taking the first lady of the United States hostage, as their fleet captain had done, was another. The swiftness of their retreat led her to believe that the catcher captains felt Yamamura had gone too far. They obviously had been looking for an excuse to turn away from the slaughter.

"Every whale is safe," sang Jan joyously.

Raquel cheered, "We did it!"

On the *Rising Sun*'s cutting deck, the sea of heads moving toward the aft lifeboat deck froze as one. The first full lifeboat had just dropped into the water. Two more, similarly crammed, were in various stages of their way down. The three boats had taken care of all the women on board. An astonished buzz gurgled up like a threatening volcano, first at the appearance of the submarine, then at the catastrophe that unfolded immediately after.

The helmsmen of *9*, in the middle of the six-pack of catchers, spun the wheel the wrong way even though his captain, like the rest, had ordered, "Hard a-port!"

Bracing for a left turn, the crew spilled about uncontrollably when the boat skidded right at full speed and head-on toward *6* heeling around. The crew on both ships spent an instant staring dumbstruck at the onrushing hulls. The gunners and lookouts, closest and most vulnerable to the inevitable impact, feverishly cut their harnesses loose. The gunners legged up the catwalks. The lookouts jumped out of their perches and slid down the ropes in a hurry.

The catchers closed, broadside threatening broadside.

"Evacuate the port side!" ordered *9*'s captain.

"Abandon starboard stations!" shouted his counterpart on *6*.

Their orders echoed below. Sirens wailed. With a rush of feet and disjointed cries, men lurched, gates clanged, hatches on deck flew open and nameless shapes fled.

The bow waves met first, rocking the advancing catchers fore to aft. Then came the impact, *9*'s port side against *6*'s starboard. The decks staggered under the men's feet. A terrible shriek rent the air. *6*'s raked bows ripped along *9*'s side like a tablesaw. Wood and metal exploded. Debris flew. The two catchers tore each other apart. The crew jumped into the ocean. A flash of orange cut a searing gash and ignited the fuel tanks. The fire spread and the sailors fled behind the curtain of smoke.

Someone on *6* had the presence of mind to release a lifeboat into the water.

The two boats passed, each sheared in half. They flopped into the water, spewing thick clouds of smoke and steam.

❄

"I hate to spoil the party," Vesprhein spoke, "but we have six bombs ticking under us."

Jan looked up at the clock above the wheel on the *Rising Sun*'s bridge. 8:21. She clapped. "Raq. Brief Paul."

"Tell him that I'm on your side and not to sink my ship," Vesprhein added.

Jan looked over to Yamamura and the bridge crew. "You can leave." Boycott followed their eager exit with his camera.

She nodded. "I want to sweep the ship."

"I will go with you," said Yamamura, startling Jan. He hadn't left the bridge with the other officers.

"Why?" she asked.

"I am responsible for every man and woman aboard. Many are lifelong whalers loyal enough to try something foolishly brave."

Jan hesitated. *Maybe the bastard has an iota of humanity.* "Give him a gas mask."

Raquel freed the one off her belt and tossed it to the fleet captain. She then gave Jan her belt pouch, which contained tear gas canisters. Boycott had already handed over his to Vesprhein. Raquel remained on the bridge.

"Why should I wear this?" asked Yamamura, holding up the

mask like something dirty. Instead of answering, Jan threw the first canister of tear gas down the steps leading off the bridge to the officers' deck below. Yamamura quickly pulled the mask on.

Jan tugged Vesprhein's sleeve. "Let's go."

"You first." Jan shoved Yamamura down the stairs. To Prophet and Larkin, "Keep the evacuation going." To Raquel, "See you at the slipway at 8:45."

Raquel's fingers intertwined into Jan's briefly. Vesprhein reluctantly tore his eyes away from his receding ship and followed the Japanese skipper into the swirling fumes filling the companionway.

The officers' cabins were empty. Flinging a second canister of tear gas, Jan and Vesprhein flanked Yamamura down another flight of steps to the administrative offices. Screensavers played on the computer atop the empty desk. They came to the door leading to the crew quarters.

"Open it," said Jan.

Yamamura obeyed. Steep, narrow stairs dropped away. Vesprhein tossed a canister. It clattered down the metal treads, spewing fumes. Jan nodded to Yamamura. He obediently went first, disappearing at the bottom behind a translucent twister of gas wisping toward the ventilator fan. Jan, two steps behind him, took them in one stride and came through the swirling curtain.

Yamamura was gone.

Vesprhein arrived beside her. "Shit."

A maze of tri-level bunk beds stretched in every direction. Evidence of hurried departure lay in the half-open trunks, closets and scattered clothes and personals. The women's quarters were strewn with hairnets, brushes, photographs, make-up and toiletries. A swooshing swell tilted the *Rising Sun* back and forth, widening the swath of litter. Jan and Vesprhein, taking separate aisles between the bunkers, swayed with the roll.

They found no sign of Yamamura.

"Let the fucker die," said Vesprhein.

"No," said Jan firmly. "I have never lost a human life, however vile he might have been and how much he deserved to die."

"What about Alfonso?" His Chilean first mate.

"He jumped."

"The bastard's probably springing a trap to kill you and claim the reward."

"I'm also worried about others he said might remain back with misplaced loyalty to him."

"The head count at the lifeboats will tell us if anyone's missing."

"By that time it'll be too late to come back for them."

She looked at her watch. 8:31.

Vesprhein grumbled under his breath and flung a canister ahead into the mess room and kitchen. They waited a minute, then went into the fog, carefully stepping across fallen benches, tables, half eaten plates of breakfast, pots, pans and groceries. The huge hot plate sizzled. They emerged into a gloomy corridor under the starboard edge of the cutting deck. Boots thumped, feet scraped and sharp voices of sailors heading for the lifeboats rose with urgency.

Jan read the faded sign on the exit at the top of a short stairway. "That goes up to the cutting deck outside."

She ascended and discovered the spring-loaded lock permitted the door to be opened only from the outside. Jan rejoined Vesprhein, peering left. A single flight of steps led below—the only way Yamamura could have gone.

"That goes to the factory," he said ominously, hoping to change her mind and give up the sweep.

Jan put a palm to his back. "Let's go."

"Do you always have to be the boss of me?" he whispered, as they descended.

"What do you think?"

Reaching the bottom, they stopped in front of a massive steel door. The latch was drawn. *By Yamamura?* "Once we're inside, we'll split up."

"No," snapped Vesprhein.

"Okay," conceded Jan and smiled. "Does that make you feel better?"

He grimaced and pulled on the handles. The moment the rubber linings around the door unstuck, a sound of gigantic machinery exploded with almost physical force. They flung their last canisters, waited for the explosion of fumes and then plunged into the reeking, musty hall of gurgling vats, automated flensers, bonesaws, grinders, conveyors, crisscrossing pipes, chains, hooks and hanging catwalks, pungent with the odors of a meat market.

The fluorescent lights seemed appropriately cold. Walkways wove narrow trails through the labyrinthine maze of running machines. Belts, gearwheels and pistons snapped emptily like the teeth of some predator waiting to be fed. The oil extracted from the six whales coated every surface with a glistening stickiness.

Jan and Vesprhein pulled up abruptly. Cold air blasted in from the open door of the refrigeration compartments. They nodded and entered, covering each other like a couple of cops on a raid. Bloody flanks hung from hooks. Massive cubes of whale meat were stacked on shelves twenty feet high. The enclosed space raised the monotonous roar of the giant compressors to an ear-rending decibel. The subzero temperatures froze the oozing blood into thick, red, crisscrossing ropes on the floor. Iced up in mid-drop, dripping flesh teethed down.

The refrigeration compartments were empty.

Back to back, Jan and Vesprhein ventured cautiously along the central aisle, peering down tortuous avenue after avenue between the hot, roaring machines. Their tear gas mixed with the stagnant gray vapor of the factory into whirling drafts seeking the ventilators. Within the spiraling columns, visibility reduced drastically.

"There's no one here," said Vesprhein with an I-told-you-so tone.

Gunfire sounded in loud rebuttal.

Three rounds ricocheted inches from them. With sharp, startled cries, Jan lost the reassuring press of her shoulder blades against Vesprhein as they dove behind separate vats, shooting blindly. The adrenaline rush receded. Jan stopped firing the same time Vesprhein did. An echoey silence stretched.

Jan couldn't see Vesprhein when he called out, "Are you all right?"

"Yeah!" Jan shouted back, regaining her composure.

"Let's get out of here."

Before she could answer, Yamamura suddenly rose beside her.

He grabbed her hair, which had spilled out of the collar, and threw her down. Her forehead hit the deck hard, cracking the eyepiece of the gas mask. She ripped it off and flung it aside. It disintegrated in the whir of the adjacent machine. Startled by the proximity, she retracted her hand in reflex and dropped her gun.

He went after the weapon.

She rolled under a cooking vat.

He turned, muzzle level. It flashed, then she heard the shot. He slid out of sight as she slid behind a stanchion. *Clang!* The bullet struck steel.

Vesprhein responded to the gunshot with one of his own, triggering a brief volley. Jan stood up, unarmed and alone. She ducked under a curtain of pipes and found herself in a gutter between two rows of steaming vats. She barely took a step.

Yamamura backed in directly in front of her.

She looked for a weapon.

Shit. Jan catapulted toward him with giant strides. Her footsteps gave her away. She knew she couldn't reach him in time, not anymore. He turned. His gun was up, cocked and ready.

She yanked the stopper at the bottom of a cooking vat. With a blast of steam, the bloody contents fell like a solid thing and tore the feet out from under Yamamura just as he pulled the trigger point blank into her face.

She flinched. The shot burned past her cheek, so close that the acrid smell of gunpowder incinerated up her nostrils, and the sound of the blast left her ears ringing. Yamamura fell, yelled and lost the gun. His thermal suit kept the boiling gore from fatally scalding him. Jan's first layer Gumby suit protected her.

The bullet cracked open a cooking vat. Being interconnected, tens of tons of molten blubber sought the small opening. Stress fractures appeared. The punctured vat came apart like an overloaded shopping bag, disintegrating into a flash flood of blood. Yamamura washed away down the slick gutter, but not before he managed to get enough of Jan's ankle. She screamed. Her knees collapsed and she splashed into the stinking red torrent.

Jan and Yamamura punched each other in the fast flowing river of flesh. Hot droplets stung and scalded their exposed faces and hands. The hard soles of Timberlands banged up a clamor on the catwalk above. Jan caught brief glimpses of Vesprhein following along. No way he could get a clear shot. Not the way Yamamura and she exchanged positions, wrestling fiercely.

Yamamura caught Jan with a blow to the jaw. Her neck jolted backward. His follow-up punch was too eager and missed. Jan found his eye and gouged it. A vessel burst, exposing raw nerves. Yamamura bellowed and smashed his head into her chin. Lower and upper teeth colliding, her head buzzed. He wrestled on top of her, blood dripping from his eye. The gutter bearing Jan and Yamamura ended, turning downward through a yard-wide open hole in the deck. With so much blood and gore, the viscous, reeking gush slowed and bubbled upward, before sinking like quicksand into the drain that emptied out of the bottom of the ship.

Yamamura tried to stuff Jan through the opening, but she wrestled him off her and rolled out of the gutter. Both came to their feet at the same time. He swung before she could and landed a looping uppercut.

She staggered backward, looking for help, buying time as Vesprhein cut across the catwalk overhead. It ended abruptly. Vesprhein couldn't jump. There was no place to land except the working machines. Jan heard him curse loudly and retreat to find another route. *Fuck.* One on one, she did not stand a chance against the squat and stronger Japanese skipper.

She backed away. He bulled into her. She fell backward on the blood-scarred conveyor, found the switch box and whacked it into his face with all her might. The power of the blow threw the switch and set the belt in motion. Yamamura staggered and made a shoelace tackle when Jan tried to crawl away. He got on the conveyor belt and pounded her.

The conveyor fed into bonesaws.

Jan clawed to break free. Yamamura kept his advantage, pinning her under his hands and knees. Head first, Jan inexorably approached the whirling rotors. The giant, sharp-edged blades, designed to powder massive, trusslike whalebone, would pulverize a human in a second.

Vesprhein's racing feet registered. He was a striating silhouette through the grating of a narrow catwalk, racing toward the retractable maintenance platform dangling directly above her.

"Ar—" Jan opened her mouth to warn Vesprhein that his catwalk stopped fifteen feet shy. Yamamura stuffed the words back into her throat with a blow.

Jan's head lolled to the side, where she saw Vesprhein take an impossible running leap. The platform was barely three feet square. It was like parachuting onto a postage stamp. The gap yawned a yard too far. He pedaled his legs but came down short.

"No!" shrieked Jan, her heart paralleling his plummet directly toward the bonesaws.

Vesprhein extended his arms. Both palms struck the guardrails around the platform and rocked it. Yamamura stopped hitting her, his eyes lifting. With a loud grunt, Vesprhein held the rails.

"Yes!" Jan kicked up, seizing on Yamamura's momentary distraction.

The fleet captain fell back. Jan kneed him in the groin. Yamamura doubled over. Jan looked up, hearing a loud, rusty shriek. Vesprhein had muscled himself up and on to the platform. He held the control box at the end of a flesh-caked cable, lowering it as fast as it would operate.

"Take my hand!" yelled Vesprhein, throwing open the safety gate. He fell flat on the platform, leaned beyond the edge as far as he could and offered down a thick, muscled and tattooed arm.

Before Jan could raise hers, Yamamura delivered a right to her temple. She fell, dazed. Her eyes lost focus.

"Huh!" she gasped as Yamamura stomped on her chest to grab Vesprhein's outstretched palm. The deafening whir of the bonesaws brought her to. Her sight sharpened. Vesprhein did not know who had his arm. He'd averted his eyes to reverse the direction of the catwalk up and away. "Arlov!"

He looked down, eyes dilating. She met his eyes for a moment, no more. Her head moved toward the blades' sweep. Fear snapped past the pain of the beating she'd taken and she fought against the moving conveyor. A blade circled in front of her wide eyes. She tried desperately to crawl away but the conveyor shook violently. Her skull entered the perimeter of the revolving bonesaw.

She gaped at the next razor whip toward her.

She had less than a moment to live.

Washington DC

The National Security Advisor smiled like a cat that had just eaten the proverbial canary and then washed it down with a glass of milk. The stock market crash, now 2100 points down and plunging, saturated the news. By the end of the day, Everett's numbers were predicted to be in single digits, a dubious first for a sitting president.

The NSA felt sorry. He had liked Everett enough to support him four years ago, delivering the crucial New England states. In return, the president had rewarded him with one of the most powerful Cabinet posts. But when he was not included in the inner circle, he'd felt used.

"Sir," his secretary interrupted over the intercom. "The special assistant is here to see you." His mole in the White House. "He says it's urgent."

Some of the cheer left the NSA's face when he saw the young man's grim expression. "What's up?"

"Sir," he said, pulling up a chair, "do you recall the partial that SIGINT picked up a few weeks ago threatening the first lady?"

SIGINT was the acronym for signals intelligence. As domestic sentinels, the National Security Agency's extensive network of listening stations and wiretaps had assimilated, through decades of surveillance and eavesdropping, an encyclopedic vocabulary of key words—plain, coded or scrambled—indispensable to foul play, assassination and terrorism. High speed, multilingual computers roamed the airwaves every second of every minute of every hour of every day all year round and locked on to any red-flag phrase or word.

"Uh-huh," nodded the NSA. "Made by an American and received by a Norwegian."

They'd caught only the tail end of the conversation and hadn't been able to identify the source or the recipient. Stretched thin by a campaign now at full tilt, with three presidential candidates to protect, the Secret Service, who'd received a transcript from the NSA, put it aside for investigation after the elections. There seemed no cause for urgency, since Jan was in the middle of the Pacific Ocean, her exact location a closely guarded secret and under the protection of Navy SEALs.

"Our listening post in Alaska picked up the Norwegian recipient on a frequency we've known the Japanese to use for illegal whale meat transfer ever since the 1982 moratorium." The special assistant opened the file he'd brought, turned it around and slid it across. "The transcript."

TRANSMISSION GRAB 1833GMT
(Operator's note: No communication on this bandwidth prior to the stated timetag)
NORWEGIAN SOURCE: THIS IS KRISTOF JONSGARD. MHA. I WISH TO SPEAK TO YOUR CAPTAIN.
JAPANESE RECIPIENT #1: HAI. (STATIC SILENCE)
JAPANESE RECIPIENT #2: YES? (Analyst's note: Probably the captain)
NORWEGIAN SOURCE: THIS IS FOR YOUR EARS ONLY. SHARE IT WITH NOBODY. THERE IS A BOUNTY OF THREE MILLION US DOLLARS FOR THE FIRST LADY. (STATIC SILENCE) DEAD.
JAPANESE RECIPIENT #2: WHO IS OFFERING IT?
NORWEGIAN SOURCE: AN AMERICAN. I DON'T KNOW HIS IDENTITY. THE MONEY HAS BEEN TRANSFERRED. DO YOU WANT TO CLAIM IT? (STATIC SILENCE)
JAPANESE RECIPIENT #2: YES.
COMMUNICATION OFF AIR 1837GMT

The special assistant waited for the NSA to look up before resuming, "Kristof Jonsgard is the secretary of the Marine Hunters Alliance. Used to be a small pro-whaling lobby, but ever since Jan got into the White House it's gone extreme. Supported by all the whaling big guns. Korea, Japan, Russia, Norway. His voice matched the recipient of that first call a few weeks ago."

"And the Japanese voice of this radio transmission?"

"We were able to acquire a pinpoint. South Pacific Ocean. I sent it over to NOIC." Naval Operational Intelligence Center, outside Washington, who tracked naval deployments all over the world. "Unfortunately they have no platform. But look at the atlas."

The NSA flipped past the transcript to a map marked with a single red X. "That's a few degrees north of Cetacean Bay." The NSA raised his eyes slowly. "So there *is* a Japanese fleet trailing the drive." Off the Special Assistant's nod, "Have you been able to ID the American voice in the first call?"

The nod turned into a sideways shake. "Cross checked the tape with everyone in the White House. Didn't pan out."

The NSA bit his lip. His first suspicion, upon learning of the threatening phone call, American to Norwegian, had fallen upon Pleasance. But the White House chief of staff was too smart to be directly involved, if he was at all.

"Sir, do you want me to put this in report form for the president?"

The special assistant knew about the NSA's confidential briefings of security around the first lady, which Everett had requested. But he did not know that the briefings had been terminated after the first presidential debate in which Leeds alleged the Japanese were shadowing the drive. The NSA had received a memo from Pleasance intimating that the president's hectic campaign schedule necessitated the vice president's taking all national security briefings. Adrian would pass it on to Everett. The NSA hadn't spoken to the president since.

"No," said the NSA. "With the bottom dropping out of Wall Street today, I think the president may be too preoccupied."

Such a conspiracy wasn't beyond Pleasance. The bastard would go to any lengths to win. *Even murder.* The NSA wondered if he should call Leeds. No point, he decided, in saying anything until he had proof. The NSA felt he'd failed his friend already by not being able to trace that anonymous call to Leeds's campaign HQ before the first debate and identify the woman who'd offered satellite pictures but then never called back.

The NSA continued, "I'll call the Navy secretary." An ally of Leeds, who'd carry out his request discreetly. "Find out if he has a ship in the area that can investigate."

Southern Ocean

"Jan!"

Vesprhein's voice struck her like a bullet. The shove of air, which the guillotine-like propellers generated, forced Jan to respond. She pulled her head out of the blade's way. Flailing a hand behind her, she found Yamamura's rising ankle with a thin, slipping grip. Seeing that her life depended on saving Yamamura's, Vesprhein put a second hand on the Japanese captain's wrist and lifted him powerfully. Jan hung on.

The rising platform carried the human chain of Vesprhein, Yamamura and Jan up to safety and stopped. Vesprhein dragged Yamamura halfway onto the platform. Without warning, Yamamura slapped away Vesprhein's hand, grabbed the vertical post of the safety gate and shook his legs violently.

"Arlov!" Jan yelled.

Her fingers slid down Yamamura's oily and bloody trouser leg when Vesprhein reappeared with a desperate expression. They slipped over Yamamura's gory shoe when Vesprhein flung his arm down, and slithered off when Vesprhein's fingers reached hers.

Too late.

Jan's fingers grasped at thin air.

"No!" Vesprhein cried out.

Time and motion slowed in her freefall. A hole opened in her stomach. The sound of the bonesaws obliterated every other. Her fall ended with spine-jarring abruptness. She thought she'd struck the blades then realized the wrenching pain ripped *down* from the tips of her fingers.

Her legs dangled. She was hanging onto the control box. Vesprhein must have tossed it over the edge earlier to haul Yamamura. She had stretched an arm out to grab it without realizing it.

Vesprhein reeled her up and reached for her when she came within arm's length. She collapsed into his arms and clutched him in a tight embrace until she stopped shivering. Finally, she found her voice between gasps. "Thank you."

He kissed her long and hard. At that moment, all doubt about joining a notorious pirate and guilt of leaving Everett dissolved. Her lips responded with a fierce passion.

A sharp clatter returned them to reality. They separated. Yamamura slid down a ladder. He released the spring and the rungs rolled back up to slow their pursuit. Vesprhein fired. The Japanese fleet captain fled the factory, slamming the massive steel door shut.

A grating screech announced he'd locked it from the outside.

They wasted precious minutes looking for another exit and found an unfastened hatchway out. It was 8:44.

Sixteen minutes to detonation.

❄

The last lifeboat splashed into the water. Boycott got a shot of the ten lifeboats running toward the four remaining catchers picking up the survivors of 6 and 9 in the water. Remarkably, the XO, who seemed so fearfully inept in Yamamura's presence, had kept the evacuation swift and efficient. Boycott captured the *Earthforce* hovering above the surface. An outboard powered Zodiac, with O'Hara and Kyle, who'd accompanied Jan on to the *Kagoshima*, had pulled Napoli, Owens and the scientists out of the sea. They made it back to the submarine. The scientists went below. Napoli stayed with Worthy on the sail. The *Stavenger* drifted uncertainly. Worthy maintained his threat to sink her if the pirates as much as twitched.

"David!" Raquel's voice reached him from the bridgewing. "Time to go."

Boycott waved back, turned off his camera and started down the midship ladder. He'd lost count of the hours of tape he'd shot. In the decade on the frontline of Green Wars, he'd filmed every atrocity and rescue. Won all the awards and accolades there were for his line of work. This voyage, though, surpassed anything he'd ever done or would do. No way he could top the unprecedented footage he'd gathered. There was enough for a season-long series and another round of acclaim.

Raquel shepherded him by and followed, waving to Prophet and Larkin, who backed off the bridgewing and followed them. They jogged along the walkway over the slaughter deck.

For fifteen seconds, as they circled around the giant funnels stacked one next to each other, all still piping hot, they lost sight of the slipway.

❄

Knight never saw Yamamura coming.

The taciturn reporter had been waiting by their lifeboat, his attention distracted toward the chaos following the collision of ships, when the Japanese captain slammed into him. Knight heard, then felt the excruciating bark of a cracking rib. With a gasp, Knight collapsed on the ramp. His gun slid off and sank into the ocean. Knight groaned to his knees but Yamamura was already in the lifeboat, firing up the motor. He roared away.

Boycott, Raquel, Prophet and Larkin arrived. Knight did not have to say anything, but he apologized profusely to Jan and Vesprhein when they ran up. The crafty fleet captain had used the catchers and smoke from the wreckage of *6* and *9* as cover to attack and escape out of sight.

"What time is it?" asked Vesprhein, twisting Jan's wrist watch: 8:49.

Eleven minutes to detonation.

The boarding party was stranded on the *Rising Sun*.

Air Force One

Everett watched the news. "For more than fifteen years,

the Japanese have been buying up US securities issued by our government to raise money. Today, by unloading them, Tokyo has indicated a loss of confidence in President Carsten Everett and the United States."

On the floor of the NYSE, it was financial anarchy, plain and simple. The Dow Jones dove past 3500 points and that was with the sell-off of only a fraction of the long bonds that the Japanese held. The aftershocks rippled overseas, where several foreign governments started emptying their portfolios of US securities. Until now, US government notes, bills and bonds had always been a sure thing. With nobody buying them, the Treasury became obliged to pick them up at face value and honor its debt.

"There is no way Washington can do that," said a reporter from the trading room floor. "Which means, as the largest creditor, Japan can conceivably put the United States in receivership."

Everett looked away. Every media outlet pounded him with blame. Despite the curbs installed by Wall Street to prevent a large-scale collapse, the Dow Jones gave up 5000 points by the time he put down at Andrews Air Force Base.

Southern Ocean

Napoli closed and opened his eyes helplessly when Jan reported what had happened. He was at a loss how to get the first lady off the factory ship before the explosives went off in nine minutes.

When the *Earthforce* had surfaced sharply in front of them, the pirates were forced to turn. They pulled up facing the Japanese factory ship's broadside just as the submarine pointed toward theirs. In the triangle created by the three vessels, listed the smoking halves and scattered debris of 6 and 9. Miraculously, there had been no fatalities. The survivors had been picked up.

"We have to skirt around to get to her," said Worthy, nodding to the film of oil spreading across the surface.

"Let's do it," responded Napoli at once.

"No!" snapped Jan's voice over the earpiece. She wore Larkin's headset radio. "You won't have enough time to pull away again. I won't let you endanger the lives of your crew."

"How are you going to get off then?"

"Yeah, how?" reacted Vesprhein. "We need a motor boat to escape the whirlpool this ship's going to create when she goes down."

Boycott swiveled his camera back and forth.

"We'll figure something out," said Jan with quiet confidence.

"We need a fucking miracle," Vesprhein growled.

"And here she comes," grinned Jan.

The water on the *Rising Sun*'s starboard broke open. As she always did, showing herself moments after the first lady appeared, Miracle blew up a playful spout. The nurses surfaced as well.

✷

6 and 9, the wrecked catchers, took their final curtsy, dipping sharply below the water. Steam and black smoke blasted up and obliterated visibility. Yamamura seized the swirling opaqueness. He drove right up the ramp of the *Stavenger*'s open slipway and climbed out of the lifeboat before it came to a complete stop. He scaled the ladder to the gangway, turned up the foredeck and swung over the guardrail of the catwalk. He sprinted on to the bridge.

"I'm Shinjiro Yamamura, captain of the fleet."

Iron Lady and Quvango introduced themselves as captain and first mate of the *Stavenger*.

"Do you want to claim a three-million-dollar reward?" asked Yamamura.

Greed sprang into Iron Lady's face. "Fuck, yeah."

"Do you have a marksman?"

"Yes."

"Bring him up."

Iron Lady nodded to Quvango, who grabbed the phone. Yamamura tilted his head toward the headset radio carelessly flung in the captain's chair. "Is that one of theirs?"

Iron Lady nodded. "Yeah."

Yamamura picked it up and put it on. The Colombian flenser, who had helped Jan deliver Miracle, loped up the companionway with a high-powered Remington with a telescopic sight.

"Target the first lady," said Yamamura.

The Colombian responded with a lopsided smile, cocked the gun, adjusted the sights and raised it. He used the tip of the barrel to open the window and wrapped his finger around the trigger.

"Where is she?" asked the Colombian, eyes pressed to the crosshairs.

Yamamura swiveled sharply. The smokescreen blown by the catchers, which had now sunk completely, thinned to gray wisps.

The *Rising Sun*'s slipway was empty.

❋

Jan and her friends were underwater. The nurses had Miracle tightly trapped between them. Jan and Vesprhein hugged the calf. Raquel, Boycott and Knight clutched the dorsal fin of the right side nurse, Prophet and Larkin the left side nurse. To Jan's dismay, the blues dived alongside the *Rising Sun*'s keel, so close, she read the time off the LED of the stern depth charges.

8:59:37... :38 ... :39 ... :40 ...

Fear filled their bloated faces.

8:59:48 ... :49 ... :50 ... :51...

Jan hung on to Miracle, who frolicked deeper and did the unthinkable: she leveled off two yards below the keel. Jan and Vesprhein furiously tried to direct her into a downward trajectory.

Suddenly Miracle's hide shuddered powerfully, almost throwing Jan off. The nurses hugged closer. Jan and Vesprhein saw why.

Sharks—twenty, thirty, perhaps fifty—swarmed in waves toward the steady flow of gore dribbling out of the scuppers from the factory drain. The nurses forced the calf into a near vertical dive.

Jan brushed past a depth charge, helplessly watching the readout roll toward zero.

8:59:57… :58 … :59 …

Barely had the leviathans plunged into the black depths, when half a dozen blinding flashes simultaneously lit up the ocean above. The six explosions sounded as one, muffled yet awesome. The sharks—wriggling, wormlike silhouettes in front of the flames—cleared the orange-red light so swiftly, the explosion was still a second away from peaking. Jan discovered the reason for their scatter: shockwaves so powerful even the giant blue whales shuddered.

Huge splinters, gouged away by the blasts, speared around them. Just as Napoli had drawn up, the *Rising Sun*'s engine room floor dropped out and fell like a stone. The screw shafts shot away like arrows. The hull around the factory peeled away, the refrigeration compartments split open and hundreds of tons of meat freed toward the ocean floor.

Vesprhein slid off Miracle. Jan lost her hold a second later. She tumbled clumsily out of control, and everyone flew backward as if they'd been shot out into zero gravity.

The crews of the *Stavenger*, *Earthforce* and four catchers became dumbstruck spectators. Four lifeboats remained to be emptied of the men from the *Rising Sun*. Rocking waves lashed outward as the shock, ejecting in a sphere, manifested on the surface as concentric circles of powerful whitecaps similar to the diverging clouds at the base of an atom bomb.

The sea noisily disemboweled the factory ship. Her bows folded. Her stern canted into the air. The ends of the long cutting deck buckled upward. Steam from the safety valve alongside the *Rising Sun*'s disappearing funnel roared to a crescendo. Oil spit up onto the ocean surface and leveled the wavecrests under a spreading blanket of black.

"Get them out of here." Napoli pointed to the four catchers and four lifeboats.

Worthy raised the loudhailer and spoke in Japanese. "All catchers and lifeboats! Leave this area immediately." Then he looked down to the missile deck, where some crew members had scrambled outside to witness the sinking of the last factory ship in the world. "Keep an eye for Jan and the others."

The four catchers, each with a packed lifeboat in tow, pulled away, leaving behind the six that had been evacuated. On the retreating decks, every Japanese eye stayed on the *Rising Sun*. She gave a violent lurch. Her bridge leaned forward at an acute angle, the stern rising fast. The towering bows twisted into the ocean.

Beginning the first turn of the dreaded whirlpool.

The *Rising Sun*'s long, mangled deck swept around. The mast snapped into a mess of rigging. The midships went under when the vessel was almost halfway around. The stern came a full circle, before being sucked into the full-blown whirlpool with a tumultuous leap of water.

"Reverse full!" screamed Worthy into the phone. "Everybody inside."

The crew scrambled down the hatch. The *Earthforce*'s screws clawed, pulling the submarine away from the widening radius of the deadly vortex. The *Stavenger* went into full-powered reverse. The killer-factory ship and the submarine barely eluded the lethal perimeter.

A funnel opened up in the ocean.

Panic gripped the four departing catchers and lifeboats. Coxswains in the lifeboats plunged the throttle all the way. Their narrow hulls jumped. The screws of the catchers turned as fast as they could go. Bow-waves increased in height and throw. Spray fell on the decks like tropical rain. The eight vessels escaped safely, but the six empty lifeboats they'd abandoned took a lap around the whirlpool's extremity and spiraled in.

❊

Underwater, Jan found herself outside the destructive cone,

looking in. Vesprhein swam up beside her. They started upward, careful not to rise faster than their bubbles. She quickly counted off the others. Nobody had perished.

Boycott ignored his pressing need for oxygen and scissored around to capture stunning images of the descending vortex. Undersea currents weakened the whirlpool quickly. Debris lost their tight spiral and dispersed randomly in all directions. Wood floated up, metal drowned. The boarding party broke out of the water, drenched in the oil on the surface.

"Here!" shouted Prophet.

He'd surfaced beside a fully inflated orange inflatable—the emergency liferaft freed from the *Rising Sun*'s officers' deck. The boarding party swam through oil, which coated their nostrils and burned all the way to their lungs. They climbed aboard, gasping.

Jan did not know the headset she'd taken from Larkin was still wrapped around her skull until she heard Yamamura's voice crackle into her ear, "This is Shinjiro Yamamura. My marksman has the first lady in his cross hairs."

Tokyo

Democratic presidential candidate, Keith Leeds, waved his arms and raised his voice, "I will declare independence for our economy, freeze repatriation of profits earned by foreign companies here and illegitimize their controlling interests in the United States of America."

A roar of laughter erupted from the Japanese prime minister and his cabinet. They'd gathered for a working dinner and the television was on. There hadn't been so much hearty backslapping among these men since the National Frontier Party's victory celebration on the night they were elected to power. Local networks tracked the collapse of Wall Street, but it was past most people's bedtime. The Nikkei Index would react adversely when it opened in the morning, but the Ministry of Finance, Takara and other big securities firms had already taken steps to ensure there would no dramatic fall on the Tokyo Stock Exchange.

Maeo raised his glass. "Yamato!"

This doctrine of purity had unified Japan centuries ago. During World War II, it filled Japanese troops with the same fervor as Hitler's Aryan supremacy. Starting in the seventies, its emphasis shifted from military annexation to economic dominance. At the end of this Wall Street session, Maeo's global policy, with the Yamato principle as its nucleus, would pay off.

The cabinet clinked their glasses proudly, ignoring the latest report on TV. "All US banks are closing their doors and terminating business for the day."

Their eyes lifted as the news on TV reported that riots were breaking out in the streets of America.

Southern Ocean

Yamamura watched Jan and Napoli snap their heads toward the *Stavenger*. The *Earthforce* had decelerated to a stop, just like the killer-factory ship, but the catchers and lifeboats headed north, dropping over the horizon. Yamamura boldly showed himself, unlike the Colombian, whose presence was indicated by the barrel of his rifle extending out of the window.

"Put Worthy on," said Yamamura. When he saw Napoli hand over the headset, the fleet captain ordered. "Empty your fuel tanks." The eco-bastard had no option but to comply.

Fuel bubbled out of the submarine. Yamamura lifted his binoculars to the orange inflatable. It rocked gently in the thickening carpet of diesel spilt by the *Rising Sun*, 6, 9 and now the *Earthforce*. Toxic stench rose as a vapor-laden mist. Jan and her eco-rogues gagged. They wiped tears and coughed violently. Yamamura relished their pain.

Half an hour later, Worthy reported, "Our tanks are empty."

"You will submerge," instructed Yamamura, "pull away at least two miles and remain underwater until we are out of sight." The longer Worthy stayed below the surface, Yamamura knew, the more battery he consumed, diminishing a sustained pursuit. He turned to the inflatable. "Madam First Lady. Jump if you want to take your chances with the sharks."

The FishEye had revealed their return in even larger numbers to feed upon the whale meat freed from the *Rising Sun*'s holds. That further diminished a threat from Worthy. He would return to save his friends. Yamamura heard the eco-maverick, who still wore the headset, order, "Clear the bridge and rig the ship for a dive." Motioning Napoli down the hatch, Worthy looked toward the inflatable. "Hang tight, Jan. We'll come back for you. I promise."

The sub's diving alarm carried across the ocean. Worthy waved to the boarding party one more time and took the ladder down. The *Earthforce*'s ballast tanks popped one after the other. Air whistled from the deck slats. The bow planes whined out. Water whooshed up the sides. The *Earthforce*'s deck tilted underwater.

"Pull out," Yamamura said to Iron Lady.

The *Stavenger* plowed toward clear water. Yamamura reached into the drawer below the chart table with a conniving smile.

❄

Jan, Vesprhein and the others watched the black sail disappear. Boycott took his eyes off the viewfinder of his camera. "Alone at last. I never thought they'd leave."

Jan smiled. The others tightly masked their nostrils with their hands. Even then, each time they took a breath, their chests throbbed with a dull ache. Larkin wheezed louder than most.

"Are you okay?" Jan asked, placing an anxious arm on his shoulder.

"Asthma," he replied in a strained voice.

"What the fuck?" Vesprhein murmured, drawing Jan's eyes to

the *Stavenger*.

Yamamura walked briskly along the catwalk to the gun platform when the ship receded beyond the oil slick. She gathered speed. He gripped the cannon for balance with one hand and stretched the other high over his head.

Glimpsing what he had in his hand, Jan gasped.

A flare gun.

Larkin's wheezing took a turn for the worse.

"Jump!" cried Prophet.

"No!" snapped Jan, who'd been privy to Yamamura's conversation with Worthy over her headset. "There are sharks."

Raquel's voice quavered, "Great. Just great."

"Paddle, all," shouted Vesprhein.

Everyone threw their hands over the side and rowed, but with hardly enough speed: the edge of the slick was at least half a mile away.

Like a comet, the flare shot high into the sky. Terror seized the faces of the boarding party. Their hands stopped working and their heads tilted up and slowly around, following the bright orange flame rise, rise, rise, rise. It reached its zenith.

And fell.

❅

The slender arm of the *Earthforce*'s periscope broke the surface a few feet inside the cleanly demarcated boundary of the spreading oil. The flare dropped a hundred feet in front of the eyepiece.

Igniting the ocean.

"Firestorm!" screamed Worthy and yanked the periscope down.

A towering plume erupted skyward and lengthened into a wall of fire that swept forward and across. The roar of the blaze could be heard in the bowels of the submarine. The periscope escaped the inferno, but steam gushed down the tube and filled the conn with a dramatic hiss. Worthy jumped a frightened step back.

❅

On the ocean surface, heat blasted in every direction. A gentle wind, which moments ago had lifted a refreshing draft toward the life raft, became the driving force behind the oil fire. Dancing wildly, the flames leapt forward. Jan removed her jacket and gave it to Vesprhein, who gratefully shrugged it on. Without a Gumby suit, he felt the physical assault of temperatures climbing rapidly into the upper 100s.

"We should take our chances underwater," suggested Prophet.

"Wait!" Jan pointed to the horizon.

A massive craft approached, flying *above* the water.

❇

The USS *Quest II* was a HYSWAS, or hydrofoil small-waterplane-area ship, the Navy's latest experimental hybrid-hulled frigate. She rode atop slender stilts. Her master, Captain Ruval Thomasson, saw the marching firestorm and reacted succinctly: "Oil fire."

He alerted all levels. The twenty-seven-strong crew in khakis dashed to action stations.

The first officer lowered his glasses. "There's a life raft in the middle of the slick."

"Who's on it?" asked Captain Thomasson.

"Can't say."

The *Quest II* had been on a ninety-day test run in the southern seas when they'd been contacted by US Naval HQ, South Pacific Sector, to investigate the first lady's drive around the fortieth parallel. Her coordinates, triangulated by Jonsgard's radio contact with Yamamura, were more than a day old. However, the *Rising Sun* carried an emergency position indicating radio beacon. The EPIRB automatically responded to immersion in water, sending out a 406 megahertz distress signal, which they'd grabbed for an accurate pinpoint when the factory ship sank.

The helmswoman pointed to the *Stavenger*, heading at full speed away from the fire. "Why's he pulling away? He can save them."

Captain Thomasson recognized the distinctive catwalk. "Isn't that the pirate whaling ship the first lady is on?" He turned toward the life raft and blanched. "Oh, God, no. She's on it."

Their sonarman's voice crackled over the bridge speakers. "Submarine in the area."

"Raise them on the radio."

"Friendly sub sir," reported sonarman within half a minute. "Paul Worthy, Captain of the *Earthforce*." He put him on the bridge speaker.

Captain Thomasson asked, "Does anyone on that raft have a radio?"

"Yes, sir." Worthy recited the bandwidth. "Request permission to go after the pirate."

"Granted." The billowing windsock atop the mast moved sharply. Captain Thomasson warned, "Surface wind shifting."

The thick black smoke crowning the oil fire abruptly changed direction and moved like a searing blast of exhaust toward the life raft.

"Full speed," he barked. "Enter the slick between the raft and the fire."

The *Quest II* rode atop a submerged hull contoured like a giant missile, which provided 70 percent buoyant lift. On the captain's order for full speed, the hull elevated higher and higher out of the water as her single, Cummins VTA-903, turbocharged diesel engine drove a three-blade, 860mm propeller faster and faster.

At maximum speed, the engineer reported from below, "Flying on foils."

The *Quest II* bulleted at sixty-six knots, faster than the fastest boats. She was completely out of the water, as she had been when Jan first spotted her, knifing across the Southern Ocean riding stiletto-thin hydrofoils.

"Tune me to their frequency," said Captain Thomasson. Within a moment, the first officer thrust a wireless handset into his hand. "This is Captain Thomasson of the United States Navy."

The first lady jerked her head in his direction, then waved and yelled to her friends over the speakers tuned to her mouthpiece, "The Navy's coming for us!"

The hydrofoil broke into the perimeter of the slick between the fire and the life raft. The crew felt the scorifying intensity for the first time.

❄

In the *Earthforce*, Worthy clenched his fist vindictively. No way in hell was he going to let Yamamura get away, especially if Jan and the others were to lose their lives. He pushed that thought away almost as soon as it entered his head and raised the Japanese fleet captain.

"Say your prayers, Shinjiro. I'm on your ass!" Then Worthy ordered, "Match his course and speed."

"Paul," floated up the chief engineer's voice, "that'll give us less than half an hour of battery power."

"I know."

The screws engaged and the *Earthforce* lunged. Worthy grabbed the periscope and hoisted it. The submarine rocked with speed. The propellers churned a long trail of raging bubbles. Struggling to keep his balance on the vibrating deck, he laid the vertical cross hair on the *Stavenger*'s mast.

"Bearing. Mark."

"2-6-6."

"Range. Mark."

"6-9-5-oh."

"Angle on the bow?"

"4-oh."

"Normal approach?" Plotted using an imaginary point ahead of the target in such a way that the *Earthforce* ran the shortest distance while the *Stavenger* the longest.

"1-7-oh."

"Make that our course." The annunciators rattled. "Are we at full speed?"

"Yes."

Worthy raised the videoscope and left it turned toward the rescue while they pursued the *Stavenger*. He groaned. *Quest II* hit the oil slick and skewered erratically, heading directly toward the firestorm.

❊

"Shit!" Jan muttered, seeing the hydrofoil in trouble.

The blaze, a hundred yards away and six fiery stories high, scorched toward the life raft. Immediately beneath the ocean surface, fish perished in millions. Their tiny corpses rose and combusted to nothing. Wisps of fire—burning droplets of oil lifted by the gust— floated down upon them. The fire burned away the oxygen and the stench of carbon made their nostrils feel like open wounds when they inhaled. Every breath was a choking, labored gasp.

Noticing Larkin's whitening pallor, Jan took her eyes off the drunkenly weaving hydrofoil. She urged him calmly, "Hang on."

Larkin slumped, losing consciousness. Prophet grabbed him.

The oil fire ate up the next fifty yards of ocean in seconds. Jan joined everyone else to stare at *Quest II*. Then she lost the fight, swerving away from them toward the mile long inferno.

Their only hope for survival was herself fighting to survive.

❊

"I need a hand!" screamed the helmswoman.

"Jesus!" Captain Thomasson rushed to her side, ordering, "Everyone! Off the decks!"

Together, the captain and the helmswoman wrestled with the heavy and unwieldy wheel. Grunting and screaming, they tried to right the rudder, but the diesel changed the density of the water. Like a race car that hits an oil slick, the speeding hydrofoil turned ninety degrees and headed for the flames. The bridge crew stared in horror. There was nothing anyone could do.

Suddenly, the steering eased.

A clear patch of ocean. The helmswoman and Captain Thomasson reacted at once and wrenched the wheel. The HYSWAS dragged around. The blaze approached them abeam once again.

"XO! Give her a hand!" he shouted.

The first officer raced over. It needed the strength of two to keep the *Quest II* on course. Captain Thomasson let go of the wheel and looked from the fire running parallel on his right to the life raft on his left. He picked up the handset. "Ma'am, we'll fire a line as we fly by. We have no time to stop or slow down. There is time for one shot."

❄

Jan threw up a hand to acknowledge that she heard him. She felt her hair start to burn and pulled up her hood. It was impossible to hear anymore. Jan's fingers entwined into Vesprhein's. He winced. Every inch of exposed skin on his body looked cooked, red and tender. She quickly imparted a reassuring, never-say-die look around the raft. Sheer will power kept her from passing out like Larkin.

Prophet clutched Larkin. Raquel gripped the edges of the liferaft tensely. Knight seemed faint, but he bravely nodded back.

Boycott remained upbeat. He grinned, "This is hot stuff. We can all watch it at my place when this is over."

Jan managed a reassuring smile, but she didn't share his confidence.

Vesprhein silently drew Jan's eyes to the rubber plastic of the liferaft. It stretched and crinkled with the heat, moments away from disintegrating.

❄

Yamamura looked through his binoculars to assess the eco-warriors' chances. *None*. "They will all burn."

"And we are going to be rich," said Quvango.

Yamamura hurried to the FishEye. "Where is Worthy?"

Iron Lady jabbed his finger.

"Port ten," ordered Yamamura, after one look at the screen.

"Port ten." Quvango whirled the wheel.

"Midships. Steady as she goes. "

Yamamura explained the maneuver to Iron Lady. "The sub is five thousand yards, matching our speed. We must weaken his torpedo angle."

Iron Lady nodded. The *Earthforce*'s angle to their bow was now sixty degrees. "But they must be seeing this. Why aren't they reacting?"

Concern probably turned the eco-maverick and crew into rubbernecks, figured Yamamura. He barked, "Starboard thirty!"

Quvango rolled the wheel the other way and the *Stavenger* slewed right like a car with bald tires on ice.

"Angle on our bow is now eighty degrees," Iron Lady reported.

"It's over," Yamamura declared flatly.

❄

In the *Earthforce*, everyone's attention stayed on the monitors playing the nail-biting race. With every passing second, the boarding party's chances of rescue diminished and the silence on all levels of the submarine deepened another notch.

"Oh shit," muttered the sonarman. His computer screen was divided down the middle, one half titled OWN SHIP and the other TARGET. Numbers beside subheadings of Range and Speed were relatively constant, but Bearings caught his attention.

Worthy tore his eyes away from the monitor. "What?"

"*Stavenger* is running parallel."

"Damn."

Worthy hoisted the attack periscope and swung it around. The eye broke out of the ocean with a high, powerful spray.

"My fault," said the sonarman. "I should have been watching the computer screen instead of the rescue and the firestorm."

"Don't worry about it." Worthy shared the blame. He should not have taken his eyes off either. The retired submarine commander had warned him about the dangers of distraction.

"They are going to fire a line," Rorque bellowed from the Control Room below.

"Keep running parallel," said Worthy. His eyes riveted back onscreen, noticing Napoli and Owens clench their fists.

A prickly hush dropped like a shroud.

❋

On the life raft, Knight collapsed. Raquel grabbed him. Ignoring his burns, Vesprhein stood up carefully. Even so, the boat rocked.

Jan gently held his ruddy legs. It was an effort to concentrate looking straight at this massive wall of flames, gobbling up the scant ocean before him. The first wave of black smoke swept over them and wiped out the sky entirely. Darkness mounted. Moments before the air turned completely opaque, the hydrofoil broke through the swirling black clouds, shielding the life raft momentarily from the firestorm. The searing heat cooled for a welcome instant.

Hearing Captain Thomasson's staticky voice over her headset, Jan shouted to Vesprhein, "This is it!"

❋

"Steady," drawled Captain Thomasson.

The helmswoman and first officer maneuvered the hydrofoil between the life raft and the fire, which blazed ninety feet away, closing at a rate of a foot per second. The air was a blizzard of sparks. The mercury on the bridge thermometer bumped the top of the tube at 160°F. The sound was an endless, numbing snarl.

Captain Thomasson stood next to the sharpshooter, a twenty-three-year-old sailor on his second tour. He could imagine the pressure this youngster must be feeling. If he failed, he would forever live in ignominy as the man who didn't save the first lady.

The sharpshooter's shoulder jerked.

The report was lost in the deafening blaze.

Captain Thomasson looked on in despair. Maybe it was that fleeting moment of apprehension that caused the young man to second guess his accuracy and readjust up a fraction.

The line sailed over the life raft. *Too high.*

Tokyo

Nobuo Tomita stared at the crush of night lights outlining a predominantly vertical city. A strong ocean breeze took the temperature into the low teens. Aiko, his young mistress, hugged her arms around her chest and stood by his side in silent support. He grudgingly admired Maeo for this bold financial strike. Republican Will Todd was now a shoo-in. Maeo would then manipulate the supply-side Republican president. With an empty feeling of disappointment, Tomita realized he had to come to grips with the reality that he was never going to be prime minister. The cold flared his arthritis and he felt every year of his age.

"Father."

Tomita blinked out of his thoughts and turned around. "Isamu?"

His surprise caused him to seek the shoulder of his mistress for support. His son and he hadn't spoken in years. After Isamu exposed Kaiyou and denied Tomita the prime ministership, the veteran had barred the activist from setting foot in his house. The resemblance between father and son was striking. Isamu bowed respectfully. Aiko gave no indication they were intimate.

"This is for you." Isamu held up a videotape.

"What is it?"

"*Rising Sun* and her fleet setting sail from Kobe."

Tomita raised his eyebrows for a moment in curious non-comprehension.

Isamu explained. Two months ago, he tipped Paul Worthy about the pelagic fleet leaving Kobe, who in turn called Jan. Last week, the eco-legend had called him after the White House had refused to divulge Jan's whereabouts. Worthy was desperate, exploring every avenue of information. He wondered if the CITES activist's father might know. Isamu had been alarmed to learn Jan and the drive were isolated, beyond contact.

Tomita's face cleared with a broad smile. Born and raised amidst factional politics, his son had easily deduced this Wall Street collapse as Maeo's retaliation against Everett. Isamu could not let the president be defeated. That would deprive environmentalists all over the world of their most powerful voice, the first lady.

Sweet irony, Tomita thought, Isamu's environmental activism, which once denied him the prime ministership, was going to hand it right back to him.

Southern Ocean

"Worthy's not making a move toward us, just keeping pace," said Iron Lady, pointing to the screen.

"He will now," said Yamamura. The firestorm dropped out of sight below the horizon and they would draw the eco-maverick's undivided attention now. "But he's running on batteries, he cannot maintain this speed."

Yamamura marched to the Fisheye. He ripped off the headset. He had no more use for it. With the fiery demise of the US Navy ship all but certain as well, there never was going to be a more opportune time than the present to end the life and exploits of Paul Worthy, who had a million-dollar bounty on his head. He told Iron Lady and Quvango his plan.

"Let's waste 'em," replied Iron Lady .

❈

In the liferaft, Vesprhein felt nothing but the instinct to survive. His body burned, but he put the pain at the back of his mind. He leaped as high as he could, his fingers groping, groping, groping. Only vapor and droplets of burning oil struck his blistered palm. His eyes misted with defeat. His legs began to fall into Jan's supportive embrace.

The coarse line slashed his palm. He closed his fingers. "I have it!" Jan pulled him down. He dropped to his knees.

"Loop it through!" she shouted.

Vesprhein fumbled the rope, got it back. He had to pass the end of the line through the hook and knot it. The line ran away, tightening rapidly. The fire stormed in from the side.

A sound like gunshots volleyed out!

The raft's stretching rubber and plastic popped holes. Air exploded out. The raft deflated.

Vesprhein slipped the line through the loop.

The line tightened to a rod.

"Don't let go," shouted Jan.

"I can't hold on."

The line slipped through his palm, cutting and opening the heat blisters. Jan tried to help. He looked over. Her sweaty hands would not let her grip the line to loop it around her knuckles either. The blood-stained line kept running.

The blaze moved within ten feet.

The plastic on Jan's headset started to melt. She tore it off and threw it away. Invisible white hot teeth inflicted more burns through Vesprhein's flimsy jacket. Air whistled out of the quickly deflating life raft.

The end slipped through Jan's fingers. "I lost the line!"

Vesprhein tried one last time to loop it around the knuckles of his right hand. Just before the line ran out, he succeeded! He hurled forward. His fist crashed into the hook. He brought his left hand in to sustain his hold. Jan hugged him from behind and anchored him.

The life raft lifted out of the water and shot forward.

Boycott toppled backward, capturing lopsided images. Raquel and Prophet held on to Knight and Larkin. The firestorm came after them. The HYSWAS and the life raft fled.

Vesprhein looked over his shoulder desperately.

❄

Worthy's videoscope lost the firestorm over the horizon. The fatal outcome seemed inescapable. Vendetta coursing through his veins, he took off the headset radio and dropped it on the chart table. "Full flank."

The *Earthforce* trembled. The chief engineer's voice crackled over the intercom, "Battery life, twenty minutes."

The sonarman reverted his eyes from the TV monitor back to the computer screen and sat up abruptly. "*Stavenger*'s heading toward us."

Without wasting a moment to express surprise, Worthy popped the periscope out of the water and snapped the handle to the high-power position. His vision cleared a rising wave and he swung the eye around ninety degrees. "Jesus."

The killer-factory ship came straight at them with furiously crashing bows. So close were the pirates, he picked up the Korean in the crow's nest pointing directly at Worthy. *Too late to come around and fire.*

He dropped the periscope, yelling, "Dive! Dive! Dive!"

The helmsman swung the steering, turned both annunciators to the extreme right and banged them against the stops. Rorque flooded the negative tanks. Air exhaled in a whirlwind. The bow and stern planes clawed the water. The *Earthforce* labored deeper as fast as her 283-foot, 2000-ton steel frame could move.

❈

Iron Lady looked up. "He's seventy feet and diving."

"Depth charge. Minimum setting." shouted Yamamura.

Right aft, two pirates stood poised beside the thrower. The killer-factory ship lurched. A welter of foaming spray arched high out of the ocean.

❈

"He'll be over us in a minute," shouted Worthy, surprised at the calmness of his voice. "Rig the ship for depth charges."

The order brought instant reaction from all levels. Sounds of watertight doors slamming shut and bulkhead valves venting echoed for the next few seconds. His eyes met for a moment with Rorque's, then the Britisher dogged down the hatch between the Control Room and the conn. Worthy looked at the gauge. The peg wavered past eighty feet. The angle of descent increased with the *Stavenger*'s fast approaching screws.

"He's coming across," said the sonarman.

The displacing water and screws of both vessels combined to create an explosive pocket of ear-rending noise.

"Rudder amidships!" Worthy hoped to escape ahead of the depth charges.

Boom! The charge detonated just forward of the *Earthforce* like thunder in an echo chamber. The sub plowed through the ball of fire. The current slammed her like a wrecking ball. The crew tumbled to the decks. The submarine swayed dizzily forward.

"Another depth charge in the water," said the sonarman.

Worthy realized Yamamura knew he'd missed. A depth charge that made contact exploded with a metallic *whabam!* "Depth charge!" shouted the sonarman again.

Worthy called down to Engineering, "Pedal to the metal, guys!"

Boom! It detonated aft of the *Earthforce*'s fleeing screws. The churn of the *Stavenger*'s screws seemed interminable above the trembling shell of the submarine. Worthy hung on to the railing. The needle of the conning tower depth gauge jiggled to a hundred feet.

"Two more depth charges in the water, starboard quarter," said the sonarman.

"Hard-a-port!" snapped Worthy.

The helmsman took the wheel left as far as it would go.

The gyro spun and the submarine listed powerfully.

BoomBoom! The detonations occurred in the water the *Earthforce* had occupied the moment preceding. Concussion waves bucked and convulsed the boat again. Lights on all levels, the digital screens and electrical systems died. People and objects catapulted around in the darkness. The twin detonations shoved the diving submarine deeper into the water, increasing their angle and momentum to a near-vertical dive.

Worthy slipped and slid toward the hatch leading down to the Control Room. There was no time to open it. "Blow ballast! Blow safety! Blow negative!"

Worthy did not hear Rorque repeat his order. Rorque should have repeated it. *Was he dead?* Then a female voice repeated it. Worthy smiled. Like dying echoes, the order was repeated, dissipating forward and aft.

But nothing happened. The *Earthforce* plummeted. That could mean only one thing, thought Worthy. *Fatalities.*

❄

The firestorm closed in from all sides.

The fast deflating life raft tossed, bounced and stayed ahead of the inferno's embrace. The exultant sensation Vesprhein felt each time they slipped away from the forks of flame kept his mind off the pain streaking up his right hand. His knuckles slammed and scraped against the hook, peeling the skin to the bone.

He couldn't stop the slide of the line coiled around his hand, only slow it. They had to be out of the slick before it ran through his fingers. There had been barely a foot of line to spare when the race began. He checked how much remained.

There was none.

The end slipped through his palm.

Tokyo

The Dow Jones kept sliding. In the prime minister's office, Maeo and his cabinet were past jubilation and into the serious business of the unprecedented actions they were going to take against the United States tomorrow.

"Gentlemen," Maeo said, "by the close of business today, Wall Street will lose at least fifty percent of its peak value. Tomorrow morning, the prospect of another day like this one will leave them with little option but to beg us for a reprieve. We will give them one in exchange for veto power on all matters of their finance until the US bonds, notes and bills we own are paid in full. Private Japanese citizens holding US securities will be able to exchange them for federal assets like land. We will reverse prior trade agreements restricting our entry into their markets and propose a five-year plan to shift the benchmark currency of the world from the dollar to the yen."

The cabinet secretary's cellular phone purred. He answered it, listened, then, with a drawn, anxious face, stepped to Maeo's side and whispered. The prime minister raised his hand and everyone fell silent.

"Tomitasen is on his way up," announced Maeo.

"What does he want?" demanded Hattori.

The cabinet secretary lifted his shoulders, nonplused.

"Good evening, gentlemen," said Tomita, walking in with a confidence in his stride that unsettled Maeo and his cabinet. Tomita held up Isamu's videotape. "This shows the *Rising Sun* and the ten catchers putting to sea from Kobe in the dead of night. There is also an interview with one of the men before he went aboard, proudly declaring he was going to kill almost two thousand severely endangered blue whales secretly."

"So?" snapped Maeo, but the color had left his face.

Hattori added without conviction, "Yes. You do not want to alienate the biggest faction—"

"Oh, no," smiled Tomita, "I don't want your support, but you will withdraw it from this government."

Maeo snorted in disbelief. "I suppose you want me to resign too?"

"Unless you want this tape to air on television tonight. Even if the Republican wins the election, he cannot stand in the way of the laws of America." He turned to Hattori, gaining confidence with each word. "This tape will ensure that the temporary ban by the San Francisco court becomes permanent, prohibiting us forever from fishing in the world's most bountiful waters. The Obata family won't stand for that. Then the US Congress will freeze all Japanese assets and we will forfeit all payments. Those bonds that you used to ruin them will now bankrupt us."

After a long silence, Maeo stood up from his chair and stepped away from his desk. The move, merely symbolic at this moment, portended the inevitable. The prime minister was relinquishing the office to Tomita, who had sought it all his life.

Southern Ocean

The ink-black interior of the *Earthforce* was a void of terror. Worthy grabbed the periscope cylinder, desperately trying to stay on his feet. Loud pops commenced. Ballast tanks exchanged water for air. Soon a continuous hiss blanketed the entire ship. The down-angle inverted into an up-angle so quickly the floor slipped in the opposite direction.

Worthy caught his breath loudly when he found himself staring at daylight from the bottom of the periscope well. The combination of the underwater current from the explosion, the *Stavenger*'s wash as she passed overhead and the *Earthforce*'s up-angle had pushed the submarine's bridge and bow well out of the ocean. The sub went dark again, intensifying the fear that gripped his guts.

He found the radio and screamed, "Mayday! Mayday! Mayday!"

✳

"Depth charges, sir, I counted at least four," shouted the *Quest II*'s sonar operator. "The eco-sub is under attack from the pirate ship."

Captain Thomasson pushed the report to the back of his mind. His first obligation was to save the first lady. The hydrofoil cleared the slick, but the life raft she towed was fifteen feet from the edge, when the line broke free.

"No," Captain Thomasson shouted. The life raft stalled, with the blaze nipping a yard behind.

The flames closed in a flash. Jan's death cry froze on her parched lips. The firestorm *stopped!* Leaned away. The momentum had cleared the life raft just beyond the perimeter of the spill and a lucky shift in the wind curved the fire away from them.

"We made it!" Jan screamed.

The life raft deflated.

"I got Patrick," shouted Raquel.

Prophet grabbed Larkin. Boycott rescued his camera. Vesprhein beamed.

"Take us around, quick," said Captain Thomasson, when the *Quest*'s sonarman alerted him of the rising shark danger from the deep. The helmswoman turned at full throttle, listing the HYSWAS like a motorcycle around a sharp curve. Loose objects flew. The decks leveled off. "Retract foils and cut engines."

The *Quest II* sank into the water with a splash and decelerated toward the floundering boarding party.

"Lower the lifeboat without cutting it loose," said Captain Thomasson. Chains rattled. The lifeboat dropped straight down over the side of the poop deck and slammed into the water. One man leaned over the rail and another kept his hand ready on the winch motor.

Vesprhein steadied it. Jan took Larkin from Prophet, who clambered aboard first. Vesprhein helped her hoist Larkin, then they gave Raquel a hand boosting Knight up and over. The two unconscious men had come to when they hit the water, but they were dazed and out of it.

"David," Jan gestured Boycott up next.

Two fins broke the surface and sliced toward Vesprhein, Jan and Raquel, panting beside the lifeboat.

Raquel's eyes widened. "Sharks!"

"Get in, quick." ordered Jan.

Raquel scrambled up with help from Jan and Vesprhein in the water and Prophet in the boat. Prophet and Raquel reached for Jan and Vesprhein.

Seeing them grab the pair in the water, Captain Thomasson ordered, "Up! Up!"

The winches reversed at full throttle. The lifeboat rose. Jan and Vesprhein clung to the end of Raquel's and Prophet's arms. Their legs left the water, dangling.

The sharks launched into the air.

Jan shrieked and lost her hold.

Raquel yelled, "Jan!"

Vesprhein let go of Prophet and dropped a second behind Jan. As they fell, they crossed the two sharks arcing out of the water, twisting for a piece of human flesh and missing with a violent collision of teeth.

"Stop!" shouted Captain Thomasson.

Jan and Vesprhein splashed into the water before the predators did. The lifeboat stopped rising with a screech. Jan and Vesprhein were gone. The two sharks crashed down, glided below the surface and disappeared out of his line of sight beneath the boat.

Captain Thomasson leaned further over the edge. The surface glistened with a dull sheen of oil droplets, obstructing visibility below the surface.

Blood erupted.

Washington DC

Air Force One commenced its landing run into Andrews Air Force Base. Everett stared out of the window. Alone. Resigned.

Defeated.

Everything had looked so good this morning. He was making a strong run for the finish. The morning news had been all about his remarkable comeback. Now the entire nation reeled under the kind of panic not seen since the crash of 1929. Civil unrest continued to spread. The National Guard requested military assistance. Everett ordered in tanks and armored cars. Every city looked like a third world country after a coup. Newspapers came out with special editions and bold headlines like, NATION BANKRUPT!

The landing gear of the president's plane touched the runway, bumped a couple of times and the jet engines decelerated with a pealing whine. Everett's Council of Economic Advisors, who had teleconferenced with the president all the way from Ohio, could not think of any way out but making a public plea to Prime Minister Maeo. Four days before the election, Everett realized such an economic surrender to Japan would seal his defeat, but it was the only way to stop the financial hemorrhaging.

Reporters thronged outside the gates of Andrews Air Force Base, but they did not get even a glimpse of the president, who quickly transferred from Air Force One to Marine One. Delta went with him. Anthony Trent, the bodyguard, climbed in after them. Pleasance warned that the media had gathered in unprecedented numbers, spilling out of the East Wing Press Room all the way to the South Lawn. When the dreaded descent toward the teeming White House began, the onboard phone rang.

Delta answered, listened and then held out the phone. "You should take this call."

His forehead furrowed, Everett put the phone to his ear. "Yes?"

"Good afternoon, Mr. President. This is Nobuo Tomita."

Southern Ocean

Raquel led the chorus of dismayed gasps when bits and pieces of flesh popped out of the crimson water. One of the sharks skimmed them off the surface. Knight retched in a rush of panic. Boycott turned off his camera and numbly sat down. The SEALs searched desperately but knew it was over.

The speakers crackled with the radio operator's voice, "Mayday, Mayday! We have a Mayday from the sub!"

Captain Thomasson grabbed the microphone, dialed up the outside speaker. "Retract the boat. Full ahead! We'll return for a body search later."

The eco-warriors and SEALs watched the ocean recede. The winch drew the lifeboat in. They allowed themselves to be helped out, still in shock. Miracle and her two nurses blew alongside. Raquel, Boycott, Knight, Prophet and Larkin sadly watched the three whales. Boycott raised his videocamera and captured a poignant image of a calf mourning over Jan's grave.

The *Quest II* pulled away.

❄

Worthy realized his Mayday call had been premature. The uproar, the screams, the rattling, the clatter—they began to settle soon afterwards. Emergency lights came on. Worthy righted himself. "Emergency speed!"

Someone heard him and rang three times. An engineer opened the main motor rheostats to pump every bit of remaining battery power into the propellers. The crew on different levels regained whatever composure they could muster to check the integrity of the craft. The conn was undamaged, so too the Control Room. Reports came in rapidly. They'd survived without a scratch, even though every level looked as if a tornado had cut through.

Worthy looked at the depth gauge. They were under again and he steadied the *Earthforce*'s rise. He upped the periscope and saw the killer-factory ship heeling around at full speed. "He's coming back."

The sonarman struggled into his chair. His screens were back up.

He grinned, "The Navy ship is on their tail."

Worthy grabbed on the headset radio.

"Is Jan okay?" asked Worthy.

"She's dead," replied Captain Thomasson quietly.

A wave of anger immobilized Worthy. He wanted to stop at nothing less than the death of the *Stavenger* and all hands on board.

"They are going to reach the iceline before we can get in range," said Captain Thomasson, "and the hydrofoil's not equipped to zigzag between icebergs." Then he added what Worthy wanted to hear, "He's all yours."

❄

Iron Lady turned angrily toward Yamamura, "You were sure they were going to die too."

Yamamura answered evenly, "They did not. We have to deal with it. But the first lady is gone and we are three million dollars richer."

The Englishman's anger dissipated. "How are we going to escape them?"

"What worked for the whales will work for us." He pointed to the line of icebergs. "In there we can run them in blind circles."

Quvango bellowed, "The sub is in front of us."

The *Earthforce* rose at one o'clock, black and gleaming under the clear sun.

Yamamura's earpiece crackled. "This is *Earthforce*. If you were planning to play hide and seek, let's go. You hide and my torpedoes will seek."

❄

"Batteries going down," reported the *Earthforce*'s chief engineer over the intercom.

"Torpedoes?" Worthy asked down the hatch.

"One and two ready," answered Rorque at once.

"Line them up."

The *Earthforce*'s beating engines stalled and whimpered.

"Target bearing and range set."

"Mark."

"We are losing power!" reported the Chief Engineer shrilly.

Worthy wasted no time. "Shoot."

The lights dimmed and the *Earthforce* went pitch black.

A microsecond *after* the submarine shook twice.

"One away, two away," shouted Rorque jubilantly.

Worthy pumped his fist.

❄

A pair of distinct profiles raced across the *Stavenger*'s FishEye.

"Torpedoes in the water."

"Bearings?" asked Yamamura.

"We can't avoid them," yelled Iron Lady. The FishEye tabulated an impact time and displayed it: 23 secs. "Less than half a minute to jump ship!"

Quvango hit the alarm bell and raced off the bridge to the catwalk. Iron Lady fled after him. Showing the same calm when his Japanese crew jumped ship after the encounter with the fin whale, Yamamura stepped up to the wheel and took it. He spun the spokes over toward the approaching fish.

In the seconds it took for the *Stavenger* to respond, the bells clamored up a chaotic response on all levels. Yamamura ignored the race of men on to the decks. He was aware of shadows scurrying along the slaughter deck toward the open slipway. When the *Stavenger* turned, she turned hard. He heard loud shouts as pirates staggered and fell.

Yamamura attempted to minimize the target area and rush into the torpedoes before they could arm. He didn't accomplish either objective.

He felt the ship jump like a rodeo bull the same time that two flashes lit up along the *Stavenger*'s waterline. Twin plumes of ocean lifted into the air and obscured the ship. The forward explosion lopped of twenty feet from her bows. Her fifty-knot speed did the rest, shredding her. She stumbled forward and deeper into the waves.

Yamamura watched the collapsing bows plunge the men into the ocean. Quvango and Iron Lady fell screaming.

The second explosion cut the *Stavenger* midship. The bridge, caught between the two torpedoes, ejected sixty feet into the air. Yamamura remained conscious. Pressurized steam melted the skin off Yamamura's body. He was struck, burned and tossed mercilessly as fire, smoke, frozen meat and wreckage hurled everywhere. Brief walls of flame erupted and died. The scientific shack blew open and the million-dollar equipment disintegrated.

Yamamura hit the water, impaled on a twisted rail that sank below the ruptured keel. He did not pass out until he died, crushed beneath the entire killer factory ship driving him into the ocean floor.

There were no survivors.

The *Earthforce* and *Quest II* returned to look for Jan and Vesprhein. Hordes upon hordes of sharks cut deadly trails across. It came as no surprise the divers found nothing.

Washington DC

Marine One put down. When the president disembarked, with Delta a politically correct step behind, the media erupted rowdily. Everett waved off the questions as he jaunted into the press room, where Zoe Zurich, had wheeled in a big-screen TV set.

Everett stepped up to the microphone. "Ladies and gentlemen, before I begin, there is someone else who will address you. The new prime minister of Japan, Nobuo Tomita."

Everett turned to the television and the LDP veteran came on the air. He spoke in Japanese. An interpreter translated over his voice. "Former Prime Minister Maeo and his cabinet are under house arrest pending an investigation into pressuring Takara Securities to sell off US securities on Wall Street."

Even though the financial giant had consciously colluded with

Maeo, Tomita concealed their voluntary involvement. Takara's importance to global finance insulated them from exposure, as also the Obata family, who were shielded by Kaiyou's manufacturing might in the US and twenty-nine other countries. Also, Tomita needed to protect the WLJ, whose support he still needed. The president and the new prime minister decided to keep the hunt secret as well. If and when it became known, Maeo would take the blame for it alone.

"I have ordered a stop to this sale and we will begin an immediate buy-back," Tomita continued. "This should begin to stabilize Wall Street at once. This collapse, former Prime Minister Maeo confessed, was designed to discredit Mr. Everett and see him lose in favor of the Republican candidate, Mr. Will Todd."

The GOP candidate and his staff issued denials for the rest of the day, to no avail. A violent backlash forced Todd off the campaign trail. He needed police protection. Keith Leeds disappeared off the news. Everett seized the spotlight. Wall Street turned around. By the final bell, the president's numbers galloped past 50 percent.

Everett collapsed into the Oval Office sofa, exhausted after a series of one-on-one interviews with every major media outlet. Delta, Pleasance, Lhea and Vice President Adrian, who'd flown back to Washington, relaxed exultantly around him. Everett buzzed the steward and ordered a round of drinks for everybody.

The National Security Advisor hurried in unannounced. "Jan is dead."

Everett shot to his feet. "What?"

The NSA recounted Captain Thomasson's report, which included the boarding party's account of the events leading up to the tragedy. The *Quest II* was towing the *Earthforce* back to Pearl Harbor.

"I'd like to be alone," said Everett.

Delta squeezed his forearm and left. He rounded his desk and sank into his chair. After this roller coaster day, he did not have any emotion left in him to feel the grief he should. Instead, he smiled wryly. He accepted her loss to be the natural and inevitable conclusion to the life she chose. She'd died on her beloved battlefield, fighting an animal rights war, accomplishing humankind's most colossal rescue. Add another 10 sympathy percent going into the weekend before the polls, he thought, matter-of-factly. He couldn't believe a thought like that crossed his mind. Had Jan's cold practicality finally rubbed off on him?

❄

Outside, the NSA smiled grimly toward Pleasance, Lhea, Delta and Adrian. "We need to talk." They herded into the vice president's office. "Now that I've fulfilled my obligation to the president, I don't see any problem revealing that she died sinking a Japanese factory ship that you so vehemently denied was tailing her whale drive."

Delta replied, "We had no overhead platforms and the first lady never indicated in her phone conversations with the president that there was any danger."

"Save your spin for damage control."

"So you're going to violate the confidentiality of your position as the National Security Advisor?" asked Adrian.

"I've decided to quit."

"No," said Pleasance smoothly. "You're fired."

The NSA shrugged, "Fine."

Pleasance hit the intercom. "Can you ask a couple of secret service agents to come in here with their sidearms."

His secretary clicked off with a gasp.

The NSA refused to be intimidated. "What are you trying to pull, George?"

"We apprehended two people, Bianca Stevens and Bruce Wilhelmson, the assistant administrator and threat analyst from the National Photographic Interpretation Center, who were assigned to watch the first lady. They confessed you offered them a substantial sum of money if they doctored the pictures to show Japanese vessels in tow."

"That's a lie," snapped the NSA.

Lhea, Adrian and Delta looked admiringly at Pleasance, who'd offered the couple clemency in exchange for signing a statement that he crafted.

Lhea picked up the thread. "Your disgrace will automatically implicate Leeds, who made the charge."

"Do you want him run out of this election like Todd?" inquired Pleasance with iron in his voice.

The intercom crackled. "The agents are here."

The NSA stood alone to one side, facing Pleasance and his three cronies on the other. His shoulders sagged.

Pleasance tilted his head with a small smile. He pressed his intercom. "False alarm."

❆

The most important political weekend in America went down in history as one completely devoid of politics. The Japanese plot behind the upheaval on Wall Street and the stunning death of the first lady dominated the news. At the center of both events, one a triumph and the other a tragedy, Everett landed squarely in the headlines, all favorable.

Yet, come Tuesday, only 54 percent of Americans showed up at the polls. Everett won easily, taking 52 percent of the vote to Leeds's 30 percent and Todd's 18 percent. The electoral college totals showed a wider margin: 412 out of 538. He paid a tearful homage to Jan in his acceptance speech.

Delta became the first female secretary of defense. Everett and she decided to wait until he was out of office to publicize their relationship. Pleasance and Lhea remained content in their posts. Random accepted the promotion to National Security Advisor.

Two weeks later, the Secret Service got around to investigating the telephone threat made by an American to the Norwegian. Lhea received their report and called Pleasance. A voice match had been made to Dale Gabon, now secretary of the interior. He'd sold his soul, obliging Pleasance's every command to feed his ambition. The morning after, he was found shot dead in Lafayette Park, an apparent suicide.

The whale drive garnered NatGeo the highest ratings ever for a cable outlet. Maeo was vilified for his role. Everett emerged without blame, thanks to Raquel, Boycott, Knight and Worthy, who decided to honor and respect Jan by concealing his part. Despite all her fire and fury, they knew she still loved Everett and would've found a way to exonerate him. So they did the same. But none of them would take the president's call. Neither would they separate fact from myth as the series elevated Jan into a lonely superhero.

Reine i Lofoten

A raw wind blustered across the tiny fishing hamlet above the Arctic Circle. The grim winter stretched a white blanket over the homes and iced up the fjords. The few hours of daylight came from a low-slung sun hidden behind thick clouds.

An old pickup followed the snowplow and parked outside the office of the Marine Hunters Alliance. The driver saw General Secretary Kristof Jonsgard waiting at the door, braving the bitter onslaught. Cutting the headlights, the driver climbed out and hunched forward into the wind. He greeted Jonsgard warmly with a bear hug, then they disappeared indoors. As they walked into the empty office, Jonsgard told the visitor, with the ban on whaling here to stay, he had to let all his staff go.

"Coffee?" asked Jonsgard in Samnorsk.

"No," replied the visitor in the same hybrid Norwegian. "I want to be on the road before the town wakes and someone recognizes me."

"I understand." Jonsgard opened his desk drawer. "Did you visit your mother?"

"Yes. I swore her to silence."

Jonsgard held out an envelope. The visitor opened it and found a key taped to a 3x5 card with a number. "As you requested, the cash is in a safe deposit locker in the Oslo railway station."

"Thank you."

"Our biggest opponent is dead, but all hunting is banned," lamented Jonsgard, hobbling with his visitor to the door.

"I know," agreed the visitor. "There is no justice."

The visitor shook hands again with Jonsgard and stepped outside. A howling wind made the light snow seem heavier. The visitor climbed behind the wheel of the pickup truck, reversed out and pulled around the corner.

"It's safe now," said the driver.

A silhouette straightened up in the back and climbed into the front passenger seat. "Did you get it?"

Jan plucked the envelope from Vesprhein's hand.

Underwater, they had almost given up. The two sharks, one ahead of the other by a body length, came charging toward them. Out of nowhere, Miracle darted between them and the lead shark. Lunging for a human meal, the shark grabbed a mouthful of the calf. Miracle thrashed into a frightened dive.

Exposing Jan and Vesprhein to the second shark.

Vesprhein grabbed Jan's arm, forcing her into a descent using Miracle as a shield. They slid under the HYSWAS to the other side. The predator went after Miracle. Two black plateaus rose. The nurses materialized out of the dark depths on either side of the lunging predator. Their seventy-ton, seventy-five-foot bodies obliterated its threat with size. As swiftly as they rose, they stopped and butted hides, crushing the trapped shark. Flesh and blood exploded to the surface.

Jan and Vesprhein broke out of the water on the other side. They heard Captain Thomasson promise to return for the bodies.

"They think we're dead," said Vesprhein.

"Let them," said Jan and dragged him behind Miracle, who blew to the surface with her two nurses. Blood trailed the gasping calf. "This way, I save Everett a scandal. He'll get the emotional vote and coast to victory. You're dead, so you have a fresh start. My death gives me the anonymity I want. Knowing Worthy's state of mind, when he hears I was killed, Yamamura and the rest don't stand a chance. The three million dollars is now ours to collect and start over."

When the *Earthforce* and *Quest II* returned to search for their bodies, Jan and Vesprhein slipped aboard the submarine through the diving hatch. The Christmas Tree blinked briefly red. Rorque Jr. did not notice. At first, Jan assumed it would be impossible to remain hidden all the way back to Hawaii and thought of showing herself to Worthy only. But lack of power forced all but three rotating crew members to be transferred aboard the *Quest*, which towed the *Earthforce*. Tinned food in the galley sustained them. In Honolulu, Vesprhein's criminal talents helped get them passports. Before flying out, Jan wanted desperately to at least tell her best friend, Raquel, then decided to wait.

"Don't you want to confront Pleasance?" asked Vesprhein, turning the pickup truck onto the narrow highway.

"In a few years," said Jan. "When my face is forgotten. When Pleasance has forgotten. I want the shock to hit so hard he will drop dead. And I mean dead."

Vesprhein laughed. He leaned over and kissed her passionately.

Cetacean Bay

Eighty-eight feet from stem to stern, the *Sea Eyes* looked like any other brand new luxury yacht. She reeked of high-class comfort and good taste. The interior was decorated with a deft, sophisticated hand in cherry wood, leather and brass, but she concealed macho hardware for long voyages and violent confrontations. Her hull was a composite of fiberglass and carbon laminates. Her combat management system allowed for the kind of surveillance above and below the oceans found on vessels of war. Her waterjet propulsion took her to speeds of sixty knots. Bow and aft, the hulls slid open into forward and rear firing, infra-red guided launchers. An Oto Melara 76mm Super Rapid gun folded out of the deck.

The *Sea Eyes* was a marriage of power and class. Muscle and polish. Speed and grace. Vesprhein and Jan.

Jan leaned against the deck rails, her golden hair flying.

"Any luck?" asked Vesprhein, appearing at her side. His arm encircled her waist.

Jan shook her head. She had never been happier and it showed. But inside, she wasn't able to shake a nagging incompleteness. She felt she never had her sunset moment of closure with the whales, specifically Miracle.

Spoiled by being so close to so many for so long, Jan realized how rare and elusive blue whales really were after she and Vesprhein arrived at the Southern Seas two weeks ago and still had yet to see one. The Austral sun dipped below the horizon, a great orange bobber dancing on a great blue sea. With ineffable sadness, Jan realized that her chances of sighting the beloved calf were fading as quickly as the diminishing light in the western sky.

"We have to chart north in a couple of days," said Vesprhein.

Jan nodded, hugging him close. Summer was gone. The chill had returned to the air. They looked out into the incredible twilight that capped off the shortening days of February. Unable to give up hope, Jan stayed out for another hour, searching the rising waves. Vesprhein remained by her side, keeping silent company. In another hour, the four main stars of the Southern Cross twinkled against the darkening sky.

Vesprhein gently nudged Jan, and they started inside. Halfway across, the *Sea Eyes* wobbled.

"Woah!" Jan grabbed Vesprhein.

A powerful, single column of water jetted up and over, drenching them. Jan's eyes lit up and dazzled. Her face beamed with a radiant, joyful smile. She rushed to the edge of the boat and recognized the familiar yet unique streamlined contours rising above the water. "Miracle!" she shouted.

The rest of the pod surfaced, emitting strong blowhole emissions, full of life, raining down a storm of glittering water all around them.

THE END

www.ingramcontent.com/pod-product-compliance
Lightning Source LLC
Chambersburg PA
CBHW020638020726
47494CB00001B/240